SWEET DISORDER

ROSE LERNER

LIVELY ST. LEMESTON, BOOK 1

Table of Contents

To Sonia,
FOR LOVING NATE ARCHIBALD
SO MUCH.

Acknowledgments

I would like to thank my editor, Anne Scott, for her enthusiasm and vision.

Thank you to my agent, Kevan Lyon, for everything.

Thank you to the Demimondaines: Alyssa Everett, Charlotte Russell, Vonnie Hughes, and especially Susanna Fraser, for always being there when I need you and for being the smartest, nicest critique group probably ever. Thank you to my generous, brilliant friends and first readers: Kate Addison, Tiffany Ruzicki and Deborah Kaplan. Thank you to Kim Runciman at Night Vision Editing for her thorough and incisive critique that, among other things, showed me how to make this story a reasonable length. I am so grateful and proud to know you all.

Thank you to Delilah Marvelle, who gave me the benefit of her awe-inspiring Regency cooking expertise, and to Peter Stinely of the Colonial Williamsburg Foundation, who kindly shared his knowledge and experience about historical printers and printing presses. Any remaining errors are of course all my own.

Thank you to my uncle, David Lerner, not only for his help with this book and for his unflagging love and support, but also for being the first person to interest me in history. You're the best.

And finally, thank you to Sonia, without whom my creative process would not be possible.

Chapter 1

Phoebe sat at the foot of her bed, her elbows propped on the deal table she'd placed under the window. She was supposed to be writing her next Improving Tale for Young People. But the shingled wall and gabled roof of Mrs. Humphrey's boarding house across the way were so much more absorbing than the tragic tale of poor Ann, who had been got with child by a faithless young laird and was now starving in a ditch.

If Phoebe strained, she could even see a sliver of street two stories below.

The problem was that she couldn't quite decide what would happen to Ann next. Tradition dictated that either the girl die there, or that her patient suffering inspire the young laird to reform and carry her off to a church, but…that was so *boring*. Every Improving Tale-teller in England had already written it. It had been old when Richardson did it seventy years ago.

But she couldn't afford to waste this precious time in daydreams. It was washing day, and Sukey, the maid she and her landlady shared with Mrs. Humphrey, would soon be back from her shopping to help. Then tomorrow Phoebe had to piece her quilt for the Society for Bettering the Condition of the Poor's auction in December, and what with one thing and another, she wouldn't have any more time to write until Tuesday. She had promised this story to the editor of the *Girl's Companion* in time for typesetting three weeks from now.

There were footsteps on the stairs and a knock at her door. *I do* not *feel relieved,* she thought firmly. Standing and crossing into her sitting room, she opened the door to discover—

"Mr. Gilchrist." Phoebe felt much less relieved.

The dapper Tory election agent stood at the top of the narrow spiral of stairs leading to her attic. Scattered drops of rain glistened in his sleek brown hair, on his broadcloth shoulders, and on the petals of the pink-and-white carnation—the colors of the local Tory party—in his buttonhole.

Drat. If it was raining, washing would have to be put off until she had Sukey again next Friday. And she'd have to keep a careful eye on the bucket under the leak in her roof to make sure it didn't overflow.

"Ah, you know of me," Mr. Gilchrist said with an oily smile. "Pleased to make your acquaintance, Mrs. Sparks."

Oh, his smile is not *oily. Prejudice combined with the urge to narrate is a terrible thing.* She smiled back. "And I'm pleased to make yours. But I should warn you, I'm Orange-and-Purple, and so are my voting friends." There was a general election on in England to choose a new Parliament. While many districts could go decades with the same old MPs, the Lively St. Lemeston seats always seemed to be hotly contested.

He tilted his head. "Your father and your husband were Whigs. But from what I hear, you're an independent woman. Decide for yourself." His expression turned rueful. He couldn't be more than twenty. "Besides, it's starting to rain and I'd rather not go outside again just yet."

She sighed. He was good at this. "May I offer you some tea?"

"I'd love some."

Maybe his smile was oily after all. Phoebe went to take the kettle from the fire, but she didn't bring out the cheese rolls from the cupboard. They cost a penny each, and she wanted them for herself.

Mr. Gilchrist waited patiently while she topped off the teapot with hot water. She didn't add any tea. A second steeping was good enough for him.

"I know you're a busy and practical woman, so I'll come straight to the point," he said as she poured. "Thank you, I take it black." A politic choice, visiting a poor widow. "Under the Lively St. Lemeston charter, every freeman of the town has the right to vote for up to two candidates in an election."

"I know that, Mr. Gilchrist." Men always wanted to explain things, didn't they?

"Also under the Lively St. Lemeston charter," he continued, clearly having no intention of modifying his planned oration, "the eldest daughter of a freeman who died without sons can make her husband a freeman."

Phoebe tapped her foot on the floor. "My husband is dead," she pointed out, since apparently they were telling each other things they both already knew.

The young man took a sip of tea. He had an eye for a dramatic pause, anyway; she had to give him credit for that. "You could marry again."

She blinked. "What?"

"Mr. Dromgoole, our candidate, would be happy to assist in finding any prospective spouse a lucrative place in his chosen profession." His smile didn't falter. Definitely oily.

"You think I'm going to get *married* just to get you extra

votes? The polls are in a month!" She set her still-empty teacup back on the table with a rattle.

"Allow me." He put a small lump of sugar into the cup, poured it half full of tea, and then filled it almost to the brim with milk.

"You found out how I like my tea?" she asked incredulously.

There was a hint of boyish smugness in his smile now. "I know how you like your men, too. If you'll just meet my nominee—"

She stood. "How dare you? Get out of my house."

It wasn't her house, though. It was her two cramped attic rooms. His eyes drifted for a moment, letting that sink in, reminding her of how much more she could have if she married.

He might know how she liked her tea, but he didn't know a thing about her if he thought she'd be happier in a fine house that belonged to her husband. These two rooms were *hers*.

He rose. "I'll give you a few days to think it over. A message at the Drunk St. Leonard will always reach me."

She went to the door and jerked it open. "Even love wouldn't convince me to marry again. An election certainly won't." She'd always had a tendency to bend the truth in favor of a neat bit of dialogue. But *love wouldn't convince me to marry again unless I were sure it wouldn't become a bickering, resentful mess like the first time* just didn't sound the same.

Mr. Gilchrist shook his head mournfully and bounded down the stairs. He passed out of sight—and there was a squawk and the sound of bouncing fruit. "I'm dreadfully sorry," he said, not sounding very sorry.

Phoebe started down to help Sukey collect the groceries, turning the corner just in time to see the girl pocket something.

"Pardon me, did you just bribe my maid?"

"It's not a bribe." Mr. Gilchrist tossed a couple of apples back in the basket with unerring aim. "It's damages for the fruit."

She considered throwing an apple at him as he disappeared around the next bend, but even in October the fruit wasn't cheap enough to justify it. "The Orange-and-Purples would never stoop this low," she shouted after him instead.

"Don't count on it," Mr. Gilchrist called back.

"I hope he's right," Sukey said cheerily. "I could use another shilling."

Nick Dymond awoke to pain in his leg and someone knocking imperiously at the door to his rooms. Moving carefully, he rolled over and buried his head under his pillow, blocking out both the knocking and the unpleasant clamor of London's early-morning traffic. Toogood would take care of it.

"I'm sorry, my lady, Mr. Dymond is not in," he heard his valet saying in the next room.

My lady. Nick had an ugly presentiment even before he heard his mother's voice. "That would be *too good* to be true," said Lady Tassell. "He hasn't gone out more than half-a-dozen times in the last two months. Kindly remove yourself from my path."

Toogood was valiant—or at any rate, the better part of valiant. Lady Tassell's skirts rustled as she swept in, the click of her boots softening when she stepped onto Nick's Cuenca carpet.

Nick groaned and swung himself gingerly upright. The

pain was always at its worst in the morning. "Toogood hates puns on his name, you know that," he called, massaging the tendons in his left thigh. Even after six months, his fingers felt awkward on the scar.

"Lying abed at two in the afternoon, I knew it," his mother said, pushing open the door to his room. So, not the morning then. "Get up and put on a banyan or something. I have a task for you."

Nick took up the walking stick that leaned against his night table and steeled himself for what he knew was coming—not the pain, but his mother's reaction to it. He stood with a lurch.

She flinched.

She was such a damn good liar. Why didn't he rate the effort? When he'd first come back from the Peninsula, she'd spent every day with him, bringing him hothouse fruit and restorative broths, criticizing his appearance, manners, and arrangements for his own comfort, and dragging him about with her to meetings, dinners, and planning sessions. He'd been too weak and unhappy to resist, but he'd hated the stares, the looks of pity and hero-worship, the questions about the battle.

And he'd hated how every damn step he took, she stiffened and pressed her lips together as if she couldn't bear it. As if she couldn't bear to be near him.

She'd expected him to—he didn't know what she'd expected. To suddenly enjoy talking about elections? To stop limping? To be happy? But after a month, when he still wasn't the son she wanted, she'd given up and left him alone.

He'd actually, contrarily, been disappointed.

Ordinarily he took pains to limp as little as possible, not to let his expression betray the tiny jolts of pain. Now he didn't bother, crossing to the pitcher and basin with uneven steps. He set down his cane and braced himself on the washstand with both hands for a moment, his breath harsh and short in his ears. He met his mother's eyes in the mirror. Her face was white and set.

It was not much to his credit that he strove never to intrude his new lameness on anyone's notice, except with the one person who most hated to see him in pain.

He breathed in and out and recited *Childe Harold's Pilgrimage* to himself.

For his was not that open, artless soul
That feels relief by bidding sorrow flow...

As he focused on the familiar words, everything faded: his resentment, the pain in his leg, his morning hunger and the smell of Toogood grilling smoked herrings and brown bread in the next room. He splashed water on his face with one hand. "Well? What's the task?"

She shook out her skirts. "Your brother Tony is in real danger of losing the Lively St. Lemeston election. I can't go myself, I'm working on Stephen's county campaign in Chichester."

Poor Tony, still trying to please Mother. Nick took his dressing gown from where it was thrown over the back of a chair and wrapped it around himself. "I've told you a thousand times I've no interest in politics." Even as a child, he'd known it was all sound and fury, signifying nothing. Politics was his mother expecting him to pretend they were a happy family on public days at Tassell Hall, when they entertained the district's tenantry and voters.

Firstborn, serious-minded Stephen and attention-craving Tony, the baby of the family, had taken to it like fish to water. Maybe for them, it *had* been a happy family.

Nick had chosen the army almost on a whim. But once in the Peninsula, the rough-and-ready life had quickly felt like home. There was no pretense in a long march or a battle or a wet game of cards round a smoking fire. Life was clear and straightforward and it *meant* something.

Nick's mother gave him a weary smile. "If I'd insisted you go into Parliament four years ago, instead of buying you a pair of colors, you'd still be walking."

Nick wished he were back in bed. "I walk. You just saw me walk."

"When you're not sulking in here."

"I'm *convalescing*."

She arched a brow. "Mmm. You're right, sulking was the wrong word. How about 'moping'? Would you prefer 'brooding'? You returned from Spain three months ago. I hoped you simply needed time, but you've barely left your rooms since I stopped making you. They smell, Nick."

"They do *not*—"

She cut him off with an exasperated wave of her hand. "I don't have time for this argument right now." She never had time for anything during an election. Nick had been born in the midst of the historic general election of 1784, when the Tories seized control of the House of Commons for good and all; she'd left him with the wet-nurse and returned to her study until the last poll closed a month later.

Nick sometimes thought she blamed the hours she'd spent birthing him for the Whigs' ensuing twenty-eight years in Opposition.

"I have a simple match I need you to make for me," she said. "No politicking required."

Nick had remained standing as long as he could, and that last comment intrigued him. He wasn't *quite* ready to show his mother the door. First point for Lady Tassell. "Please sit." He was careful not to sound grudging, so he wouldn't have to accord her another point for oversetting him. He eased himself down onto the edge of the bed. "Matchmaking?"

She sat with a regal sweep of skirts, smiling. In that moment she actually looked happy with him. He hated how warm it made him feel. "I knew that would get your attention," she said smugly. "There is a certain young woman in Lively St. Lemeston who could make her husband a voter, if she had one. Alas, she is a widow."

"A recent widow?"

His mother waved her hand. "Oh, a couple of years. Plenty of time to get over her grief. It wasn't a happy marriage, by all accounts. You remember Will Sparks, don't you?"

Nick had stopped spending Christmases in Lively St. Lemeston with his family years ago. He remembered the name but not the face. "The newspaper editor."

She gave him that pleased look again. "You *did* read my letters."

He shrugged, not eager to admit either that he'd read them only sometimes and then with variable thoroughness, or that he'd been grateful to get them. "Is she pretty?"

She sniffed. "You're always such a *man*, Nicky. Would you refuse to go if she weren't?"

Just like that, he'd managed to say the wrong thing. And just like that, she assumed he'd fall in with her plans. "I'm not going either way."

He'd known her his whole life. He knew that slight, still pause meant he'd hurt her feelings. But her face didn't change a whit. "I thought you'd say as much," she said after a moment. "Every cloud has a silver lining. Your father owes me a hundred pounds."

He blinked. "You *bet* him I wouldn't go?"

"I bet him you couldn't do it at all, when he suggested you for the job. But I think he'll probably agree this means I win."

She had never had the slightest bit of faith in him. Nick tried not to let it sting. Why should she have? It was only in the army that he had found something worth working for, worth fighting for. He'd been useful there, even valuable. He'd become someone to be relied on.

Now he was useless again. His wounded leg, as minor an injury as it was in the grand scheme of things, couldn't stand up to forced marches or sleeping on cold, sodden ground.

He stood, lurching just a shade more than necessary. "Enjoy your winnings."

Her jaw clenched. She had wanted a fight.

He waited, meeting her eyes blankly. After long moments, she rose in an agitated flurry of ruffles and petticoats. "Very well. But your allowance is stopped as of this moment."

"*What?*"

"If you won't contribute to this family, I see no reason why this family should contribute to you. Find someone else to pay for your calf-bound editions of *Childe Harold's Pilgrimage* and whatever it is you've been eating."

He had no other source of income, and no means of procuring one. How was he even to begin looking? Asking hat in hand for employment from a succession of men who would see his leg and pity him—all those eyes on him—the idea was anathema.

Anger and hurt were a lead weight on his tongue. His thoughts slowed. He'd been like this since he was a boy, going silent and blank when he should have flown into a fine rage. "Toogood is an excellent cook," he said finally.

She made a violent, frustrated movement.

He tried again. "Mother, you can't—"

"I think you'll find that I can," she said tightly. "Just behave like a dutiful son for once in your life and go to Lively St. Lemeston. Prove me wrong. I'd be overjoyed to lose this bet." She sounded tired, suddenly. She *looked* tired, the wrinkles around her eyes and mouth deepening.

He'd seen her tired before, of course, giddy and incoherent from lack of sleep before important votes in the Commons, or snappish and sore-throated from sixteen hours canvassing. But he'd never seen her look faded. She'd aged while he was away.

He drew in a deep breath, reminding himself that Byron did it. He went out every day with his deformed foot, and he let them stare. He went to Almack's in knee breeches with that skinny leg of his, and to the devil with them all. If Byron could do that with half of London breathing down his neck, Nick could manage Lively St. Lemeston.

He had survived the siege of Badajoz. This was nothing. "I'll go," he said. "But I'm making you a bet too."

"I'm listening."

"If I get that woman married off, you can never wince when you look at me again."

Her lips parted, her eyes filling with tears. "Oh, Nicky, I—"

"Don't apologize. Just make the bet."

She held out her hand. It was older than he remembered, the veins more prominent. But when he shook it, her smile made her look young. "The coach will take you this afternoon. And see if you can keep Tony away from women while you're there, won't you?"

He would get this match made by hook or by crook. And then he'd walk away and—

His imagination failed. It didn't matter. *One step at a time,* he told himself, just as he had in hospital when every step was a small, blessedly finite agony. *One step at a time from here to the door, and we'll worry about what's on the other side when we get there.*

Nick leaned on his walking stick, giving himself a few moments to catch his breath. Of *course* the widow lived at the top of two flights of very steep, very twisty stairs.

After six hours of jouncing about on bad roads the day before, followed by sleeping in an unfamiliar bed in damp weather, his leg had already been protesting. He'd waited until the sun came out this afternoon, and still his leg whined all the way from the Lost Bell, Tony's inn headquarters: past the Market Cross and down the quaint streets, up the uneven garden path to the widow's lodgings, past hedges and bushes strewn with drying clothes and past the open kitchen door, and into the house. Now, after the stairs, it shouted at him that it wanted to go home and sleep.

You and I both, leg. He rapped on the low attic door. There was no answer. After half a minute dragged by, he tried again. No answer. The wretched woman wasn't home. The staircase yawned behind him like a drab, dirty descent into Hell.

Men had probably journeyed into Hell with more grace

and less cursing, but eventually Nick found himself back out on the threshold. He closed the door and leaned against it. The maids at their washing in the kitchen couldn't see him from this angle. He shut his eyes and silently recited Byron until the ache in his leg receded.

"Are you ill, sir?"

He started upright. The plumper of the two maids stood before him. The water from the washing had splashed all down her front, and it was chilly enough that the points of her nipples showed even through several layers of wet cloth. There was so much of her, breasts and hips and thighs and—

She cleared her throat loudly. "*Sir?*"

He hurriedly raised his eyes to her face. It was a lovely face, heart-shaped, with great dark eyes, finely arched brows, and an annoyed rosebud mouth. The tips of her thick dark hair curled wetly.

"Yes, I must have eaten something that disagreed with me," he said. "I'm Mr. Dymond, and I'm looking for Mrs. Sparks. Do you know if she'll be in later?"

The maid's eyes widened, and she tried to dry her hands on her skirts. "Maybe," she hedged. "What did you want to speak to her about? Wait a moment, did you say Mr. Dymond? But I've met him, he's—"

"I'm sorry, I should have said Mr. Nicholas Dymond. My brother is the candidate."

Her eyes narrowed. "You know Mr. Sparks is dead, don't you? He can't vote." Her Sussex accent wasn't as strong as many of the folk he'd spoken to here, but a warm burr coated her words like a honey glaze.

It would behoove him to win her over for the sake of Mrs. Sparks's vote, but he didn't quite know how. Flirting with a voter's wife was safe; she knew you didn't mean it. A maid might think you were trying to bed her. His mother had impressed upon them all from a very early age the folly of womanizing during an election.

How would Lady Tassell handle this? A smile, flattery, and a bribe, no doubt. She had small armies of servant spies across England, and they all thought her a paragon of kind generosity.

He smiled at the maid. Her hands twisted in her skirts. "I do know," he said reassuringly. "But there's nothing to stop her taking another, is there? If you could tell me of anyone she might be sweet on, I'd be very grateful. You must know all the news hereabouts." He pulled a shilling out of his pocket and pressed it into one nervous hand.

Her fingers were cold and damp. Even with the sun finally out, it was a damnable day for washing.

The other maid, holding a linen shift trimmed with faded green bows and red rosettes, appeared at her elbow and plucked the shilling from her fingers. "That's mine, I believe. And Mrs. Sparks isn't sweet on anyone."

"Sukey!" The maid flushed, then turned on him, eyes flashing. "I thought better of the Orange-and-Purples, I really did. I'm *not* getting *married* for your dratted election, so you can stop flirting with all the servants in the vicinity."

Sukey winked at him. "Oh, don't stop on my account."

Nick stifled a groan. He wasn't cut out for this. He couldn't manage even the simplest bit of politic dealing. "Mrs. Sparks, I take it."

Chapter 2

Despite Nick's dismay, he couldn't help thinking this meant that was *her* shift in Sukey's hands. *Her* petticoat and underthings were draped over the rhododendron behind her. Under her wet dress, right now, she must be wearing brown-and-white striped stockings, like the three pairs hanging from a nearby tree branch.

"Yes," she said sharply, "and yes, those are my underthings you're ogling. Sir."

Nick straightened, collecting his wayward thoughts. "My humblest apologies, madam."

She raised her eyebrows. "Really? The very humblest? *Ne plus ultra?*"

There was no purpose even in an ordered retreat; he had no reinforcements, no main army to rejoin. He had to stay and fix this. But first he needed to discover the lay of the land. "Did you like being married?" he asked bluntly.

"No," she snapped, and then pressed her fist into her mouth as if she couldn't believe she'd said it. "I mean—yes," she amended after a moment. "Sometimes. I—it wasn't Will's fault. Lord, I'm a beast."

This was interesting.

"Of course you're not a beast, ma'am," Sukey said. "Men are impossible to live with, that's all." She put a hand on her mistress's shoulder.

As if that made her remember how cold she was, Mrs. Sparks shivered. "I'm impossible to live with too," she said sadly. Then she shot him a glare. "Which is why I live alone."

He sighed. "So do I. Although I'm sure it will be no time at all before my mother is trying to matchmake for *me*. She bullied me down here to talk to you, you know."

He didn't like how calculated his words were. But it worked. He could see it, when in her mind they became fellow pawns in his mother's game. She smirked. "If this is an example of the delicacy of her stratagems, you have nothing to fear."

"Unkind, but just." Her lips twitched. He almost had her. "Listen—perhaps you don't want to marry again, but do me a favor and at least come to the dinner my brother is throwing for the voters on Thursday? Meet a few potential husbands. I hear there's to be dancing, and it will convince my mother that I'm at least making inroads into your spinsterhood." Damn, that last bit sounded rather indecent.

She flushed, evidently agreeing.

"Why not, ma'am?" asked Sukey. "It would do you good to get out for an evening. I can't remember the last time you wore something really pretty."

It wasn't meant as an insult, but Nick winced as the blush deepened into angry shame on Mrs. Sparks's face. "I don't *own* anything really pretty," she said harshly. "I dyed my best gown black when we laid Will out."

"There, you see?" Sukey said. "That means it was more than two years ago. Two whole years of drudgery and scribbling. It's about time you—"

Mrs. Sparks began to vibrate like a teakettle. Nick found it inexplicably charming.

"It's not a very formal affair," he interrupted before she could boil over. "Pin an orange-and-purple rosette in your hair and you'll be the height of fashion. Please say you'll come. I'd like to know there will be at least one familiar face in the crowd." His mother wanted him to dance. He had planned to ignore that, but now, if his leg would permit it, he found himself wanting to dance with Mrs. Sparks. Although if she stepped on his feet, he imagined she would do so very firmly.

Her face softened. He was close to success, so close. "I don't have time," she said, still sharply but with rather less conviction than before. "Drudgery and scribbling is time-consuming work, and unless *you* wish to do my washing and piece a quilt for the Gooding Day auction, the rest of my week is—"

"So if I help with your washing and make a donation to the auction, you'll come to the party?"

Her jaw dropped. "You're going to help with my washing."

"I did my own plenty of times in Spain." Of course, he had had two good legs then. Now the prolonged exposure to the chill and wet would probably have his thigh aching all evening and into tomorrow. But he could see that the novelty of an earl's son doing her washing had her hooked, and in the first heady flush of victory, that pain seemed far off.

"But you said you were ill," she protested.

"I'm feeling much better. Why don't you go upstairs and dry off? Maybe you can get some scribbling done while Sukey and I finish here. That should save you enough time to allow for the party on Thursday."

She hesitated, looking from him to the maid.

Sukey grinned at her. "Yes, ma'am, Mr. Dymond and I will be just fine. I'll tell him all about what sort of men you prefer."

Mrs. Sparks sighed. "That's terribly kind of you, Sukey. But really, if all three of us work, we'll be done in two-thirds the time." Nick hid a smile; Mrs. Sparks had a precise mind. She was also generous in her estimation of his skills as a laundress. Then she smiled, rather maliciously. "We'll give him the table-cloths." Sukey laughed.

He found out why quickly enough—soap had to be rubbed into every last stain before laying the twisted linen on the kitchen bench and beating it with Mrs. Sparks's pad-dle-shaped battledore. Then the tablecloths had to be soaked in the trough and scrubbed with his fingers, and examined again for stains. If there were any left, the whole process was to be gone through again. But Mrs. Sparks was kneeling beside him, doing the same thing to her worn gowns. Her cheeks were pink from exertion and the heat of the fire, and when she rubbed the cloth together vigorously, her bosom bounced. There were worse ways to spend an afternoon.

Phoebe tried not to be too aware of Mr. Dymond's shoulder pressed against her own as he struggled with her tablecloths. It had been cruel of her to assign them to him, only she hated doing them so much. The third time he cursed at a stubborn stain, she took pity on him. "Here, let's switch, you can take the—" She was suddenly conscious she was holding one of her dresses. The idea of his hands on it seemed terribly intimate.

"No, no," he said airily. "I can do this."

If it was a matter of masculine pride, there was no use in arguing. She shrugged and hid her relief.

She still couldn't quite get over the oddity of the situation. She'd only ever seen him before at church, at Christmastime when his family was in residence. He'd sat in the Tassell pew in the front; Phoebe's family felt lucky to have their own pew at all, a few rows from the back.

He'd been a handsome boy even then, but he'd grown into something special, and now here he was in her landlady's kitchen, close enough to touch. He was too fine and fancy for washing day, the watercolor of his honey-blond hair, blue eyes, and soft features turned to an expensive oil painting by the dramatic slash of dark eyebrows, sharp cheekbones, and firm mouth.

Half an hour ago he had looked like a distinguished fashion plate with his old-fashioned walking stick, and now his hair was frizzing from the wash-water and his expensive coat was wet to the elbows. But he didn't complain or show any sign of shrinking. And when it came time to pound the linen with the battledore—well, he had splendid shoulders. She caught Sukey eying them too.

Not to mention, he was tall. She smiled smugly. "Here, help me get the sheet onto the line." She carried the wet bundle up into the yard, and he followed with his walking stick, of which he seemed very fond. Generally she and Sukey had to struggle with this, and more often than not they trailed the end of the sheet in the mud and had to wash it all over again. Mr. Dymond had no trouble at all. He lifted the sheet over the line from his great height and, without even stretching, straightened it so it hung neatly.

They were almost done. Laundry day wasn't so bad, now that she lived alone. When she'd had to do all Will's things, she had spent the day before, the day of, and the day after in a grumpy, resentful haze. *Surely it isn't that difficult not to spill soup on one's shirt,* she'd thought to herself, and *Tobacco is a filthy habit, only look at these stains on his cuffs.*

She really *had* been impossible to live with, hadn't she?

"Sukey, why don't you go upstairs and build up the fire?" she suggested. "Mr. Dymond and I will finish the bed linens, and you can get some soup heating. And make a new pot of tea. You must come upstairs and dry off, Mr. Dymond. The Orange-and-Purples would never forgive me if I let you catch cold." It was a perfectly ordinary thing to say, but it felt daring. She was cold enough not to mind the heat in her cheeks.

"Some tea sounds like heaven." There was something startling about his smile, every time—it entirely changed the shape of his face. Strong lines appeared on his smooth skin and his eyes gleamed a brighter blue. Even his dark, winged brows took on a more welcoming curve.

Sukey straightened her shoulders, removed all expression from her face, and said woodenly, "Of course, madam."

It was her imitation of a butler in a great house, the sort of impassive, well-trained servant who didn't blink at anything. She liked to bring it out when Phoebe got snappish with her or—Phoebe's cheeks warmed further—when she was teasing that Phoebe had done something very shocking indeed. "Just ring if you need anything, madam, sir."

"I'll wring your neck," Phoebe said, flicking water at her, and Sukey laughed and went up the stairs. Silence stretched. She should really move into Sukey's place at the other end of the trough and not kneel so close, but they were almost done. She reached for the last pillowcase. "Thank you for helping with this. And don't mind Sukey."

"Oh, I don't. My valet's just as bad. He's going to wring *my* neck when he sees the state of my coat and shirt. It's a good thing I didn't take him to Spain. He would have thrown himself off a mountain. Or thrown me, maybe."

"No laundresses?"

"Sometimes in a billet." He followed her outside to strew the last few things on the hedges. "Never on bivouac. And we had to carry everything. Well—the men had to carry *everything* on their backs. I owned a mule in the baggage train, but that still meant only two spare shirts and two spare pairs of socks, and in the winter everything was damp for weeks on end. Sometimes I thought I'd never be warm and dry again." His mouth went grim. "I was, though."

She heard it in his voice, even though he didn't say it: *Some men weren't.* She shivered, abruptly ashamed of her laundry-day whining. He looked fine and fancy, but that didn't make him a china figurine who'd sat on a mantelpiece all his life. He'd suffered greater privations than hers.

He took her shivering for cold. "You'd better change out of those wet things. Your lips are turning blue."

She must look a fright. "You're just as wet as I am." She wished she didn't sound so sullen. What did it matter what he thought of her appearance?

"Am I?" He looked down at himself in surprise. "I never understood the fellows who stood about complaining of the Spanish climate—the quickest way to get warm is to build a fire, and the best way not to feel the cold is to think of something else."

"What did you think of, generally?"

He smiled a wonderful, wicked smile that made his blue eyes glitter like winter ice, and let the moment drag out until she'd supplied a hundred naughty answers in her own mind.

"Mr. Dymond!" She tried to sound disapproving without much success.

"Oh, I'd compose poems, mostly, or recite them," he said

innocently. "What did you think I was going to say?"

"I think it's time to dump out the laundry water."

He eyed the trough, a wary expression crossing his face.

"It *is* heavy, but Sukey and I are usually too lazy to carry it out bit by bit in buckets. Would you rather—"

He squared his shoulders. "No, no, it's quite all right." He bent and gripped the handle at one end of the trough. She grabbed the other.

"Watch the top step, it's higher than the path," she said as they maneuvered up the kitchen stairs and out into the garden. His face looked a little set. "Are you sure—"

"Quite sure." They made it over the top step without incident. He smiled at her—and she forgot entirely about the loose stone in the path. She tripped and dropped her end of the trough, water sloshing over her in a great dirty wave.

That wasn't the worst of it. Mr. Dymond lost his balance completely, sprawling on the ground with a pained grunt that utterly mortified her.

"Oh God, I'm so sorry, we should have used buckets, are you all right?" She shut her mouth firmly before she could say, *You shouldn't have smiled.*

"That dress you're in needs to be washed," he said, and they both started laughing. His laugh was as attractive as his smile; she was watching him very closely when he stood.

She stopped laughing. "You've sprained your ankle."

"No, it's fine."

"It's not fine," she insisted. "You're limping."

The humor fled his face, leaving it as harsh and sharp as a woodcut illustration. "I didn't twist my ankle. I'm lame. Now can we dump out this water?"

She could think of nothing to say that might not further

offend him, so she picked up her side of the—now much lighter—trough and they carried it to the street and back in silence. How had she not noticed? He had been careful to walk behind her, she realized, and she had thought nothing of it except to wonder if he was watching her arse.

She opened the door to the back stairs, suddenly aware that they were very steep and very narrow, and that she lived two flights up. Behind her, Mr. Dymond drew in a deep breath. He hadn't been ill at all earlier. He'd been resting after going up and down the stairs. She glanced over her shoulder, and he gave her an unconvincingly bright smile. "After you, ma'am."

His footsteps mingled with the rap of his stick on the uneven wood. She looked back once or twice, but in the dim stairway she couldn't see much of anything. At the top, she opened the door and went through into her modest lodgings.

Even setting aside their small size and the steeply sloping eaves, they weren't as well kept as they could have been. Sukey's two afternoons a week were somehow always filled to bursting. Slippers and an umbrella sat by the doorway, and shawls and her pelisse were flung about the room while their pegs hung empty. She should have waxed the worn patches in the wood of the floor months ago.

She had meant to re-cover the cushions on the ancient carved-oak settle too; stuffing spilled out of several seams. Her little table, its surface marred with teacup rings, was littered with books, notes, and old magazines and issues of the *Lively St. Lemeston Intelligencer*. A plate of crumbs from her morning sandwich and the unwashed teacups from Mr. Gilchrist's visit yesterday perched haphazardly atop the clutter.

She simply wasn't a good housekeeper. It was her one fault that had never bothered Will.

She turned to catch Mr. Dymond's reaction as he stepped into the light, his height making the ceiling look even lower.

His face was set, his knuckles white on the handle of his walking stick. Of course he had other things on his mind than the state of her sitting room.

"Here, you must sit down," she said in alarm, hastily tossing a shawl and a volume of *Robinson Crusoe* from the armchair onto the settle. She looked around for Sukey, but the maid had disappeared, along with the teapot. She must have gone downstairs to fetch hot water from Mrs. Pengilly while the soup heated in the kettle. Phoebe hoped she would steal a spoonful of the landlady's fine tea as well.

"It's nothing, I assure you." But he walked to the chair and stood before it, waiting politely.

She sat with a flurry directly on top of *Robinson Crusoe*. He was already lowering himself carefully into his chair, so she pulled the book out from under her without standing and set it beside her. "It's not nothing. You should have said something, I shouldn't have asked you to—"

His face had softened in amusement at her fumbling, but at her words his jaw set. "It will pass." His educated speech was more precise than ever. "I assure you I can still manage a little washing and a flight or two of stairs."

Men. "Maybe so, but you're obviously in pain. I—"

"I have nothing to complain of. Better men than I lost hands, arms, legs, even their lives. I should be grateful."

That was what everyone had told her when she lost her baby five months into her pregnancy. That she was lucky to be alive. That it was the will of Providence. That other women lost half-grown children. It was all true enough, but—"Pain is pain. It hurts."

His mouth twisted. "What a profound tautology."

"Is there anything I can do to help?"

"You can not talk about it."

She remembered what he had said downstairs; that he recited poetry to himself. She wanted desperately to go and change out of her soaked clothes, but she offered, "I can read to you, if you like."

He looked mulish for a moment. Then he seemed to remember that he had meant to charm her. His face smoothed out. "Do you like Lord Byron's work?"

It was pointless to try to talk to him as one human being to another. He didn't see a fellow soul when he looked at her. He saw two votes. "No," she said. "Not every woman is precisely the same as the next, you know. We don't all copy Lord Byron's verse into our commonplace books from memory simply by virtue of our sex. I haven't read a word of his silly poem, and I don't intend to. I do not care a straw about his tragic past or his tragic profile or how many women he had in the East."

He blinked. "You sound like my mother."

That brought her up short. "I do?"

She had made that speech before, or something close to it. Byron was all the rage; he came up in conversation. Suddenly, she remembered that there had been a time when she had read every fashionable book she could get her hands on. She'd pored over the lists of new publications that London booksellers sent to the newspaper.

Now she sounded like someone's mother.

"She thinks him an embarrassment to the Whigs. She called his speech on hanging the frame-breakers 'theatrical.'"

"I cried over that speech," Phoebe admitted, subdued and strangely unsettled. "Jack—that is, Mr. Sparks, my brother-in-law—printed it in the *Intelligencer*." Did she dislike Byron at all? Or had she simply spouted an unexamined opinion, to be contrary?

"It was brilliant," Mr. Dymond said hotly. "But it was not in the style of the House of Lords. Passion and compassion have no place in well-bred politics."

She hid a smile. He wasn't, after all, much more tactful than she was. "I didn't mean to be rude. As I said, I haven't read his lordship's work. I might like it. Plenty of others do."

He smiled. "No, I do believe rudeness comes to you quite unconsciously."

She felt both embarrassed and pleased. She had never been a girl who got on well with strangers, unlike her father or her sister Helen, who made friends wherever they went. Will had called her "hedge-pig", sometimes. She'd been glad to spend the last two years mostly on her own, seeing only family and the same small circle of friends.

But now she remembered the deep, visceral enjoyment of flirting. The nervous flutter in her stomach that came from looking at men and seeing them as *men*, not merely fellow rational beings. Mr. Dymond leaned towards her, his blue eyes brilliant even in the filtered light from her unwashed windows. Was he aware of the casual invitation in every line of his athletic body?

"I'm going to change my clothes," she said abruptly, heading for the door to her room. "You'd better take off your wet coat and boots and put them by the fire before you take a chill. I have an old coat of Mr. Sparks's you can borrow."

She had only one dry dress; she wore it every laundry evening now. It was the favorite dress she had dyed black when Will died. She hadn't had the heart to include it when she sold her other black things. Looking at it now brought on a complex wave of guilt.

Will had liked her in the dress. She'd married him in it, the first time she'd worn colors since her father's death. When she had pushed down the last bubble of blue-and-green fabric into the tub of black dye, she had cried like a child—for her dead hopes and her dead husband and a small traitorous bit because she'd wanted to keep her pretty dress.

The cheap dye she'd used had rubbed off on her skin as she sat with Will's body. All her mourning dresses had turned her skin black that year, in hot or damp weather. Every time she saw it she'd felt a fresh pang, as if the color was trying to help her conceal the relief in her heart, or maybe sink in and extinguish it. She missed Will, but she was happier without him.

She couldn't put that dress on and go in the next room and flirt with another man. She couldn't do that to Will.

Besides—Phoebe remembered how she'd felt in those early days with Will. The first day they'd gone out walking together, when this dress was nothing but a bolt of cloth on a shelf, she'd felt so alive, so hopeful and anxious. She felt the same now, but the dress was old and black and she'd learned feeling this way didn't lead anywhere good. It was better to be alone.

Sukey poked her head in the door. "He looks tol-lol in his shirtsleeves," she whispered. "The arms on him! Hadn't you ought to forget to lend him a coat?"

Phoebe thought that was a wonderful idea. There was only one just way to punish herself: not allowing herself to see his shirtsleeves at all. "He won't be very handsome when he's frozen to death," she whispered back severely, pulling Will's old coat out of the wardrobe. "Here, go and give him this."

Chapter 3

Nick was pleasantly surprised by the Honey Moon, the sweet shop owned by Mrs. Sparks's prospective husband. The many-paned window sparkled, the jars of sweetmeats displayed inside were colorful and tempting, and the sign—a crescent moon the shape of a man's profile, mouth gaping to receive a piece of fruitcake—was neatly painted and scrupulously clean.

He was even more impressed when he walked inside and saw the small case of cakes and biscuits beside the counter. It had been unfair of him to expect rustic mince pies and honey-sweetened Banbury cakes. The carefully sculpted tarts, Naples-biscuit towers and candied fruits would have graced a London confectioner's. He was immediately seized with a powerful craving for sugar.

It appeared he was alone in that among the inhabitants of Lively St. Lemeston. Apart from himself, the shop was entirely empty. He rang the bell on the counter.

A harried young man of about his own age appeared through a swinging door, his floury apron tied over a floury shirt and floury breeches. His head and hands at first seemed an oasis of color, but on closer inspection they were dusted in fine white powder, down to the tips of his outsized ears. He beamed at Nick. "Good morning to you, sir, may I get you something or other?"

"I'm Mr. Nicholas Dymond, here to see Mr. Moon," Nick said, his eye caught by a marzipan pig.

The young man's smile only intensified. "I'm Robert Moon. I'm that glad to make your acquaintance, sir." He shook Nick's hand fervently, leaving it covered in paste. "Oh—plague take it—I'll fetch you a wet cloth." He ran back into the kitchen, returning with the promised cloth and a dark, moist slab of cake. "I be working on the recipe, and I'd be that honored by your opinion."

He ushered Nick over to one of the small tables by the window and pulled out a chair for him. Once Nick would have thought the man was merely obsequious; now he wondered if Moon thought him a cripple. He sat, trying not to let his unease show. Moon watched avidly as Nick sliced off a corner of cake with his fork and lifted it to his mouth.

Rich flavor spread over his tongue, sugar and lavender and a dark hint of tea. The texture was perfect, dense and smooth.

"Do you like it?" Moon asked anxiously.

Nick took another bite, this time getting a taste of the lemon glaze and the sharp tang of lemon zest. "It's remarkable."

He had been sincere, but Moon's ears drooped. "I put in more than I ought of sugar, didn't I?"

Nick tried to imagine this praise-hungry young man married to prickly Mrs. Sparks and failed. He would give her cake and she would say, *Mmm, it's very good, but I prefer jam tarts and anyway I'm busy,* and he would droop like a blade of grass in the rain. Nick smiled at the image of her bent over her work, licking crumbs from her fingers and cursing when she smeared lemon glaze on her manuscript.

He, on the other hand, was painfully aware of the weight

of Moon's expectations. He leaned forward and looked the man in the eye. "I meant what I said. I'm fond of sweets, but it's rare they're so utterly satisfying. I feel as if I'd just taken my first bite of real food after three days of foraging."

To his relief, Moon's face lit with joy. It was how Nick must have looked when his mother had been briefly happy with him, that same helpless gratification. Relief faded into a slight queasiness. Lady Tassell was going to pay Moon's debts if he landed Mrs. Sparks. That was why he was so eager to please.

Don't think of it as playing lord of the manor. Imagine he's a nervous young recruit. He lounged a little in his chair, letting authority settle over him like a comfortable cloak. "Sit." He waved at the chair opposite him. "So you want to marry Mrs. Sparks. Do you know her well?"

Halfway into the chair, Moon's eyes widened in panic like an unprepared schoolboy called upon by his professor. "Not— not *very* well," he said in a tone that meant *not at all.* "But I know she helped her husband with his newspaper; she's not afeared of hard work."

"I believe she supports herself with writing children's stories, doesn't she?"

Mr. Moon gave a shaky smile. "Yes! And she'd surely have my blessing to go on with it at night, when we've finished down here."

If the Honey Moon was successful, Mrs. Sparks wouldn't need the income earned by her pen. Perhaps she wouldn't want it. It was only the poet in him cringing in sympathy at the thought of giving it up or cramming it into a few exhausted candle-lit hours; he had no reason to believe Mrs. Sparks felt the same.

Moon fidgeted. Nick leaned in and asked gently, "You are

really going to marry a woman of whom you know nothing?" *For money* lingered in the air unsaid. His question was rude enough already, aimed as it was at a man unlikely to risk rudeness in his answer. But part of Nick wanted Moon to take this chance to back out, to say, *No. I won't.*

But Moon's anxious face smoothed out, as if here he felt sure of his ground. "If I don't, I'll lose the *shop.*"

Once, when Nick had been very small, he had begged his mother to stay past the daily quarter of an hour she allotted each of her children during elections and read him another story. It must have been the general election of 1790, so he had been six—did other children calculate their ages by election years? She had smiled wearily and smoothed his hair. *I can't, Nicky. I have to work.*

It will only take another five minutes, he had said.

I can't spare five minutes.

But, Mama, I miss you.

She'd wanted to, he thought. Tears had stood in her eyes. But she'd said, with this same quiet certainty, *I miss you too, Nicky. But we mustn't be selfish. For want of a nail, the kingdom was lost.* He'd always hated her blind insistence on following her head over her heart, her refusal to swerve even for five minutes to give happiness to someone she loved.

He used to compare it to Evangelical fanaticism. Since then he'd been in the army. He'd seen officers who knew sacrifices were necessary for a goal that *could not* be sacrificed. He'd seen fallen men piled atop one another in the breach in the wall at Badajoz. He'd climbed over their bodies, because the city had to be taken. He hadn't faltered.

The vital importance of a city was easy for Nick to understand, a confectionery or an election less so. But he could see in

Moon's face that he would sacrifice far more than his domestic happiness to keep this place. "You'll be at the Orange-and-Purple party Thursday evening, won't you?" he asked. "Mrs. Sparks has promised to be there."

"Then I'll be there." Moon looked like a man preparing to face the firing squad.

"Have you given any thought to how you'll court her?" Nick asked as delicately as he could.

Mr. Moon froze. "I thought you were looking after that side of things!"

Nick smothered a groan. "I'm working at it, but Mrs. Sparks may be a hard nut to crack. Don't take it to heart if she snaps at you, will you? She can be a bit blunt, and her first marriage—"

"They fought like Kilkenny cats," Moon said glumly. "Do you think she likes sweets?"

Nick had no idea.

"She must," Moon answered for him. "Everyone likes sweets. Especially with a splendid figure like hers."

He tried not to think about Mrs. Sparks's figure, but it was too late. He wouldn't mind feeding her sweets—that rosebud mouth closing around a bite of cake, her tongue darting out to lick icing off his fingers. Her eyes drifting shut. The heave of her breasts as she sighed in satisfaction.

He shifted uncomfortably in his chair. He was supposed to be helping Mr. Moon, not daydreaming about the widow's mouth. He could do this. He *would* do this. Even if he had no bloody idea how.

Phoebe thought perhaps she could afford a new dress.

No, that was foolish; she had only half a pound put by and she needed it to patch the roof. That was far more important than feeling pretty. No matter how much she wanted to prove to a handsome lord's son that she was *not* a draggletail, thank you very much. He'd thought she was a maid!

But that was foolish, too. To the Honorable Mr. Nicholas Dymond, there wasn't much to choose between Mrs. Sparks, printer's widow, and Sukey Grimes, maid-of-all-work. It was like asking a man in an air-balloon to tell the difference between a beetle and an ant crawling on the ground below.

You look *like a beetle, as round as you are,* a nasty little inner voice said. *Vanity will only expose you to ridicule.* It sounded like her mother.

I don't care, she thought defiantly. *I don't care about Mama's opinion and I don't care about Mr. Dymond's, either. I am going out on Thursday to enjoy myself, not to please anyone else. I work hard, and I deserve to feel pretty.*

She pulled on her boots and headed for the Lively St. Lemeston circulating library, where her younger sister Helen sat behind the desk three days a week for a small salary and the right to have the first look at the London fashion magazines.

On her way, she passed Market Square at the center of town. Carpenters clustered around the half-built hustings, the raised wooden platform on which speeches would be given and votes cast come the polls three weeks from now. Most of the structure was there in skeleton, and the steps were mostly complete, but the floorboards, sidings, and distinctive sloped roof were entirely absent. Since carpenters were freemen and the candidates paid for the work, construction tended to drag out as long as possible with little protest.

As she walked up the steps of the boarding house that held the small library, her brother-in-law, Jack Sparks, strode out the door and nearly bowled her over. For a moment he looked so much like Will that she caught her breath. Tall and stocky with fine fair hair standing out from his head like dandelion fluff, he even moved with the same swift intensity she'd once loved. Later it had made her stomach turn over anxiously when she saw Will coming: *What's he angry about now?*

Jack had never had the same effect on her. She smacked him on the arm. "Watch where you're going!"

He started back. "Phoebe? What are you doing here?"

"I'm here to see my sister, you clunch."

His frown smoothed out. "Oh, of course. Give Helen my regards." He headed down the steps.

"Jack, wait."

He turned back with a sigh. "I'm in a bit of a hurry."

"This won't take long. I was hoping you might advance me that half-a-crown for my election poem."

Jack shifted uncomfortably. "Actually, Phoebe, I don't need the poem after all. The *Intelligencer* is going to be neutral in this year's election."

He couldn't have surprised her more if he'd told her he was emigrating to Canada. "Neutral? But the *Intelligencer* has been Whig since your father founded it!" The Sparkses had always been the most dyed-in-the-wool Orange-and-Purple family in Lively St. Lemeston. Jack, being the last Sparks, had taken it upon himself to be Orange-and-Purple enough for a small army.

"He and Will would understand." A spasm crossed Jack's face. "I think." He pulled some coins from his pocket. "Of course I'll still pay you the money. Here are two shillings, and

I'll owe you sixpence—"

Oh, how she wanted those coins. "Jack, you don't have to pay me if you don't want the poem."

Jack drew himself up. "You're family, and I made you a promise. I feel enough of a turncoat as it is. Take the money."

She put out her hand, but something stopped her. "Do you need the money yourself? Is everything all right—?"

"Of course it is." He grabbed her wrist none too gently, twisted her hand palm-up, dropped the coins in it, and crushed her fingers shut around them.

"Jack, if you need help—"

"Let it alone." His thick, straight brows drew together and his face set. It was an expression that brooked no opposition, and while it didn't drive her to oppose him on sheer stubborn principle, as it had on Will's face, it still annoyed her quite a bit.

"Don't tell me what to do—"

The door opened behind her, and a man in his thirties came out. "I'm sorry to interrupt, sir, but if you would give me a hand with Miss Jessop's chair, I'd be grateful."

Jack seized on this pretext with relief, hastening past Phoebe up the stairs. "Of course. My sister and I were just finished talking." He held the door as the servant pushed the incumbent Tory MP's daughter through in her wheelchair and then lifted her out of it so Jack could carry the chair down the short flight of stairs. "Pardon me, Phoebe," he said pointedly. "You're taking up most of this step."

Phoebe's jaw dropped. "No, pardon *me*." She pushed past him, skirting around the servant and his charge with no difficulty whatsoever. The chair might be a great long wood-and-leather thing, with two heavy wooden wheels away and back from the seat and a small one jutting out in front below the footrest, but the steps were wide enough to accommodate three or four like it. She slammed the door behind her, only to flush when every head in the quiet library turned to look at her.

All but one. Helen remained bent over the newest *Belle Assemblée*. "Good morning, what can I do for you?" she said without looking up when Phoebe's shadow fell across her desk.

Phoebe's heart filled with helpless affection. "Morning, Ships." She reached out to run her fingers over her sister's painstakingly braided coronet of shining dark hair.

"Fee! How are you?" Helen ducked away with the ease of long habit. She was a very orderly girl and hated having her hair mussed.

"I want to remake one of my dresses. I'm going to Mr. Dymond's voters' dinner on Thursday. Would you like to come?"

A shadow passed over Helen's face, her smile turning strained and the skin around her eyes tightening. "I can't, I'd planned to start embroidering kerchiefs for the Gooding Day auction. But I'd love to help you remake one of your dresses."

Phoebe frowned. Helen could be a little self-contained and anxious, but surely the shadows under her eyes hadn't been so dark last week. And surely even Helen wouldn't turn down a party simply because she'd already settled it in her mind to embroider kerchiefs. "Is something wrong?"

"No, no, of course not." Helen's smile brightened again. That smile could light up a room. "I have a bit of a headache, that's all. Mama was in a tear this morning."

That explained everything. Mama in a tear was worse than a barrel of ale for making your head ache. "Ugh. Poor Ships."

"Ugh indeed."

"Do you know what's wrong with Jack? He was jumpy when I ran into him outside just now, and he told me the *Intelligencer* won't be partisan in the election."

"Couldn't say." Helen flipped back through the pages of her magazine. "I was reading."

Phoebe laughed. "Of course you were."

Helen was no longer listening. "Is your dark blue dress clean?"

"I washed it yesterday."

"Perfect. Look here, it says that 'for evening, dark blue trimmed with white, and faun trimmed with blue, are very general'. If we buy a length of white lace, I can trim the bodice and the sleeves and add a white belt of sorts to raise the waist-line—waists are shorter this month, it says. It's a shame it hasn't a demi-train, but…" They both knew neither of them would ever own a gown with a demi-train. "And you must buy a new shawl in some rich color. I saw a Turkish one with dark red flowers at the milliner's that would do splendidly."

Mr. Dymond liked Lord Byron; he would like a Turkish shawl. Phoebe was ashamed of herself for the thought. "You're a gem, Ships."

"I know." Helen smiled at her again, but she still looked tenser than usual. Phoebe wondered for the thousandth time if she ought to ask Helen to come and live with her—and concluded, for the thousandth time, that she couldn't afford it. She was never sure if that was true, or if she was selfishly clinging to her privacy.

"Here," Helen offered, "why don't you look at the magazine until my shift is over and see if there's anything you particularly want to try?"

This was supreme generosity, but Phoebe could imagine nothing that would make the time pass slower. "No, you keep it." She paused, embarrassed even as she opened her mouth. "Have you got any Byron?"

Helen raised her eyebrows. "Byron? You, Fee?"

Phoebe searched for words to explain her sudden feeling that she was missing something, had closed herself off from something and now wanted it back. She shrugged.

"Well, it doesn't matter," Helen said. "There's a three-month waiting list on both cantos of *Childe Harold* anyway."

So Phoebe went to read *Pamela* for the tenth time. *I've become about as lively as this town,* she thought.

Nick rapped at his brother's door. He could hear raised voices, to his dismay if not his surprise.

Tony yanked the door open, gave Nick a nod of welcome, and turned back to his wife. "Can't you at least make an effort?"

"I *am* making an effort," Ada said stiff-lipped, as her maid added a few extra ringlets to her coiffure. "Just because I don't want to wear an orange-and-purple gown—"

Nick hated the smell of burning hair. He also disliked shouting. He leaned against the wall and tried not to be noticed.

Tony switched tactics. "You'll look splendid," he cajoled. "Like a Persian princess. Nick, wouldn't she look splendid?" Nick didn't answer. Tony and Ada both glared at him. It was almost like spending time with his parents.

"I don't want to look like some shameless heathen princess," Ada said. "I want to look like an English lady, and I'll wear my own clothes!"

Tony sighed and gave up the fight. "But you'll dance with the voters, won't you?"

"Tony, they'll paw at me—"

"Oh, for heaven's sake, stop *whining*. This is an important night for us, and you're giving me a headache." He turned away, rubbing at his temple with the heel of his hand.

Nick was getting a headache too. He had always hated these sorts of parties, his mother hissing at him to smile at the voters' wives and daughters, but don't smile too much, remember your manners and for God's sake look as if you're enjoying yourself, and if you do it wrong, the world will end. He'd thought he was done with them.

"Oh, I won't embarrass you in front of your precious voters," Ada spat, jabbing pins into her dark brown hair.

Nick had never liked Ada; he had thought her proud and stiff from her first Season, when Lady Tassell had invited her for tea and whispered to him and Tony that her father had a great interest in West Sussex. But now he was uncomfortably reminded of himself at fourteen, saying the same thing to his mother as he yanked the knot tight on his cravat.

"How can you stand it?" he asked Tony. "It's like public days at Tassell Hall all over again."

Tony glanced at him. "I never minded as much as you did. And it's worth it to win the seat."

"Why? What do you want the seat for?"

Tony gave him an irritated look. "What do you mean? Every seat the Whigs have is one step closer to Reform…"

Tony kept talking, but Nick stopped listening. It was the same smooth answer Lady Tassell always gave, the same recitation of party goals and agreed-upon doctrine. It didn't explain the heart of it. It didn't explain why Tony cared.

He realized Tony was waiting expectantly for his response. "Sorry," Nick said.

Tony sighed. "*You* aren't going to embarrass me tonight, are you?" He didn't even sound angry, only resigned.

Nick felt sorry and ashamed. It wouldn't kill him to make an effort for once. He met Tony's eyes and shook his head.

Tony didn't look very reassured, but he didn't pursue it. He went to his wife, put a hand on her shoulder and leaned in to whisper coaxingly in her ear. She stilled and trembled like a nervy horse, meeting his eyes in the mirror. "I just don't know what to say to them," she said softly.

"Just smile," Tony told her. "You're so pretty when you smile."

Nick saw the corners of her mouth tilt upwards a little, a hopeful curve, and Tony smiled back. Maybe there was a chance for the two of them after all.

"I won't have to eat any more of that awful curried blood pudding, will I?" she asked.

Tony stepped back sharply. "Ada, the butcher is one of our key supporters!"

It was going to be a long night.

Helen would be there soon to help her dress for the party. Phoebe was embarrassed by her own excited anticipation. It had been so long since she had gone to an evening gathering of more than three or four. She had forgotten how overblown one's hopes could get, as if a few hours could change everything.

To distract herself, she sat at her writing table and thought about poor Ann, still feverish in a ditch. Perhaps the girl could die in childbirth, but her child could survive and grow up virtuous and poor in the home of a passing Good Samaritan.

She had written a dozen tales with babies in them since her miscarriage. She'd thought herself inured to it. But tonight, imagining a swooning Ann holding her crying newborn child for the first and last time, she was swamped with fresh longing and grief.

All the better to write the passage, she told herself, blinking back tears and taking up her pen.

Someone banged on the door so loudly the hinges rattled. It couldn't be Helen; her sister always knocked quietly. She wiped at her eyes as she stood, ready to be annoyed if it was Mr. Gilchrist again.

But it *was* Helen, her face blotched and wet, her lips trembling and her chest heaving. Helen had cried like this as a child, shaking and heaving and uncontrollable, sometimes for half an hour at a stretch; the last time Phoebe had seen it had been at their father's deathbed five years before. "What's wrong, Ships?" Phoebe tried to sound calm. "What's happened?"

Helen tried to draw herself up and walk into the apartment, but she stumbled blindly over the threshold, and when Phoebe caught her she collapsed gratefully into her arms. "I'm sorry, Fee," she choked out. "I'm so sorry."

For a moment Phoebe was so frightened she couldn't speak. "S-sorry for what?"

"I'm—I'm in a family way," Helen said, and then went stiff and silent, gulping down her sobs convulsively, waiting for Phoebe's response.

Chapter 4

Panic stopped Phoebe's throat like an accidentally swallowed boiled sweet, turning an ordinary moment into a life-or-death struggle. She strove for breath, irrationally angry at Helen for making her feel this way. *How could you be so stupid?* Luckily the lump of panic stopped the words before she could say them.

"Mama told me—she told me not to come home again," Helen sobbed. "She kept asking me how I could be so stupid. She called me a—"

"Mama is a harpy. You know she is." Oh God, what was she going to do? "Who is the father?"

"Don't ask me that. Please, Fee."

"What? Why not? Ships—"

"I can't talk about it. I can't tell you—it doesn't matter. I can't marry him."

"Why not?"

"I just can't."

"Ships, did he hurt you?"

Helen shook her head jerkily. "It was all my fault. Mama was right, I'm a stupid sl—sl—" She couldn't even bring herself to say the word out loud.

"Don't say that. It isn't true. This man is responsible. If you—God, if you really can't marry him—" What was going to happen to her beautiful little sister? She drew in a deep breath. Helen was counting on her to be strong and worldly, and know what to do. "He can at least help with money."

Helen shook her head. "He can't. He said there's no money, and if I tell anyone, he'll ruin me. He'll tell everyone what I did."

"*What?*" Phoebe couldn't comprehend the magnitude of this atrocity. Someone had bedded Helen and then *threatened* her? Helen was practically a baby herself!

"What am I going to do?"

Phoebe poured her sister a lukewarm cup of tea, her hands shaking. "Drink this, sweetheart. It's going to be all right, I promise." Helen obeyed, her sobs quieting. Phoebe tried to think. Then she tried to think about something other than tracking down the piece of filth responsible for this horror and ripping him into tiny pieces. "How—how far along are you?"

"Six weeks." Helen pulled a delicately embroidered handkerchief out of her pocket and blew her nose.

"And you're sure?"

Helen nodded. "At least, six weeks ago is when we—" She flushed. "My courses are usually regular as clockwork, and they're a month late."

Phoebe took a deep breath. She felt a pang even asking, but she said, "There are—herbs you can take. If you don't want the baby."

Helen's hands moved to cover her stomach protectively. "No." She swallowed. "I mean—is that what you think I should do?"

I don't know. "What do you want to do?"

Helen shook her head helplessly. "I don't know. I don't know what to do."

"If you got married, you could keep the baby. Otherwise, you'll have to give it up." Phoebe couldn't imagine giving up a child, but women did it all the time, didn't they?

"I—who on earth would I marry?" Her mouth contorted as she evidently began going through the men she knew.

There were dozens of men in Lively St. Lemeston who would kill to marry Helen, illegitimate child on the way or no. But God, she was so young. Only sixteen. Too young to be pushed into a choice the magnitude of which she couldn't possibly understand. Marriages could go wrong so easily.

On the other hand, Helen had never been pregnant before. Her child hadn't started to kick. To have that, and then give it up—

But if Helen didn't want to cause abortion and didn't want to marry, then there was only one other choice that wouldn't ruin her. "I'll take care of this," she told her sister. "I'll take you away, and you'll have the baby somewhere far away. We'll find a nice family to raise it, and no one will ever know."

"How—we can't possibly afford that." Helen's eyes looked huge, her features so small beside her wide handkerchief.

No. They couldn't. But there were two families in town at the moment who could, and would, to secure Phoebe's marriage and her vote. The Dymonds and the Wheatcrofts.

Phoebe could feel all her anticipation and hopes dying in her breast as she thought it, but that didn't matter. All that mattered was Helen. "You are *not* going to die in a ditch, Ships."

Helen frowned. "What?"

"Never mind. Here, let's fetch out the blue dress."

Nick tried to keep his hand light and relaxed on his walking stick, but Moon's anxiety radiated from him in shimmering waves, like heat from the Spanish ground. He laid his other hand on Moon's back, and Moon jumped.

"I'm sure she'll like you," Nick lied. "Don't worry."

"I'm not very good with women," Moon said for the fiftieth time.

Nick took a sip of punch to hide his sigh. Orange and purple ribbons were wound around the columns in the small but elegant local assembly rooms. His mother had donated a large sum for their construction just before the by-election of 1792, as had Lord Wheatcroft. The rooms were full of voters, clusters of professional men and their well-dressed wives and children in a sea of tradesmen and their families. Almost everyone wore either orange or purple or both, or at least a rosette or armband, even though Nick knew that about half of them had no intention of voting for Tony and had only come for the free food and punch.

Tony was in his element. He'd just finished whisking a middle-aged woman across the dance floor and was now surrounded by voters, who were all laughing at something he'd said. True, he'd been here for nearly two months getting to know all of them, but Nick suspected it would have been exactly the same in a room of strangers.

He shoved a stuffed egg in his mouth just as the tipsy voter beside him said, "Honored to meet the Hero of Badajoz, sir. Did you kill a lot of Frenchmen?"

Oh God, not this Hero of Badajoz nonsense again. Yes, he had killed a lot of Frenchmen. Did that really make him a hero? And why could Englishmen never pronounce Badajoz properly? Nick smiled, shook his hand, and pointed apologetically at his full mouth, chewing until the man lost interest. But as he turned to gather more conversation stoppers, a little girl no higher than his waist asked, "Can you still ride a horse?"

He almost choked on the egg. "Not very well, I'm afraid. Maybe when I've healed more…"

"That's terribly sad," she said earnestly. "I love horses."

So did Nick. He smothered another sigh.

"Can you dance? What about climbing trees?"

Looking around for a likely parent, he spotted Mrs. Sparks in the doorway. His sigh turned into a smile. She had worn something pretty after all, a dark blue dress edged with white lace that showed off her ample curves, and a bright, rich Turkish shawl that clung to them. It brought out the drama of her creamy complexion and dark eyes and hair. "Excuse me," he told the girl, and turned to Moon. "There she is. Wait here, I'll bring her over and introduce you." He wanted to warn her not to be too sharp with the poor confectioner.

She forced a friendly smile when she saw him coming towards her. It threw him; she'd made very little effort to please when he met her. But he smiled back anyway, saying, "Good evening, Mrs. Sparks. You look very pretty." She looked even prettier close up. Her thick hair was coming loose from its pins, the orange-and-purple rosette half-dangling above her ear. It would be improper to reach out and push it back in, but he imagined doing it. He imagined tracing the delicate curve of her ear, running his finger down the line of her neck. She'd shiver and blush…

Her face grew tight at the mild compliment. "Thank you, Mr. Dymond. You're too kind."

"Is everything all right?"

She opened her mouth, then shut it, shaking her head.

"No. I—may I talk to you for a moment? Privately?"

"Of course," he said at once, making a *wait a moment* gesture to Moon. "Will the porch do?"

The Orange-and-Purples wanted to install gas lighting in the town's main streets, but the Pink-and-Whites were bitterly against it. Very little light from the flickering street-lamp or the candles inside reached the steps of the assembly rooms. It was cold, and he couldn't see her face. She wrapped her shawl tightly around her shoulders and didn't speak.

"Please, if I can help—" He should have said *we,* speaking for his Party, but he didn't.

"You can, sir," she said in a small, tense voice that was somehow also trying to placate him. "I—well, they say pride comes before a fall, don't they? I'm that sorry if I was rude earlier. I've reconsidered your very generous offer and I find—it isn't too late to meet that man who wants to marry me, is it?" As she spoke, her Sussex burr grew thicker with agitation.

A few days ago, she had recoiled at the very idea of marriage. Something was terribly wrong. "Of course not. Are you—"

More words spilled anxiously from her mouth before he could finish the sentence. "I hope if I marry him, I may count on—that is—"

"The Dymonds always stand by those who have stood by them," Nick said gently, borrowing the words from his mother. "What sort of trouble are you in?"

"I—you must promise me you'll keep what I'm about to tell you a secret. Will you promise me? Can I trust you?" She huffed out a breath. "Lord, how stupid to ask a man if he can be trusted, but—can you?"

Tony or his mother would have told him to say yes at once.

"I like to think I'm an honorable man," Nick said at last. "I wouldn't break a confidence without an overwhelming reason. But if what you have to say concerns electoral fraud or other wrongdoing by the Tories, I might have a responsibility—"

Her death grip on her shawl relaxed. "It doesn't. It's entirely personal."

"Then I believe I can be trusted." Keeping a secret, at least, he could manage.

She half-laughed, not sounding very amused. "Let's hope you're right." She looked about. "My sister—" She stopped again, took a deep breath. "My younger sister is in the family way. If I marry your man, I need you to help her have the child in secret and find a family to raise it."

When Lady Tassell had given him this task, it had sounded a joke. The favors his mother traded in had always seemed so small: an apprenticeship here, a new roof there. But suddenly Mrs. Sparks was offering a great price for a great favor. He had won his bet already, and he couldn't be glad.

His mind raced, but he saw no way out. Paying to raise a child would be expensive. His mother would only do it for a vote. He couldn't afford it himself, especially if his parents stopped his allowance. "I'm sorry."

She half turned away, a sharp movement in the gloom. "No, you're not."

I'm not my brother, I don't care about your votes, he wanted to say, or *I know what it's like to watch the life I planned vanish like a mirage in the desert.* But his feelings wouldn't help her. "Can't your sister marry?"

"She doesn't wish to."

"Neither do you."

The white lace dipped as she shrugged. "I've done it

before," she said lightly. "I can do it again."

Would he sacrifice so much for Tony? "Have you spoken to her about aborting the child?"

Her face turned towards him. "She doesn't want to. I won't ask her to. I…"

"Yes?"

"I lost a pregnancy once. Not on purpose. It just happened. I won't ask her to do that for me."

He knew she wouldn't thank him for saying it. "Surely a few days of her pain for a lifetime of your freedom is not—"

"It's a lifetime for her child." Her voice was flat. "Can you help her?"

"My mother can."

Mrs. Sparks nodded. "Don't—don't tell her yet. I hope you don't mind if I see who the Pink-and-Whites have picked out for me. I'm an Orange-and-Purple born and bred, but—"

"Of course not."

There was silence for long moments.

"Who do *you* have picked out for me?"

"Mr. Moon, the confectioner." He tried to sound enthusiastic. "Do you like sweets?"

There was another pause. "Oh yes," she said unconvincingly.

"You don't like sweets?" Mr. Moon sounded stunned. "But—"

Phoebe shifted uncomfortably. "That's how I look when people tell me they don't like reading," she said, trying for a friendly laugh. Mr. Moon's eyes widened anxiously. "…You don't like reading."

"I've naught against it, but it's really for women, isn't it? Novels and magazines and all that?"

She blinked, confounded. Who on earth had picked this man for her? He was handsome enough if you didn't mind big ears, but...

Behind him, Mr. Dymond's dark brows drew together like a blackbird settling its wings huffily into place after being shooed to a new perch on the roof. *He* liked reading. She shouldn't have wanted to laugh, not when her future hung in the balance.

Mr. Moon glanced over his shoulder and caught Mr. Dymond's frown. "I'm agreeable to *your* reading, though. I know you write stories. I'd not begrudge you..." He trailed off. "Well, it's extra income, isn't it?"

Had Mr. Dymond impressed on him that she wasn't to be stopped writing? She felt warm for a moment before realizing that he'd been coaching Mr. Moon on how to win her over so his brother could get her vote. "Yes. It is."

Mr. Moon nodded, looking as desperate as she felt. He didn't want this either; he must need something from the Dymonds, although she didn't know what just yet.

She didn't *have* to have a husband who read. "Here, how's this? I'll come round every day or so this next fortnight and bring you something to read, and you can give me a sweet, and perhaps we'll convert each other in the end."

"I'll have you by the end of the week, that's smack!" Moon had a sweet smile.

But if this were a story, you'd describe it as 'gormless', she thought.

Behind him, Mr. Dymond was smiling at her too, admiration and sympathy and encouragement and a few other things all intermixed. She couldn't think of one word that would sum that smile up.

You can't rate men on how difficult they are to write about. Or on how charitably you would describe their smiles, either. At least Mr. Moon seemed mild-mannered enough, unlikely to become a petty domestic tyrant or berate her for trifles.

"What sorts of flavors do you like?" Mr. Moon asked, and she jolted her gaze back to him.

"Um..."

"Citrus, brandy, rum, anise...?"

She grimaced before she could stop herself. "I don't like anise." His shoulders sagged a little. "Citrus. I like citrus." He smiled gratefully, and Phoebe tried to resign herself to a lifetime of lemon cake.

Chapter 5

"Ships, you can't wear the same dress for the rest of your life," Phoebe said. *And I can't afford to buy you new ones, either.* Besides, there was already enough gossip about why Helen had suddenly fled her home to live with her sister; a new wardrobe would only make it worse. Most people seemed to have settled on *Their mother is impossible to live with* as an explanation for now, but there was no guarantee that would last. "I'll go with you."

Helen had two shifts. Every night she took one off and washed it, then wore the other until morning when the first one was dry, when she put it back on and washed the second one. She hadn't been able to do that last night, and she was far too fastidious to sleep naked. She had been wearing the same shift for a day, a night, and a morning, and her discomfort showed in every movement. But she said, "I can't go home. I can't face her."

Helen didn't even seem able to face Phoebe; she kept her eyes carefully on her own face in the mirror as she slowly rebraided her hair. The tender skin around her eyes was dark from lack of sleep, almost bruised looking. It only made her great dark eyes look greater, and very deep.

Phoebe hugged her around the waist, pressing a kiss to the top of her head. "You can face anyone. You're my beautiful sister."

Helen's eyes met hers in the mirror for a brief second, so uncertain it broke Phoebe's heart. "What if I go back and she—what if the neighbors hear?"

If this news got out, Helen would never get over it. *Was he worth it?* Phoebe wanted to demand. "All right. I'll go before my appointment with Mr. Moon."

The loose left side of Helen's hair danced as she nodded quickly. "Thank you, Fee."

"Don't worry about it. I'll take Sukey with me to help carry."

"A whacking crate of books is the only thing heavier than a washtub," Sukey grumbled good-naturedly.

"It's not a crate. It's a hamper with six books in the bottom. And I only brought the first volume of each."

"Ooh, you separated the volumes?" Sukey put on a wide-eyed expression. "It must be love."

Separating volumes offered too much chance that one would be lost and all three would be useless. As a rule, Phoebe never lent books at all. If someone was going to spill coffee on one of her precious books, she wanted it to be herself. But this was important, so she steeled herself. "It isn't love," she said. "But it might be marriage."

Sukey gave her a remorseful look. "I'm sorry, ma'am. I hadn't ought to have teased."

Phoebe shrugged. "Don't worry about it."

"Maybe it won't be too bad. You'll never go hungry, anyway."

Phoebe nodded glumly.

"Have you spoken to that Mr. Gilchrist yet?"

"I've been putting it off."

Sukey nodded. "He's a tricky one. But he wants your vote more than Mr. Dymond."

"I think you're right."

Sukey laughed. "No need to sound surprised."

"Sorry," Phoebe said, abashed.

"Do you think you might get an advance bribe from him? The grocer won't let you go on tick much longer."

Phoebe sighed. "It's not a bribe," she said halfheartedly. "It's—patronage or something."

"Or you could send Miss Helen to talk to the grocer. I'm sure he'd extend your credit then."

"Absolutely not!"

Sukey shrugged. "You can't do everything for her. Bad enough you let her talk you into fetching her clothes."

Phoebe glared. "If I *could* do everything for her, I would."

"Yes, and she knows it."

"She's a sixteen-year-old girl, and I'm her older sister. She ought to know it." Poor Helen had nobody else; it was up to Phoebe to be a whole family to her. "It isn't as if she can count on Mama."

"Could be worse. My mother would beat me black and blue if I got myself in trouble like that."

"And if she did, no doubt *you'd* come to me for help as well," Phoebe snapped, wishing for the millionth time that Helen hadn't chosen to confide in Sukey. She thought the maid could be trusted, but thinking wasn't the same as knowing.

"I suppose I would, at that," Sukey said amiably.

Everybody came to Phoebe for help, because they knew she'd give it to them. She didn't mind, most of the time. The shameful truth was that it made her feel important. But today she couldn't help wishing there was someone to help *her*.

Helen would always do anything she could, of course. When Phoebe had needed nursing and cheering after her miscarriage, Helen at thirteen had done more than her share. But it wasn't the same as having a father, or a husband, or a best friend her own age. Someone who could make her feel safe. How long had it been since she'd really confided in Martha Honeysett, her closest friend as a girl? What had happened?

"Well," Phoebe said cheerlessly. "Here we are." Even after five years, even though she did it at least once a week, she hated walking down this street to this door knowing that her father wouldn't be there to open it.

It seemed unfair that it should still be the same street, the same house with the same spindle tree crowding the windows, covered in the same distinctive pink-and-orange berries. *That tree ought to pick a party and stick to it,* her father used to say, and laugh heartily at his own weak joke.

She squared her shoulders and rapped on the door. She squared them even further as the doorknob turned and the door opened. She pasted a smile on her face. "Good morning, Mama."

Sukey curtseyed behind her. "Ma'am."

"Good morning, Phoebe, darling." Her mother looked her up and down in that way that made Phoebe feel angry and ugly all at once. Mrs. Knight reached out to straighten Phoebe's kerchief. She tried not to flinch away. "What a colorful dress."

Phoebe's dress was a practical dark lavender. But she knew what her mother meant. Five years after her own husband's death, Mrs. Knight still wore black. "Thank you." She tried to say it blandly, but it came out defiant anyway. "We've come for Helen's things."

Mrs. Knight sighed heavily. "You're taking her side?"

Phoebe's hands clenched into fists. She hid them in her skirts. "Why won't *you*?"

"Because I value her happiness over her approval. Her behavior is unfeminine and selfish"—two of Mrs. Knight's favorite words—"and I won't encourage it. She has to marry the father of that baby before her child is born a bastard."

"The father of that baby, whoever he is, doesn't deserve to touch the bottom of Helen's boot."

"Helen didn't seem to think so, if she was thinking at all. But you girls never think, you only do what feels good."

Phoebe could feel every muscle in her body tightening at the injustice of this. She'd heard it from her mother her whole life. Even reading by herself had been a selfish pleasure; it was read aloud to the family or nothing. If she broke a plate while washing the dishes, it was because she was careless and didn't think of how hard her father worked to buy those plates.

Sukey shifted awkwardly beside her, and Phoebe just managed to hold on to her temper. "I've come for Helen's things."

"Those are my things," Mrs. Knight said. "I paid for them and since Helen has decided to no longer be part of this family, I'll have to sell them to make up for the lost income."

No one, not even Will, had ever been able to make Phoebe so angry with so few words. "You don't decide who is and isn't part of this family," she said tightly.

"'Family', not 'familry', dearest," Mrs. Knight corrected her, even though her own speech was rarely more genteel. She wiped away tears. "This would have broken your father's heart."

"Yes. It would have." Mr. Knight would never have allowed her to put Helen in the street. Never. "You haven't told anyone about Helen, have you?"

"I'm too ashamed," Mrs. Knight said, in a throbbingly tormented voice worthy of Mrs. Siddons. "Besides, I still expect her to come to her senses and post the banns."

"May we discuss this inside?"

For one unreal moment, Phoebe thought her mother would deny her the house as well. But Mrs. Knight stepped reluctantly back, and Phoebe and Sukey went past her into the parlor.

Sukey set down her basket and waited, and Phoebe sat in her father's wing chair. She breathed in deeply, smelling the old leather and the faint, faint aroma of pipe smoke that still lingered. Maybe that was only her imagination—five years was a long time for the smell of smoke to linger. But she pressed back into the chair, ignoring the disapproving look on her mother's face.

Mrs. Knight never sat in this chair. She kept it as a holy relic to be preserved, as she did all Mr. Knight's things.

When he had been alive, she had complained that the chair was ugly and that she hated the smell of smoke, and if he would only think of his family instead of being selfishly concerned with his own pleasure, he would sell the chair and give up tobacco. Precious little good it did Mr. Knight to be worshiped now.

"Mama, I'm going to take care of all this. I'm marrying a man who wants to be made a freeman before the election, and my husband's patron will pay for Helen to have the baby in secret. He'll find a family for it." She hated that in spite of everything, she was careful to pronounce 'family' the way her mother liked. "It will all come right, and Helen will be able to go on with her life—"

"Go on with her life?" Mrs. Knight gaped at her, her face

flushing bright red, the first sure sign of uncontrollable rage. "Go on with her life without her child? What woman could be happy, knowing she had done that? Knowing that somewhere she had a child being raised by strangers?"

As always, her mother's condemnation sent pricks of shame sparking across her skin. Her stomach shrank to a hot-cold knot. The worst of it was the fear that her mother was right. What if Helen was never happy again? What if thoughts of her child tormented her forever?

But if Helen were unhappily married, or ruined in the town, that would hurt her even more surely. She had agreed to this plan. "What choice does she have? I won't see her married off against her will!"

Mrs. Knight trembled. "*You* won't see her? You aren't her mother. And you'll sell yourself to secure this disgusting bargain? How any daughter of mine could be so unnatural—"

Phoebe's face burned. This was her most secret shame: her mother's rage that so repelled her was also her own. Soon she would begin to shake, and things would come out of her mouth that she had vowed to keep forever buried. "What kind of natural woman puts her frightened child in the street?" Her voice was quavering already.

"That girl is a liar. I told her that since she lived under my roof she would obey me, and she said, fine as you please, that in that case she wouldn't live here, and stormed out like a child!"

"She *is* a child!"

"A child who lifts her skirts for a man she must have been meeting in secret, for *I* never saw him. Who is the father, then? Did she tell you? Does she even know?"

Outrage choked Phoebe. She rose jerkily from her father's

chair, her heart pounding like a drum. "You—you—"

"Ma'am," Sukey said desperately, "we're going to be late to see Mr. Moon."

Oh, how she hated to let Mrs. Knight have the last word—and *such* a last word. "We must be going," she said with an effort. "I've obligations to see to."

"Don't walk away from me," Mrs. Knight spat. "I'm your mother."

"Can I choose to no longer be part of your family either?" Phoebe asked flippantly, and then froze in horror at what she'd said. She flinched even before her mother's hand came up like a whip and slapped her, hard.

"You'll speak to me with respect!"

Phoebe shut her mouth tight. *I won't speak to you at all then.*

Sukey yanked on her arm, pulling her sideways and forwards around her mother. "It was lovely to see you, Mrs. Knight."

Mother and daughter glared at each other, and then Sukey tugged Phoebe out the door. The fresh air cleared her head a little, and she was able to go down the sidewalk, taking in huge lungfuls until the trembling in her limbs subsided.

"I hope I didn't overstep, ma'am," Sukey said at last, sounding worried.

Phoebe's face burned again, this time with humiliation. She must have looked like a lunatic, or a child throwing a tantrum. Was this what awaited poor Mr. Moon? A shrieking harpy for a wife? "No, I—*thank* you," she said in heartfelt tones. "If we'd stayed I would have said something awful."

Sukey blinked. She didn't understand that what Phoebe had said was cruel in a sort of general way; the things she had never, ever said were quite specific and far more hurtful to a woman, the foundation of whose life was a delusional memory of a happy marriage. "We'd better wait before going to the sweet shop," Sukey said. "It will take a while for that to fade."

Phoebe had forgotten her mother's slap. She pressed a hand to her cheek. Her fingers felt freezing against it. "I told Mr. Moon nine o'clock, and we're already late."

Sukey waved a hand. "He's busy. He won't even notice." That didn't make Phoebe feel any better.

Sure enough, when they entered the Honey Moon a quarter of an hour later, Mr. Moon was not waiting anxiously. The shopgirl looked up from washing the windows. "Good morning, madam, may I get you something?" Sussex was thick in her voice, but she spoke carefully. The shop was neat and colorful and seemed the object of much care. Phoebe wouldn't be marrying a sluggard, anyway.

"Good morning. I'm Mrs. Sparks. If you'd tell Mr. Moon I'm here and that I'm sorry I'm late—"

The girl, a pretty blonde with a round, fresh face, bit her lip. "He went out, ma'am. He said to tell you he's that sorry, only you weren't here and the milkwoman jostled us ten pounds of butter and he had to go and see about getting us some more."

Phoebe felt deflated, and petty for feeling that way. "Of course a confectioner can't do without butter." She tried to smile. "Have you any idea when he'll be back?"

"Half an hour?" the girl hazarded. "Only it might be longer if he has to go to the dairy in Warnham. If you'd clap down and wait, I'll bring you a slavven of cake."

Helen was waiting at home for her clothes, and Phoebe had a dozen chores she ought to be doing and poor Ann's story to finish for the *Girl's Companion*. "What's your name?" she asked. After all, if she married Mr. Moon, she would be the girl's employer too.

"Betsy, ma'am."

"Well, Betsy, please tell Mr. Moon that I understand completely, but I can't wait. Is there a time in the afternoon that isn't usually as busy? I could try to come round again."

Betsy glanced ruefully about the empty shop, but she said, "There's generally a lull abouten three, ma'am. He's baked something wonderful for you, only he told me to hold it clutch. He wants to give it to you himself, to see how you like it."

"Are you wanting to leave the books for him, ma'am?" Sukey murmured.

There was no real reason not to. But it didn't feel safe, leaving a stack of her precious books in some corner of the kitchen or behind the counter to be forgotten. And Mr. Moon hadn't wanted to give her his cake by proxy, either. She shook her head, offering, "I'll carry them home." Sukey hesitated, then handed them over.

By the time they passed the steps of the circulating library, only a few hundred feet up the gently sloping street, the basket had already become unbearably awkward and heavy. She ought not to have made Sukey carry it all morning.

Jack was coming down the steps as they passed. She was glad to see him; they hadn't spoken since their strange conversation Monday. Besides, if she asked him to walk her home, he would perforce offer to carry her basket. "Jack!" she hailed him. "There must be even less happening in Sleepy St. Lemeston than usual, if you have so much time for reading."

He gave her a spooked look. "What are you doing here? Helen doesn't work today."

It had been a difficult morning. It would have been nice

if Jack had been happy to see her. "This is the main street of a small town," she reminded him sharply.

He glanced back at the door of the library anxiously. "Don't talk so loudly."

Phoebe had a voice that carried, and her father had been hard of hearing. It had been Mrs. Knight's constant complaint that they embarrassed her with their vulgar shouting.

On another morning Phoebe would have tried to get to the bottom of Jack's difficulties. Today, when Nicholas Dymond came out of the Lost Bell across the street and his face positively lit up when he saw her, she hissed at Jack, "I won't talk at all, thanks," and turned to Mr. Dymond with the best smile she could manage. It was better than she had thought it would be.

"Mrs. Sparks!" he said. "I thought I heard your voice."

Phoebe felt her face fall. "From inside the inn?" Jack was walking away by this time, but she heard him laugh behind her, and Sukey snickered.

Mr. Dymond squinted at her. "Does this question have any particular significance?"

She shrugged, her arms slipping on the hamper. She rested it briefly on her hip to secure her grip.

There was a pause. "May I carry that for you?"

"Can you?" She didn't see how he could, with his cane. It was too large to fit under an arm.

He frowned. "I'm not a cripple, Mrs. Sparks."

There was a cough behind them. Phoebe turned—and saw, to her dismay, crippled Miss Jessop being settled in her chair.

"Would you like me to carry your basket, Mrs. Sparks?" the young woman asked, her gray eyes wide and innocent. "It would be the easiest thing in the world for me to hold it on my lap while Jeffrey wheels me along."

Mr. Dymond closed his eyes tightly for a moment and sighed. "I beg your pardon," he told Miss Jessop. "The truth is, it would be very difficult for me to carry Mrs. Sparks's basket, and it is even more difficult for me to admit it. I hope you will forgive my really unforgivable choice of words."

Miss Jessop raised her eyebrows and smiled at him. "I can forgive anything to a man who apologizes so well."

His blue eyes glinted wickedly. "Anything?" Phoebe felt suddenly jealous of poor Miss Jessop, who was very pretty despite her thin frame and carroty hair.

The young woman's pale cheeks turned pink, but she answered without hesitation, "Anything but the cruelty of not allowing Mrs. Sparks to introduce you." Phoebe felt even more jealous. She had a certain talent for sarcasm, but archness was beyond her.

Of course, Miss Jessop was a gentlewoman and her father's hostess. She had probably been trained in the social graces by governesses of higher social station than Phoebe.

"Miss Jessop, may I present Mr. Nicholas Dymond," Phoebe said blandly. "He is in town to help his brother with the election."

Miss Jessop's eyes widened. Glancing up and down the street, she sighed. "Alas, I suppose I must add being an Orange-and-Purple to the list of things I cannot forgive. I'd better go before someone tells my father we were speaking." She turned to Phoebe. "Unless you do need help with your basket."

"No, thank you. It isn't very heavy. But it was kind of you to offer."

Miss Jessop's gray eyes glinted warmly. "I am always kind to people I want to be friends with. We must talk some other time."

Phoebe blinked. "I—yes, we must." She hoped she didn't sound as startled as she felt. "Some other time." It occurred to her belatedly that Mr. Jessop was said to dote on his daughter, and that he had the ear of the Lively St. Lemeston Tories. If she could win over Miss Jessop, it might mean something for Helen if the time came when she needed to sell them her vote.

"I would love to," she said more enthusiastically. "You must—" She was about to invite Miss Jessop to her home, but remembered the stairs and changed tack. "Perhaps we could meet at the Honey Moon one day. I hear they have splendid sweets."

"What a lovely notion," Miss Jessop said eagerly. "Perhaps tomorrow morning?"

Phoebe had planned to spend the following morning writing, after her meeting with Mr. Moon. "Of course. Is half past nine too early?"

Miss Jessop looked as if she rather thought it was, but she said, "Not at all, Jeffrey will bring me."

Phoebe turned to smile at Jeffrey and realized he was ogling her bosom.

On a large scale, Phoebe believed firmly that the passage of time brought progress and improvements of all sorts. But sometimes in the short term—this morning for example—it seemed to bring only a succession of ever greater indignities. She waved as cheerily as she could at Miss Jessop as Jeffrey wheeled her away.

"I thought you would still be at Mr. Moon's," Mr. Dymond said. "Did it not go well?"

"He wasn't there." Mr. Dymond frowned, and she hastened to add, "Their butter wasn't delivered and he had to go looking for more. I understood."

His eyes stayed on her face. "You really didn't mind? You look a bit frazzled."

She tried to put a hand up to her hair without losing her grip on the basket. "Do I?"

He smiled, that warm curve that somehow made his honey-colored hair seem brighter, and plucked something out of her hair.

It was a dead leaf. The heat that flooded her face was half embarrassment and half simple lust. He had touched her hair.

He did it again, reaching out to push a pin in more firmly. This time, his fingers lingered, smoothing what she hoped were only a few errant strands. The heat spread. Meeting his eyes from this close felt suddenly intimate. She swallowed, lips parting breathlessly, and his eyes dropped to her mouth.

Sukey pinched her. Phoebe jumped, and Mr. Dymond let his hand fall, smiling so naturally Phoebe was left to wonder if she'd imagined the desire in his eyes.

It was foolish to like him this much, and yet—women must react this way to him all the time. It was natural and harmless.

It *would* be harmless if she could avoid standing in the middle of the main street gazing into his eyes, anyway.

"I didn't mean to insult you," he said. "You only look as if you've had a trying morning. I've had a very calm one full of toast and marmalade, so you can tell me all about it without fear of oversetting me."

She hesitated. Her arms were tired, and ordinarily being asked if something was wrong made her irritable and close-mouthed. Yet here she was dying to confide in Mr. Dymond.

Sukey elbowed her encouragingly. "I don't want to keep you standing," Phoebe said. "Is your leg—?"

His forehead creased for a moment. Evidently he didn't

like to be asked if something was wrong either. He smiled less warmly than before. "Keeping it in one position is the worst. I'll walk you to your door."

As they went, Phoebe's feet felt like lead. "I promised my sister I would get her clothes from our mother's house, but I couldn't. And now I've got to go in and tell her, and she hates not being neat, and wearing clothes that don't fit—" Her voice wavered.

Luckily Mr. Dymond was watching where to place his feet on the clinkers that paved this part of town and didn't look at her. "Why couldn't you?"

It was too humiliating.

"She had a row with her mum," Sukey said finally. Phoebe wished she could sink through the ground and disappear.

But Mr. Dymond frowned in instant concern. "A bad one?"

Mutely, she nodded.

"About your sister?"

"She said Helen had chosen not to be part of our family any longer." She could feel Sukey's skepticism like a palpable thing: *You aren't telling him what* you *said.*

His expression darkened. "Did she mean it?"

"Probably not. But I—I got so angry with her, and now I don't have Helen's clothes." It all pressed in on her, an angry weight on her chest. She was the only family Helen had left. Soon her sister would grow big and have to leave her employment, and it would be up to Phoebe to support them both. She didn't have money for new clothes and she didn't have *time* to deal with this, she had to get poor Ann's story done and send it to London—

But she didn't. All she had to do was marry. The weight on

her chest grew until her heart flailed desperately to free itself, pounding against her ribs.

"We'll get the clothes," Mr. Dymond said.

She darted a glance at him. "What?"

"Do you still have a key to the house?"

She nodded.

"And the servants?"

He'd seen her tiny lodgings. After that, it shouldn't embarrass her to admit that her mother didn't keep a full staff. But it did. "She has a girl come in most mornings. Not today, though. Are you suggesting burglary?"

His eyes twinkled. "I'll invite her to dine with me. You can fetch the clothes while she's out."

"You—you'd do that?"

He smiled. "She isn't *my* mother. She won't bother me."

It was dreadful to contemplate Mr. Dymond having dinner with her mother. What would Mrs. Knight say? What would she tell him about Phoebe? Would he pity her? Or worst of all, would Mrs. Knight charm him as she could sometimes unexpectedly do, so he'd think Phoebe an ungrateful, unnatural child?

She had promised Helen. "Thank you."

"It's nothing. Really."

"Ask for her advice. Say you've heard many Orange-and-Purples speak of my father with respect. She loves that."

"I *have* heard many Orange-and-Purples speak of your father with respect," he said quietly.

Her eyes stung. "Everybody adored him." *Except my mother.*

He pulled a gleaming gold watch from his pocket. Any further confidences died in her throat; that watch would feed her and Helen for years. "It's half past ten now," he said. "By half past eleven she'll be out of the house."

Chapter 6

Phoebe Sparks's childhood home was a low brick townhouse with a roof of rippled Sussex stone, a spindle tree pressed against one side. Nick stopped to pick a few pinkish-gold leaves.

Either Mr. Knight's practice had not been a lucrative one, or he had not been wise with money. Despite its welcoming appearance, the house was small compared to its neighbors, and the man had left his widow and daughter with only enough for a maid "most mornings"—some of whose wages might be paid by Mrs. Sparks, for all he knew.

He might know, by the end of this meal. He had offered to help out of instinct—here, finally, was a simple problem with a simple solution that could be effected by one simple action—but had quickly recognized an unrivaled opportunity to pump Mrs. Sparks's mother for information that would help him marry her off.

He rapped at the door with his walking stick. It soon opened to reveal a stout, tired-looking woman with wispy silver hair. Mrs. Sparks's dark eyes and stubborn chin looked out of place in her faded countenance. She was dressed in black so old it had streaked and paled to a patchy dark gray.

"You must be Mrs. Knight," he said with a smile. "I'm terribly sorry to drop in upon you like this. I'm Nicholas

Dymond, Mr. Anthony's brother, and I've come to help with his campaign."

Her eyes narrowed suspiciously. "I've spent enough of my time talking to your brother. I even had my daughter take him on a tour of the town, with special attention to the Voluntary Hospital. I'm not sure he really took what we said seriously."

Nick wasn't exactly shocked to hear it, but he said, "It's only that he's young and lively. He might not always *seem* serious, but the well-being of the borough is very near to his heart. It was he who suggested you would be a splendid person to advise someone new to the campaign on the real interests and situation of the people of Lively St. Lemeston." He'd have to remember to tell Tony that, later.

Her shoulders unhunched and her mouth lost its ill-humored twist. *A golden key unlocks all doors, but flattery oils the hinges,* Lady Tassell used to say. He'd always writhed in vicarious humiliation watching people swallow her lies. Didn't they know what she would say about them later at the supper table? And now here he was, following her example.

"I'm very busy." Mrs. Knight's dark eyes were still narrowed. "A woman alone, you know, cannot afford to waste daylight hours." For a moment he was struck by how like her Mrs. Sparks was. Except that Mrs. Sparks had been sincere, and her mother clearly only wished to be a little more persuaded.

"I promise I won't take up more of your time than just the dinner hour," he said earnestly. "And I believe the Lost Bell is serving jugged hare today."

She sighed wistfully. "Jugged hare was my husband's favorite. I used to make it for him whenever I could—he received presents of game quite often—but since his death it seems like so much work for one meal…"

"Come and dine with me, and tell me all about him. I've heard him spoken of by everyone with the greatest respect and affection, even after so many years."

Her eyes brimmed with tears. "He was a saint. Wait a moment, I'll get my pelisse."

"…which is why my dear Mr. Knight believed that a Police Act was an absolute necessity."

"That was very forward-thinking of him." Since the question of increased policing for Lively St. Lemeston had occupied no one until the last year or so, either Mr. Knight had been forward-thinking indeed, or Mrs. Knight simply prefaced all her own opinions with *as my late husband always said.*

"He was very clever," Mrs. Knight said proudly. "The girls take after him in that."

Nick smiled. "And after you as well, clearly."

Mrs. Knight looked genuinely surprised, as if she hadn't just delivered an oration worthy of being read in the Commons. "Oh, well, I suppose I'm not a dullard. But the girls really have talent."

"Mrs. Sparks writes stories for children, doesn't she?"

Mrs. Knight sighed. "She could wring tears from a stone with those. She began after she lost the baby, you know. It was poetry, when she was younger."

"Really?" He tried to quash his guilt. Some people—evidently Mrs. Knight among them—thought the topic of poetry quite neutral. But Nick guessed that Mrs. Sparks would consider it deeply personal.

Mrs. Knight sniffed. "Well. It was novels to start with, when she was only ten or eleven, those awful Gothic things. She got them from the maid—we gave that girl a stern talking-to! Mr. Knight would have none of it. He always said novels weakened the mind. Phoebe threw a pretty tantrum, but in the end she came around to his way of thinking. Both the girls looked up to him. I wish he were here now."

Nick spared a moment to be grateful that his father had never paid the slightest attention to what his sons might be reading. "Did Mr. Sparks like to read?"

"He *was* a printer, wasn't he?" she said snidely. She met Nick's eyes, inviting him to share in her ridicule.

He smiled uneasily. He had forgotten how touchy the middling sort could be about slight gradations of rank. He supposed a man who worked a press, even if he was a successful newspaper editor, would seem low to a lawyer's wife.

Mrs. Knight speared a piece of hare with more force than necessary. "There were weeks they ate oatcakes and potatoes because he'd sent away to London for the newest account of some good-for-nothing's voyage to the South Seas."

"Did he order books for Mrs. Sparks as well?"

"Oh, she was just as bad. When he took sick, she had nothing but a great useless library and a brand-new cast-iron printing press for his newspaper. They bought it broken, if you can believe, and spent everything they had left on fixing it. She sold the library to pay the doctor, and his brother got the press and the paper. So much for providing for his wife."

"Did your husband like Mr. Sparks?"

"Oh, very well—as a supplier of legal forms!" She chuckled.

Nick laughed politely, despising himself for it.

"Sparks would never have dared to come courting when Mr. Knight was alive. Dove in like a vulture, with Mr. Knight not cold in his grave. I could never credit how they'd go walking and she'd come back singing, as if nothing was wrong." She sighed. "It's painful for a mother to see her daughter's faults. I know she loved her father with all her heart, but she always did think of herself first."

It was becoming obvious that Mrs. Sparks had heard a great deal about her faults growing up. "She speaks of him with great affection," Nick said evenly.

"When she was small she preferred me, you know." Mrs. Knight toyed with her fork. "And then all at once I couldn't do anything right."

There was something terribly pathetic in the admission. Nick wondered if his own mother felt so wronged and mystified by his resentment. "Did something happen?"

"Ask her! I've never understood it."

"Did *you* ask her?"

"Oh yes, again and again, and got an earful of recriminations and accusations. She never forgets a thing, that girl. She remembers slights from when she was four and expects me to somehow atone for them. But when I try, it's never good enough. I always did my best."

"I'm sure you did." He was surprised at how quickly poor Mrs. Knight had made him angry. The polite replies were becoming difficult. Soon he'd be reduced to monosyllables.

Just because Mrs. Sparks also had a difficult mother, that was no reason to feel this—not even sympathy, but an intimation of kinship. Half the world had difficult mothers, at a low estimate.

"But here, I've been boring you with talk of my children when you wanted to hear about the borough. Now the magistrates say…"

He'd wanted, of course, to hear about her children. The borough interested him not at all. But he didn't have the heart to pry further. He listened with half an ear as Mrs. Knight explained, in detail, Sir Samuel Romilly's recent reforms of the penal code, the Lively St. Lemeston system of magistrates, and the obstinacy of the corporation, who liked to have the whip hand in this town. It was just like being at home.

When he had safely deposited Mrs. Knight at her house, he headed for Mrs. Sparks's lodgings to make sure her mission had been successful.

The door was opened by a vision of loveliness. A lovely mouth, lovely dark eyes, and a lovely straight nose were arranged in perfect harmony in an oval face, peaches-and-cream skin a startling contrast to her neat coronet of dark, dark hair. A neat, serviceable dress of faded rose, kerchief embroidered with neat rows of green vines tucked neatly into its neck, showed off her trim figure.

Indeed, "neat" was the first word that came to mind after "lovely"—and then, close behind, "haunted". It was her eyes that did it; they were so large and fine and surrounded by such dark lashes, and the soft skin beneath them was so translucent, that they stood out starkly in her face like a plea. There was something about her, some tension and contrast of light and dark, that told a man she would be easy to bruise, that made him want to bruise her and protect her from bruises all at once.

She started back, her gaze falling from his and fixing on the floor. "Mr. D-Dymond," she said with an effort. "Please come in. I'm Helen Knight."

Oh, Christ. This was the pregnant little sister. Of course she was, and he'd been staring at her as if she were a portrait or a whore. He tried to smile. "It's a pleasure to meet you."

Her eyes darted to his with something like suspicion. "Thank you."

Mrs. Sparks appeared in the doorway of her bedroom, the same suspicious look on her face as she glanced between him and her sister. She had the same eyes, he realized, the same lovely mouth and straight nose, the same peaches-and-cream skin and dark hair. But somehow she had missed her sister's blinding beauty.

It wasn't her different build. Perhaps it was that neatness, the self-contained precision and grace of Miss Knight's movements and dress. It gave her an otherworldly quality that drew the eye with its improbability.

Mrs. Sparks was emphatically *here*, vibrant and determined, stray bits of hair and cuff and shoelace poking at the world as if to say, *Stop shilly-shallying and listen to me.*

He hadn't come here to see if she'd got her sister's clothes, he realized. He'd wanted to see her. He was nursing a *tendre* for her, in fact.

This was inconvenient, to say the least. "Mrs. Sparks." He bowed.

"Thank you for your help with that errand," she said meaningfully. "I would have taken care of it myself, only I was fetching Helen's things." She hadn't told her sister about the quarrel with Mrs. Knight, he surmised.

"It was on my way," he said. "I was having dinner with your mother. I believe she knows more about the borough than my brother's election agent."

Mrs. Sparks smiled, but there was a sour twist to her lips.

"Did—what did—what did you talk about?"

Guilt squirmed a little in Nick's chest; he knew Mrs. Knight had said a number of things Mrs. Sparks wouldn't have wanted him to hear, and he had encouraged her. "Mostly the borough," he prevaricated. "She didn't much like your husband, though, did she?"

Mrs. Sparks glowered. "She doesn't much like anybody."

"That isn't fair," Miss Knight said tightly. "Will—"

"—made me happy," Mrs. Sparks finished. "She couldn't forgive either of us for that."

"He made you happy at *first*," her sister muttered.

"It was my fault things went wrong with Will." She gazed up at Nick with those big eyes, looking as haunted as her sister. "I'll do better this time. Mr. Moon needn't worry."

Nick had no idea what to say.

Miss Knight's eyes brimmed with tears; she looked like a painting of grief. "I'm so sorry, Fee," she whispered.

Mrs. Sparks looked, for a moment, almost annoyed. She straightened her spine just the tiniest fraction. "I don't—" she began, and stopped. "You don't have to be sorry."

A fat tear rolled down Miss Knight's cheek. Her lip trembled. She stared straight ahead and said nothing.

"I've heated some milk for cocoa," Mrs. Sparks said desperately. "It's by the bed. We'll talk when Mr. Dymond is gone."

Miss Knight gave him that suspicious, searching look again. "You shouldn't be alone with him."

Mrs. Sparks raised her eyebrows nearly to her hairline. Her sister flushed scarlet, stumbling over her hem in her haste to leave the room.

Mrs. Sparks's shoulders sagged. "I didn't mean to imply that she was throwing stones in a glass house—oh drat, I suppose I did. I don't mean to be short with her. I only—she keeps apologizing, and I've said I don't blame her several hundred times already. What's the use in saying it again? Oh, and I'm keeping you standing, please, sit down—" She sat on the very edge of her worn comb-back armchair, as if she might need to leap into action at any moment. She looked frazzled to the bone, and it was only two in the afternoon.

Nick lowered himself onto the window seat. "You're doing the best you can. You can't do more."

Her jaw set. "This isn't the best I can do. It can't be."

"I wouldn't think less of you if you did blame your sister," he said carefully. "She's put you in a very difficult situation."

Her eyes flew to his, half-afraid and half-hopeful. "I don't understand what happened. I don't understand how—but I left her there with our mother. I should have looked after her better. My father would be so disappointed in me." She covered her mouth with the tips of her fingers, as if they could trap words that had already escaped—or, he realized, to hide that her lips were trembling.

During elections, his mother had used to regale them at supper—when she came to supper—with accounts of her canvassing visits and the various tales of woe she had heard. *My heart went out to him,* she used to say. *My heart went out to her.* He had thought it an empty phrase, but now he felt it, a sudden vertigo in his chest as if a narrow piece of the world had tipped sideways and his heart was falling towards her.

Did Lady Tassell really feel this way in every house she stopped in? Or was this different? Was this a connection between him and Mrs. Sparks?

His mother also said, *Never confide in a voter.* He was about to break that rule. "My mother doesn't support the war."

She blinked. "What?"

"We've been at war with France almost continuously since 1793. And her opinion has never changed in all that time: that it is a reactionary war to oppose the will of the French people, who freely chose Bonaparte to lead them, and an unconscionable squandering of British money and British lives. She used to weep over the casualty lists and call it a tragic waste."

Mrs. Sparks frowned. "But you were in the army. She was so proud of you. At Christmas she always asked the vicar to pray for absent soldiers."

He hadn't known that. For a moment he faltered—but what his mother did in the borough had nothing to do with how she felt. "She loves me and she made the best of it, but she wasn't proud," he said, a bitter taste on his tongue. "She thinks she shouldn't have let me go." He gestured at his cane. "To her, I'm a tragic waste. Proof of a political idea, and symbol of her failure. She wants to fix me, and she can't, and she hates it."

"What did she want you to do?"

"Politics."

"She must be proud now, then," she said uncertainly, perched on the edge of her armchair with her mouth scrunched up and a piece of hair falling over her ear, and he wanted to kiss her. If he wanted to kiss her *now*, in the midst of the most soul-baring conversation he'd had in a long time, then he really wanted her. This was not good.

It was terrible, because the truthful answer was, *No, she isn't proud. But I'll do everything I can to force you into this marriage you don't want, because I think maybe then*—"I don't care if she's proud. I only—I only want her to see me when she looks at me. Not some idea in her head—just *me*."

He could see she understood completely. Her lips parted,

and then closed. "Do *you* think your injury was a waste?"

"No," he said at once, as if he were sure. As if he had never lost a soldier under his command or a friend, and gone to sleep that night in his leaking, icy tent wondering whether the war was worth it. As if, breathless with pain in the hospital, he hadn't listened to men dying and suffering all around him and thought that his mother had been right all along.

But doubt always came like a thief in the night. It came when you were alone. He had hardly ever been alone in the army. Christ, he missed that certainty and companionship. "I would do it again. We all sacrificed for something we believed in. Something I still believe in."

She drew in a deep breath and steadied like a raw recruit given a few encouraging words and a clap on the back. "I believe in my sister."

He was going to win his bet with his mother. He looked away. "Talk to your sister. She's apologizing because when she looks at you, she sees her guilt that she's forcing you into marriage. And when you look at her, you see your father's disappointment. I don't care whether he would have been disappointed. He would have been wrong." He couldn't turn his gaze back to Mrs. Sparks's face. When he looked at her, he was supposed to see his chance to show his mother the truth of himself. He wasn't supposed to see *her*.

Footsteps came rattling up the stairs. Mrs. Sparks catapulted out of her chair. Nick rose politely. When his leg had been whole, he'd never realized how annoying the rule about never sitting in front of a standing woman could be. To top it off, he hit his head on the eaves.

"Sorry!" Her rosebud mouth made a twisty little knot of embarrassment. "You're much taller than most of my visitors."

With her leap out of her chair and his step forward to the higher part of the ceiling, she was exactly at kissing distance. She had to tilt her head back to look up at him, eyes wide, and for a moment he felt flooded with strength and confidence. He could lean down and kiss her expressive mouth, and all their doubts and fears would melt away and everything would be perfect…

A loud rap sounded at the door. Mrs. Sparks started violently and went to open it. Nick's fingers curled with wanting to slide into her soft, thick hair.

Her visitor was short and narrow and brown, with longish hair and a boyish, foxlike face. The pink-and-white tea rose in his buttonhole proclaimed him a Tory. "You're looking lovely today, Mrs. Sparks. Lavender is a good color for you."

"Thank you, Mr. Gilchrist. Please come in," she said with the same forced friendliness she'd used on Nick at Thursday night's party. Was this the Tory election agent?

An even worse suspicion struck him. Was this the man the Tories had selected to be her husband? They would never suit, if so. There was something decidedly oily about his smile.

And if that weren't enough reason to dislike him, he'd bounded up the stairs, probably two at a time, and wasn't even breathing hard.

Gilchrist looked around the room. His eyes narrowed for a moment when he saw Nick. "So, was I unjust?" he asked innocently. "Did the Orange-and-Purples' agent prove more principled than I? Or just handsomer?" The election agent, then.

Mrs. Sparks flushed bright red. "Keep a civil tongue in your head," Nick snapped.

Gilchrist actually looked abashed for a moment before

flashing a bright, apologetic smile. He was much younger than Nick, perhaps about twenty. "And more chivalrous, it seems," he said lightly. "My apologies, Mrs. Sparks, I didn't mean to embarrass you. Shall I come back at a more convenient time?"

Mrs. Sparks swallowed. "No. You were right, the Orange-and-Purples are just as unscrupulous as your lot. But some changes in my circumstances have overtaken my own scruples. Mr. Dymond, if you wouldn't mind, I'd like to speak with Mr. Gilchrist. You said—you said I might."

Nick gritted his teeth. He hated the idea of Mrs. Sparks having to toady to the little rat when she'd obviously given him an enthusiastic shove-off pretty recently. "Certainly, madam," he said. "You know where to find me. Good afternoon."

She nodded briefly, the connection between them snapped as if it had never been. Perhaps it hadn't. To her, there might be little to choose between him and this smug Tory.

"Be careful on the stairs," Gilchrist said with showy concern. "They're tricky even without a cane."

Nick's teeth ground together. But as he pulled the door shut, he saw Mrs. Sparks gave Mr. Gilchrist a glare on his behalf. That cheered him—until he realized that she might equally well have been offended on behalf of her stairs.

Chapter 7

"If you would just wait here a moment," Phoebe said to Mr. Gilchrist. "I need to speak to my sister."

"Of course." His bright brown eyes were already going around the room as if planning where to snoop first.

"I'll only be a moment," she emphasized, and slipped into the bedroom. Helen was sitting on the edge of the bed, carefully sipping cocoa and rereading a fashion magazine from a few months ago—a sure sign something was wrong. Helen was fond of saying that a month was as good as a year when it came to modishness.

"I'm sorry I was short with you earlier," Phoebe said.

Paper crinkled as Helen glanced up nervously. "It's all right. I didn't mean to imply you would be guilty of any impropriety."

"Oh, Ships," Phoebe said helplessly, sitting on the bed beside her. "I don't blame you for what's happened. I don't think less of you. Honestly."

Helen pressed her lips together so tightly they turned white. "How can you not?"

Phoebe sighed. "I slept with Will before our marriage."

"You *did*?" Helen snapped her magazine shut without even marking her place.

"We couldn't wait." A month while the banns were read

and the wedding prepared for had seemed like an eternity, with Will in arm's reach, solid and handsome and the only thing that had made her feel glad and alive in so long. "It can be hard to resist. I know that."

"He *was* hard to resist," Helen muttered.

"You said he didn't force you," Phoebe said through lips suddenly stiff with dread.

Helen shook her head, and Phoebe could move again. "No. No. He was very persuasive, that's all."

She couldn't help asking again. "Helen, who is he?"

"He can't marry me, and he can't help me. So there's no use talking about it."

What did that mean? Was he married already? Or was he poor, or sick, or dead? As petty as it was, besides her worry she was hurt that Helen didn't want to confide in her. She was so tired of being petty, of feeling small and mean and angry. She was tired of this tightness around her eyes. "I'm sorry," she said. "I don't want to pry. I want to say that—you apologized, and—" *I forgave you,* she had been going to say. But she hadn't, had she? Not in so many words.

"I forgive you." It felt wonderful, the resentment sloughing off like an old, dead skin.

Helen took a deep breath and smiled, the most relaxed smile Phoebe had seen from her in days. "Thank you, Fee." She put her head on Phoebe's shoulder, careful not to disarrange her hair. "I'll try to stop apologizing. And—be careful. The Dymonds have a bit of a reputation."

"They do?"

"As heartbreakers. Read the London papers if you don't believe me."

Phoebe hadn't read a London paper in months. It was an

unsettling realization. Once, she'd read a dozen every day.

She had no trouble believing Helen, however. "Mr. Nicholas has been out of the country for years," she said anyway. "I doubt he was included in the gossip. But I'll be careful."

Helen relaxed further. "Thank you."

The cupboard door snicked shut in the next room. Phoebe winced, though there was nothing secret in her house. "I've got to talk to Mr. Gilchrist before he starts taking up the floorboards."

Helen swallowed. "Are you going to tell him about me?"

Phoebe bit her lip. "I think I'll wait and see if I like the man he's picked out for me." The less people who knew, the better. Probably it had been foolish to tell Mr. Dymond.

Helen nodded, standing. "You don't have to meet him if you don't want to," Phoebe said. "He's obnoxious." But Helen followed her with a wary, stubborn glance. Well, if her sister wanted to bore herself to tears playing chaperone, Phoebe had no objection this time.

But you were quite eager to be alone with Mr. Dymond, weren't you? Mr. Gilchrist had been far too near the mark with his dig about Nick's good looks.

When she opened the door, the Tory agent was lifting the lid of her oak chest. Suddenly Phoebe felt cold and naked, because there *was* something secret in the shallow drawer at the base of the chest, wrapped up with lavender and wormwood to keep away the moths. The baby clothes for her child that was never born. Her hope and her grief laid out for anyone to see.

Had he seen them? There was no way of knowing. He let the lid fall and turned with a cheeky smile—and his jaw actually dropped when Helen walked in behind her.

He swallowed audibly and straightened his pink waistcoat. "You—" His voice cracked. "You must be Mrs. Sparks's sister. The resemblance is quite striking."

Phoebe laughed. He was so *persistently* oily, it was impossible not to be a little charmed.

Helen threw her an exasperated glance. "Yes, I'm Helen Knight. You're very perceptive."

"It comes with the profession." He bowed low over her hand, much lower than a gentleman *should* bow to the daughter of a country lawyer. "Of course I'm honored to make your acquaintance, Miss Knight, but"—he faltered, then continued with an heroic effort—"I was hoping to speak with your sister on a matter of some importance."

Phoebe was impressed at his fortitude. "I have no secrets from my sister, sir. This concerns her as well, since she's quarreled with our mother and has come to live with me. The fact of the matter is—I am quite without funds and in danger of falling into debt." She gestured at her tiny, precious rooms, at the bucket under the leak in the roof. "I can't live like this anymore," she lied. "I'd like to at least meet the man you want me to marry."

Mr. Gilchrist smiled like a triumphant villain in a melodrama. "You won't regret it."

"I regret it already," she said dryly.

I made a sacrifice for something I believed in, Mr. Dymond had said. *I would do it again.*

"You'll like the man I found for you. Walter Fairclough is new in town, just come from Lewes where he owns a flax manufactory. He wanted to be closer to London, so he's bought the gunpowder works just outside town. I don't mean to run down the Whigs, but their Robert Moon—his little sweet shop is neck-deep in debt. And the debt's creeping up the chin, if you know what I mean."

Oh no. That well-loved shop. The Whigs must be prepared to pay his debts if he married her. It explained everything.

"If you want to get away from scrimping, I recommend Mr. Fairclough. He's eager to be part of local society, and a Lively St. Lemeston wife would help enormously."

"I'm not part of local society," Phoebe protested. Men who owned factories didn't want wives like her, did they? "Not even close. If he wants his way smoothed, he'd do better elsewhere."

Mr. Gilchrist patted her hand soothingly. She glared at him. "Everyone knew and respected your father," he said. "That means something. Besides, Mr. Fairclough comes from simple stock himself. And he's a great admirer of your work."

Phoebe felt her cheeks warming. "He's read my work?"

"He loves to read, and so does his daughter."

Phoebe's breath caught in her throat. "His daughter?"

Mr. Gilchrist smiled like a fox in a henhouse. Had he seen those baby clothes after all? "He's a widower. His daughter is a lovely little girl, eight years old. Mr. Fairclough quite dotes on her. Do you like children, Mrs. Sparks?"

A daughter. A little girl who liked to read. Phoebe tried to keep her face blank. "Most people like children, Mr. Gilchrist."

Mr. Gilchrist's smile widened. "If you'd like to meet him, he and I will be dining at the Drunk St. Leonard tomorrow at noon. We'd be honored if you and your sister would join us."

She took a deep breath and nodded slowly. "We'll be there."

She went back to the Honey Moon at three, alone this time. Helen had offered to accompany her, but Phoebe felt obscurely embarrassed at the idea of Helen watching her try to make small talk with a man she might be married to in a couple of weeks. She carried only two books, since four of the ones she'd chosen last night had seemed suddenly ridiculous when she looked at them again.

Betsy was measuring out candied apricots for a customer, but she gave Phoebe a bright smile. "Mr. Moon will be glad to see you. I'll take you back as soon as I've finished here." She was good at her job, Phoebe thought; the man she was helping clearly liked her, and not only because her striped apron hugged her small, curvy body. She was friendly and genuine and knew to ask after his mother, who had had the ague last month. That was in Mr. Moon's favor, that he hired good people to work for him.

Soon the customer was on his way with his candied apricots and a few currant pastilles Betsy had given him gratis to see how his wife liked them. "Come on into the kitchen. Mr. Moon's preserving nectarine chips, but he'll be glad you've come back. He was that sorry to have missed you."

Did everyone in the shop know their fate depended on her goodwill? "I was sorry to have missed him as well."

"It's only that we can't do without butter." Did Betsy's little laugh sound forced?

Phoebe felt exhausted, suddenly. She wanted to go home and take a nap. But Helen was at home, counting on her to be strong. When she had lived alone, no one knew if she chose to take a nap in the middle of the day. She gave a forced little laugh of her own. "I'm very fond of butter myself."

Betsy's gaze flicked to her generous bosom and waist.

Phoebe braced herself, but Betsy just smiled gratefully and said, "So am I. This is the kitchen. Isn't it splendid?"

The first thing she noticed was the overpowering smell of burnt flour and charcoal, underlaid with fruit, peppermint and a morass of other things. It wasn't altogether awful, just very, very strong. She breathed through her mouth and looked about her.

The kitchen was a narrow, high, charcoal-blackened room with a row of low ovens and stoves along the left wall. It was very close despite the open windows near the ceiling, but after the October chill outside and in her own rooms—she couldn't afford to keep the fire very high—Phoebe rather liked it. The right wall was lined with wooden tables, a wide marble slab lying on the nearest. Shelves were mounted on the wall above, filled with pots, pans, rolling pins, and molds of all shapes and sizes.

Mr. Moon stood at a table paring and slicing a crate of bruised hothouse nectarines with great speed and efficiency. She could smell them as she got closer, a heavenly scent. She rarely allowed herself the luxury of a nectarine. Perhaps this wouldn't be so bad after all.

He set down his knife and fruit with a start. "Mrs. Sparks! I'm so glad you're back." He reached out to take her hand, realized that his own was covered in nectarine juice, and flushed. "Pardon me. And pardon me for being out earlier. I wouldn't have missed you for the world—"

"Please don't apologize," Phoebe said fervently. "Betsy told me about the butter. I don't mind at all."

"That's very kind of you." Mr. Moon smiled in relief, and Phoebe's chest felt tight. Here was one more person whose happiness was now her responsibility. She was almost tempted to accept him at once and spare them both the agony of uncertainty, this impossible weight on everything they did and said. But he turned away to wash his hands, and thankfully the moment was lost.

"I made a few different kinds of sweets for you. Well, I made six. But this morning I saw that most of them were much too sugary for you, so I only want you to try two. They're in the pastry room through here. Would you like to see?"

At her nod, he led her through a swinging door into a narrow room the twin of the first, but far cooler. Barrels and casks lined the left wall, shelves of supplies above them. Along the right, farthest from the heat of the ovens, were low wooden ice chests. More shelves held jars of preserved fruit, candy and pastilles. That wall, too, had a swinging door in it. "What's through there?" she asked, for something to say.

"The ice room. We keep the ice there." He flushed. "I suppose that was obvious from the name." He opened one of the ice chests and pulled out a china plate. "I call this one a raspberry dozzle. Dozzle, you know, the folk hereabout use to mean—"

"A small amount, I know." Lord, did he think her some sort of great lady? Of course her mother would consider him even further below her than Will, but not everyone could be a lawyer. "I'm Sussex born and bred, just as you are."

"I'm sure I didn't mean to offend." He held out the plate uncertainly, indicating two pale puffy biscuits cemented together by a thin layer of red jam.

She took it and bit in. To her great relief, it was delicious. The biscuits were a light, nutty meringue, and the jam had a tart flavor that counterbalanced the sugar perfectly. She chewed slowly, making sounds of sincere pleasure. "Mmm, splendid."

He smiled, but he kept his eyes on her face as she ate the rest. It was delicious for two more bites, but by the third, she had had enough. She swallowed the last of it hastily, wishing for some tea or milk to wash the taste out of the back of her throat. Instead, he presented her with another pastry, a wedge of layered cream and dough. "This is puff paste with pistachio cream."

Don't make a face, she told herself. *Just don't.* But as her teeth sank through the perfect pastry into the smooth, flavorful custard, her lips contorted despite her best efforts.

His face fell. "You don't like it."

"I don't like custard," she said miserably. "I don't like whipped cream or jelly, either. I hate the way it feels when I bite into it. It's the texture, that's all. It tastes lovely. I love pistachios. You're a wonderful baker." It was so cold in the room. Sugar clung to the roof of her mouth. She would have given half a crown for an olive or a pickled oyster.

He shook his head. "Don't trouble over it. I'll find it. There's a pastry for everyone, that tastes as if it was created by the Lord just for her."

"What's yours?"

He smiled. "Lemon cheesecakes. I could eat a dozen trays and not be quotted. I make them by my mother's recipe."

"She must be proud."

He shrugged, leading her back to the main kitchen. The warmth was a relief, as was no longer being alone with him. "I suppose."

She laughed. "My mother taught me to write, but she isn't always happy with what I do with it either."

They shared a quick look of perfect understanding. He had nice eyes. Perhaps she would find him handsome, in time.

He was tall, at least. She'd always liked tall men. "You brought books for me?" he asked.

She plucked them off the counter and dusted flour off the covers. "Ye-es." She cradled them, feeling suddenly protective. "*Robinson Crusoe.* Maybe I could read it to you while you work?"

"That would be nice," he said, more as if he hoped it were true than believed it. "Would you like a nectarine?"

"I'd love one."

He dug in the crate for a mostly unbruised fruit and handed it to her. She bit into it with relish. Juice ran down her chin. Smiling self-consciously, she wiped it off with the end of her sleeve.

He smiled back. "You like that better than the dozzles, don't you?"

She nodded apologetically and opened the book, careful not to drip juice on the pages. "I was born in the year 1632, in the city of York, of a good family, though not of that country, my father being a foreigner of Bremen, who settled first at Hull," she read. "He got a good estate by merchandise, and leaving off his trade, lived afterwards at York…"

Oh God. She had chosen it as the most exciting and manly of her books, but now it sounded terribly dull and long, and what, after all, did it matter where Robinson Crusoe's father had lived?

Not knowing what else to do, she struggled gamely on. Mr. Moon looked up earnestly from his nectarines every now and then to show he was listening, while Betsy and the kitchen boy tried to pretend she wasn't in the way as they reached around her for the sugar, the walnuts and a hundred other necessities.

Nick sat in the bay window of his room at the Lost Bell, watching the sleepy street below: the small shops, the knots of men and women talking familiarly together, a few maids with baskets out shopping. He'd always liked Lively St. Lemeston. He'd wished he'd lived here and been part of the odd, merry Christmas customs instead of swooping down to give alms to poor widows on Gooding Day and gifts to the servants and tradesmen on Boxing Day. He'd tried to imagine living in the same place all year.

Everyone here was a known quantity to each other. They all had their place in the whole. It reminded him of an army camp in the evening, calm and purposeful, with a certain logic even in the disorder.

The army had felt more like a home, a place where people shared their lives with each other, than any of his family's residences ever had. This town was a home, but it wasn't his.

He couldn't stop thinking about Mrs. Sparks looking up at him with her luminous dark eyes and saying, *I believe in my sister.* No one had ever believed in him like that. And—this was harder to admit—he had never believed in anyone like that.

Why couldn't he write to any of his friends in the Peninsula? He'd tried, but even in the hospital he hadn't managed it. He wasn't one of them anymore. His concerns were no longer theirs. And the Oxford friends to whom he'd written such detailed letters describing the Spanish countryside—he couldn't write to them either.

He swung himself off the window seat with a deliberate lack of care, the jolt of pain a punishment for...too many things to name.

He knocked on the door of the common room devoted to Tony's campaign. Tony himself opened it with a sheaf of papers in his hand, looking harassed. Nick had expected him to be out canvassing. He'd thought only to foist himself on a bored election agent.

"Yes, Nick?" Tony asked impatiently.

"I wanted to help. To learn more about the campaign."

For a moment he thought his brother would say he didn't have time to schoolmaster him, but Tony swung the door wider. The room was filled with tables, all covered in stacks of notebooks and paper. Even the bed was strewn with documents.

"A list of voters, accounts of canvassing visits and their results," Tony said, gesturing to one table. He went round the room, naming the functions of various piles of paper. Their mother's handwriting threaded through everything, even apart from the heap of instructive letters she'd been sending Tony. "And here we have the heart of the campaign." He smiled bitterly. "The checks and the cashbox. The venality of voters is an ever-unfolding wonder."

To Nick's surprise, he found himself saying, "We *are* their patrons. It's only fair we show it."

Tony chuckled. "I never thought I'd hear *you* parroting Mama."

Nick grimaced. "Sorry. And what are those?" He pointed at the pages in Tony's hand.

Tony gnawed at his lip. "My speech for the hustings. I should probably let Mama write it for me."

Nick smiled. "You can do it. You wrote half my Latin compositions at Harrow, and you were three forms below me." Even then, Tony had felt like a stranger: a better student, better dressed, a better conversationalist. He had always seemed to know what he wanted and how to make people give it to him, while Nick had gone into most situations wondering what the devil he was supposed to do, and why he never seemed to care enough to find out.

Nine years old. Tony had been nine years old when he started Harrow. He couldn't possibly have been the prodigy of *savoir-faire* Nick remembered. Had Tony wanted an older brother who gave him more than a clap on the back and some smuggled cigars in exchange for an extra Latin essay?

Of course, Tony had had Stephen for that.

Tony's laugh was tired. "Yes, and I've often wondered what your masters made of the sudden swells and ebbs of your vocabulary."

"They thought I wasn't applying myself the rest of the time." They'd been right about that. They'd just been wrong in thinking his laziness concealed talent. "Speaking English is enough for me."

"Mama told me you learned Spanish," Tony said. His tone made Nick feel that he'd failed something yet again, that Tony agreed with his Latin masters.

"Yes, by speaking it." He tried for a self-deprecating but careless smile. He knew he only sounded defensive. "I couldn't learn a word out of the grammar I took with me on the ship. What do you want your speech to say?"

Tony pushed some papers aside to sit on the edge of the bed. "Christ, Nick, I don't know. 'Vote for me and I'll sponsor the damned gaslight bill'? These people don't care about politics. They don't care about what Liverpool's government will get up to in London. They don't understand that their sons—" Tony glanced at Nick's leg, and Nick could only suppose that a comment about the war had been intended. "All they care about is what the Whigs can do for them. And apparently it's not enough."

"It's been a long campaign," Nick said. "You're worn out. You know that's not true. Most of the people I've met seem to take their Orange-and-Purple loyalty very seriously." Incomprehensibly so, in Nick's opinion. "Mrs. Sparks feels guilty for even considering marriage to a Tory."

Tony gave Nick a look of abject horror. "She's considering marriage to a Tory?" He drummed his fingers on the table. "Did she tell you why?"

Nick sighed. "I don't think she's very impressed with Mr. Moon."

To his surprise, Tony looked relieved—but only for a moment. "Oh God, I'm going to lose this election."

Nick felt an edge of panic. "Of course not," he said confidently. "What are the numbers?"

"Fifty votes for Jessop, so he's assured a seat. The real contest is between Dromgoole and me for the second seat. Our current count is twenty-six for Dromgoole, and twenty-five for me. And one voter with his two votes still not spoken for." Tony's mouth twisted. "I don't know what Mama will say when I tell her I've lost Jack Sparks."

"Mrs. Sparks's brother-in-law?"

Tony nodded. "The Sparks family has been Orange-and-Purple probably since the Great Rebellion, and *I* lost Jack Sparks. He avoids me and my agent in the street, and when I go to his press, he's never there. Once I swear he slipped out the back door." Tony rubbed at his eyes. "I can't bring myself to tell her. How will I look her in the eye if I lose this election? It was supposed to be easy!"

"Tony, how could it be easy? She's been fighting Wheatcroft for this borough at every election since before we were born. You'll notice the only safe candidate is Jessop, and he's a Tory. I don't know what she said to you, but—"

"Leave Mama out of this. It's not her fault. It's mine." Tony looked him in the eye, manfully taking the blame for something that was entirely not his fault. "Perhaps I'm not cut out for politics, after all."

Politics were Tony's army. He'd been politicking since he was in short coats. "Of course you are." Nick held onto his cane as he bent over to clear the spot on the bed next to his brother. The angle was awkward, but he managed it. "Do you know why Jack Sparks is avoiding you?"

"*No,*" Tony said indignantly, his gaze dropping—but whether because he did know, or simply because he was discouraged, Nick couldn't have said. He didn't really know his brother all that well. Not as well as he should. He tried to remember if he'd written Tony a single letter from the Peninsula, besides a short one congratulating him on his marriage.

"Are you sure?" he asked anyway.

"Of course I'm sure," Tony snapped. There was a pause. "Why, do *you* know?"

"How would I know?"

"You've been spending enough time with his sister-in-law."

And nevertheless, she's thinking about marrying a Tory. Perhaps Tony hadn't even intended the accusation, but Nick heard it. "I'll see her again soon. I'll ask if she knows what's going on with Sparks."

Tony gave him an uncertain look. "I don't know if that's a good idea…"

"I'll be tactful," Nick promised. "The two of them are close. If she doesn't know, she can find out."

"And she'll do that for you?"

Nick felt his face heating. "It can't hurt to ask."

"Oh, believe me, if there's one thing I've learned these past two months, it's that it can always hurt to ask," Tony muttered.

Nick put a hand on his shoulder. He half-expected Tony to pull away, but instead his brother pressed back against the touch. Nick felt a sudden warmth in his chest. "She won't marry a Tory," he said. "We're going to win this thing."

Chapter 8

The following morning, Phoebe made sure she was in the Honey Moon at nine o'clock sharp. There was no one in the front of the shop, so Phoebe let herself into the already warm kitchen. Mr. Moon was pulling a tray holding tin cake-hoop out of the oven, paper tied around the bottom to keep in the dough. "Good morning," he said with his usual anxious cheer. Betsy and the kitchen boy gave her slightly more convincing smiles, but the whole thing still made Phoebe itch.

She gave him a cheery wave, then wished she hadn't. He was only a couple of feet away, after all. "Good morning."

Betsy elbowed him. He set the cake on the counter with a clatter. "You look very fine this morning." He glanced at Betsy, who gave an infinitesimal nod.

Phoebe didn't know whether to laugh or cry. "Thank you. You're very kind."

His shoulders relaxed with the satisfaction of a job well done, and picking up a spatula, he transferred pastries from a tray onto plates for cooling. Every counter was covered in fresh-baked sweets except for one, where Betsy was laying out yesterday's nectarine chips and dusting them with sugar. The kitchen boy—a spotty lad of fourteen or fifteen with light brown skin and beautiful green eyes—was draining syrup into a pot from a large preserving pan of greengages.

"We make all the pastries in the morning," Mr. Moon explained, "before the kitchen gets hot. The butter must be cool when they go into the oven."

"I write best in the morning, too." She tried not to wish she were home writing now.

Sweat beaded on his forehead from standing at the ovens. She had used to like it when Will worked up a sweat printing the *Intelligencer*. His fine blond hair darkened and spiked, his shirt clung to his shoulders as he worked the press, and when a drop of sweat rolled down his neck she had wanted to lick it up.

She tried to appreciate Mr. Moon's arms, which were objectively rather fine. But all she felt was a compulsion to wipe his forehead with a handkerchief before he dripped onto the pastries. She searched for something, anything to say.

The kitchen boy took the pot of syrup and set it on a stove. "See that it boils very smooth," Mr. Moon instructed him. "And your clarified sugar should…?"

"Blow very strong."

Mr. Moon smiled. "This is Peter, my apprentice." Peter turned to look at her, his eyes immediately fixing on her breasts.

"Nice to meet you, Peter."

He glanced up, saw that she had caught him looking, and ducked his head until his scraggly dark hair covered his eyes. "Nice to meet you, ma'am. Is it true you live in a haunted attic?"

Mr. Moon smacked his spatula on the counter. "*Peter*. Manners, if you please."

"It's no matter," Phoebe said, since she was trying to make a good impression. "No, people say Mrs. Pengilly's attic is haunted, but it isn't true."

The boy's face fell. "So you've never seen the ghost?"

"I'm afraid I don't believe in ghosts."

"Well, that's why, then." Peter turned back to his pot, satisfied.

Phoebe didn't tell him that her lack of belief was more of a wish than pure truth. Mrs. Knight, who thought the supernatural very vulgar, had hated that Mr. Knight was a believer who insisted on passing along to their daughters all manner of tales of the fairies and ghosts who inhabited their corner of the world. "What does 'blows very strong' mean?" she asked Mr. Moon, seizing the opportunity to make conversation.

He opened his mouth to tell her, then looked at his apprentice. "Why don't you explain it, Peter?"

Peter drew himself up. "Sugar's got different degrees," he told her slowly, clearly trying to soften the thick burr in his voice. "First, her's to be—" Mr. Moon cleared his throat. "I mean, it must be clarified to remove impurities. Then, when you boil it, it can be smooth, blown, feathered, crackled or caramel…" He went on explaining, dipping a scummer into the sugar to show how a drop pressed between thumb and forefinger stretched into a thread when he drew his fingers apart. Phoebe listened with a great show of attention.

"It's the first thing a confectioner must know," Mr. Moon told her when the explanation was over, looking very proud of his apprentice. "Good, Peter."

"I didn't know you had an apprentice," she said.

Mr. Moon glanced at Peter, and it occurred to her that perhaps he had needed the bond money from the boy's parents. But after a pause, he smiled. "Peter has a gift. It's best to have an early start in the trade. In any trade, don't you know."

Betsy snorted. "You never apprenticed."

"And I've no established custom, have I, or the freedom of the city," Mr. Moon said, more heatedly than she'd yet heard him speak. "If I'd apprenticed, I'd be a freeman and we could have a stall in the market—" He drew in a deep breath and looked at Phoebe. "My pa owned the bakery in Runford," he said, naming a village seven miles west, near the Dymond estate. "It was my grandfather's and great-grandfather's afore him. The bettermost bread in three counties, Pa used to say. And I sold it to come here."

Phoebe didn't want this shop to go under. All she had to do, to ensure it and Helen's security both, was marry the man. Why couldn't she say the words? "Where did you learn the trade, then?" she asked.

"The Dymonds kept a confectioner. He taught me things, sometimes. I always had a powerful sweet tooth."

"Mr. Moon had one afternoon off a week from the bakery," Betsy said. "And he'd walk an hour each way to Lenfield House to slave in the Dymonds' kitchen."

The tips of Mr. Moon's large ears turned red. He laughed. "My ma says I have syrup in my veins instead of blood."

"Is that a compliment?" Phoebe asked.

He shrugged. "She does like syrup."

"It's a compliment," Betsy said firmly. "We made you a saffron cake."

Mr. Moon started. "Faith, so we did!" He fetched a paper-wrapped hoop from the next room. Expertly separating the cake from the sides with a knife, he popped it out, set it on the counter, and cut her a warm wedge.

She took it, conscious of three sets of eyes on her. It was a beautiful yellow color, and Phoebe knew that saffron was terribly expensive, but—it was studded all over with caraway seeds. She hated the taste of caraway seeds. "How beautiful," she said with a nervous smile, and put it in her mouth. Ugh. "Mmm. Delicious."

"Do you mean that?" Peter's green eyes were suspicious. "I put a shilling's worth of saffron in it."

"Hush, Peter," Betsy said sharply. "How you'll ever contrive to have a shop of your own with such manners I don't know. He don't intend anything by it, ma'am."

Phoebe swallowed. If only he hadn't cut her such a large slice. "Of course I mean it."

Mr. Moon shook his head. "It isn't the one, is it?"

"No," she said honestly. "Sorry."

He sighed. "Well," he said with an attempt at cheer, "what book did you bring for me today?"

"*Tales from Shakespeare.*" It was in very plain language—intended, she thought, for children—and got right to the heart of the stories, which she hoped would give it an advantage over *Robinson Crusoe.* Flipping hastily through the book, she stopped at *Macbeth.* That was a nice manly play, wasn't it? "When Duncan the Meek reigned King of Scotland there lived a great thane, or lord, called Macbeth…"

She was soon caught up in the story, but when she remembered to look up, Mr. Moon wasn't really listening at all, but demonstrating to Betsy how to lay sugar-dusted nectarine chips on a tray to fit the greatest number. Phoebe had to give him credit for doing it silently.

Peter, on the other hand, said loudly, "Hey, don't stop, you're getting to the good bit. Lady Macbeth'll do the king herself, won't her?"

Phoebe grinned at him. "Wait and see."

Peter was very disappointed by Lady Macbeth's fate,

especially when Phoebe explained that Banquo was an ancestor of the Stuarts. Peter, it developed, was a good Whig and despised Jacobites.

Wheels squeaked in the front of the shop. "That must be Miss Jessop. I asked her to meet me here." Phoebe hesitated. "Peter, would you like to borrow the book?"

He reached for it eagerly, and she snatched it back. "*Never* touch a book with sugar on your hands. Never." He hurried to wash them.

Mr. Moon came suddenly to attention. "Miss Jessop? The Tory MP's daughter? I didn't know you two were friends."

Phoebe's heart sank. "It's nothing to do with the election. I don't think, anyway. But—Mr. Moon, I owe it to you to warn you, I'm dining today with the Tory election agent and"—she felt cheap and humiliated and guilty, admitting to more or less taking bids for her vote and her hand—"the man he wants me to marry," she said baldly. "I'm Orange-and-Purple, through and through, and you've all been very kind, but this is the rest of my life. Our lives. I—"

Mr. Moon looked stricken. Betsy's eyes hardened. And poor Peter, who stood to lose his apprenticeship, slowly traced the words of *Macbeth* with his finger, so rapt in concentration he hadn't even heard what she said.

"I'm sorry," she mumbled. "I'll see you tomorrow morning." She took up her pelisse and fled to the relative chill of the front of the shop.

Miss Jessop broke into an anxious smile at the sight of her. Phoebe couldn't remember the last time so many people had wanted to please her. Most likely the election of 1807. She bobbed a half-curtsey. "Good morning, Miss Jessop."

"Oh please, call me Caroline."

Phoebe didn't want to. Not until she understood what was going on here. "Then you must call me Phoebe." She took a chair reluctantly.

"I shall." Miss Jessop twisted her hands together in her lap. "What shall I have to eat?"

"I'm not—I really couldn't say. I don't love sweets as some people do. But everything is very good." She would have to do better than that if she married Mr. Moon. She'd have to pretend to adore everything so as to sell it.

Betsy hurried out of the kitchen, tying the strings of a clean apron. "Good morning, madam. What can I fetch you?"

"Have you any meringues?"

"Yes, madam, baked fresh yesterday. With raspberry jam."

"Splendid. I'll take two, and a packet of those almond comfits in the window. Jeffrey, here's sixpence if you'd like to buy yourself something. Would you like anything, Phoebe?"

"No thank you." Phoebe was very aware of Betsy's accusing eyes on her. "I just had a lovely slice of cake."

Miss Jessop's eyes lit up when the meringues came. "Oh, they're beautiful." She picked one up and bit into it. Her eyes fluttered shut and she very nearly moaned. "It's like a bite of heaven. They're delicious," she called after Betsy, who had gone back to the counter. Betsy smiled more broadly than Phoebe had ever seen her.

"Are you sure you don't want one? They're extraordinary." Miss Jessop held out the plate to Phoebe.

"I had one yesterday," she said awkwardly. "You're right, they're very good."

Miss Jessop set down her meringue. "I'm sorry, this is all very cloak-and-dagger, isn't it? I wasn't sure what else to do. I've something to confide in you, and really it isn't my place, only—only Jack wouldn't."

Phoebe blinked. "Jack...*Sparks*?"

Miss Jessop blushed. "Yes. He's asked me to marry him."

Phoebe tried to absorb this. "And—you've said yes."

Miss Jessop's smile burst across her sharp-featured face with startling radiance. "I have." The smile dimmed when Phoebe said nothing. "Do say you won't be angry with him. He feared you would be, because I'm a Pink-and-White. He regards you as his family. His only family. He hasn't the faintest idea I'm telling you all this, but he was so worried. I was sure you couldn't really be so prejudiced." Miss Jessop did not look at all sure.

It isn't prejudice, it's principle, Phoebe thought automatically, but given her own circumstances it would be ridiculous to say it. At least Jack was following his heart, not Lord Wheatcroft's pocketbook. So this explained the non-partisan *Intelligencer*. And it explained Jack's consternation at seeing her at the library, if he had been secretly meeting Miss Jessop there.

"I'm not angry with Jack," she said. "But—are you quite certain of your wishes? The printing office doesn't make very much money, and neither does the newspaper."

Miss Jessop's brows drew together. "I didn't choose Jack for his money."

"There's nothing petty or self-interested in worrying about money," Phoebe said sharply. "It isn't easy to be poor." Miss Jessop couldn't know what it was like, to worry you wouldn't be able to pay the grocer's bill next month. To kiss your husband's forehead and feel that he had a fever, and to have to decide whether to call the doctor, and what you could sell to pay him. "Will your father help you?"

"I don't know. He doesn't much like the Sparkses." Miss Jessop poked at her meringue, watching the surface crack. "There's money settled on me from my mother's family, but the trust provides that if my father doesn't approve of my husband, he can keep hold of the purse strings until my children are of age."

Phoebe looked at Jeffrey. "I could only afford one servant girl on Will's income."

Miss Jessop colored. "Simply because I have been used to being waited on hand and foot doesn't mean I can't grow used to another way," she said, an edge in her voice. "Jack will take care of me."

Who will take care of Jeffrey? Phoebe thought sourly. From the look on the man's face, he was thinking the same thing. "But you'd be dependent on Jack for everything. What if you quarreled or—?" She'd been confined to her bed for a week after her miscarriage, unable to escape Will's hovering and his snappish fear for her. She'd pretended to sleep for hours on end just to get away, face turned towards the wall.

"Believe me, I know that better than you can." Her mouth twisted bitterly. "You'd think, with all the wonderful mechanical strides our great nation is making, that someone would invent a chair I could direct myself instead of always needing someone else to push me. But I suppose there isn't as much money in that as there is in machine-looms to put men out of work."

Phoebe felt ashamed. Miss Jessop might never have been poor, but she had used a wheelchair all her life. And she had almost sounded like a Whig, there.

Miss Jessop took a deep breath and returned her face to a semblance of calm. "If Jack mistreated me, I daresay my father would take me back. But I don't think it will come to that."

Phoebe didn't know what to say. She wished she could be happy for Jack, but she could only see endless difficulties for him in this marriage, so many added responsibilities Miss Jessop could not share. What would Miss Jessop do on washing day? Could she learn to cook? Could she even bear him children? And surely, after years of being unable to leave their lodgings above the printing office unless he carried her down the stairs, she would come to resent him.

"We love each other." Miss Jessop's hands were tight on the arms of her chair. "I'll be a good wife to him. You think I'll be a burden, but it isn't true. I'll manage the advertisements and the books, deal with the newsagents as you used to do. I can do that."

With her education, maybe she could do it better. Unexpectedly, the idea irked Phoebe. "I didn't say—"

The shop's bell rang, and Jack walked in. Phoebe stood abruptly. He looked between the two of them, his round face darkening. "Caro," he growled. "What the—what the blazes did you do?" But his eyes lingered on Phoebe.

When she married Will, Jack had taken to bringing her his articles for the *Intelligencer*, to fix any errors in grammar or spelling before they could aggravate Will. Jack hated being corrected, and he'd taken even her mildest suggestions with a bad grace—but even though he was six years older than her, he'd always looked at her with this same burning desire for approval when he handed her the pages. She doubted anyone had ever cared so much what she thought, about anything.

Her eyes spilled over with tears. "Jack, I'm so happy for you!" she said, suddenly meaning it, and held out her arms.

He seized her in a great bone-crushing Sparks hug. "Thanks, Fee," he muttered in her ear, and set her down out of the way. He and Miss Jessop grinned at each other like fools, fierce matching grins. Maybe Jack knew what he was about after all. "You'd no call to meddle," he said, trying to sound stern.

Miss Jessop sniffed, her eyes gleaming. "I did if I ever wanted to be married. You'll call on me at home now, won't you?"

Phoebe almost laughed at the look on Jack's face. When they were younger, they had sometimes spat on the pavement outside the Jessop house as they walked by, if the MP had recently done something to upset them. "This very afternoon," he promised. "And I'll wear my best suit."

Phoebe hurried home. She didn't know why she was hurrying, except that her stomach jittered and her thoughts crowded her mind, jostling each other. The brisk motion and the breeze on her face made her feel a little calmer. Only a few days ago everything had been fine, and now her life was topsy-turvy and in a fortnight she would be married.

Married.

She swallowed bile and panic together, and kept them down. She believed in Helen. She could do this.

I need to write, she thought. Writing always calmed her. It was an application of leeches for the brain, drawing out excess thoughts and containing them. Banishing thoughts of Helen, confectioneries, and elections, Phoebe began to spin a new ending to her story, one in which Ann's sister rescued Ann from her ditch and, after a touching reconciliation, nursed her and her child back to health.

She knew that wouldn't wash with the *Girl's Companion.* If Ann bore a child out of wedlock without repercussions, there was not much Improving about the Tale. Perhaps she should go back and add in some early details of Ann's corrupt mother pandering to the villain, and Ann being borne along despite her sister's good counsel. Then the moral could be about the terrible consequences of choosing money or pleasure over the claims of family rather than simply avoiding sensual temptation…Phoebe would have to punish the mother and perhaps have Ann lose her health or wear black for the rest of her life to pacify the editors, but it could be done.

She burst through her door and headed to the bedroom and her writing table, mind racing—and Helen twisted round to look at her from the dormer of the window, where she knelt on the chest to shelve Phoebe's scattered books. "How did it go with Mr. Moon?" she asked anxiously.

Phoebe glanced around. The settle cushions were mended. Her cups and plates were in a neat cluster on the newly oiled table. Her notes were stacked with the corners aligned, no doubt all out of order—or worse yet, Helen had read them through in ordering them. She spotted Sukey behind the table, sanding the floor on her hands and knees.

Sukey knew Phoebe hated anyone rearranging her things. Helen ought to know it too; they'd shared a room growing up. The maid watched Phoebe curiously to see if she'd make her sister eat carp-pie.

Phoebe swallowed her frustration. "I'll tell you later, Ships. I want to write now."

"But we're meeting Mr. Gilchrist in an hour," Helen protested. "Don't you want to get ready?"

"I am ready."

There was a pause. "Oh, you're wearing that?"

Phoebe looked down at her brown dress. "You redyed this dress only last month." Helen had added a red ribbon at the waist. Phoebe *liked* this dress.

"Yes, to hide the ink-stains."

"And I can hardly see them."

Helen sighed. "At least let me do your hair."

Phoebe hated when Helen did her hair. It always pulled at her scalp and gave her a headache, and she grew fidgety sitting still for so long. But mill-owning Mr. Fairclough would expect his wife to present a respectable appearance to the world. "Well…"

There were footsteps on the stairs—footsteps, and the knocking of a cane. Phoebe's heart beat faster. Damn. "It's Mr. Dymond," she said. "I'd better see what he wants."

Helen dropped the second volume of Wordsworth's *Poems*. "Mr. Dymond?" she asked, scrambling to pick it up. "Why would he—"

"Can't you hear his cane?" Phoebe resisted the urge to check her book for damage.

"Oh, Mr. Nicholas Dymond, of course. Fee, I'm so sorry, the corner's bent."

Phoebe's surge of protectiveness was entirely unjustified. The corner might already have been bent. Until a few minutes ago, it had been stacked hugger-mugger under three other books and a teacup. "No matter."

"I'll put it under your dictionary to straighten it." Helen hurried into the bedroom.

Phoebe had the door open before Mr. Dymond had even raised his hand to knock. He really was handsome; he stood out from her shabby stairwell like the shiny red ribbon on her old brown dress. "You could just throw a pebble at the window," she said, trying to prevent her friendly smile from widening foolishly.

His blue eyes glinted and his mouth curved warmly. "Would you come down if I did?"

Another quarter inch and her smile would *definitely* be foolish. "Maybe. If I'd a mind to."

Sukey made an amused noise behind her. Phoebe stood aside to let him in, but he said, "Would you like to take a walk with me? It's a fine day, and who knows how many more we'll get before winter sets in."

"Go on," Sukey encouraged her. "You've done enough cleaning for one day."

Phoebe's home had always been a refuge; having her beloved little sister here shouldn't make her want to leave so badly, but it did. Mr. Dymond's height only made her rooms look smaller and more cramped. "Helen was going to do my hair," she temporized.

Mr. Dymond's dark brows flew up. "Oh, don't change your hair!" He laughed, ducking his head rather like Peter that morning. She wondered whether his hair had been long enough in the army to cover his eyes when he did that. "I'm sorry, that was unforgivably rude."

Helen appeared accusingly in the doorway. "Good morning, Mr. Dymond. What were you saying?"

"Ships, Mr. Dymond and I are going for a walk."

Helen frowned. "Fee—"

"I'll be back in time, I promise." She took her pelisse off the peg. "Let's go."

Chapter 9

She resisted all the way down the stairs, but once in the sunlight she couldn't help fishing. "You really think my hair is all right? Helen thinks I'm slovenly."

He glanced at her. He had the sort of lashes women always claimed to envy (*"What does a man need with such long lashes? They ought to have been given to a girl"*) but actually were quite glad of, right where they were. "You're not the *most* un-slovenly person I've met," he said. "But you know, 'a sweet disorder in the dress—' Oh, blazes. I was about to be very rude again. Please, pay me no mind."

Her face felt as if it were on fire. Her father had been fond of Herrick; she knew that poem. *A sweet disorder in the dress / kindles in clothes a wantonness.* The fire spread down her neck and over her bosom, until she was acutely aware of the heat trapped between her breasts and corset.

He bit his lip. "You know the poem, don't you?" She nodded. "I shouldn't have quoted it to you. The Cavaliers aren't really suitable for respectable women."

She sighed. "Few things are." She didn't want to see the hustings rising inexorably in the town square, marking the dwindling time until the polls; turning the other way, she led them down to the river and her favorite wooden bridge over the Arun. The birch and poplar leaves were yellow against the gray sky, the water the flat rich color of slate. Only the grass was bright and green from the recent rains. It would flourish until the frosts and snow began.

She enjoyed the rustle of dry leaves under their boots, the swish of his dark greatcoat beside her. She sneaked a glance at it, how splendidly it draped across his strong shoulders. Even in the pale autumn light, his hair shone warmly, like honey.

"How are things going with Mr. Moon?"

So quickly and efficiently he shattered the illusion that they were walking out, the two of them. Phoebe considered what to say. "Not—*badly.* He's a pleasant young man, and he cares very much for his business. That's in his favor."

"Hardly the words of a besotted woman," Mr. Dymond said ruefully.

She felt a flash of resentment. "My heart doesn't start and stop at my command. Or yours, *or* your mother's for that matter."

He grew serious. "Of course not. It needn't be Mr. Moon, you know. If there's another man you would prefer, we have no stake in the matter."

"There isn't." Phoebe had been thinking of this for days. But try as she might—making lists of the town's bachelors and then tossing them on the fire before anyone could see, cataloging the faults and virtues of acquaintances she ran into on the street—there was no one. It wasn't that she lacked a woman's natural urges. There were a number of men she wouldn't have objected to bedding. But marriage? "I suppose I'm too choosy."

"An unhappy first marriage would make anyone choosy."

"I was choosy before that. I don't mean to sound puffed up, but I think—I believe, anyway, that there were boys who might have wanted to court me if I'd given them any encouragement.

But I was shy, and none of them seemed to have so great an advantage over books as to be worth the effort."

"Mr. Sparks must have been a very prepossessing man."

She closed her eyes, and there was Will, big and broad and vibrant with his fair hair standing up from his head and catching the light like a halo. "He was. But he'd asked me to go walking with him before. He'd published a couple of my poems in the *Intelligencer*—youthful drivel I'd be ashamed of now, but he liked them. I pretended I thought he didn't mean it—the compliments and the invitation both. He was a dozen years older, and my mother thought the ink on his hands made him lower than me."

"But then your father died," Mr. Dymond said.

Had she told him that? No, her mother must have. She knew exactly what Mrs. Knight had told him: that she hadn't waited long enough. She wanted him to understand. "I was desperate to get out of that house. Everything there—his chair, his books, his pipe, the plate he used at dinner—"

She cut herself off. A tendency towards lists was one of the weaknesses of her prose. "Will took me out walking in the sun. And then he'd take me home. I knew my father wouldn't be there, and that when I went in, my mother would show off her red-rimmed eyes and try to make it out that she missed him more than I did. Just because I'd laughed a little with Will. Sometimes I'd cry when we passed the spindle tree, and Will would put his arm round me. I wanted to be out with him more and more, I wanted him to hold me more and more, and I thought it was love. Maybe it was, but I don't know if I'd still want to marry him if I met him now for the first time."

She couldn't imagine why she was telling a stranger all of this. Maybe it was *because* he was a stranger. Mr. Dymond hadn't known Will, he didn't know her.

He didn't know that she'd left her grieving eleven-year-old sister in that dreary house to go walking with Will, to marry him and escape.

In a few weeks he'd be gone, and her confession with him. It was like King Midas's barber shouting his secret into a hole in the ground—although that hadn't worked out so well, had it?

She slid her eyes towards him and felt a jolt. He was so near and solid. His eyebrows were dark slashes of ink on a page, the realest thing there was.

It was Will all over again. He was here, and handsome, and she wanted desperately to escape from her own life.

"I know exactly what you mean," he said, and she almost laughed because it was so precisely what she wanted to hear, so precisely what everybody always wanted to hear. "I was madly in love with a nurse in the hospital in Spain."

"Really?"

He watched the river. "You can't imagine the power of a woman's smile in a place like that. I lived to see her. I lay awake composing sonnets to the perfection of her nose. I spent hours imagining what her ears must look like."

"Her ears?"

"She was a nun. I never saw her without her veil."

A Spanish nun! For a moment she was so blinded by the romance of it that the pathos of his situation, alone in a foreign hospital with no one to smile at him but a nurse, didn't strike her. That, she supposed, was his point—that the romance had distracted him, too.

When she had been sick, she'd had her family. "Was it very bad in the hospital?"

A shadow crossed his face, but he shrugged. "No one likes to be in hospital."

"Tell me."

He shook his head, smiling. "I'm afraid it's not fit for a woman's ears."

Of course. They weren't equals. This wasn't friendship between them. He was kind to her out of chivalry, soft-heartedness and a dash of political self-interest, not because he liked her or would dream of confiding in her himself.

Mrs. Sparks's face fell. Nick had hurt her feelings.

Lady Tassell had another rule that went hand-in-hand with *Never confide in a voter*. *Nobody likes chatting with a Sphinx.* You had to give in order to get, but if you gave too much, you lost.

He'd used the rules with his men in the army. There was an art to maintaining a proper distance without being standoffish, revealing enough about himself to seem human without compromising his authority. But of course, his men had never expected to be his equal. When he'd encouraged Mrs. Sparks to confide in him and given her only that small story about Sor Consuelo, she'd seen at once that he was treating her like a subordinate. Voter and patron.

He had invited her on this walk to find out about her brother-in-law. For Tony's sake he couldn't like her; he couldn't help her or confide in her. He had to marry her off and be done with it.

But he couldn't do that if she was offended, now could he? He'd give her something small. "The conditions weren't the best in the hospital. There were rats and flies, and the smell—well, my nose stopped smelling it after a while."

Her own lovely nose wrinkled. A little more, and she'd be glad enough when he stopped. He kept his eyes on the path. "But the boredom and loneliness made everything a hundred times worse. The bullet broke my leg, and the surgeon had cut the wound open to take out a piece of bone that had split away. It was a long incision, and"—he hesitated a moment, figuring out how to avoid the word *thigh*—"so placed that if infection set in, they would have no choice but to amputate at once. I kept it clean with injections of sweet oil. That also kept the maggots away, it turned out."

She covered her mouth with her hand.

"Sorry."

"Don't be sorry," she said. "I was a newspaper editor's wife. I've read accounts of prisons and workhouses. You won't shock me. I want to know." And he believed her; she wanted to know. So few people did. They wanted to shut their eyes and their ears—

But was that true? Or was it only what he had told himself, because he didn't want to tell the story? Would his brothers really have flinched back? His friends from school, his fellow officers? Hell, some of them had *asked* him, and he'd ignored them or played it off with a joke.

He'd never wanted to talk about it with anyone, until now. Somehow Mrs. Sparks drew it out of him with her simple friendly curiosity and those serious eyes.

"Please," she said. "Go on. If there's more."

"There was nothing to do, no one to talk to. The two other officers in the cell with me—the hospital was in an empty convent—were delirious or unconscious most of the time.

And every other day, Sister Consuelo would come into that room and look at my wound." He didn't mention the feel of her hands on his thigh, but it had been the one good physical sensation he had had in those days. "She'd tell me I was healing nicely, and then she would smile at me. I felt as if the whole world were a lantern and she'd lit the candle."

Everyone had thought he was healing nicely. Then one day he had tried to stand and fallen. They'd realized the bone had healed thin and weak, and that he'd have to sell his commission. Consuelo had hovered over him. He'd wanted nothing more than for her to leave.

"Didn't your friends visit you?"

"They couldn't. My regiment was immediately posted away, and the hospital was some distance from the battle anyway. They took us there in carts, half-a-dozen miles over wretched roads, and when we arrived…"

"Yes?"

He'd gone too far. He gave her a crooked smile. "It's an ugly story, and today is such a lovely day. Tell me instead about the cake Mr. Moon—"

She scrunched up her face, half in self-deprecation and half in distaste.

He laughed harder than he could remember laughing in a long time, as if talking about his pain and sorrow had brought all his emotions closer to the surface—the joy and laughter, too.

"I don't like sweets." She sighed, but her eyes were twinkling. "I'd much rather hear your ugly story. If you wanted to tell it to me."

If he told her, she would see him for the weakling that he was.

In that moment, he wanted her to. He wanted her to see him, weakness and all. "They brought us there in carts and lined us up in the courtyard to wait for the surgeon. The bullet was still embedded in the bone, and it hurt like the devil." She shuddered, frowning. "I'm sorry, shall I stop?" he made himself ask politely.

"Oh!" She shook her head. "Of course not. Just—please don't say that word."

"What word?"

She blushed. "You know. 'His former name is heard no more in Heaven.' It's bad luck to say it aloud."

Enough of a country girl to fear the devil's name, enough of a scholar to quote Milton. He smothered his smile. He shouldn't curse in front of her anyway. He shouldn't be telling her any of this. "The surgeon was throwing the severed limbs into the courtyard as he took them off, to get them out of the way. When a new hand or leg would come flying down past our noses and land in the pile, it made the most terrible sound I've ever heard. The weather was wet and warm, and we could smell them. I lay there for hours, men dying in agony all around me. I was sure they would take the leg. They would have if I'd been an enlisted man. I couldn't see past that night into living as a cripple, into leaving the army."

He was surprised at how flat and calm his voice sounded. His reaction to the memory felt dull and muted, as far away as his voice. But he must feel something, because he couldn't *stop*. "I couldn't think past the operation. I tried to ready myself by imagining it, and I couldn't. Each time, I couldn't go any further than the saw scraping against the bone."

She put a hand on his arm, her eyes bright with unshed tears, and he confessed the deepest, darkest secret of all. "I wanted my mother."

He'd been sure that she wouldn't flinch at the sick thumps from that pile of limbs. He'd never seen her flinch away from anything.

"I wanted my father desperately after I lost my baby," Mrs. Sparks said. "I would have given anything for him to tell me everything would come right in the end. He was the only person I would have believed."

Why couldn't he accept that answer? But it was different. He knew it was different. She was a woman. "I should have been able to bear it." He hadn't had any trouble with the battle. He'd led his men over heaps of the wounded without turning a hair. He'd shown great personal heroism, everyone said. He'd even made a rousing speech at one point.

While he had been sniveling in that courtyard, three of his best friends and half his men had died. Any one of them would have made a better civilian than he did. There were days when he wished he could trade places. He hated himself for that. He should be able to bear it. "Before that night, I was a soldier. I was a man. Now I'm nothing."

"You're not nothing," she said sharply. "No one is nothing. We all matter. All of us."

He laughed bitterly. "And God loves the sparrows, but—"

She actually glared at him. "I'm a woman of no family and little income," she said. "I was a newspaper editor's wife, you know. I thought I would be one all my life. I thought I'd raise my children in the press room. I thought I'd *have* children. And no matter how angry I was with Will, no matter how bad our marriage was, I—" Her voice broke and her face crumpled. "I miss him."

He stared at her, paralyzed by the immediacy of his

response. He wanted to kiss her tears away. He wanted to hold her. He wanted to pour his heart into hers.

"But I found something new. I have my own life now, and I'm not nobody."

On the transport ship coming home, when he'd seen the coast of England for the first time in four years—all around him men had been overcome with emotion, and he'd felt nothing. Now here it was, hope rising white and shining from the dark sea in his heart.

He wasn't supposed to feel this way. Not about her. He could not—should not—*would not* kiss her, no matter that she made him feel the world was new, no matter that she was beautiful or that her well-worn boots and ill-tied bootlaces peeking out from under her petticoats made him want to lift her up and push her against the nearest tree. She would wrap her legs around him, and when he thrust into her, those boots would thump against the backs of his thighs—

He couldn't pick her up anyway. Not anymore.

"I'm *not*," she repeated, evidently taking his silence for disagreement.

"No," he agreed. "You're not. You're one of the somebodiest somebodies I ever met."

Her eyes narrowed. "I don't think that's a compliment."

"It is. I'm not always good with words, but—"

She laughed. "'And little of this great world can you speak, more than pertains to feats of broils and battle'? It's about as convincing when you say it as when Othello did."

He frowned, feeling obscurely attacked. He might write poems and letters, but his mother and brothers had the glib tongues, not him. "Believe me, I am showing the depths of my esteem for you in every action."

Her eyes sparkled with amusement, at once the darkest and brightest feature of the landscape. "I'm afraid I hadn't noticed. What does your disrespect look like, I wonder?"

He'd been so firm against temptation in his mind, and then somehow he'd led the conversation right here, confusion and turmoil coalescing into one simple, logical action. "It looks like this," he growled, and curled his free arm around her waist and pulled her to him.

Chapter 10

I t went as smoothly as if Nick had planned it. Maybe he had. His walking stick was in just the right spot, and he was holding it firmly enough that his leg didn't even begin to give. He barely noticed the faint jolt of pain because he had apparently also planned for exactly where her mouth would be. By the time her body fetched up against his, he was already kissing her.

It felt so good. She felt so good, all of her, her soft breasts and the stiff busk of her corset, her strong legs, warm and heavy and real. She kissed him back with so much energy. She went up on her tiptoes to reach more of him, slinging an arm around his neck for balance so their lips wouldn't have to part for more than a second. He'd noticed she was careful, usually, not to do anything that might overbalance him. She'd forgotten to be careful now. Her breath was hot on his cheek, and when she stretched upwards her breasts dragged against his chest. She made a small sound and clutched at him harder.

The pain in his leg was distant and dull compared to the warm, vivid pleasure of her kiss. It felt like sprinting, that exhilarating rush of energy you got when you held nothing back, just ran with every ounce of strength you had. No, better than that—it felt like battle, that thrill of intense physical risk, because underneath it all was a pulsing awareness of the enormity of what he was doing.

He slid his hand up to tangle in her hair. It wasn't as soft as he'd imagined; there was a firm springiness to it that was somehow better. He traced the perfect curve of her ear with his thumb—

The town clock chimed the hour.

She pulled away so hastily he almost did lose his balance, setting his weight on his left leg with a painful crunch.

"I'm late," she gasped, turning away to look towards the town. "Good God, what am I *doing*?" She glanced back at him, her eyes wide with horror. "I'm sorry, I'm late to meet Mr. Gilchrist, I have to—" She picked up her skirts and ran full-tilt down the path.

He couldn't have caught up with her, so he just watched her go. She looked splendid running, all bouncing *derrière* and glimpses of rounded calf. Her hair was coming loose. He wanted to learn to draw so he could capture the bold lines of her. He wanted to touch her again. He wanted—

He wanted a whole hell of a lot, but he couldn't have any of it. She was late to meet the Tory election agent.

He'd lost control. He'd risked her reputation and her future when she could least afford it, and worse, he'd failed Tony. He hadn't found out about how it was going with Moon, he hadn't asked about Jack Sparks—he hadn't done anything he was supposed to.

If his mother knew, she wouldn't even be disappointed. She'd just sigh and say, *It was my own fault for sending you. I knew you couldn't do it.*

And yet—for all that, his heart was racing in the most pleasant way. He hadn't felt this alive since Badajoz.

Phoebe realized she was smiling at Helen's frowning face in the mirror as she hastily repinned her hair. Could her sister tell what they had been doing? She didn't think so—her hair was messy enough on its own, and running accounted for her flushed face.

She was the most selfish woman alive, snatching a moment's pleasure at the expense of every finer feeling. It was one thing to daydream about kissing a handsome young aristocrat, and quite another to actually do it.

But she didn't know what could be a finer feeling than his lips on hers.

"We're late." Helen didn't say, *And you look like a slattern,* but it was clear from the sweep of her eyes that she was thinking it.

"A sweet disorder in the dress kindles in clothes a wantonness," Phoebe said giddily.

Helen looked down at her own neat clothes, her face shuttering. "I don't think wantonness is the note we wish to strike."

All the guilt and shame she should have been feeling crashed down on Phoebe at once. "I kissed Mr. Dymond," she confessed, turning to face her sister. "Do you think wantonness is in the blood?"

Helen went white. "I warned you. I told you they had a reputation."

Phoebe didn't want to blame Mr. Dymond. She didn't want the kiss taken away from her. "I provoked him into it."

Helen looked at the ground, clasping her hands tightly. "So did I. And then he expected—he thought I was—"

Phoebe felt cold and sharp, like a knife. No matter what,

her sister was not going to have to marry this man. "Thought you were what?"

Helen shook her head.

"Won't you tell me what happened?" she asked gently, for the hundredth time.

"I can't," Helen whispered.

The sight of her sister too ashamed to speak filled Phoebe with inchoate rage. "He was a muckworm, Ships." She wrenched open the door to the stairs. "It wasn't your fault. You didn't make him a muckworm. Come on, we're late."

Helen followed her. "Mr. Dymond is a muckworm too, or he wouldn't have kissed you."

Phoebe noticed she didn't defend her own seducer. "Don't worry. He isn't going to take any liberties I don't want him to."

"But what if you say no, and he's angry? He could tell everyone you kissed him."

"He won't," Phoebe promised as they half-ran towards the Drunk St. Leonard.

"How do you *know*?" Helen held her skirts up with one hand and her hair carefully in place with the other.

Phoebe just knew. "He wants my votes," she said flippantly.

"What if you give them to the Tories?"

A knot began to grow in her stomach. Mr. Dymond wouldn't betray her, would he? He esteemed her. He had said so. But he'd also implied that showing respect meant not kissing her, and then he'd kissed her. Did he feel differently now? Was he shocked that she hadn't stopped him? *You threw yourself at him like a two-penny whore,* a voice whispered. It sounded like her mother.

Her sister was hearing that voice a hundred times worse. If Phoebe gave in to it, that meant Helen's shame and fear was right. And it wasn't.

Only, Phoebe's freedom was forfeit because Helen had followed her desires, so maybe it was.

"It's a tangle," she told Helen as they fetched up below the swinging wooden sign of a haloed, bearded fellow quaffing a mug of ale. "But do you remember that William Blake poem—?"

"This isn't the time for poems." Helen seized Phoebe's hand, crushing it in a fierce grip. "Promise me you won't do it again."

She didn't want to. "Ships—"

"Promise me."

There had been shadows under Helen's beautiful eyes for weeks. Phoebe couldn't let her worry over this, not when she shouldn't be kissing Mr. Dymond again anyway. He might not even want to.

"I promise."

Helen's taut, thin shoulders relaxed. "Well, come on then. We're late."

"Only by"—she glanced at the Town Hall clock—"twenty minutes."

Helen rolled her eyes. "To other people, that's a lot to be late by."

Mr. Gilchrist and another man were seated close to the door, Mr. Gilchrist recounting an amusing anecdote with an air of desperation. He chuckled nervously at the funny parts to fill the silence left by his companion, who was—Phoebe's heart sank—checking his watch.

And the watch was expensive—less valuable than Mr. Dymond's, to be sure, but its chain was finely worked and it lay heavily in the stranger's hand. At least it was brand-new, and his Kerseymere coat did not quite sit easily on his shoulders. He hadn't been born to prosperity.

"And the grocer's lady said to the cheesemonger's wife, 'Nothing goes after *cheese*,'" Phoebe finished for Mr. Gilchrist. "I'm so sorry I'm late." The election agent lapsed into relieved silence as both men stood to greet them. The stranger glanced at Helen, his eyebrows going up, and then at Phoebe. He looked briefly disappointed as he realized which of the sisters must be his prospective bride, but Phoebe had expected that. She hadn't expected him to hide it so quickly.

He had a set of pale, piercing eyes, and she thought a physiognomist would have admired the lines of his skull, clearly revealed by the close crop of his graying straw-colored hair. There was a restless, wolfish energy about him; he snapped his fingers shut around his watch and dropped it in his pocket with a movement that would have been jerky if it hadn't been so precise.

He wasn't handsome, exactly. And he looked older than she had expected. She couldn't guess whether that was because he *was* older or because he had driven himself hard. There were few lines on his face, but they were deeply etched.

Maybe, Phoebe thought, to her own surprise.

"No matter." He smiled—or rather, bared his teeth. "I know a woman is never on time. I had scheduled an extra half an hour a-purpose."

Phoebe didn't know quite what to say to this. Fortunately, Mr. Gilchrist jumped in with one of his oily smiles. "Mrs. Sparks and Miss Knight, allow me to present Mr. Fairclough. Miss Knight is Mrs. Sparks's younger sister." He put a faint emphasis on *younger.* Helen bristled beside her, but Phoebe was rather grateful to the young man. "Please do sit down, ladies." He pulled out Phoebe's chair first, but he lingered a little behind Helen, looking at the top of her head, before moving smoothly back to his own seat. "Mr. Fairclough is a great admirer of your poetry."

"You mustn't flatter me, sir," Phoebe said.

Mr. Fairclough raised his head. His smile was startlingly boyish and engaging—and startlingly brief. Why, he was as uncomfortable as she was, that was all. "I don't flatter." He rearranged his fork and knife. "I bought my daughter your mourning poem. She misses her mother, you know. She was glad to have it."

He referred to one of the poems Jack printed for her and sold in his shop. She had written it about her miscarriage, and revised and published it after Will's death. It was among her best work and she chose to sell it, but she often felt awkward discussing it with strangers. Mr. Fairclough had lost his wife, though. He looked as if he understood. "I'm so sorry for your loss," she said.

He nodded in acknowledgment. "Are you fond of children, Mrs. Sparks?"

"I am." She glanced self-consciously at Mr. Gilchrist, wondering again if he had seen the baby clothes in her trunk.

Mr. Gilchrist looked very bland as he said, "Do you have that darling miniature of your little girl, sir?"

Mr. Fairclough opened his watch and turned it to face her. The lid held a miniature depicting a girl of seven or eight with carefully tended blond ringlets, a sharp chin, and her father's piercing eyes.

Phoebe tried to hide the covetousness in her breast. "She takes after you."

"She's prettier," Mr. Fairclough said with satisfaction.

"Cleverer as well." He eyed Phoebe. "I'd like to have more."

Phoebe flushed. "So would I." There was something shocking in considering marriage, and children, and all that entailed, so early in an acquaintance. Of course it was always on one's mind when meeting an eligible man, but in a distant way. She and Mr. Fairclough might really be married and sharing a bed in a fortnight.

The memory of her kiss with Mr. Dymond intruded guiltily. She had wanted him so badly, and now half an hour later she was thinking about bedding Mr. Fairclough. Had she grown unchaste and indiscriminate without the regulating pleasures of the marriage bed? Or had Mr. Dymond's kiss uncovered all her long-buried desires? Her body felt awakened, aware. She had ignored it for years, and now it clamored for attention.

Ashamed and self-conscious, Phoebe couldn't find much to say through the meal. Mr. Fairclough was either equally anxious or a man of few words. The conversation was carried chiefly by Helen and Mr. Gilchrist, who talked with determined gaiety of the weather and tomorrow's St. Crispin's Day celebrations before discovering a topic that interested them both: the latest London fashions.

Mr. Gilchrist was perfectly willing, even eager, to explain the desired cut of the new style of sleeve and what exactly a Spanish button was. A dozen times, Phoebe met Mr. Fairclough's eyes with shared amusement. It was plain he cared as little for the finer points of fashion as she did.

When Mr. Gilchrist suggested a stroll after dinner, it seemed natural that he and Helen should fall behind still chatting of hussar cloaks and coquilla nut bracelets. Phoebe and Mr. Fairclough, brisker walkers, ended up ahead.

"You are new to Lively St. Lemeston, I understand," Phoebe said to break the silence.

He nodded. "I spent most of my life in Lewes, processing flax for the sailmakers up North. My brother manages the manufactory now. Lately Mr. Jessop put us in the way of a large contract with the navy. I knew him from the Ministerialist party in Lewes."

Ministerialists, ha! Tories never called themselves plain Tories; it was always a grander name. *Don't let your prejudices spoil a good thing,* she admonished herself. "How splendid that you were able to do your part for King and country. I suppose you will be selling the government your gunpowder too?"

He laughed. "I hope so. I shan't make much money from pheasant hunting."

She laughed back, turning her face up to his—and saw that they were passing the windows of the Honey Moon. Mr. Moon paused in serving trifle to a customer to gaze stricken at her. Cream dripped unnoticed from his spoon to the counter.

She faced ahead and tried not to think of him, or Betsy or Peter or the way everything in the front of the shop was kept so lovingly clean while the kitchens were a busy, well-used mess. She could not marry to please a confectionery.

"My parents took us to Lewes once," she said. "We went to see Sarah Siddons when she toured in *Macbeth*. Helen was only nine and cried so hard at the assassination scene that we were obliged to leave the theater. I'm not sure I've quite forgiven her to this day."

Mr. Fairclough frowned. "Nine is too young for *Macbeth*."

"Well, I know that," Phoebe said hastily. "I was quite angry at my parents for bringing her, too. I wanted one of them to stay at the play with me, but my mother was frightened by

Lewes's bustle and wouldn't hear of being separated." Phoebe had sulked for weeks afterwards with all the single-minded resentment of sixteen.

"It's a big city." He gave her one of his brief smiles. "I saw Sarah Siddons when she was in Lewes. This was seven years ago?"

Phoebe nodded. "Do you think we were at the same performance?"

"Could be."

"Wouldn't that be a marvelous coincidence?"

"Not so marvelous," he said, frowning again. He fixed his piercing eyes on her. "I was already a man of middle age then. You were a young girl."

Mr. Moon was a boy next to this man. She resolutely didn't think of Mr. Dymond. "I don't think a difference in age is a bar to happiness."

"You may meet a younger fellow later, one you like better."

She stiffened. "I keep my vows, sir."

He nodded. "Good. I like you, Mrs. Sparks. I'd like you to meet my daughter. If she don't take a dislike to you, and you want to marry, we shall. Are you free tomorrow?"

She *was,* but she felt suddenly cornered. Perhaps in the morning, she wouldn't feel so certain she preferred him. And then, this was giving her vote to the Tories, and maybe condemning the Honey Moon to bankruptcy. It would be a strange upheaval for poor Miss Fairclough to meet her if Phoebe wasn't sure.

But if she stalled, would he be angry that she was less decisive than he? "I don't know," she said finally. "The polls will open Friday fortnight. We'll need a few days to obtain the license. That gives us ten days. I'd like to meet you again once or twice before I risk your daughter's feelings. I like you too, but marriage is a great step, even at election time."

He nodded, his eyes warming. "You don't let yourself be rushed into a deal. Good for you. May I take you driving Monday morning, then?"

She agreed. "How was Mrs. Siddons's mad scene?"

He whistled. "The hairs stood up on the backs of my arms."

Phoebe sighed.

"She'll do it again," he said. "I know she retired this summer, but these actors never really retire, do they? She'll get up a revival at Drury Lane, or one of her brother's provincial theaters. I'll take you."

She drew in a breath at the idea, eyes widening, and he gave her another of those startlingly boyish smiles.

When the men left them at their door, Mr. Gilchrist bowed over her hand and murmured, "I told you I knew your taste in men."

"You have the oiliest smile, did anyone ever tell you that?" she murmured back.

He blinked, looking injured. "Frequently. I don't know why. Will I see you and your sister at the Pink-and-White Literary and Philosophical Society supper this evening?"

She glanced at Helen, who nodded resignedly. "I look forward to it," Phoebe said, half-expecting to see the sun falling from the sky or some nearby rocks melting. But nothing of the kind transpired.

Chapter 11

"Do you think they'll expect us to be wearing pink-and-white rosettes?" Helen ruthlessly repinned a tendril of Phoebe's hair that had, against all odds, come loose on the walk to the Drunk St. Leonard.

"If they do, they will be disappointed. They shall have to content themselves with my hair, which looks lovely. Thank you, Ships." Phoebe's escape from hair-arranging at dinner was now being paid for. She counted no less than six separate braids, woven into a tight coil at the crown of her head. Four fat curling-iron ringlets dangled, their arrangement and shape about as natural and artless as Lord Wheatcroft's ornamental trout stream. The odor of heating hair still lingered in her nostrils.

Helen smiled, her face lighting up with pride. "*You* look lovely. That dress really does become you." Phoebe was in the same blue dress she had worn to the Whig dance, but she was hardly the only voter in town with only one set of Sunday best.

Besides, since Thursday it had sprouted several inches of white embroidery around the hem, the neck, and each sleeve. Helen had spent hours refurbishing Phoebe's wardrobe over the last three days, sewing until her sight blurred and her fingers cramped. Helen liked sewing and she had good reason to avoid her own thoughts just now, so Phoebe hadn't said anything, but she worried there was some sort of penance in it.

Opening the tavern's front door, they were greeted by a great wave of sound. Six trestle tables had been pushed together to fill much of the room's length. Mr. Jessop was seated at the head of the table with his daughter. Mr. Dromgoole and his wife took the foot, and each side was filled with voters and their families on a hodgepodge of chairs, stools, and benches.

Her eyes found Mr. Fairclough immediately. He showed to advantage in the boisterous company, quiet and a little withdrawn, a nearly full mug cradled in his hands. She waved to catch his attention—drat, would he find that vulgar? But he gave her one of his brief smiles and stood, indicating the empty chair beside him. There was only one.

"I was hoping my sister could sit with us."

"By a stroke of luck there's an empty seat by me," a familiar voice said. She turned to see Mr. Gilchrist a little way down the table on the other side, also guarding an empty chair. She shot a suspicious glance at Mr. Fairclough, who shrugged, his eyes creasing in amusement.

It was difficult to be angry when they were so pleased at their small subterfuge. "Helen, if you'd rather not, we'll find other seats."

Helen rolled her eyes and smiled. "It will be a sacrifice, of course," she said, but she was speaking more to Mr. Gilchrist than to Phoebe, already walking towards him. Phoebe felt a pang. This was how Helen's life should be. She should be free to flirt and talk and enjoy men's attentions. She shouldn't have to worry they would expect something of her. She shouldn't have to guard a shameful secret.

"Sorry about that," Mr. Fairclough said in her ear as she

sat. "I wanted you all to myself."

Having assumed Mr. Gilchrist wanted Helen all to himself, she warmed at this new interpretation, but didn't know how to reply. Looking down the table, she recognized the greater part of the guests, ranging from Tory worthies of the town to a few artisans and tradesmen. She saw several lawyers her father had faced in court again and again—he representing some small fellow in danger of bankruptcy or imprisonment, they the interests of the corporation, the landlord, or the bank. She saw their clients, too, and the magistrates who almost always ruled in their favor.

One of the men at the table had begun a local petition a few years ago, opposing the expansion of the franchise. She and Will had started a contrary one and got twice the signatures, but the Tories' names had been higher and more respectable. 'The better sort,' Mr. Jessop had called them, and somehow only the Tory petition was presented to Parliament.

Wait till the next election, Will had said. *We'll get our man in then.*

This was the next election. Will was dead, and she was at this supper. Will and her father would hate that she was here. She hated that she was here.

"Don't worry," Mr. Fairclough said. "They don't bite."

She tried to clear the trouble from her face. "And you, Mr. Fairclough? Do you bite?"

The corners of his eyes crinkled again. "Only sometimes."

She liked him. She would probably even like him to bite her. If she left, she would have no choice but Mr. Moon.

"What are you doing here?" someone hissed in her ear. She jumped. Jack. *Jack* was here? He was wearing his Sunday best, too—although he wore boots instead of his buckled shoes in unmistakable disrespect for his hosts. Miss Jessop wouldn't be pleased.

"I could ask you the same thing," she hissed back. "*Later.*" She turned to Mr. Fairclough. "Mr. Fairclough, this is my brother-in-law, Jack Sparks. He publishes the town newspaper."

Mr. Fairclough held out his hand. "The *Mercury*?"

Jack's face darkened. The *Mercury* was the monthly Tory newsletter. (*If you can even call it that*, Will had told her hundreds of times. *By the time they bring that thing out, none of it's news anymore.*) Since Jack ran the only press in town, the *Mercury* was printed in Lewes and shipped in at Lord Wheatcroft's expense.

"Mr. Fairclough is new to town," Phoebe interposed hastily. "No, Mr. Sparks's paper is the *Intelligencer.*"

"I see." Mr. Fairclough sounded less friendly. Phoebe elbowed Jack, hard.

"It's an honor to meet you," Jack said, but his eyes strayed to Miss Jessop halfway through their handshake. The seat on her right was taken by Mr. Anti-Reform Petition. She cast Jack a longing look. He returned it, his fair hair wafting sadly down over his forehead.

"Spill something on his coat and take the chair," Phoebe suggested.

"I wish it were that simple," Jack said miserably. "Even if the chair were free, Jessop wouldn't let me have it. She's forbidden to see me."

Her heart sank. "Is there any more of that cider?" she asked Mr. Fairclough.

Phoebe had almost forgotten what real cooking tasted like. When Mr. Fairclough filled a plate for her without asking what she wanted, she didn't take him to task but simply set to eating. Roast goose, hot potatoes dripping with anchovy sauce, a roll still hot from the oven, bacon, and fricassee of turnips…heaven.

You look like a pig with a trough, her mother's voice told her. *He filled your plate too full. You don't have to eat it just because it's there.* She drank more cider to shut the voice up and tried not to listen too closely to the election talk around her. But eventually the main course ended and the desserts were brought out.

"Of course we expect our representative to guard against further bills in favor of the Papists," Mr. Fairclough said to the man on his left as he began to fill her plate with sweets. Across the table, Jack poured another mug of cider.

"I don't much care for sweets," she said.

"After all, we don't know where their true loyalties lie," he continued, heaping chocolate cream on her plate. "With the Crown or with Rome?"

"Mr. Fairclough, I don't much care for sweets," she tried again, louder.

He carefully selected a jelly-covered sword knot and set it next to the chocolate cream. "Napoleon was crowned by the Pope, wasn't he? Who's to say they—"

"Whatever their faith, they are still Englishmen!"

A dozen heads swiveled to look at her. Helen shook her head in warning and Jack covered his eyes with his hand—but only for a moment, as it was difficult to drink cider in that position.

Mr. Fairclough blinked. Then he smiled, relaxing. "No,

Mrs. Sparks, you must consider the matter logically. Allow the Catholics into public office and the military, and who's next? The Jews?" There was general laughter around the table at the folly of this idea.

Phoebe thought the Dissenters were likely to be next, and as they were far more numerous than Catholics and predominantly Whiggish to boot, she could see why the Tories opposed it. She repressed the cynical comment with an effort. "My father always said we worshiped the same God."

His smile widened into a snicker. "Mrs. Sparks, have you ever even spoken with a Jew?"

"Yes, I have." She flushed at his look of disbelief. "Jewish peddlers come through town all the time."

There were snickers all round the table at that. "And there you have it," Mr. Fairclough said. "You must—"

"I've never spoken with anyone from Manchester either," she said, goaded. "Should they be denied the franchise on that account?"

"It might be best!" someone called out, and suddenly everyone was telling stories about brainless Northerners and showing off their impressions of an incomprehensible Northern accent. Mr. Fairclough's was actually rather good, which only irritated Phoebe further, especially when he set the heaping plate of sweets down in front of her with, "Owt else you fancy, ma'am?"

"I don't much like sweets." Her self-deprecating little laugh depleted most of her remaining self-control.

He blinked. "Why didn't you say so?"

Phoebe was reaching for the cider jug when Helen appeared at her elbow. "You've got to get Jack out of here, he's drunk as a wheelbarrow."

Phoebe threw Mr. Fairclough a nervous glance. "I can't take care of Jack tonight."

"A wheelbarrow with no wheel."

"Ships, a wheelbarrow with no wheel is just standing still." But she looked around for Jack. His chair was empty. Then she spotted him weaving his way towards Miss Jessop, who was glancing anxiously between him and her father. Phoebe thought the young woman would have fled, but her chair was quite hemmed in.

She looked at Mr. Fairclough. "He's my family."

"Not strictly speaking," Mr. Fairclough muttered, but he stood to pull back her chair.

"My sister will keep you company until I return."

Helen frowned. "Are you sure you can manage Jack by yourself? He's rather heavy."

She wasn't at all sure, especially since she herself had had more than one pint of cider. But she couldn't simply abandon Mr. Fairclough. "I'll be fine," she said confidently.

Luckily Jack's drunken progress was slow. She reached him just as he set one broad palm on the table by Miss Jessop's glass of syllabub.

"We were just leaving," she said brightly, buttoning her pelisse to illustrate the point. "It was lovely to see you both." She tugged none-too-gently on Jack's arm. "Come along, Jack. If you make a scene, you'll be sorry in the morning."

"But I love her," Jack said in a stage whisper. "Caro," he said louder, "I love you." Miss Jessop's cheeks bloomed a bright red. So did her father's; he rose from his seat in a clear threat.

"Father, he's drunk," Miss Jessop said sharply. "Please don't."

Mr. Jessop looked from Jack to his daughter. His mouth

twisted in disgust and he sat abruptly. "Get him out of here," he said loudly to Phoebe.

Her cheeks burned with fury and embarrassment; the MP had just publicly branded them as beneath him. But if Jack had been a gentleman—or if Mr. Jessop had chosen to treat him as one—his behavior might have warranted a challenge. It might still, if she couldn't make Jack leave. Her heart hammered in her chest. "Yes, sir, I will," she murmured, bobbing a curtsey. "Thank you, sir."

"I won't be swept under the rug like—" Jack began.

"Jack, please." She let her voice crack, hating that she was reduced to pleading. "I need you to come with me. Please."

He turned his head, his eyes struggling to focus. "But Phoebe—"

"Please, Jack. I need your help."

"Of course," he said at once.

Phoebe's heart swelled. That ploy would have succeeded with very few people in the world; even Will had never been one of them. "Come outside with me. Please."

"But—" His head twisted almost halfway round to watch Miss Jessop as Phoebe dragged him across the room and out the door. She grabbed up his coat as they passed his chair. "Phoebe, what's going on? What were you even doing there?"

"I'll tell you tomorrow," she said gently, helping him into the overcoat on the front steps. "You're too bosky to keep a secret right now. Let's get you home before you fall over."

His brow furrowed. "Thought you needed help. Did you lie to me?"

Phoebe's head ached. "You'll thank me tomorrow."

He drew himself up as best he could. "I don't need to hide behind anyone's skirts—" His eyes widened in panic. Before

Phoebe could move out of the way, he doubled over and cast up his accounts on the flagstones—and on the newly embroidered hem of her blue dress.

For a moment she simply stood there, unable to believe it had happened. A lump rose in her throat—but she swallowed it. Jack was on his knees, heaving. She knelt down beside him and fished his handkerchief out of his coat pocket, wiping his mouth with it.

"Sorry," he muttered.

She smoothed his fine, fair hair back from his forehead. "What are sisters for? Come along." She wiped the sick from her hem as best she could with the handkerchief and left it there next to the pool of vomit. It was an unkind thing to do to the Drunk St. Leonard's staff, but she *couldn't* go back in there with her soiled dress to tell them what had happened. Not when Mr. Jessop would see.

She helped Jack to his feet and began their slow progress down the street, hoping he wasn't drooling onto her shoulder. Luckily it wasn't far to the printing office.

"I miss you," he said.

She almost dropped him. "What?"

"I miss you. And Will."

For what seemed like the hundredth time that week, Phoebe blinked back tears. "I miss him too."

"I used to love press day. When it was the three of us."

"So did I." The post would come in and the three of them would go through the latest London papers, racing to fill the last column or two and typeset it. Then, when it was run off and in the hands of the newsmen, Phoebe would make supper and they'd take the evening off. It had felt like a celebration, every week. Even after she and Will had begun to quarrel, on that day she still felt that they were one flesh.

"Now it's just a relief when it's over," he said. "Only I know I've got it all to do again the next week."

Phoebe stumbled. "No. You love the paper."

"I did when it was the three of us. Now it's still the same work, and only me and my apprentice to do it. I like Owen, but he isn't you and Will."

She felt a horrid creeping guilt. She should have stayed with the paper, with Jack, instead of trying to earn her livelihood as a writer. Jack had asked her to. She'd thought he was only being kind. "I didn't mean to abandon you."

"I hate the rooms upstairs now. I'm all alone there."

She felt another stab of guilt. She'd thought he must like having the place to himself, instead of taking a narrow pallet in the front room while she and Will slept—or more often, that last year, fought—in the bedroom.

She'd imagined he felt precisely what would allow her to do as she wished. How had she been so selfish? "I'm sorry," she said inadequately. "But soon Miss Jessop will be there with you."

He shook his head heavily. "Her father will never let us marry. Never."

"He will. We'll find a way to convince him. I promise. What exactly did Mr. Jessop say, when you saw him?"

There was no reply. She twisted her head to look at Jack just as the arm around her shoulder went limp and his head lolled forward. Their temples cracked together, and it was all she could do to break his fall as he tumbled over, utterly insensible.

They were under a streetlight. She thought of the picture they must make, a pool of light in a dark street illuminating a sleeping drunk and a young woman, both in their Sunday best, the woman's fine skirts stained with vomit.

Jack began to snore gently.

The spirits of the wise sit in the clouds and mock us, Phoebe thought. At a certain point you had to laugh, and that's what Phoebe did. She pressed her forehead against the cold pole of the streetlight and giggled uncontrollably.

Footsteps came down the street. They'd see her. They'd think her quite mad. That only made it funnier, though.

Then she heard something else—a faint tapping, a slight unevenness in the step. Her heart leapt with instinctive happiness. She caught her breath, sputtering a little bit. Then she remembered their kiss and how she had planned to appear dignified and aloof at their next meeting, and that set her off again.

It probably isn't him, she told herself. *It's probably old Mr. Bickerstaff out for his evening constitutional.* But when she raised her head, she could see at once that it was Mr. Dymond, carrying a wrapped bundle under his free arm. He passed into the light of the next streetlight over, and his quizzical expression sent her into whoops again.

She had almost got control of herself when he reached her. He looked from her to Jack, then back at her, then at Jack again, and visibly gave up. "Mrs. Sparks," he said with a slight bow, just as if everything were perfectly ordinary. "How serendipitous. I was on my way to see you."

Her heart leapt again. "You were?"

He hefted his bundle, giving her that schoolboy headduck and regarding her through his lashes with a practiced repentance she was sure had served him very, very well when he *was* a schoolboy. It was serving him well now. "I know it's late, but I wanted to tell you how sorry I am for my conduct this morning. I ought never to have treated you in that fashion, and I can only hope you'll believe that I still feel the utmost respect for you."

It was a practiced apology—but he had taken the trouble to practice, for her. And when he'd come across her in this ridiculous situation, he was so set on apologizing that he'd delivered it just the same.

He looked lovely in the glow of the streetlight, his fine features splashed with shadow like an ink drawing.

"Oh, don't mind it," she said, and then felt like a fool.

But his face brightened. "I brought you a ham."

"A ham?"

"Well, I know you don't like sweets…"

That set her off again, making mortifying high-pitched squeaks as she struggled to catch her breath.

"Let me guess, you don't like ham either."

She shook her head frantically. "I love ham!" With a super-human effort, she put on a straight face. "I promise I wasn't laughing at you, only—it's been an evening."

His mouth curved with amusement. "I can see that. May I have the pleasure of an introduction?"

She looked down at Jack, still snoring faintly, his cheek on her boot. *Don't laugh. Don't laugh.* "Mr. Dymond, may I present my brother-in-law, Jack Sparks." She held her aching sides. "I can't possibly get him home unless I drag him by the arms."

The shadows deepened on Mr. Dymond's face, and she realized that he was regretting his inability to carry Jack home himself.

"I'll manage somehow," she said hastily. "Actually—if you

could wait here with him while I go and look for the night watchman. He should be...well, around somewhere. If the corporation would stop living in the past and support a Police Act—especially in winter, when it's dark so early—" She cut herself off. "I know it's a great deal to ask, especially when you've already purchased me a ham. Would you mind very much bringing it by tomorrow? I'd love to have it. I haven't been able to buy a whole ham since last Christmas."

He chewed at his lip. "I think we can manage him together. Just wait here while I put the ham back in my room."

Chapter 12

When he returned, Mrs. Sparks was waiting where he had left her, her elusive brother-in-law propped up against her legs and the lamppost. Her earlier amusement had passed, leaving her looking tired and a little worn, but her face brightened when she saw him. "Thank you again, I—"

He smiled, knowing his leg would hurt in the morning because he'd helped her. Maybe all day, and maybe the next day too. Before, he'd never had to think twice about something like this. It was a small enough burden, but he resented it sharply. "It's nothing."

Together they heaved Mr. Sparks upright and got his arms about their shoulders. Mrs. Sparks gave the unconscious man a light slap. "Wake up, Jack, we've got to get you home. Come on, wake up."

He stirred, mumbling something unintelligible, and put one foot in front of the other with just enough strength not to be entirely dead weight. Nick concentrated on his steps, on not tripping over the gaps in the flagstones, on holding tightly to Mr. Sparks. It kept his mind off Mrs. Sparks's arm pressing against his and the way her generous hips jolted Mr. Sparks's side into his with each step they took. He was doing this because Tony wanted their votes. Not because of how wonderful she looked in a fit of laughter, like a warm fire and roasted

Spanish chestnuts on a rainy day.

They turned left at the Market Cross and there, about fifty yards down on the left side, was a crisp black-and-white sign painted to look like a printed sheet of paper.

SPARKS PRINTING

Home Of The Lively St. Lemeston Intelligencer
"Labour to keep alive in thy breast, that little Spark
of Celestial fire called Conscience."

He recognized the quote. It was printed on each newspaper, below the title and next to the price and date. "There seems to be a fashion for name puns in this part of the world. My valet is quite distressed."

Mrs. Sparks fished the key out of her brother-in-law's pocket and let them in. "Why?"

"His name is Toogood."

"Oh dear. That is too good to pass up."

It was dark inside and nearly as cold as the street, but Nick could make out shelves filled with goods, a counter, and a few racks of books, pamphlets, and prints. Behind the counter were hulking objects Nick could not make out in the dark. The room was full of strong smells: linseed oil, turpentine and lye, wet paper and something burnt.

"Can you hold him on your own while I fetch a candle?"

Nick nodded.

"Wait here, then." She made her way surely through the dark and crowded room, and Nick remembered that this had been her home. Mr. Sparks's arm dragged at his neck. He shifted. Pain lanced through his leg, but he gritted his teeth and held on, running through some verses from *Childe Harold* about the sweetness of labor and risk.

Mr. Sparks moved, letting out a loud snore, and Nick squeezed his eyes shut and prayed not to drop him.

Mrs. Sparks's footsteps returned; she appeared in the doorway, carrying a candle. It lit her lovely, heart-shaped face with a flickering glow.

Nick gave her a casual smile, wiping the strain from his expression.

She smiled back, the corners of her eyes crinkling. They looked black and mysterious and beautiful in the half-light, and he really forgot the pain in his leg, forgot everything but wanting to stand there and look at her, and make her smile again.

"I'm sorry, I had trouble finding the tinderbox." She turned back to set the candle down before hastening to them. "I don't want to risk him on the stairs. I've brought some bedding. He can sleep on the hearth."

The back door led to the kitchen. Even at night, enough moonlight came through the windows and mixed with the candlelight to give it a crisp, cheery air. Mrs. Sparks scuffed a toe over the swept floor and sighed. "It was never this clean when Will and I lived here."

They deposited Mr. Sparks in a chair for the moment, and she spread a sheet and a folded quilt a safe distance from the hearth.

In the candlelight, he saw the quilt was patchwork, hundreds of small hexagons forming a complex and delicate pattern. The central ordered design gave way to a muted shift of colors, like a formal rose garden shading into parkland. "What a remarkable quilt," he said as they heaved Sparks onto it.

"It is, isn't it?" She stayed on her knees for a moment, her fingers tracing a slender line of green cotton. "Helen made it for Will and me when we married."

"Perhaps you'd better fetch something else. He might be sick again."

Her nose wrinkled. She glanced from her brother-in-law to the quilt and back, then shrugged. "It's his quilt now," she said, a little sadly. "No worry of mine. Serve him right if something of his gets ruined as well." But she rearranged the soiled hem of her skirts so they didn't touch the quilt. Since last he'd seen the dress, the white lace had put forth innumerable embroidery shoots that twined up the sides as if to swallow Mrs. Sparks whole. It was engaging, meticulous work; at a guess, he would say it was her sister's too.

"I've never yet made a stain Toogood couldn't get out," he offered. "I wager he could have your dress looking as good as new in a couple of days."

Her look was almost worshipful. "Oh, would you?"

He swallowed. "It's nothing."

She glanced down. "It isn't. It's more than I know how to repay."

Nick saw his opportunity. "Do you know why Mr. Sparks has been avoiding my brother and his agents? Here, let me." She was lifting her brother-in-law up to get his coat off. He knelt and hoisted Sparks up with an arm under his neck.

"Thanks." Mrs. Sparks pulled the left sleeve off and then came round for the right one. There was a pause as they both realized that unless they changed tack, she would have to press right up against Nick to get to Sparks. It suddenly felt quite a bit warmer in the cold room.

He'd promised himself he'd behave. "Here," he said

reluctantly, "you lift him up from the other side and I'll get the coat off."

"Oh, of course!" She retreated, but her hand skimmed up his arm as she cradled Sparks's head, and even that was enough to make his cravat feel entirely too tight. He pulled away, Sparks's jacket in his hand. Then she knelt to pull off her brother-in-law's boots.

Nick immediately imagined himself in Sparks's place. There was something seductively domestic about the idea of coming upstairs to one's bed after a long day and being helped to undress by one's wife.

That, and her position gave him a splendid view down the front of her dress.

"Brace him for me, will you?"

He started. "Of course."

"He's in love with the Tory MP's daughter, that's why." She tugged the right boot off and set it on the floor with a snap. "He's trying to appease Mr. Jessop."

Nick was distracted by this extremely unwelcome intelligence. "But he's one of the strongest supporters we have in the town." His newspaper was influential too, in the whole district.

The left boot was proving difficult. She pulled and pulled, with no luck. "That's why Mr. Jessop will never let them marry." She yanked so violently that she and the boot tumbled backwards together. For a moment he could see the stripes on her stockings before she dragged the hem of her dress down. "I promised him we'd fix it, but I don't see how. You should have heard how Mr. Jessop talked to us at the Tory supper."

"How?" Nick demanded, feeling instantly protective. "Wait—you were at the Tory supper?" So that was why she was in her best dress, her hair a bewitching morass of tight braids he wanted to trace with his fingers to see where they ended. He rolled Sparks onto his side and stood.

She pulled a blanket over Sparks, not bothering to make it neat. "We were." She sighed, brushing past him to take a bucket from the corner and set it by her brother-in-law. She had known where it was without searching.

If her husband were alive, she'd still be living here and Nick would be hounding the pair of them for their vote, or perhaps he'd be in London and altogether out of the picture. It was a disturbing idea.

"Can Sparks support a crippled wife without her dowry?"

"I didn't think so." She took off her gloves to lay a small fire on the andirons. Her hands were small and sure. "But maybe I've been narrow in my views. She might have some difficulties with the housekeeping, but Jack has a maid for that anyway. It's the paper he needs help with. She probably even knows French and could translate some of the Continental news."

"And how does Miss Jessop feel about all this?"

"She loves Jack. She says she doesn't care about her money. But I've heard she stands to inherit five hundred pounds. That's not something to turn one's back on lightly."

To Nick, five hundred pounds didn't sound like much in the way of a dowry. But from the way Mrs. Sparks said it, it was a fortune to her. "If Sparks had five hundred pounds, would you still have to marry?"

The kindling caught, illuminating her face. He saw that she hadn't even considered it—and that she was considering it now with a desperate wistfulness.

But she soon shrugged the thought away. "Even if Jessop agrees to the match, he won't agree before Helen starts show-ing. The key thing is to keep him from shipping Miss Jessop off to some relative out of town or—oh, I'll think about it tomorrow." She set the screen before the fire and stood. "I've got to get back to Mr. Fairclough."

"Who is Mr. Fairclough?"

She threw up her hands. "He's the man the Tories want me to marry. I rather like him, and now I've abandoned him, and I've been gone an age. I have to go home first because there's vomit on my dress, and he'll want me to explain why I'm in different clothes than I was an hour ago and I'll have to tell him, and he'll think even worse of Jack than he does already." It had been a long week for her. She sounded overset, her voice wobbling alarmingly. "He doesn't even know about Helen."

He wanted to put his arms around her. He wanted to kiss her again.

God, he wanted to kiss her again. With the low firelight wrapping her in shadows and warmth, she looked like everything in the world he couldn't have, home and hearth and hot, simple pleasure. The shadow under her lower lip made his mouth go dry. His stomach tightened with the effort of holding still, holding back.

He pinched himself, hard, and jerked his gaze away to Sparks, lying on that magnificently painstaking quilt. It must have taken months. He wanted that too: a family that would lavish so much love and effort on him that a gift like that could be left behind.

But he had one, didn't he? His mother had written him every day when he was in Spain, two or three closely written sheets, and he'd tossed most of them in the fire half-read. He'd rarely bothered with a reply, and still the letters came, every day for four years. Why didn't he know how to be satisfied with that?

"You really don't care about the quilt?"

She straightened her pelisse, brushed off her knees, picked specks of dust from her cuffs. He thought she was considering the effort of getting a different blanket. But when she spoke, she said, "A few years ago I lost a child I was carrying."

She'd said something about that at Tony's dinner last week. "Yes, I remember. I'm sorry." But he felt a flame lick up the inside of his ribcage, that she was going to confide in him again.

"I didn't take it well. It was as if a black fog had rolled over me and settled, expanding until it filled every crevice in the ceiling and crack in the floorboards." She glanced at him, eyes crinkling. "I'm sorry, that was rather turgid prose, wasn't it? But for days after I was physically well enough to walk, I couldn't even drag myself downstairs for meals. It took a while for the feeling to lift. I lay in our bed for weeks looking at that quilt." She took a breath. "Will *died* under that quilt. It meant hope to me, once. I didn't want to take it with me. I should have anyway. I think I hurt Helen's feelings."

"I'm sure she understands," he said, because he couldn't bring himself to say *I understand*. He couldn't bring himself to admit that after he was well enough to walk, he'd lain in bed for months staring at the ceiling. "It must have hurt, to see the possibilities you'd counted on lost so quickly."

She reached up to fidget with the soft curls that usually clustered at her neck, but they were all pinned into place. Her hand dropped. "It did. That was it exactly." She shook her head as she led him back through the press room. "Poor Will couldn't understand it at all. He cried and raged and got on with things while I just lay there, and it frustrated him no end. Jack took over all my work on the paper so Will wouldn't nag me about it. Sometimes I could hear them shouting at each other because Jack had bungled some task of mine."

"What got you through it in the end?" he asked, trying to sound as if the matter could have no personal bearing on him beyond his natural concern for her.

"Writing," she said at once, shutting and locking the shop door behind them. "I hadn't written much since I married, just a few incidental pieces for the paper. I loved the *Intelligencer*, and it consumed all my time and energy."

He offered her his arm. The formality of the gesture felt out of place, but the way she tucked her hand into the crook of his elbow was—just right.

"After I lost the baby, I lost that feeling about the paper too. One morning I was reading a collection of stories for children—a gift for the baby—and I thought, *I wouldn't have done it that way. I would have done it like* this. And that was it. I wrote until I couldn't hold the pen. I covered the margins of a week's worth of unsold papers."

"How did Will take it?"

"Not very well. I did go back to helping with the *Intelligencer*, but it was never the same and I think he knew it. We'd already been quarreling a little, but after that—" She sighed. "Jack told me tonight that he hates working on the paper alone. I abandoned him when Will died, just as I abandoned Helen after our father..."

She called herself selfish, but to his eyes she was painfully ready to make everyone's well-being her responsibility. Who was fighting for her well-being? As far as he could tell, all she wanted was to not be married, and she couldn't even have that.

She reached up to massage her nape, stretching so that the graceful line of her neck, curving upwards to meet her ear, caught the light of a street-lamp.

The memory of their kiss surged up with disconcerting force. The inside of her elbow at the back of his neck, her breasts crushed against his coat, the way she'd stood on tiptoe and kissed him as if she couldn't get enough. He remembered how close she had felt, how close he had felt to her, how much he had *felt*—

He wanted that again.

But when had Nick, in civilian life, ever taken responsibility for anyone's well-being? She could lose everything by kissing him. "I'll talk to Mr. Jessop," he said, counting stones in the pavement until the moment passed. "Maybe we can come to some agreement about your brother-in-law's suit."

It wasn't fair. She was trying so hard to be good and unselfish and get along with Mr. Moon and Mr. Fairclough. Why had the evil one sent Mr. Dymond to tempt her? They were alone in the near dark, had been for a good half hour, and all she could think about was that dratted kiss.

Sometimes it seemed simple, the way she wanted him, an animal hunger no different from her eyes lingering on a fat pink ham when there was only sixpence in her pocket. He smelled lovely and looked delicious and that was all.

But it *wasn't* all, and it wasn't simple. She hadn't been tempted to confide in either of her suitors, and yet she kept telling Mr. Dymond things she'd never told *anyone.* The excuse that he was a stranger and so it was like shouting secrets into a hole in the ground was wearing thin. You couldn't put your hand on a hole in the ground's arm and feel muscle and heat through the fabric of its greatcoat. A hole in the ground didn't have soft, spiky hair or the most adorable way of firming its mouth when it was determined about something.

Mr. Dymond had a beautiful mouth.

"You don't have to walk me home," she said. "It isn't that late. The night watchman is around somewhere."

"It wouldn't be that late in London. Here I can only see a few houses with a candle burning. And the night watchman is seventy-five, isn't he?"

"He may be seventy-five, but he was a prizefighter in his youth," she said, though privately her dislike of walking alone on dark, empty streets was as much a reason for her support of a Police Act as her belief in the advance of modern life and the inefficacy and immorality of capital punishment as the sole deterrent of crime. "I don't imagine there are many men in town who could best him even now."

"Then if we meet him, he may walk you the rest of the way."

He was concerned about her well-being, and tonight of all nights she couldn't turn that away. Mr. Fairclough wanted to marry her, and he hadn't tried to help her with Jack, or taken her part in front of Mr. Jessop.

Of course, Mr. Fairclough hadn't been raised to treat women like hothouse flowers. He disliked Jack and relied on Mr. Jessop's patronage. It was easy for Mr. Dymond to help. He was Mr. Jessop's equal.

But he wasn't family—she might not even be Orange-and-Purple, anymore—and he had helped her without hesitation. It had hurt him; he would never say so, but as they turned into Mrs. Pengilly's back garden she could see that his limp had worsened.

"I'll wait here while you change," he said.

"You really don't have to."

He smiled at her. "I want to." His warm tone said he couldn't think of a thing he'd rather be doing than waiting in the chilly street to walk her to a Tory supper.

The house was dark. Mrs. Pengilly had been having trouble sleeping, so Phoebe tried to be quiet climbing the stairs. She didn't bother to light a candle, just guessed which dress was which by feel and picked her second-best. By dint of some squirming she unbuttoned the blue dress and pulled it over her head.

She could smell Jack's vomit turning sour. Had Mr. Dymond been able to smell it? She hated the idea of giving him the stinking bundle to carry to his valet, but she couldn't have afforded to toss it out even if Helen hadn't slaved over it. Reluctantly she folded the stain over itself and bundled the dress into her spare pillow tick.

Her second-best dress was a plain green one with no embroidery, but it fit her splendidly—by which she meant that when she wore it, even more men than usual stared at her bosom. No matter how she stretched, though, she could only do the top three buttons and the bottom one. The two in between were out of reach. Sukey had long since returned to the boarding house for the night, and it would be beyond rude to wake up poor Mrs. Pengilly. There was no help for it. She put her pelisse under one arm, took up the pillow tick, and went downstairs.

It had started to drizzle, but Mr. Dymond's smile was warm as ever as he pushed off the wall he'd been leaning against.

"I need you to do up a few of my buttons," she blurted out and spun around, afraid of what she would do if she could see the expression on his face.

Chapter 13

There was a pause, and then she heard him lean his cane against the wall. Even though she'd expected it—waited for it—anticipated it with eagerness and dread—she still gasped when the backs of his fingers brushed her shift. His hands stilled for a moment, and then he briskly did up her buttons and gave them a businesslike pat.

She yanked on her pelisse. "Thank you."

"Think nothing of it," he said a little too cheerily.

Her own laugh was high-pitched, almost giddy. "I'm trying not to," she said, and then was astonished at her own boldness. He brought that out in her. She liked it, and wished she didn't.

"Shall we?" He swiped up his walking stick from against the wall with his right hand and tossed it to the other. She'd noticed it was a habit he had, an airy gesture he saved for awkward moments. Was he trying to seem less affected than he really was? The idea warmed her further.

They walked the quarter mile to the Drunk St. Leonard in silence. She was getting to like walking with him, the characteristic little lurch in his step vibrating up her arm. She was getting to like him altogether too much.

Still, where was the harm? In two weeks she would be married and he would be in London, and even the prospect of missing him had a sharp, exquisite flavor. So when he said he'd bring the ham round the next day, she answered, "I'd like that, thank you."

He smiled and nodded towards the tavern door. "Give 'em hell."

When he looked at her like that, as if he thought she could do anything, she almost didn't care about bad luck.

Nick eyed his cravat narrowly. "Do I look all right for church?"

Toogood glanced up from where he was soaking the hem of Mrs. Sparks's dress in a solution of hartshorn and soft soap. "Eminently respectable, sir." The rest of the dress lay crumpled on the table. It didn't lie entirely flat. The bodice in particular was still stretched, hinting very gently that it had last night contained the most splendid bosom in Sussex. The dark blue wool was soft, and worn at the cuffs. She was too poor to buy a new dress. She couldn't even afford a ham. She was beneath him in every way—

Beneath him. Mmm. She'd look lovely and debauched beneath him, her breasts pulled wantonly to the sides by their own weight. If she held them up for him with her hands, plenty would spill over the ends of her fingers. How much darker would arousal make those eyes? Would she let him watch them go black, or would she shut them?

"Thank you, Toogood." He smacked the door shut with his cane on his way out.

When he reached Tony and Ada's room, his brother was engaged in sketching a bird on the windowsill in the margin of a closely written and heavily crossed-out page that was probably his speech.

He hastily covered the paper when he saw Nick. The movement frightened off the bird, and Tony's shoulders slumped miserably.

"Was it a rare one?"

"I think so." Tony gave up any pretense of working and hastened to complete his sketch while the details were fresh in his mind. "A warbler, but not a sort I've seen before. A migrant, probably."

"You're not on about birds again, are you?" Ada asked from the dressing table, where she was adjusting the bow on her bonnet.

Nick looked down at the sketch. It was a lovely thing; the bird almost seemed to watch him with its bright dark eye. "Have you ever thought of doing this professionally?"

Tony laughed. "And be a mad naturalist who does nothing but lurk in fields all day? No, thank you. I'll stick to the odd monograph."

"Have you been going out birdwatching?"

"Yes, in the early mornings. It's one of the few times of day when no one wants to talk to me."

Nick had opened his mouth to ask if he could come along, but that stopped the question in his throat.

"I think he's meeting a woman," Ada said. "Don't try to go along."

"Oh, hell," Tony said. "I didn't mean—of course I'm happy to talk to *you*."

Ada pressed her lips together and swept past them out of the room.

Hard to tell if Tony meant it. There was no reason for Tony to be glad to talk to him. "I'd like to come out with you some morning," Nick said anyway. "I'd like us to…" He didn't know how to finish that sentence.

To his relief, Tony looked pleased. "You're really interested?"

Nick nodded.

Tony grinned. "And if I tell you to be silent or still—"

"I shall be a statue," Nick said, elated at this minor victory.

Tony bit his lip, his eyes going to Nick's cane. "It won't be too hard on—that is to say—it's very damp in the mornings, the air doth drizzle dew and all that. I don't mean to imply that you—"

"I'll be fine," Nick said before Tony could tie himself into a complete knot. He wanted to say more: *You can say the words, you know*, or *Don't be afraid to talk to me.* He was aware of the hypocrisy of the thought. He didn't want to talk about it either.

"Splendid. Meet me here at six o'clock—let's see, not tomorrow morning, I've a Fox Club dinner tonight and will be just crawling into bed at dawn. Let's say Tuesday."

Tony watched him carefully when he said *six o'clock*, as if that would put Nick off. True, it was earlier than he'd been waking up since he'd been back in England, but he'd gone without sleep plenty of times in the army. "Oh, and I found out why Sparks has been avoiding us," Nick said, grinning, as they joined Ada for the walk to church. Maybe he was cut out for this brothering stuff after all.

"You did?" Tony looked as if he dreaded the answer.

"He's in love with Miss Jessop."

Tony's jaw dropped. "That's the whole mystery? He's turned his back on his party for a *girl*?"

Ada sniffed. "I think that's sweet."

"He's *very much* in love with Miss Jessop," Nick said. "Jessop emphatically does not approve. I'm going to try to change his mind after church."

"If he does, he'll want Sparks's votes." Tony turned up his collar against the drizzle. "Better to convince Sparks that voting against the son-of-a-bitch is the best way to get his own back."

Nick was a little shocked. But he was reluctant to break the fragile rapport he'd just established with Tony—and to be honest the same thought had occurred to him. There was nothing to be gained in playing holier-than-thou. "Mrs. Sparks asked me to talk to Jessop," he prevaricated. "Things are at a delicate stage with her. She likes the man the Tories have picked out for her." He smothered his jealousy at the thought.

"And if you do this, you think she'll marry Moon?" Tony sounded as if he knew the answer was no, but couldn't help hoping. Ada yawned ostentatiously.

"I don't know," Nick admitted. "She's trying to make a go of things with him. She's been visiting his shop. But the best we can hope for may be that Sparks uses Miss Jessop's dowry to help Mrs. Sparks with her difficulties, and we get his vote but not hers."

"That's not good enough," Tony said. "I need both votes to beat Dromgoole."

"I can't force her to the altar," Nick snapped. "I don't know what you and Mother were about choosing Moon anyway. They've nothing in common." Damn. He held his breath, certain the secret of his kiss with Mrs. Sparks was written all over his face. His brother would be furious.

Tony opened his mouth, obviously to say something scathing. But perhaps he was as reluctant to risk their accord as Nick, because what came out was a forcedly good-humored, "Do you know what Mrs. Sparks's difficulties are, by any chance?"

Nick gratefully accepted the change in topic. "I do. But

she's asked me to keep it quiet until things are settled. It's a delicate matter."

Tony gave him a searching look, as if he might say more, but they were caught up by some townsfolk in their Sunday best and the opportunity was lost.

After church, they dined with a couple of wealthy voters and their families. It was two before Nick could politely make his excuses. He stopped at a flower-girl's cart and bought sunflowers.

The Jessops' house was newer than Mrs. Sparks's by half a century at least, with a clean neoclassical facade. The neatly painted green door was opened by a maid in a gray frock and white cap, who took his card and murmured that she would enquire if Miss Jessop were in.

"Show him in, I'm bored to tears," the young woman's voice called from the rear parlor. The maid looked uncertain, but did as she was bid.

The house was decorated in dark colors, the walls hung with still lifes and an unsmiling portrait or two. English oak predominated in the furnishings without a fanciful classical, Egyptian, or Eastern touch anywhere to be seen. The solid, elegant style had been common fifty years ago but not precisely smart even then. Either Jessop really was conservative down to the marrow of his bones, or he worked hard to give the appearance of it.

The fire was kept very high in the parlor, and Miss Jessop wore a warm day dress patterned in dark greens and reds. Her pale face topped with carroty hair was the one bright spot in the room. She lit up when he entered.

"Sunflowers!" She held out her arms for them and bent her head to breathe them in. Her hair blazed even brighter by the contrast. "They smell sweet when you get close enough, you know. Like candy."

Even that made him think of Mrs. Sparks, who didn't care for candy.

Miss Jessop was safe to flirt with. They both knew it didn't mean anything. He bent his head near to hers and breathed in. "Lovely," he said in a low voice, keeping his eyes on her face.

She laughed, a light sound in the dark room. "You almost carried that off. I'm impressed."

"I carried it off," he said with mock wounded vanity.

She shook her head. "Something that shopworn only comes off if you mean it." A smile lingered about her lips as she said it, as if she was remembering something—and then it turned sour. She really was very pale.

But that was fashionable in England, even if it was hard for him to get used to after Spain. Mrs. Sparks's skin might have a light golden overlay, like a perfectly baked tart, but she wasn't a lady. Maybe Miss Jessop's pallor was merely stylishness and indolence, and not that she was trapped in this house like a flower in a pot.

Maybe it was only Nick who felt uncomfortable and trapped indoors these days, yet still disliked to go outside and let people see him.

"Here, Peg, put these in water, will you?" she asked. The maid took the flowers and went out, leaving them alone. Miss Jessop turned to him eagerly, lowering her voice. "Have you a message from him?"

Nick blinked. "From who?"

Her face fell. "Mr. Sparks, of course." She gestured after the vanished flowers. "I thought…"

"The flowers were from me. I suspect Mr. Sparks is still recovering from last night's drinking. He wasn't at church."

"I noticed." She sighed. "Then you must take a message. My father's forbidden him the house and has me under constant watch. Tell him I shall contrive to be alone under the Market Cross for five minutes Tuesday at nine o'clock."

He frowned. "My dear girl, if it came out I was aiding in the seduction of the Tory MP's innocent daughter, it would do my brother a deal of harm in the election."

Her gray eyes narrowed. "I'm not a girl, Mr. Dymond. I'd have been in caps years ago if I weren't vain of my hair. You want Mr. Sparks's vote, don't you?"

"Of course."

"If you help us, you shall have it."

In the end, it wasn't much of a dilemma. It was unlikely there would be any more scandal than there was already. Five minutes in public in broad daylight could hardly ruin the girl, and Sparks would be pleased. So would Mrs. Sparks—but that was entirely beside the point, Nick told himself. "I have your word for his vote?"

She nodded. "And—can I borrow five pounds?"

His eyebrows rose. "What for?"

She bit her lip. "For Jeffrey, my man. He's been turned off for helping Mr. Sparks and me."

Damn. "Miss Jessop, you must see that I can't possibly give money to a servant who has connived at a young gentlewoman's illicit behavior. Not during an election."

Miss Jessop made a restless, unhappy movement. "I knew I shouldn't ask him to help. But I didn't know when I would get another chance. I didn't want to be my father's hostess for the rest of my life."

"Of course you won't be," Nick said uncomfortably. "You're a very pretty girl."

She snorted. "Don't be dense. Besides, plenty of women who can walk go their whole lives without finding what Mr. Sparks and I have. As my father's hostess, I have a wider circle of acquaintance than most women, and Mr. Sparks—" She shut her lips, as if on something private and precious.

The certainty, the intensity of her desire—Nick felt a faint embarrassment, and for a moment, an envy that ate at his chest like acid. Envy for a woman who couldn't walk.

It wasn't his leg that kept him from feeling like a whole man, he realized. It was something far deeper, a lack within himself. He had never wanted anything with such a bone-deep conviction. Sometimes, it seemed, he could go all day without wanting anything at all.

The maid reappeared in the doorway, Mr. Jessop on her heels looking suspicious.

"I'm glad I found you at home," Nick told him, trying not to look at Miss Jessop's sharp, unhappy face. The brash sunflowers looked out of place in a delicate porcelain vase with a shepherd and shepherdess painted on the side. "I was hoping to speak to you on election business."

"I'll show you to my study." Mr. Jessop's gaze lingered on his daughter. "Are you comfortable where you are, Caroline?"

"I have the bell if I should want anything," Miss Jessop said with polite, angry distance. She didn't look at her father. "Thank you for the flowers, Mr. Dymond."

Chapter 14

"Out of the question," Mr. Jessop said. "Do you know what Sparks called me in his paper after Brand's reform bill was defeated?"

"No, sir." His mother had cut out the article and enclosed it in a letter, gleeful comments scrawled in the margin. Nick hadn't read it. "But that was two years ago. Ask for an apology, if you like. I promise you would get it."

Jessop snorted. "I daresay I would. I'd have respected him more if he had not been so willing to abandon his principles and his party in the midst of an election for the sake of his own convenience."

"I'm not best pleased myself." Nick injected understanding into his voice. "But we must both try to remember that he doesn't view it as a mere convenience, but as his entire future happiness."

Jessop looked unimpressed. "He meets the girl in a sneaking sort of way, courts her behind the backs of any of her friends who might advise her against him, and tries to force my hand by asking her consent before my own? My daughter might not see through such stratagems, but I flatter myself I'm a little older and wiser."

Older, certainly. "You put the worst possible construction on it. The truth is he was loath to tell his own friends he was walking out with a Tory until he was sure it was a lasting attachment. Partisan stupidity is to blame for this muddle from first to last. Surely we, as reasonable men, shouldn't allow that sort of prejudice to stand in the way of a love match."

Mr. Jessop's tolerant laugh set Nick's teeth on edge. "You young people and your love matches. When you're my age, Mr. Dymond, you will realize parents really do know best what will bring their child happiness. I'm profoundly grateful I never married any of the young ladies I found myself in love with."

"You think Miss Jessop is more likely to find happiness in an arranged match than with the man she has chosen herself?"

Jessop sobered. "I don't know that my daughter will marry at all. Her condition has kept her from receiving the attention she deserves. I don't believe a fair-weather friend like Sparks will long regard her infirmity as anything but a burden, himself. Even if she were whole, I'd hesitate to allow a match so far beneath her station. Better to be comfortable and beloved in her father's home than poor and resented in her own establishment."

Nick's throat was so tight with revulsion that he couldn't speak. There was a hot weight on his lungs that would become rage if he allowed it to spread. Here, in a few sentences, was so much of what he had hated in his own upbringing: his mother's confidence in her own superior understanding not only of the world, but of Nick himself. Her certainty that the few small things he might have to offer were already known to her.

"I know you mean well," Jessop said gently. "You're a good lad, and we're all proud of you." His gaze fell meaningfully on Nick's leg.

Nick's hand had been resting on his thigh; he dug his fingers into his flesh until his mended bone ached, to keep from making a fist. Mrs. Sparks wanted him to help her brother-in-law. He could imagine the look on her face when he confessed to knocking Jessop down for being patronizing.

He could imagine the look on Tony's face, too. It made his gut hurt, but it was almost tempting—an easy, quick, simple pain, and an end to this pretense that he could be of use in any capacity that required more than physical courage and a knack for making himself agreeable.

Mr. Jessop leaned forward. "Have you given any thought to leaving the Whigs? The Opposition benches are no place for a soldier."

Nick blinked in disbelief. "I thought you valued sticking to one's principles."

"And it's principle I'm speaking of, not this party nonsense. Loyalty to your country and your King, and offering him your support in the struggle against Napoleon's tyranny. Who could refuse to listen to a hero's voice?"

You aren't listening to me right now, Nick thought. He opened his mouth to say that 'the Whigs opposed tyranny, both abroad and at home,' and one or two similar polite catch-phrases before taking his leave.

"Opposition has turned the Whigs into a bunch of petti-fogging old women," Jessop said. "Men of action belong in the Ministerialist party."

"Is that why when the men in my regiment needed new boots, it took over a year for England to send them?" Nick was horrified. Had he really said that? But when he opened his mouth to apologize and smooth the moment over, more words tumbled out. "Is that why when they came, the contract had been given to a pinch-penny profiteer who glued on the soles instead of sewing them? Do you know what a man's feet look like when the soles of his shoes have fallen off and he's marched thirteen hours without them?"

Jessop had gone rather pale; it brought out his resemblance to his daughter. "I wasn't on the committee for funding the War Office, so I can't—"

"The army fights this war while you sit in committees to decide how many farthings should go to feeding and clothing us, and how many can be diverted to feed and clothe the Regent. If you imagine I would be proud to join you, you are very much mistaken." He set his cane on the floor with a sharp click and stood. "I hope you will reconsider allowing Sparks's suit. Talk to your daughter. Let her—"

"I can manage my family without your help, thank you." Red blotches bloomed on Jessop's pale skin. "Good day."

Nick bowed, painfully aware that his visit had accomplished nothing except to completely alienate the Tory MP.

Nick's leg was sore, and his arm ached from carrying a heavy ham without being able to switch arms. He had bad news to convey, and two flights of stairs to climb to deliver it. For all that, he couldn't wait to see Mrs. Sparks.

But when he turned the last corner, he heard a chorus of female voices. She wasn't alone. Why had he expected her to be alone? She had a life in which he had no place; she had a home in Lively St. Lemeston, and people she belonged to.

The door opened before he reached the top. Mrs. Sparks gave him a welcoming smile. "I thought I heard you. Here, let me take that ham." He followed her up the last few steps. "Look, ladies, Mr. Dymond has brought us a ham!"

They appeared to be engaged in some sort of sewing project. Workboxes were scattered across the room, as were heaps of mangled old clothes, bags of scraps, and old newspapers for piecing. It was a small room, so the effect was impressive when six pairs of female eyes were raised from their work and fixed on him.

Most were friendly, one or two were wary—and Helen Knight's were hard and accusing. Nick swallowed. Had Mrs. Sparks told her sister about their kiss?

"Oh, how lovely," a plump, blond young woman said warmly from the settle. "Thank thee, sir. And really, I must thank thee also for finally convincing our Phoebe to consider remarriage."

Nick felt cold. He had to stop thinking of their kiss as if it meant something. It was nothing, a moment in time. There were more serious things at stake.

"Martha," Mrs. Sparks hissed at the Quakeress. She tucked the ham under one arm and gestured at the empty spot on the settle. "Won't you sit, Mr. Dymond?"

His leg ached, but he was damned if he would show her less than respect. "Not before you, madam."

"Nice manners, that boy," an elderly woman in the old armchair whispered loudly to Miss Knight. "That whole family has lovely manners."

"You mean they're all shameless flirts," Miss Knight muttered. She bowed her braided head over a length of dark red worsted, carefully measuring out diamonds with a wooden ruler and chalk. Her body was as unyielding as the straight back of her chair.

"That too," the old woman said.

Mrs. Sparks rolled her eyes and began moving things off

the wooden chest by the window onto the floor. She had given him her seat—the only one available. He ought to protest, but his leg hurt. He hesitated.

"I haven't more chairs," she said in a small, defiant voice, flushing, and he realized she was embarrassed by her tiny lodgings. There would have been nowhere to put another chair, even if she owned one.

"When Mrs. Meade took sick, I *offered* to hold the meeting at the boarding house," a woman in her forties said. Her mouth turned down at the corners, giving her the look of a bulldog. "There's no need to cram us in here like—"

"You're just afraid of the ghost," the old woman cackled.

Miss Knight set down her ruler with a snap. "There is no ghost."

"Oh, there's a ghost," the old woman said with great enjoyment. "I've heard her wailing many a time, poor thing." There were several shudders around the room. Mrs. Sparks plopped down on the chest with a sigh.

Nick sat. "Is this your house, then, ma'am?"

Mrs. Sparks started. "How remiss of me! This is Mrs. Pengilly, who owns this house." She pointed at Martha and the sallow, dark-haired woman next to her. "Mr. Dymond, this is Mrs. Honeysett, chairwoman of the Lively St. Lemeston Society for Bettering the Condition of the Poor's Committee for the Encouragement of Charitable Subscriptions and Bequests, and her sister-in-law Miss Honeysett." Lastly, she indicated the bulldog and her companion. "This is Mrs. Humphrey, who runs the boarding house across the street." Mrs. Humphrey nodded at him. "And this is her lodger Miss Starling."

"It's a pleasure to meet you," Nick said. "How do you all do?"

They assured him they were very well, except for Mrs. Humphrey, who announced, "I feel rather faint. It's been a long time since breakfast."

Mrs. Sparks popped up off the chest. "Oh yes, the ham."

Nick reached for his stick and pulled himself to his feet, wondering if the creaking in his leg was audible to everyone or just him. Damn Mrs. Humphrey anyway.

"Flirt," Miss Knight muttered.

Mrs. Sparks flushed. "I haven't enough bread for everyone, but if you don't mind waiting while I run to the bakery—"

"Fetch mine from the kitchen, dear," Mrs. Pengilly said. "And bring up the jar of mustard, won't you?"

"Thank you," Mrs. Sparks said, not meeting any eyes at the revelation that she couldn't afford mustard. "I'll be right back. Pour Mr. Dymond some tea, won't one of you?" She whisked away down the stairs.

Everyone looked at Miss Knight, who didn't move. Mrs. Honeysett smiled brightly. "Milk or sugar, Mr. Dymond?"

"Both, thank you."

Miss Knight sniffed, as if his preference in tea were a sign of weakness. Mrs. Honeysett's smile broadened nervously. "Please convey our greetings and support to thy brother."

Nick was always surprised at how deep party loyalty ran in these provincial towns. Of course Mrs. Sparks's friends were Orange-and-Purple. He leaned down and took his tea from Mrs. Honeysett, holding the saucer awkwardly in one hand. "Thank you."

There was a short silence, broken only by the rattling of his cup.

"My leg is rather troubling me today," he said at last, seeing no alternative. "Sitting is easier than standing, but changing from one to the other is the worst. Mrs. Sparks will be back at any moment."

"Have you tried wrapping it in red flannel?" Mrs. Pengilly asked. "My Harry's knee was shattered by an angry horse, and he used to swear by red flannel when the pain was bad. But it must be red, mind."

"Did you get that at Badajoz?" Mrs. Humphrey asked him, pronouncing the J in the English fashion. There was no reason anyone should know how to say it, and yet it always irked Nick.

"Yes." He tried to think of something to follow that with.

Miss Starling offered timidly, "I prefer willow bark for aches and pains. But it's most effective in a hot bath."

Miss Honeysett shook her head. "Our maid used to be a lace-worker and has the most terrible pain in her wrists, and nothing will do for her but sticking them in a bucket of ice water."

"Don't be stupid," Mrs. Humphrey said. "A man can't fit his whole leg in a bucket. But crushing the ice and putting it in a bag, with a paper on which the verse has been written in which Christ heals the lame, is a sure remedy."

Miss Honeysett pushed her thick glasses up her nose. "Sacrilege."

"My valet likes to alternate hot water bottles and ice," Nick said tentatively. "It does seem to help."

So, when Mrs. Sparks returned with the bread and a small clay jar that Nick supposed to be mustard, they were enthusiastically swapping remedies.

She fetched a knife and some plates from her cupboard with great haste, and sat down to carve. Nick eased himself gratefully back onto the settle and drank his tea.

Mrs. Sparks was a conscientious hostess, making sure

everyone had a large enough slice of ham, cutting Mrs. Pengilly's bread for her when her hands shook on the knife, and generally managing everyone to within an inch of their lives.

"Thee'll be a splendid mother," Martha Honeysett said with a smile. Mrs. Sparks froze. "I always thought it a shame thee was so set on not marrying again. Doesn't thee think it a shame, Dorothea?"

Miss Honeysett shrugged. "Marry in haste, repent at leisure, my mother always said."

"*My* mother always says that if you haven't anything nice to say, don't say anything at all," Miss Knight snapped.

Mrs. Pengilly leaned across and said in her loudest whisper to Mrs. Honeysett, "That girl must have her courses, she's been out of sorts all morning."

Miss Knight's face flamed, her chalk grinding audibly against her ruler. Mrs. Sparks glared at her landlady.

"So tell me what you ladies are working on," Nick interjected.

"We've brought our old clothes and scrap bags, and we're each making a quilt to sell at the Gooding Day auction," Mrs. Honeysett said. "The proceeds go to the poor old women and widows of the town."

Where would he be at Christmastime? He could come to the auction, if he liked; his family would doubtless be in attendance. But Mrs. Sparks would be married.

"I'm going to make two," Miss Starling said. "Since I'm just doing plain hexagons while you're all doing such lovely patterns."

"Maybe you should do hexagons, Fee." Miss Knight took a pair of scissors and began to cut her red worsted into identically sized diamonds. "It would be easier."

Mrs. Sparks smiled. "You don't appreciate my artistry?"

There was a pause. Then Miss Knight's lips curved, her sly smile the mirror of her sister's. "The human form is notoriously difficult," she said innocently.

Mrs. Sparks laughed and reached for a piece of newspaper, her eyes meeting Nick's. Covetousness went through him like a shock. He wanted a home and good company. He wanted to belong here. "Helen is making a complicated and perfectly symmetrical star-shaped pattern out of hundreds of six-inch by two-inch diamonds," she told him as she cut out a—a top hat, he thought, and pinned it in place on a sheet. "I'm doing four scenes from *Belinda*. See, this is the duel between Lady Delacour and Mrs. Luttridge."

He squinted, prepared to say something polite about a jumble of cut-out newspaper—and the pattern snapped into focus. It was charming and lively and full of personality, and he could tell which figure was which. "It's splendid. You must sew tiny buttons onto their coats."

"Now that is clever." She smiled. "I know they aren't perfectly in proportion, but I need the quilt to tell a story if it's to hold my attention until it's done."

"Last year she did scenes from *Otranto*." Mrs. Honeysett grinned at her. "It was beautiful, of course, but we were terrified it wouldn't sell."

Mrs. Sparks's eyes met his, glinting with laughter. "Conrad being crushed by the giant helmet *was* a little gory." A room full of her friends, and she chose him to share her amusement. It wasn't fair, that he should like her more with every word she spoke.

"People like a novelty." Mrs. Pengilly struggled to manage

her scissors with arthritic fingers. Mrs. Sparks laid her own quilt by to help her. "I could do it myself just last year," the old woman said in frustration.

"I know," Mrs. Sparks said.

Mrs. Humphrey carefully snipped the sleeves off an old dress. "Scenes from Byron would fetch more."

"Yes, but Phoebe doesn't like Byron. Unaccountable woman." Mrs. Honeysett gave her friend a teasing poke.

To his surprise, Mrs. Sparks glanced at him and blushed. "Maybe I was too hasty," she said haltingly. "It's the worst sort of snobbery to condemn a book without reading it, merely because it's popular."

"She tried to get it from the library on Monday, only we haven't enough copies," Miss Knight revealed.

Mrs. Sparks's blush deepened, and she bent her head low over her work. Monday. Not long after their first meeting. "I would be happy to loan you my own," Nick said.

"I'll wager he's got the real thing, on nice paper," Mrs. Pengilly said. "Not these provincial printers' copies, full of errors in the typesetting."

Mrs. Sparks set down the scissors with a clack. "Not in Jack's."

"Maybe not," Mrs. Honeysett said, "but Mr. Sparks is only publishing one page a week, inserted in the *Intelligencer*. Thee couldn't expect us to wait until he'd got through it."

Nick had come for a reason—but there were ham sandwiches and a roomful of Byron readers, and his leg could use some rest. They asked him a great deal about Spain, since it was the setting of Canto I, but he found he rather liked talking about it when the focus wasn't on his own supposedly heroic experience. It was another half an hour before he said reluctantly, "Mrs. Sparks, might I speak with you for a moment on election business?"

She set aside Mrs. Pengilly's pattern. "Of course." She glanced at her bedroom door, hesitated, and said, "We can talk in the kitchen. Excuse us, everyone."

Mrs. Humphrey had mostly stayed out of the conversation once she had realized Nick wasn't going to talk about battles, but now she gave him a hard look and said to Mrs. Sparks, "Don't give up your independence unless the money is very good indeed."

There was a very awkward silence.

"Really, Mrs. Humphrey," Mrs. Honeysett said with a glance of pure dislike. "Thee makes it sound some sort of sordid exchange. Phoebe is merely accepting help setting up a new household."

"Indeed." Miss Honeysett's eyes were skeptical behind her glasses. "Marriage is a sacrament. Remember the moneylenders in the temple."

"I've always wondered"—Mrs. Pengilly's voice followed them down the stairs—"why were they selling doves? As pets, or to eat? I suppose they'd make as fine a pie as pigeons."

Chapter 15

"Don't mind Mrs. Humphrey," Mrs. Sparks said. "She's a dreadful woman."

"She seemed to have your best interests at heart," Nick said.

Mrs. Sparks snorted. "Do you know she goes through the clothes we bring and selects the least worn sections for her own quilt? She isn't even making it for herself. There is something almost comically mean in pettiness with nothing to gain." She took a seat at the kitchen table. They'd done laundry in here a scant week ago. He hadn't known her yet, but he'd liked her already. It wasn't fair, that she wasn't a gentlewoman and that they couldn't be friends.

Or lovers, he thought traitorously, taking a chair. Sitting didn't help the ache in his leg. It would stop hurting when it was good and ready, hot water bottles and Biblical verses notwithstanding. Life wasn't fair, and anyway who was to say he deserved better?

"It isn't fair," she said, echoing his thoughts. "You walk in here and an hour later, you're getting along with my friends better than I do."

"Don't be ridiculous," he said, startled.

"I'm not. You have a silver tongue."

"I'm just friendly."

She took up the poker and jabbed at the fire. "Maybe that's all it is. Maybe I'm not friendly."

"They're *your* friends. They were only being polite to me. You can't really be angry with me because I got on with your friends."

She shook her head. "I get along with you better than I do with them, too. I daren't confide in any of them about Helen, and you—I thought it was because you were just passing through. Like talking out loud to a bird on the windowsill." She glanced at him, looking embarrassed. "Wait. Other people do that, don't they? Talk to birds?"

"I don't know. I do sometimes, though."

She pointed at him accusingly. "There you go again. You make people feel comfortable. As if you understand them. It's not fair."

She made him sound like his family. He wasn't like them. But—people did confide in him, didn't they? He'd never had dinner alone at an inn or taken a sea journey when someone or other hadn't regaled him with their whole history. He'd thought he must just have that sort of face. "That isn't why you confided in me," he said, suddenly angry. "We share something. You know we do."

She chewed at the corner of her lip in frustration, a tic she shared with her sister. "Maybe that's what isn't fair," she said at last.

She was angry for the same reason he was: that this couldn't go anywhere. He was a bird on the windowsill. He hated this feeling, this shut-out, gnawing envy he'd felt all his life. All around him were boats on their way somewhere, while he drifted rudderless. Until he'd joined the army and been given a purpose.

He'd tried to give himself a purpose last night, and he'd already failed in it. "My silver tongue was no good against Mr. Jessop."

She sighed. Her perfect breasts, pillowed on her perfect round arms and dainty hands, rose and fell. "What did he say?"

Nick recounted the conversation and passed her the five pounds for Jeffrey. Mrs. Sparks pocketed it with only the shortest of lingering glances at the crisp bill and wrinkled her nose. "'I'd respect him more if he stood on his principles'! Who condemns a man for trying to compromise with him?"

"Mr. Jessop didn't seem much for compromising."

"He's a stubborn old son-of-a-bitch," Mrs. Sparks said darkly. "Pardon my language."

"Pardoned."

"Did you know he voted against the first three Slave Trade Bills?"

"I did know," Nick said. "My mother told us all about it at the time."

"Of course." She looked at him uncertainly. "Did she ever talk to you about my father?"

He nodded. "She said he was well liked. That he was good with words, and that his jokes were funny." He hesitated, but told her, "She said he was stubborn. And I believe nearly all our conversations during the last election contained some mention of how much she wished he were still with us."

He had thought it the most callous, self-serving way to consider a dead man—as a great loss to the Orange-and-Purples—but Mrs. Sparks smiled proudly. "He was splendid at shoring up waverers. He made everyone feel so sure, and safe." Her smile faded. "I wish he were here."

"I would have liked to meet him."

"He would have liked you." She gazed out the window, distracted. "He would have known what I ought to do about Jack and Miss Jessop."

He heard the note of self-recrimination in her voice. "I think what you really mean is that you're angry with yourself for *not* knowing." She shrugged. "It's a sticky situation. You aren't obliged to be omnipotent, you know."

She turned back to look at him, mouth curving reluctantly. "Thank you."

"You don't have to thank me."

She ignored him, thinking. "Listen, if Mr. Jessop won't budge, there's no need for Jack to keep up his neutrality. I'll pass along Miss Jessop's message and the money to him. I'll tell him how earnestly you tried to help. Then—Tuesday is press day. I'm going to go and help Jack. If you turn up, you can talk to him about his votes, and about printing the Orange-and-Purple circulars again, and all that."

It was exactly what he was supposed to want, so he smiled and said, "Thank you, I'd love to." But he wished they hadn't become voter and patron again quite so soon.

Once the committee had packed up their work and left, Phoebe forced herself to spend some time writing. The story about Ann wouldn't conclude. She decided it had become too personal, and wrote three pages of a new Improving Tale about a young wife who didn't show proper consideration for those less fortunate.

You're just giving up on Ann and her baby, then?

It was laughable to feel guilty about abandoning a product

of her own imagination. Really, she ought to just let both of them die in that ditch; it was the properest ending for an Improving Tale. Authors did it all the time. Phoebe had never been able to. She always felt obscurely that she had created them and that therefore their happiness was her responsibility.

You aren't obliged to be omnipotent, Mr. Dymond had said. Was she so stuffed with pride that she really believed she could solve any problem? That if she failed at anything, it was a fault in her nature and not mere human fallibility?

She had always felt that her father could solve any problem. She had known that if she needed him, he would move heaven and earth for her.

She'd wanted to live up to his example, to make other people feel as safe and loved as he had made her feel. Because—she saw it now—she had been so lost without him. She couldn't bear to feel so helpless, or for anyone else to feel that way. She had wanted to fill the hole he left in the world.

It was natural for a child to view her father as omnipotent. But only God really was. Maybe what helped people was just the knowing you'd do the best you could for them.

It had been her father's love, not his power, that had made her feel so warm and happy. But it was her love she'd been keeping wrapped up tight in her heart all this time. It was her love that Helen and Jack and Will had wanted. And she hadn't known how to give it to them, ever since she'd been unable to keep her child safe.

She didn't understand what was changing. She didn't understand how Mr. Dymond made her want to love again, made her feel all at once as if she had love to give, as if her love was worth having. She'd known him a week, for heaven's sake!

He was right, though. They shared something, and she

knew it. But it didn't matter. She had an appointment with Mr. Moon in a few hours. Any love she had to give to a man, she'd be giving to him, or to Mr. Fairclough.

At the moment she almost felt as if she could do it.

She felt less optimistic after her visit to the Honey Moon. Mr. Moon had let her into the back of the closed shop with a smile, but he showed little interest in *The Newgate Calendar* despite the many gruesome descriptions of shocking crimes (though he had asked to borrow it for Betsy, who apparently combed the papers every week for good murders). Phoebe had barely managed to swallow his chocolate puffs. If she didn't find another Whig soon, she'd have to marry Mr. Fairclough.

The prospect wasn't quite as distressing as it should have been, especially when she thought about his daughter.

On the way home, she knocked on the printing office's shutters to pass on Miss Jessop's message and money, and tell Jack about Mr. Dymond's conference with Jessop. He was very interested in the message, but took the news with surprising lack of discouragement. "I like Nicholas Dymond" was all he said, sounding distracted as he circled something in pencil on the proof of page two of the *Intelligencer*. "Looks like he'd blow over in a stiff wind, but he's got ballast. I wish he were running instead of Mr. Anthony."

Phoebe had yet to speak with Anthony Dymond for more than a moment or two. She remembered him from Christmases at church as a beautiful young man who very much enjoyed being fussed over. But that was only to be expected when a boy had blond curls, melting blue eyes, and strong limbs in addition to being a politician and the baby of his family. "Just because Mr. Nicholas isn't as solid as a Sparks doesn't mean he's frail," she said, thwapping him lightly on the arm and trying not to think about Mr. Nicholas's strong shoulders or long legs. "He helped drag *your* heavy carcass home last night."

"Mmm. Don't remind me. I couldn't keep down breakfast *or* lunch."

"That's very sad," she said unsympathetically. "You cast up your accounts on my best dress, you know. And embarrassed me in front of half the town."

"The half we don't care for," Jack pointed out.

Phoebe took a deep breath. "Jack, I may be marrying Mr. Fairclough."

Jack dropped his pencil. "*What?* The man who bought the powder mill?"

"Yes. I like him, all right? Even if he is a Tory."

"You *like* him? I should hope you feel more than that, if you're considering marriage. You realize if you marry him, he'll be a voter?"

"I—Jack, you have to swear on Will's grave you won't repeat this. Not even to Miss Jessop."

He thought about it for a moment. "It doesn't concern her or her father, does it?"

Mr. Dymond had hesitated too, and asked her if it concerned election fraud. She felt pleased by the integrity of her friends. Not that Mr. Dymond was a friend, precisely—oh, for heaven's sake, this wasn't the time to dither about Mr. Dymond. "No, it concerns me and Helen."

"All right, then."

"Swear."

"I swear."

She waited.

"On Will's grave," he added after a moment. "Fee, what—?"

Jack's apprentice Owen was having Sunday dinner with his family, but Phoebe leaned in anyway, lowering her voice. "Helen's with child." Jack's jaw dropped. She hurried on. "I need someone to help cover it up, and the Dymonds and the Wheatcrofts are the only people who might want to help me. If I help them."

"Don't be an idiot," Jack said at once. "I'll help you, of course. We'll take her to my aunt in Lewes, we'll find someone to take the baby—"

Oh, how she wanted it to be true. "I can't afford it, Jack. I barely have enough saved for two stage tickets to Lewes."

"I'll pay for it. I'll find someone to take the baby, I'll advertise in the *Intelligencer* for a family if I have to—"

Tears threatened. She knew Jack had about five pounds in the bank after his last order of stamped paper from London. "You can't afford it either, you know that. And you mean that as a joke about advertising, I know, but—we don't know how to go about something like this. Every person we ask about finding a family would be someone we know, someone who knows Helen. Lady Tassell can ask about among her friends and no one will ever trace it back to us, but if you do it—I won't risk Helen being ruined over this. I won't."

"But to *marry*. To marry a Tory—"

"You're marrying a Tory."

Jack buried his head in his hands. "Damn. *Damn.* I was going to."

"Don't despair, Jack, we'll work something out."

"I have worked something out," Jack said heavily. "I was going to ask her to run off with me. Anthony Dymond gave me twenty quid on the sly to help us—ostensibly to pay the Whigs' printing costs, but it was pretty clear what he meant. I was going to ask you to put out next week's paper for me. We can't now, of course. I can't leave you to face this alone."

Phoebe sat in her chair, stunned. "Run off together?"

"If we went Tuesday, we'd be back in time for the hustings."

"But, Jack, the scandal. What will your readers think?"

"They'd think it was damned interesting and wish I'd print a story about it."

"People won't receive you," she said. "They'll whisper and gossip, and Miss Jessop will have left all her friends—"

"Caro isn't you. It won't break her heart the way it would you. She's used to people whispering anyway. The people in this town are a regular Greek chorus, only with less Christian charity."

That was people everywhere. Everywhere in England anyway. Phoebe was sure of it. And they wouldn't forget. In twenty years, people would still be saying, *They ran away, you know. Spent four days on the road together before they were married. Stay away from their daughter, young lady, she's likely no better than she should be.* "Jack, you can't."

He nodded. "You're right. If I'm not here, who's to stop you doing something stupid and martyrish like marrying Fairclough? Only what am I to tell her? He's keeping her prisoner there, blast him. She can't even move from one part of the room to another if he doesn't like it. I promised her I wouldn't let him do this."

Phoebe tried to imagine using a wheelchair and living with her mother. It had been bad enough in that house when she could sneak off with a book, or dawdle at the library after going to market, or run off to Martha's after a row with her mother. If she were unable to even back away when her mother started carping, she'd be thinking about slitting her wrists inside a month.

Besides, if Jack stayed, he'd try to stop her marrying. He'd convince her somehow that they could do this on their own, because she wanted so badly for it to be true.

"You're right," she said. "You can't leave her there. You have to go."

He shook his head. "I'll wait till after the election, at least. I'll see this business with Helen settled, and then we can go."

She was almost annoyed with him, that he was making her talk him into acting selfishly. "He was very clear with Mr. Dymond that he would rather see her single for the rest of her life than married to you. What if he locks her up or sends her away where you can't get at her?"

Phoebe had never understood the phrase 'an agony of indecision' until now. Jack's face contorted. He rubbed hard at his eyes, then grabbed a fistful of his hair as if he'd tug it out by the roots. "You're my sister," he said tightly. "I'm not leaving you."

The floor had been swept not too long ago. She knelt down beside his chair. "Jack. I'm your sister because your brother married me. Because he made an unbreakable bond between him and me, and even though he's dead, we're still family. That's what marriage is supposed to do: make two people one person, make someone else bone of your bone and flesh of your flesh."

He half-chuckled, half-snorted. "You and Will couldn't agree on a single damn thing. You're about to marry a stranger to help your flesh and blood. Don't get mystical about marriage now."

Drat him, he was right. But she still believed it could be

something more—a sacrament, like Dorothea Honeysett said. That was what God intended, surely. "Do you think you and Miss Jessop are going to be like me and Will?"

He shook his head.

Phoebe hoped he was right. "If you want to marry her, you have to put her first. Always. And if you can't do that, you'd better not marry her."

Jack's mouth twisted. "Will did love you. He just—he raised me, you know, from when he wasn't much more than a boy himself. He was used to being in charge."

She turned away, sitting on the floor and leaning against the wooden arm of his chair. "I didn't mean it as a criticism of Will. We were neither of us very kind to each other. I—I've always wanted to apologize to you for that. You loved him, and I made him unhappy. We made your home a misery, and you've never held it against me."

His hand came down on the top of her head. "You were unhappy yourself. I remember how he used to make you cry. And you sat by him in bed without sleeping that last week. After he died, you just slumped down right there and cried yourself to sleep."

She'd apologized to Will so many times that week. She would never know if he'd heard her—not in this life, anyway. "I can't even remember it. I just remember you waking me in a panic after I'd slept dunnamany hours, sure I'd taken sick too." She reached up and laced her fingers with his. "I know you want to help me, Jack. But you can't. It's enough help to know you want to."

There was a pause. Jack said quietly, "Fairclough won't want you seeing me, if you're his wife. He'll expect you to put him first."

Phoebe felt a chill. Was Jack right? She knew very well that she wasn't making a match of the kind she and Jack were speaking of. She felt terribly lonely, that she would never have someone who put her happiness first out of all the things in the world. But that was selfish. She had Helen and Jack. She was lucky. "If that's the case, he can go hang, and I'll marry Mr. Moon."

"At least he's Orange-and-Purple," Jack said. "And you'd never want for sweets."

"I don't like sweets."

"Don't you?" Jack scrubbed a hand through his hair. "You're sure you'll be all right?"

"I'm sure."

"I've left you half of a column on page three for the news that comes with tomorrow's mail, and if anything important happens locally, you can take out the second paragraph about Mr. Neale's litter of sheepdogs and put it there…"

Phoebe mentally wrote *put out a newspaper* under *help Mrs. Pengilly write a letter to her son, finish the* Girl's Companion *story,* and *get married* on her list of things to do that week.

Chapter 16

Mr. Gilchrist was there when she got home, smugly helping Helen with her quilt pattern. It wasn't something one would think could be done smugly, but the Tory election agent was managing. The Pitt Club should nominate him for some sort of Smugness Award. She was sure they must have one. If not, a number of their members were sadly misdirecting their efforts.

Phoebe, examining her last few thoughts, was forced to admit that she was in an absolutely foul mood.

"Now a moss-green one," Helen said. "No, no, that's forest green. The moss green is directly to the left of that one."

"Of course, how foolish of me." Mr. Gilchrist handed her a cotton diamond.

"Thanks."

He smiled.

Phoebe wished swearing didn't make her so nervous, because it would have relieved her feelings wonderfully. Did Mr. Gilchrist plan to pursue her sister now? That was a complication she couldn't begin to see how to deal with. The worst of it was that Helen looked happier than she had all week.

Helen blushed when she saw Phoebe. Mr. Gilchrist did not. He stood politely. "Ah, Mrs. Sparks! Just the woman I wanted to see."

Phoebe doubted that.

"You and Mr. Fairclough were getting along swimmingly last night, unless my eyes deceived me."

"Your eyes didn't deceive you," Phoebe said grudgingly. "I like him. But talking to him about politics makes me want to throw the sugar at his head."

"Then don't talk about politics," Mr. Gilchrist said. "Problem solved."

"How clever of you," she said. "Why didn't I think of it? Don't worry, I'm sure he told you I've agreed to go driving with him tomorrow."

"Yes," Mr. Gilchrist began, "and—"

"I'll be in the bedroom if you need me, Ships." Phoebe went in and shut the door. Mr. Gilchrist stayed another hour and a half. Phoebe quietly tried a few obscenities. It didn't help.

On Tuesday, Nick dragged himself out of bed before dawn and into his clothes, examining himself in a mirror to make sure there were no dark circles under his eyes. He would see Mrs. Sparks later to help bring out the paper.

That wasn't a reason to want to look his best. He was trying to marry her off to Moon. But he held the candle up to the mirror anyway. He was in the clear; evidently he hadn't gone entirely soft in the last six months.

When Nick got there Tony was just slinking out of his room, a satchel over one arm and a rolled-up blanket under the other. Around his neck hung a set of field glasses Nick recognized as his own present, from the shop where he'd purchased his officer's kit. "Shhh," Tony said, yawning. "Ada's still sleeping."

"Has Ada ever come out with you?" Nick asked when they were downstairs.

"Ada couldn't be quiet for five minutes if her life depended on it. This is my time to be away from all that, anyway." He flashed Nick a grin. "We've yet to see if you receive a second invitation."

Nick resolved on the spot not to speak until spoken to. He followed Tony down the cobblestone streets in silence until they became country lanes. Tony turned off into a field and stopped within a little stand of trees, spreading the blanket and settling down on it. Nick lowered himself into a sitting position and took the sandwich Tony offered him. It was ham, which, like everything else these days, made him think of Mrs. Sparks.

Tony pulled a leather-wrapped flask out of his satchel and poured them each a thimbleful of coffee. At first that and his wool greatcoat kept Nick warm, but as they sat, Tony sketching intermittently, the chill and damp crept in. His leg began to protest being kept in one position. At first he tried to shift every few minutes, but Tony asked, frowning, "Is your leg all right?" and after that he was too self-conscious.

It wasn't a problem. He was good at this. He thought about Mrs. Sparks's warm laugh and watched Tony draw, and the chill and damp and pain faded just enough to be bearable. Every so often Tony pointed out a particularly interesting bird, whispering, "Rare vagrant," or "I've never seen that sort of warbler in Sussex before." Nick trained his field glasses on them obediently.

They really were very pretty, birds—strangely and efficiently made. He liked it best when they took flight. That impossible moment when they went from stillness to soaring made him catch his breath every time. Beside him, Tony sighed and grumbled that he had almost captured the shape of the crest.

After a couple of hours, Tony stood. "We'd better go back," he said reluctantly. Nick's leg almost gave out, but he hid it and offered to carry the blanket and satchel. To his mingled relief and humiliation, Tony wouldn't give them over.

"You're my little brother. Stop coddling me."

"I'll stop coddling you when you start taking care of yourself," Tony returned sharply.

Nick had nothing to say to that.

"You were good company." Tony ducked his head shyly. "If you've ever a mind to come again, you'd be welcome. Not that you'd probably want to, I know it's a dashed odd way to spend one's time, but—"

Just like that, it was all worth it. "I'd love to," he said, and meant it.

When Nick arrived at the printing office Tuesday morning, Jack Sparks was nowhere in evidence. Mrs. Sparks was seated at a table going through the day's mail, and a stocky adolescent was setting type by the window. She glanced up as the door opened, looking relieved to see him. "Oh, wonderful. It's going to be tight getting the paper out on our own, so if you could stay for even a few hours—"

"On your own? Where's Sparks? Is he all right?"

She frowned. "What do you mean, where is he? He's gone to Scotland with Miss Jessop."

Nick's jaw dropped. "He's done *what*?"

Her frown deepened. "Your brother gave him the money. He didn't tell you?"

"No! I was just with him—but we didn't talk much. H—" He remembered just in time not to say *hell*. "The hot place. Ruination." That didn't do much to relieve his feelings. Nick dropped into a chair. Tony had meant well, he was sure, but... he groaned and buried his face in his hands. This was a disaster. He had been speaking to Miss Jessop and pleading the couple's case only the day before yesterday. The Dymonds' involvement would be suspected immediately. Not only that, the reputation of one of the most influential Orange-and-Purples in the town would be tarnished forever. Lady Tassell would be furious.

"It'll come right." Mrs. Sparks didn't sound at all sure. Her pencil tapped out a faint, anxious rhythm on the edge of the table.

Nick realized this was even worse than he'd thought. "He's left you to face the gossip alone, hasn't he?"

"There won't be much about me," she said. "He's only my brother-in-law."

"Gammon. You're here, aren't you, covering for him? They'll say you helped him abduct a gently reared girl from her home. They'll say—"

Her rosebud lips were so pale they almost disappeared into her face, but her eyes were determined. "I know what they'll say," she said quietly. "But they'll forget about my part in it soon enough. It's not an interesting enough tale."

"Maybe not, if you're not here when their flight is discovered." He stood up. "Come along, I'm taking you home."

She gave him a shocked look. "Someone has to put out the paper."

"Owen can do it."

"Don't be ridiculous, there's still *days* of work to be done."

"He's right, ma'am," Owen said. "I can do it. It'll only be a few hours late."

"A *few* hours late? A few *hours* late?" Evidently there were some things that were unthinkable to a newspaperman's widow. "The paper will be in enough trouble after this without being *late.*"

Her conviction was charming, but Nick was unswayed. "Come along." He yanked her out of her chair by the upper arm. "Owen will say Sparks was late, we got tired of waiting and left in a huff." He let go of her for a moment to fish in his pocket and toss the apprentice a shilling. The young man pocketed it with a nod.

Nick was pleased to find that Mrs. Sparks did not resist him very strongly. She needed someone to occasionally overrule her quixotic streak, that was all. Or did that make him Sancho Panza? He was still searching for a better metaphor when the front door banged open, almost taking off his nose. The bell slapped back against the door with a jangle-thunk.

"*Sparks!*" roared Mr. Jessop.

Nick released Mrs. Sparks, cursing inwardly.

"Where is Sparks?" Jessop demanded.

Mrs. Sparks drew herself up, trembling with what could probably be mistaken for indignation. "He is out running errands," she said coldly. "If you tell me the nature of your business, I—"

Mr. Jessop lifted the panel in the counter and headed for the kitchen door. "He's hiding her up there, isn't he?"

Mrs. Sparks's eyes widened angrily. She was a better liar than Nick had thought. "My brother-in-law would *never*. You must have been misinformed."

"Then you won't mind my going up to look?"

She raced back to block his way. "I most certainly do mind!"

Nick was very much hoping it wouldn't come to blows, when a liveried Jessop footman burst through the door. "Sir, I've found their trail!"

Jessop turned. "Their trail? My daughter is not a fox, young man."

"Of course not, sir," the boy said. "They got on the stage-coach going north. The crippled soldier who begs by the coaching inn was sitting in her chair. I recognized it at once, sir. He told me they'd gone a couple of hours since. The chair wouldn't fit, and they just gave it to him."

"Good God." Nick hoped he was projecting the right air of stunned horror. Since he was feeling rather stunned and horrified, he thought he might be.

Mr. Jessop collapsed into a chair, white as a ghost. "She's gone," he said, his voice like a moan. "She's gone."

Mrs. Sparks stood with her hand over her mouth. "Oh God. He really—Jack really—"

"There, you see? I knew it!" But even the triumph of being right couldn't bring animation to Jessop's features for more than a moment. "The blackguard has stolen my girl." He cupped his hands before his mouth, almost as if in prayer. "And they left her chair. How will she manage without her chair? She always liked to have her own, hated the Bath chairs you could rent in town…"

"You have had a shock, sir," Mrs. Sparks said. "Let me fetch you some brandy." Jessop didn't respond, but she hastened from the room anyway.

"I am most sorry," Nick said. "I never thought anything of

this nature would occur."

"Of course you did not. What honorable man would think of such villainy? To abduct a poor crippled girl…"

"Sir, you must put that sort of thinking from your mind," Nick said carefully. "It seems clear Sparks did not abduct your daughter. She is old enough to know her own mind, and went with him quite willingly."

Jessop's face contorted. "She was always such a good little girl."

Nick had yet to meet *any* child who was not a holy terror in one way or another, and suspected Jessop's mind was clouded by either nostalgia or a poor memory. "You must consider, sir. If they are married, revenge against Sparks will harm your daughter as well."

Jessop's eyes widened. "You think I should turn the other cheek? To that Whiggish son-of-a—" Mrs. Sparks came in, holding a glass mostly full of brandy, and Jessop reflexively checked his language. He took a healthy swig and grimaced. "Swill. Of *course* the cad buys terrible brandy."

Nick met Mrs. Sparks's eye, smothering a smile in spite of everything.

Some color came back into Jessop's cheeks as he drank, but he still looked dazed. "Oh, and during an election too. How *could* she? She was always such a staunch Tory."

Nick wanted to put a hand on the man's shoulder, but thought it might be considered presumption. "It will all come right, sir. If you treat this as a somewhat amusing youthful piece of idiocy, if you receive the couple when they return, if you are generous in the matter of settlements—"

Jessop gaped. "Give him *money*? You want me to reward him for this piece of infamy?"

"Mr. Dymond is right, sir," Mrs. Sparks said, with a respectful bob. "Gossip thrives on story."

"Of course you would agree with him—wait, what?"

"Story," Mrs. Sparks repeated. "People love a good story. If you tell everyone exactly what happened and accept Mr. Sparks and your daughter, there's no story. There's no hero and villain, no 'what really happened' or 'what happens next'. People may not entirely forget, but they'll stop talking after a few months."

Jessop groaned. "A few months? The election will be over next *week*!"

Mrs. Sparks frowned. "Your daughter will have to live here forever," she said, a faint note of censure in her voice.

Jessop colored. The enemy was surprised; it was time for a flank attack. Tony and his mother would kill him, but the time for caution was past. Tony had put Mrs. Sparks in this position. "The Dymonds will back them," he said. "Publicly. If you refuse to see them, if you spread accusations as to Sparks's conduct, if you make it a question of party—you know no one will speak of anything else. No one will ever forget it. And your daughter will bear the brunt of it."

Jessop threw back the last of his bad brandy.

Nick gentled his voice. "You'll want to see her. She will want to see you. Don't create enmity between you. You gain nothing by it."

"People will say I tolerate wickedness," Jessop said. "'If thy right hand offend thee, cut it off.'"

"If you cut her off, people will say you failed to temper justice with mercy," Nick said. "People always have something to say. No one has the right to make this decision for you, not even your party. What does your heart say?" What would his own mother do, in this situation? If he eloped with Mrs. Sparks tomorrow, would he have a family when he returned?

Why had his mind immediately gone to eloping with Mrs. Sparks?

Jessop buried his face in his hands, but not before Nick saw his expression crumple. "Her mother left her to my care. I've failed her." It was terrible. He should have been saying these things to people who liked him.

"None of us can change what's already happened," Mrs. Sparks said. "In the end, you don't know what your wife would have thought or done. You only know she would want you and your daughter to be happy."

It was what Nick had tried to tell her, about her father. He swallowed.

Jessop stared at her for long moments. Then he stood up. "I'm going home."

"Drat," Mrs. Sparks said as the door shut behind Jessop. "He's taken Jack's glass with him."

"I thought that went well." Nick wasn't sure himself whether he meant it or whether it was a joke, but she began to laugh. She laughed so often, and yet not often enough.

"The spirits of the wise sit in the clouds and mock us, as my father used to say." She rubbed at her eyes. "I'm sorry I dragged you into this. I know you came to talk to Jack. You don't have to stay. Owen and I have a lot of work ahead of us; I don't suppose we'll be good company."

If Nick left, he would have to confront Tony about this mess. If he stayed, he could talk to Mrs. Sparks. It wasn't much of a contest. "I haven't anything else to do."

The morning passed in a blur of correcting proofs, printing, and folding. Owen ran the press. He was quick, and the cast-iron press was much faster than the old wooden one Will had taught Phoebe to use. But even going full out, the last sheet wouldn't be off the press until suppertime.

Mr. Dymond took the damp papers from the press and hung them to dry, while she folded the sheets in half as soon as the ink wouldn't smear. He inserted this week's page from *Childe Harold*, thankfully printed in advance. Then she counted them out and bundled them for the newsboys and riders, who came in throughout the day for papers and their pay.

She dealt with Jack's employees, but Mr. Dymond dealt with the customers. Phoebe had always liked the rush and bustle of the day, but it didn't leave her much energy for smiling and chatting. When it had been her and the Sparks brothers, Jack had usually dealt with the crowds eager to have the week's news ahead of their neighbors. Phoebe and Will brought out the newspaper, taking swigs of ale every time a customer remarked in delight and surprise, *The paper is still damp!*

This week was worse than usual—swarms of gossip-hungry townsfolk who'd heard about the elopement and wanted details. Mr. Dymond managed them with a friendly cheer she probably couldn't muster *any* day. The fiftieth time someone said, "Whatever is a gentleman doing selling newspapers?" his reply was as natural and engaging as the first, though she suspected he disliked the cracks about his being in line for a new profession.

She felt a nagging guilt at taking advantage of his good nature, but he made press day feel almost as festive as it used to. And he asked her and Owen questions, loads of them, as if he was really interested in the press and the paper.

"What are the parcels you give the newsmen?" he asked.

She looked up from running a folding bone down the crease of a barely dry *Intelligencer*. He had put on a leather apron over his fine clothes. Fine beads of sweat ran down his neck into his cravat, which had long ago lost its starch, and there was an inky fingerprint on his chin. He had so far been too polite to take his coat off, but she had hopes for the near future.

He frowned, and she realized she had been staring. "Sorry, woolgathering," she said hastily. "The riders carry parcels and orders from the shops along with the papers. They go regular as clockwork once a week, so they're more reliable than the tinkers and cheaper than the mails. In Will's father's day they carried letters, but that's against the law now. I'm all for progress, but the Royal Mail isn't half as reliable—"

A surprisingly mournful expression crossed his face.

"I've never seen anyone look so sad at the inefficiency of the mail before," she said.

He shook his head, chuckling obligingly at her feeble joke. "You're the heart of this district, with arteries going all over Sussex, bringing people news and hope and parcels. I miss being part of something like that."

Her first impulse was to say something self-deprecating about it only being a newspaper—but she didn't believe that, did she? She did think the *Intelligencer* was the heart of the district. "You will be again," she said.

"Maybe. In the army—" He sighed. "You must be sick of my starting sentences that way. Everyone must. I'm afraid that when I'm old, I'll still be saying it. My little grand-nieces and -nephews will mouth it behind my back along with me. I don't—"

She folded a newspaper with great care, not looking at him. "Not grandchildren?"

She could see out of the corner of her eye that he wasn't looking at her, either. "I don't know if I shall marry."

"Admiral Nelson was missing an arm and an eye, and girls swooned as he walked down the street. At least, I know they would have done here, if he had ever visited."

"It isn't that."

He didn't elaborate further, and she was afraid of revealing too much if she pressed him. She covered her unease under a pretense of being too busy to talk. But eventually the paper was out, the press was cleaned, and Owen began putting out the candles.

Mr. Dymond stood and collected his cane. "May I come again tomorrow?"

Yes! "You really want to come again?" she asked dubiously. "I know this must all seem very boring—"

"I don't know why people always say that about things they love," Mr. Dymond said. "I don't think it's boring at all."

She felt warm from the inside out. "It would be a great help."

Chapter 17

Nick steeled himself and rapped on Tony's door. By now his leg was in agony and he wanted nothing more than to eat supper and sleep, but he'd rehearsed this conversation on and off all day, growing angrier as he went. If he wanted to sleep, he had to have this out.

But when Tony answered the door, clearly on his way to speak at some club supper or society meeting, Nick searched for that anger and couldn't find it. He only felt sad.

"Nick?" Tony checked his watch. "Ada and I are on our way to the Carpenters Guild supper, but I can spare a minute."

"You gave Mr. Sparks money to take Miss Jessop to Scotland?"

Tony drew back, looking wary. "I did."

"We talked about this." Nick leaned against the doorframe to take weight off his leg. "You did this to ensure Mrs. Sparks would marry Moon."

Tony's brows rose. "You think she'll marry Moon, then? I thought she was inclined towards the Tory."

Nick winced. "That isn't the point." He held on to his indignation. "It's going to be a terrible scandal. People were by the printing office all day asking about it. Mrs. Sparks's reputation—"

"*You're* going to lecture me about Mrs. Sparks's reputation?"

A sarcastic edge crept into Tony's voice. "I'm not the one dancing attendance on her."

Nick flushed. "Is there—?"

"Gossip? Of course there's gossip. People in this damn town have nothing *else* to do. I've been asked about the two of you a dozen times or more, and I haven't gone poking my nose in your business about it either."

Guilt swamped Nick. He might say he wanted to help her, but so far, he'd brought Mrs. Sparks nothing but trouble. "She's a respectable woman," he said firmly. "This elopement—they could have married here with banns, if they didn't want her dowry."

"No, they couldn't. The first week Jessop heard the banns read, he'd ship her off to the North. Besides, Sparks is the newspaperman in this town, and now he'll be more loyal than ever. I did us all a favor."

He hadn't done Mrs. Sparks a favor. But Tony was right about the most important thing. Nick couldn't wish Miss Jessop back in her father's house. His brother had meant well. "I'm sorry I ripped up at you."

"Don't worry about it."

Nick smiled with an effort. "Sparks's press is Whig again. If you've anything to be printed, I can bring it in tomorrow morning."

"You're going back tomorrow morning?"

Nick nodded.

Tony pursed his lips, looking concerned. "I know I said I wouldn't poke my nose in your business…"

"Poke away." Nick tried to sound amused.

"I don't think you should see so much of her."

"Mother sent me here solely to get her vote. Would you

rather I ignored her?"

"If you want her vote, you'll throw her together with Moon."

"She's *been* spending time with Moon," Nick said. "Frankly, I'm not sure that's to our advantage."

Tony sighed. "Go and put a hot water bottle on your leg, you look about to swoon."

Nick turned to go.

"Wish me luck?" Tony blurted out behind him.

Nick's heart swelled. He turned back and clapped his brother on the shoulder. "You don't need it. You were born for this."

Tony didn't look as if he believed it.

Phoebe was a little surprised and very pleased that Mr. Dymond did come back the next day, and the day after. He went through the London papers while she turned Jack's near-illegible notes into articles about the election. She showed him bizarre local contributions, and he showed her inexplicable advertisements and marriage notices for people with funny names. They went for walks before dinner and after closing up for the day, so his leg wouldn't grow stiff, and they found plenty to talk about then too.

He didn't berate her, or question her judgment, or demand she work faster. Oh, he disagreed with her once or twice about whether something ought to be included—the paper would have been half military news if he had his way—but that only added to the fun. She felt guilty for making the comparison, but she'd always wanted working on the paper with Will to be like this.

She kept wondering if Mr. Dymond would kiss her again. So far, he hadn't.

"I'm that glad you're not averse to early rising," Mr. Fairclough said. "Doesn't it take your breath away?"

Phoebe smiled. "It does, a bit." She didn't often get to ride in a carriage, and from this height, there was something magical about the stands of tall, slender trees and the fallow fields gilded with the pale morning light. Apart from a few laborers on their way to work and a milkwoman with her cart, the only other people out were two gentlemen pedestrians in casual morning wear, one carrying a satchel and the other a stout walking stick.

A walking stick? Phoebe looked again, and saw that same morning sun glinting a warm gold in the taller one's hair. Suddenly the figure resolved into—

"If it isn't the Dymond brothers, trudging along." Mr. Fairclough crowed with laughter. "Think I can spatter them with mud?"

Phoebe thought of Toogood's fastidiousness. "Oh, don't."

Mr. Fairclough slowed the horses. "If you don't like it," he said in that terse way of his, with a smile. She really did like him. So long as they didn't talk about politics, everything was fine.

Mr. Nicholas Dymond was not a possibility.

"It's only that I've been spattered with mud on this road a hundred times," she hastened to add. "I hate it."

"They've laundresses," Mr. Fairclough said cynically. "When I was a boy…"

They passed the brothers as he was talking. Mr. Anthony looked furious to see her with a Tory. Mr. Nicholas, on the other hand, simply looked as startled as she felt. Their eyes met, and a shock went through her whole body.

"Well?" Mr. Fairclough said.

"I'm sorry, what did you say?"

Later, when Mr. Dymond arrived at the printing office, all he said was, "How are things going with Mr. Moon?" She couldn't think of an answer that would be encouraging.

On Friday, Owen finished typesetting pages one and four, locked them in the chase together, and printed a couple of proofs. "Go home early," Phoebe told him. "You've been wonderful this week. You deserve it."

The apprentice didn't wait to be asked twice, cleaning the ink off the form at double speed. Ordinarily he slept in the kitchen at the shop, but just now he was staying with his sister, as her husband was away and she hated being alone in the house.

After Phoebe and Mr. Dymond had each read the proofs through twice, she dug out the box of pages of *Childe Harold's Pilgrimage* that were to go in this week's papers.

> *On yon long, level plain, at distance crown'd*
> *With crags, whereon those Moorish turrets rest,*
> *Wide scatter'd hoof-marks dint the wounded ground;*
> *And, scath'd by fire, the green sward's darken'd vest*
> *Tells that the foe was Andalusia's guest…*

"Good," she said. "It's war stanzas this week. We've already got fourteen letters about last week's."

"What was wrong with last week's?" Mr. Dymond asked, immediately indignant.

"It contained the phrase 'adulterate joy', apparently."

"Apparently? You haven't read it?"

She shook her head. He made a disappointed face. She *felt* disappointed, in herself. "I used to love reading travels and geographies," she said. "I wanted to see the mountains and olive trees of Spain so badly it was like a pain in my chest."

Mr. Dymond turned his face to the window, taking in the boring English street. He looked as if his chest were hurting to see Spain at this very moment. "They're beautiful."

"I'm sure they are." Her chest did hurt—but it hurt for *him*. It hurt with how much she wanted him to turn towards her again, to touch her. She knew she would never see Spain. "I used to see possibilities for myself. It used to seem as if maybe one day I could visit Spain, or the West Indies, or Giza. As if even if I didn't, there'd be no room in my life to regret it. I thought…"

His gaze came back to her, blue eyes steady. He waited patiently for her to go on.

"I think I stopped seeing possibilities after I lost my baby. I—I stopped seeing them for the world as well. I lost interest in the *Intelligencer*. I lost interest in politics. I still believe in progress here"—she tapped her forehead—"but in my heart, I stopped. I hate it. I hate that I've become so small. All there is to my life is two rooms. I don't even read the London news-papers anymore." She picked up the *Times*, then dropped it with a *thwack*. "I don't recognize half the names in these pol-itical articles. What's happened to me? I used to care about things. I used to want things."

He chewed his lower lip. "You still want things. You must. You move with so much purpose."

That stopped her. She flushed. Was that how he saw her? It wasn't the usual sort of compliment, but she liked the idea.

"I'm sorry, that was both strange and overfamiliar," he said. "But I mean it. I feel invigorated just being near you."

There was no one about. No one would ever know what she said next. And he made her want to be the person he saw—a bold, purposeful woman. She grinned at him, heart pounding. "I wasn't talking about *that* sort of wanting."

His eyes darkened. "Neither was I."

It wasn't at all the same, that sort of wanting and what she'd been speaking of. Or was it? Since meeting him, she had more energy than she'd had in months, maybe years. He'd woken up her body, and the mind and body were connected.

But it wasn't just her body that wanted him, was it?

"If you could have anything, right now, what would it be?" His eyes were fixed on her with a curious intensity, as if he were hungry for her answer. Hungry for her desire.

For a moment, she let herself consider the possibilities—and just like that, it was too late to lie. She wanted him desperately, and maybe she could have him. She could ignore that and go back to her small boring life, or she could be bold and take what she wanted. She'd been that woman, once. She wanted herself back.

She should ask for a kiss. It was small, and safe, and the least shameful of all her desires. But it wasn't what she'd been thinking all afternoon. Not when she kept catching him sneaking glances at her bosom. Her nipples ached, her breasts feeling heavy and swollen. She wanted to be shameful. She wanted to be shocking and forward and get exactly what she wanted, just this once. "Will you touch my breasts?"

His face went slack, as if he felt too many things to decide on an expression. His throat worked soundlessly, his eyes going to her bosom like a needle to the pole. She sat and waited for him to reach out a hand. She let the silence fill with their mutual understanding of her desire.

There was a man with a static-electricity machine at the Whitsuntide fair; for a penny he had let her stand on a resin cake and electrified her body. When Will had reached out to touch her, miniature lightning had stretched from a point on her skin to his finger, bright and painful like a burn. She felt like that now. She was charged and humming, and if Mr. Dymond put out a hand, the energy within her couldn't help but leap towards him, making the candles in their tin sconces look dim.

"We'd better go into the kitchen," he said.

"Oh. Oh, of course." He was going to do it. He was really going to do it. She was the worst sort of wanton, encouraging a man she had no intention of marrying to fondle her like— *like a whore,* she made herself think. But she led him into the kitchen and drew the curtains closed. She faced him, trying not to shake, light-headed with shame and eagerness.

Then he did put out his hand, slowly, to cup her left breast, shaping it through her clothes and squeezing gently. He rubbed up and down, his palm hard against her. Pleasure spiked in her nipple and radiated out like heat from a hot stove. He had taken off his gloves for the work they had been doing; his bare hand stood out against the dark fabric of her dress, her neckline shifting under the pressure of his fingers. When she glanced up, he was watching her face. "Is that what you wanted?" he asked.

Her face flamed. She shouldn't be doing this—but that only made it better. Having begun with honesty, she found she didn't want to stop. "More." He drew his hand back, and she said, "Please," then flushed with shame at the naked intensity in her voice.

He grinned. "Don't forget 'thank you.'" He felt for the pins at her bosom. She helped him pull them out, and he plucked the kerchief from her dress with a sharp tug. Though she couldn't feel it with any sharpness through the thick fabric of her corset, even the slight friction and shift in pressure made her gasp. He lifted the kerchief to hold it over her eyes. She gasped in shock.

"May I?" he asked.

He could see her, and she couldn't see him. She couldn't know what he would do. "Yes."

He tied the linen at the back of her head. Phoebe was exposed, uncertain, and painfully aroused. She felt a change in the air a moment before he cupped her breasts, lifting them, weighing them with his hands. "So perfect." He raised them as high as they would go, until it almost hurt—then let go. They fell with a bouncing jolt that *did* hurt, splendidly and gloriously, her flesh already sensitized beyond belief.

His fingertips pressed into her as he sought her nipples. Would he be able to feel them through the fabric? He rubbed circles in their vicinity—so lightly, and there was so much fabric and stiff linen between his fingers and her skin, that for a moment she wondered if she would feel it herself when he found them.

Twin streaks of pleasure shot through her. She cried out in surprise, her knees threatening to buckle—and his thumbs jammed into her flesh, hard. It hurt for a brief, agonizing second, and then heated, feverish sensation flooded through her, centering between her legs. He did it again. Her nipples throbbed. Oh God. This was wicked. Wicked, and unbearable. She was afraid of his touch, and on the verge of begging for it.

He let go. "Turn around," he said in a low voice.

She nearly stumbled as she obeyed him, breath stuttering in her throat. As she shifted, she became suddenly aware of how wet she had become. She felt for the edge of the kitchen sink to ground herself. He didn't steady her; his own balance must be tenuous without his walking stick.

He unbuttoned her dress swiftly. "I thought about this last week, when you asked me to do your buttons up."

"So did I." She half-expected her voice to have changed, to be something guttural and rusty. Instead she sounded bizarrely normal.

He left her dress on and put his hands on her waist, pulling her carefully back against him. She could feel, faintly through layers of petticoat, that he was hard. She pressed back instinctively; his hands stopped her before she could overbalance him. "Careful," he said. "Don't move."

She stood, breathing hard, as he slid his hands around to gently cup her breasts again.

"I could have you like this." He had leaned in without her realizing. His lips brushed the curve of her ear below the blindfold, his voice low and intimate. "If you put your hands flat on the table, I could pull up your skirts and take you."

She moaned.

"Do you want me to?"

She did. "I think it's your turn to want something."

He froze for a long moment. She should have said yes. She should have just said yes, and now he was going to pull away and they would never be able to look each other in the eye again and everything was ruined, everything.

"Not yet," he said, warm, rich amusement in his voice. "We haven't finished with what you asked for. Pull down your bodice."

Chapter 18

S he tugged at her cuffs, pulling her sleeves off by feel. Her dress sagged around her waist. He unbuttoned her flannel petticoats, and she pulled her arms out of those, too. She must look ridiculous, improbable amounts of fabric bunched everywhere. "You'll have to unlace my corset."

He loosened the laces, creating a small gap between the front of the corset and her shift. Cool air rushed in, but the linen of the shift stuck to her skin. She realized she had been sweating. Her skin would be marked with lines from the seams of her corset; maybe without the stays her bosom would sag more than he had expected. Maybe this would turn the moment's fairy glamour to cold reality, her breasts nothing special or magical after all but only the same boring flesh she saw every morning and evening. She hesitated.

He bent down and kissed her shoulder. "Do you want me to lace it back up?" His voice's cultured accents suddenly sounded alien and distant. He was such a gentleman. She liked that about him, but just then she would have been reassured by rough, common lust.

Liar, she told herself. *You only want him to make this easier for you. You want him to take the choice away so you don't have to be brave.*

She yanked her corset down, its stiff wooden busk jutting

forward awkwardly. She could feel her shift still clinging to her skin, probably transparent with sweat.

He bit off an impressive piece of profanity. "Sorry. Turn around."

She did, fighting the urge to cover herself or pull off the blindfold. What did he see? Without the firm pressure of her corset and clothes, she felt unanchored. The cool air of the kitchen caressing her skin felt obscene. Her shift pulled free of her skin, chill air rushing in. She started. He gave a husky laugh. "Put your arms up." She obeyed, and he pulled the shift over her head.

"Show them to me."

Her breath came shallow, half from arousal and half from nerves. Awkwardly, she put her hands under her breasts and lifted them. Her nipples caught on the buttons of his coat. She hadn't realized he was so close.

"Christ, yes," he said. "I knew they would spill over your hands like wine."

"Touch me."

She could hear the smile in his voice—the smile and the hunger both. "I've been in h—er, the hot place—since I met you, you know. Knowing I couldn't have this. That I'd never, ever know what your breasts tasted like or what sounds you'd make when I nipped you with my teeth. Now I will. I want a few more moments of torment."

She couldn't see him, but she knew what he looked like, the wicked glint in his blue eyes, the way one eyebrow and the corner of his mouth turned up slightly and those two little things changed his whole face. Maybe he could wait, but she couldn't. She leaned forward, dragging her nipples up and down over the fine fabric of his coat. It felt unbearably wonderful.

He trembled. His arm brushed against her; she guessed that he gripped the edge of the sink for balance. His other hand settled over hers and his mouth closed around her left nipple.

He was gentle at first, simply surrounding her with wet delicious heat; the feeling was like a dash of cayenne, turning to cool peppermint when he moved away to blow gently, to mouth and lick at her other nipple. Just as she was about to melt into a puddle at his feet, he sucked *hard*. She made a grotesque sound, hips jerking.

She felt the light touch of his teeth, as he'd promised, tiny needles of pleasure before he flicked gently with his tongue. She made another terrible needy noise and leaned back against the sink to steady herself. Apart from his hand on hers, he touched her with only the very tip of his tongue. She felt as if he'd entered her. Her intimate muscles clenched helplessly around nothing. Was it possible to achieve the height of pleasure only from this?

If she did, though, it would be over. She wasn't ready for it to be over.

"Wait," she rasped. "It's your turn to want something."

He stopped just long enough to say, "I want this." She gave in. Her pleasure grew until she was frantic with it. When he finally drew his mouth away and let go of her breast, she was shaking and weak and ready to spread her legs right there on the kitchen table, please, please, *please*.

"Sorry," he said. "I just need to sit down, so I can use both hands."

To his surprise, there was a flicker of disappointment in her face below the blindfold. What did she want instead?

Nick had never really understood men who complained that women were difficult to please. All you had to do was pay attention, follow their lead without being obvious about it—women enjoyed a masterful air—and with a little trial and error you could easily discover what they wanted. They might find it embarrassing to ask in words, but they moved their hands, spread their legs wider or drew them together, made sounds of pleasure or disappointment or demand.

Nick had a reputation as a generous lover, and he was proud of it. And after all, there was no point being selfish. A man who spilled his seed in the presence of a pretty, willing woman was never unsatisfied.

"You don't want me to use my hands?"

"I—" She broke off, embarrassed, and pulled the kerchief from her eyes. She looked down at herself. He looked, too. She was an erotic, wanton mess, her clothes in disarray, her corset gaping, her heavy dark hair—already disheveled after a long day's work and her habit of rubbing at the back of her neck while thinking—about to come entirely loose from its moorings. She breathed hard, face flushed and bare breasts heaving. *I did that,* he thought.

Her nipples gleamed wet with his saliva. She noticed and went to rub them dry with the kerchief. She hadn't thought it through, and her eyes widened when the rasp of linen gave her unexpected pleasure. Nick's mouth went dry.

"Do you want me to use my mouth?" he asked her, grateful his voice didn't crack. "Down there?"

She gasped as if she liked the idea, but she didn't nod.

"You want me inside you."

She squeezed her eyes shut and nodded. "Please."

His own need had been present all along—but it had been at the back of his mind, sequestered away while he focused on hers, on the smell and taste of her and the sounds she made. Now it rushed back like blood into a frozen limb, fierce and painful. He hesitated. "There's no place—"

He hated his leg at that moment, hated it with a concentrated disgust that could have corroded steel. He had used to like to take women in odd places, standing. Now he wasn't sure he could make it all the way through the act without collapsing. His earlier offer to take her from behind had been an empty promise. It had already been foolish pride to stand so long without his cane; his leg would give him hell tomorrow. None of the chairs looked as though they could take the weight of two, the floor was hard, and the table was completely covered in parcels, newspapers, correspondence, scissors, and a thousand other odds-and-ends.

Reality was rushing back in, and he could tell from the look on Mrs. Sparks's face that she was deflating like a balloon in the face of his inability.

"We could put a tablecloth on the ground," she suggested in a small voice. "Unless you don't want to. I'm sorry, that was terribly forward of me, I—I'm sorry—never mind."

"Shhh. Of course I want to." Nick had yet to meet the man who would turn down an opportunity to fuck a beautiful, eager woman.

She pulled a tablecloth from a chest in the corner, and together they spread it on the ground. Moving with a fierce erection only exaggerated his limp, but she didn't say anything and neither did he. Then he couldn't help himself. "It's not going to be very comfortable on this tiled floor."

She frowned, crossing her arms over her bare chest as if growing really self-conscious for the first time. "Will it hurt your leg?"

It would, but, "That isn't what I meant." He had meant that if he were whole, she wouldn't have to be on the floor.

"You didn't answer my question." The excited flush was fading from her cheeks, and her crossed arms were starting to look more annoyed than modest.

"Everything hurts my leg," he snapped. "If I didn't do anything that hurt my leg, I would lie in bed all day, and then my leg would hurt from lack of exercise."

"Well, is there something we could do to make you more comfortable?"

There was, of course. They could use the bed upstairs. She could be on top. He didn't want to ask for either. "I'm a man, damn it. I don't need to be babied. I was merely concerned for your comfort."

"And I'm concerned for yours."

He struggled to sound calm. "If you've changed your mind…"

"Is that supposed to shut me up?"

Yes, Nick thought.

"Of course I haven't changed my mind. Will it be easier for you"—she flushed—"in a certain position? Or—?"

"I assure you, it's all the same to me." He tried to sound merely obliging, but he could hear the edge in his voice. That carefully cultivated young-man-about-town indifference, meant to hide his own reaction to criticism. He hadn't intended to use it with her. He could see the moment she lost her temper.

"Exactly how demanding do you want me to be? Would

you like an opening statement and witnesses, too?"

How had this gone so wrong? This had never happened to him before. Had he forgotten how to do this in the last six months?

Only it *had* happened to him before, hadn't it? Never this quickly, and not in the middle of lovemaking, but his liaisons with women generally did end with, *Don't I mean anything to you? Aren't you even going to try to stop me leaving?*

His answer was always unhappy, resentful silence. If they wanted to leave, what did it matter what they meant to him? "I don't—I didn't say anything. I expressed concern for your comfort. Women are incomprehensible! What do you *want*?"

"I want you to show even a quarter of the enthusiasm I have!"

"You didn't seem dissatisfied with my performance a few minutes ago."

She hunched over, brows drawing together like soldiers standing back-to-back. "No, you're very skilled. I don't—I don't need skill, or to be satisfied with your *performance*. I wanted desire. I wanted to share something with somebody who wanted me just for me, who didn't need any favors or votes or—this week is the last time I'll ever be able to choose who I bed, and I chose you."

She sounded on the verge of tears. Nick cursed himself. She had wanted him to help her forget, and he had botched it beyond recognition.

Next week she would be married to someone else. Next week Moon or Fairclough would have the right to bed her whenever they liked.

"I chose you too," he said. "Don't cry. I'm sorry. Come here." He put an arm around her, leaning back against the sink for support and smoothing his fingers coaxingly over her bare, round arm. "Let me show you how much I want you. I'll make you forget about everything but what's in this room, right now—"

She looked away. "You always know what to say."

He squeezed her shoulders. "It's a gift."

She shook her head. "It's theft. You don't mean it. You just know what I want to hear."

His heart pounded, his panic out of proportion to her words. "Can't it be both?"

She shook her head. "You told me that if you care about someone, you should see them for who they really are. You see me. I *let* you see me, and I want to see you, but you won't—"

He gave her a cajoling smile. "If you wanted me to disrobe, you had only to ask."

She glared at him. "It isn't funny. If you told anyone the things I said today—if anyone found out we had done this—I risked everything for this, including my pride, because I wanted it so badly. It wasn't easy, and you won't even risk telling me what part of your body you want me to touch."

"I can't think of a place I'd complain about," he protested. He ought to be feeling ashamed that he'd touched her at all, and instead she somehow made him ashamed that he hadn't helped himself more freely to her body. He didn't understand. He'd tried to be chivalrous. He hadn't taken advantage of her or tried to push her into anything. When had that become a bad thing? Was he supposed to play the Pirate and the Captive Heiress with her?

"I didn't want to forget," she said. "I wanted something to remember. I wanted it to be worth the risk I took."

He felt sick. Everything had been going so smoothly, and

now suddenly he was being judged and found wanting by someone who a quarter of an hour ago had been begging him to fuck her. He had no idea what to say.

She reached up to ruffle his hair, as if he were a puppy or a confused child. Her fingers felt good against his scalp. She felt good in the curve of his arm. He didn't want this moment to end. "You have a lot to give," she said. "Someday you'll find someone you want to give it to. Thank you for—" She coughed. "Well. I enjoyed it."

"So did I." It didn't sound convincing even to him, which was ridiculous because it was the truest thing he'd said in years.

She sighed, reaching for her shift and pulling it over her head, shoving the ends of the fabric down under her stays. "You'd better help me lace back up."

He could still have her. That was the devil of it; he knew he could still have her if he only said the right words in the right way. But anything he said now would sound false. He could tell her what to do, but if he was telling her what to do because she told him to, did that count?

And even that…he tried to imagine asking her to lie down so he could fuck her tits, and his throat closed. He didn't understand why. What was the worst that could happen? She'd make a funny little face and say it was perverse and she'd rather not. That wouldn't be so terrible.

He couldn't do it.

She put her arms back through the straps of her corset, and pulled the sleeves of her petticoats and dress over her arms. He laced her stays for her, and buttoned her clothes, and tried to think of something to say.

"I'm sorry," she said in a small voice as she repinned her hair. "I told you I was hard to live with."

He wished he could take that uncertainty out of her eyes. "It isn't your fault." That, at least, he was sure of. "I've been— I've been more honest with you than I ever have with anyone."

Her rosebud mouth twisted and her eyebrows arched just a bit. He wanted to kiss the corner of her eye. "I threw myself at you. It wasn't your responsibility to be thrilled about it. It's like having your plate made up for you at table. You don't have to worry about making the wrong choice or taking too much, but you never get exactly what you want."

You're the one who wasn't happy with what you got, he thought.

Chapter 19

Phoebe trudged home, feeling wrung out and empty. Jack was gone, and even if Mr. Jessop decided to be kind, it would be a terrific scandal. And now she had ruined things with Mr. Dymond. She was too much, just as her mother always said: too hungry, too loud, too demanding, too change-able. Never, ever satisfied. He'd been generous and debauched, driven her to ecstasy, and still she'd taken some notion into her head that it wasn't enough, that she had to have it all. She'd never even touched him or given him one scrap of pleasure in exchange for what he gave her.

He'd looked so confused and frustrated and unhappy. What was wrong with her? What right did she have to com-plain that she was just a pleasant-enough distraction for him, a nice bit of fun fallen into his lap? Wasn't he the same for her?

And now he wouldn't be back to help her with the paper, and the one bright spot she could see in the rest of her life had winked out like a snuffed candle.

Marriage is hardly a tragedy, she told herself. *Stop whining.*

She was just so tired. Her whole body ached as if she'd fallen down stairs. Fallen back to earth, more like. If she could have just kept her mouth shut, she'd be sated and relaxed right now.

Helen would be waiting for her at home; there was no way

even to quickly pleasure herself before bed. There was nothing for it but to eat some ham, work on her quilt, and go to sleep, and hope she'd feel better in the morning.

Nick ignored entirely Toogood's complaints about the state of his clothes. He tried to listen when Tony came by to complain about Ada, the freemen, and Lively St. Lemeston generally, but only managed about half an ear until Tony said, "You have to end this thing with Mrs. Sparks. Or if you have to bed her, can't you at least wait until after the election?"

"I don't have a thing with Mrs. Sparks." It was true, now. He'd made it true somehow. At least the gossip would stop. That should have seemed important, but it felt like a paltry gift to give her when she'd wanted so much more.

"I know you." Tony gave him a rueful smile. "You don't care about the election or her votes. If you're spending time with her, it's because you like her. The last thing I need is a scandal, Nick."

It was a fair assessment of his character, which was why it hurt. "I do care about the election." It didn't sound true, any more than his words to Mrs. Sparks earlier. "You're my brother. Of course I care."

Tony sighed. "Thanks." He sounded about as convinced as Nick had been convincing. "I just—I need to win this election, Nick. If I don't—" He stopped, as if even finishing the sentence would be painful.

"If you don't, you'll run in the next one, or Mother will find you a pocket borough." He was trying to be reassuring, but Tony gave him a vicious glare.

"You don't understand. I've been getting by in all this political stuff by the skin of my teeth. If I can't pull this off, everyone will see—"

He broke off again, but Nick thought he understood. If Tony failed, everyone would see he was a failure.

"You can't let everything have so much symbolic weight. If you lose the election, it will mean that Dromgoole got a few more votes. That's *all* it will mean. Men who've been Whig leaders for decades lose elections all the time, and a place is found for them in another district."

Tony shook his head. "Nick, I know you're older and wiser than I am, and have seen more of the world. And if I want advice about"—here his attempt at tact ran out, because he said—"sleeping in the rain or eating raw wheat or being shot, I'll ask you. But you don't understand. You don't know what it's like to try your damnedest and never be good enough."

"Tony, of course I do. Why do you think—?"

But Tony barreled on, "You told Mama plainly enough that she couldn't rely on you, and she doesn't. But she's counting on *me* to win this election. And I can't do it."

Nick opened his mouth, but despite all the words swirling inside him, nothing emerged. Tony was right. Nick had maneuvered very carefully so that he would never be in the situation Tony was in. By the time Tony was six and Nick was nine, Tony had been charming voters with his antics and Nick had been standing vaguely by the wall thinking about something else and not doing anything that could call his mother's attention onto himself, because he couldn't stand the constant weight of expectations and criticism.

"She'll be proud of you whether you win or lose," he said finally. "This is your first election. It's just target practice. If she were really so determined to win, she'd be here instead of canvassing the county for Stephen."

He could tell at once it had been the wrong thing to say. "Maybe *you* haven't noticed that I grew up while you were in Spain," Tony said tightly. "But Mama has. She isn't here because this is a small borough and she trusts me to take care of it for her on my own."

This was why Nick had given up on making his family happy. There was no pleasing them. "Mother doesn't trust anyone to take care of anything on his own!"

Tony's face turned red. "You're just jealous because she doesn't trust *you.*"

It was infuriating, how she had the whole family snookered. "Claiming to trust people is just her way of keeping a hold on them. Look at you, tying yourself in knots trying to please her. I'm glad I'm well out of it."

Tony sneered. "Well out of it? You're here, aren't you? Sent to be nursemaided by your little brother because left to yourself you can't even be arsed to get out of bed in the morning!"

Everything stopped. Was that how Tony saw their time together? Was that how Tony saw *him*?

Nick had no idea what his face looked like, but it must have been bad because Tony covered his mouth with his hand, stricken. "Nick, I didn't mean that. I was angry. Of course you were convalescing. You're a hero, I know that, and I've been glad of your company. Your *support.* I'm a rat, a rat who's *very sorry*—"

"No," Nick said with difficulty. The last time anything had hurt this much, he'd had a bullet in his leg. He felt as if he were coming apart and re-forming, but he wasn't. He'd been this way all along. "You're right. I'm no hero."

"Don't." Tony's fingers splayed across his eyes. "Don't try to make me feel better. This campaign was supposed to teach me how to be a statesman, but mostly I'm learning that I'm a snake."

As always, Nick's stream of words dried up when it mattered. And he saw now that it wasn't because he was a man of action. It was because while he did generally know the right thing to say—sometimes it was even true—that wasn't enough. It had to be felt in order to sound convincing. His mother and Tony were good at that because in the moment, they felt it.

Nick was good at it too, when it didn't matter to him. But now all at once it was as if he were watching Tony from a distance, as if Tony were a stranger and not a brother whom he loved.

Mrs. Sparks had been right. Yes, he wanted her. Yes, he'd dreamed of touching her breasts. But he hadn't said those things because they were true. He'd said them to please her.

"I'm going to bed," Tony said at last. "I'll be less of a beast in the morning."

Nick summoned up a smile. "It's a little brother's duty to be a beast. Don't worry about it." He could hear the weariness in his voice. He had to offer something more. "I'll stay away from Mrs. Sparks for a few days."

"Thanks, Nick." Tony smiled gratefully back, clapped him on the shoulder, and headed off to his own room, leaving Nick's thoughts still in a whirl.

Nick had thought his family was glib, while he had a knack for getting along with people. He'd thought they were manipulative, while he was agreeable and easygoing. But all along he'd been just like them, presenting what he thought people wanted. The problem wasn't that it was true, or that it was false; it was that it had a life of its own, independent of his own impulses. It made his own desires irrelevant, hid them away so safely he sometimes couldn't find them himself.

Was this why army life had suited him so well? Not because he was a man of action at all? Getting along with his fellow officers, charming his men into loyalty, and ignoring his own desires: those were his talents. He was good at forgetting that he was hungry, forgetting that he was cold and wet. He was good at forgetting that he was lonely or sad or afraid.

He'd always focused on his partner in bed because he was afraid to focus on himself. Why? Was he afraid that if he didn't satisfy, she wouldn't want him anymore? Was he afraid that if he really wanted her, if he really let himself feel how much he wanted her, he would feel how much it hurt when he lost her?

Nick felt that he ought to lie awake for hours, tossing and turning and thinking over his new insights, but instead he fell asleep with the ease of an old campaigner.

Phoebe would have liked to toss and turn, but she didn't want to wake Helen. She'd got used to sleeping alone, and now she missed it. Helen might help keep her warm, but she also stole the blankets, put her feet precisely where Phoebe wanted to put her own, and made Phoebe self-conscious about every movement or tiny cough.

What if it were Mr. Dymond in the bed with her?

At once she was suffused by heat. She tried to push the top blanket off without shifting the mattress, but the sudden cool only made her feel exposed, reminded her of chill air on her naked breasts. If Mr. Dymond were in bed with her, he could curve against her back, lift up her nightdress, and enter her from behind, easy as anything.

She'd never sleep at this rate. She slid back the covers and swung herself out of bed as quietly as she could. It was cold, and she couldn't remember where she'd put her flannel night-rail, but she padded into the next room, shut the door behind her, and curled up in Will's armchair with a blanket over her.

Even the smooth, chilly wood against her backside felt intimate and erotic, the carved saddle seat cupping her like a caress. She held her own breasts, remembering how hot and large his hands had felt. Her thighs parted of their own volition. She squeezed her eyes shut and pinched her nipples hard, imagining Mr. Dymond, shirtless, pushing her legs apart and undoing his trousers. She pictured the play of muscles in his arms and shoulders, sliding one hand down to her—

The door to the bedroom opened, candlelight spilling across the floor. Phoebe hastily dropped her hands and tried to look as though she had been lost in pensive thought.

"Fee? Are you all right?"

"I'm fine," Phoebe said cheerily. "I just couldn't sleep."

"All right, now I *know* something's wrong," Helen said severely. *She* had known exactly where her wrapper was. Its flannel ruffle danced an orderly minuet around her neck and down her front. "If it wasn't, you would have snapped at me for asking."

Phoebe sighed. "I'm just worried about Jack. And it's been a long time since I put a newspaper together. I can't rely on Mr. Dymond to help me all week." Or ever again. How had she made such a hash of things?

Helen came over and held the candle near Phoebe's face,

looking at her with a suspicious expression. "Mr. Dymond's been helping you a lot."

Phoebe's heart raced. She shrugged. "He's a kind man, and besides, he's bored in Lively St. Lemeston. Don't be so uncharitable." Ugh, she sounded like their mother. "I mean—"

Helen pressed her lips together. "You've been keeping your promise to me, haven't you?"

"What promise?"

Her sister's lips parted in breathless outrage. "You promised me you wouldn't let him kiss you again," she said in awful tones. In the midst of everything else that had happened that week, Phoebe had completely forgotten. Her stricken expression was plainly visible to Helen, who drew herself up like an avenging angel. "Fee!"

"I didn't—" Phoebe cleared her throat. "He didn't kiss me."

"Then why are you looking so guilty?"

Even the shame pooling in the pit of her stomach curled lower, caressing her secret places. It wasn't fair, that women be formed to want this so badly, and then be so heavily punished for it. "We did…other things," she admitted almost inaudibly.

Her sister's eyes flew wide. "Without kissing?"

Phoebe covered her face with one hand. "I'm sorry, Ships. I should have remembered my promise. But I wanted him so badly, and I thought—oh God, everything's gone so wrong." She pinched the bridge of her nose until it hurt to keep from crying.

Helen pulled a chair up beside her and sat. "What's gone wrong, sweetheart? What did he do to you?"

Phoebe turned her head to look at her sister. "You told me he didn't force you. Did you lie to me?"

Helen shook her head vigorously. "But men don't always

have to force women, do they? I wanted to please him, and I thought—I thought it would feel good. It felt good when he kissed me, but—"

Phoebe clenched her teeth together to keep from shouting, throwing something—doing *something*, not to feel as angry as she did. "It does feel good, Ships," she said. "It feels splendid. It hurts the first time, but he should have been gentle with you. He should have taken care of you." *He should have kept his filthy hands to himself.*

"Was *Will* gentle?"

In spite of everything Phoebe giggled at the skepticism in her sister's voice. 'Gentle' wasn't the first word most people would have chosen to describe Will. But... "Will thought he was going to break me in half. He was afraid his—his member was too big."

Helen blinked. "Was it?"

Phoebe rolled her eyes. "Of course not. Will worried about everything, you know that. He didn't even want to stay inside me that first time after I said it hurt." He had been so gentle and slow, and taken so long as a result, that it really had become uncomfortable and he had had to pull out and finish himself off with his hand. But she had felt like a goddess anyway. Walking home, the soreness between her legs had been a promise that her life was changing.

Helen looked away. "He didn't stay inside me either. He... he..."

"You can tell me, Ships," Phoebe said softly. "You can tell me anything."

Helen ran the ends of her braids through her fingers, testing that they were the same length. "He said he was being careful and I had nothing to worry about. I don't know how he got me with child. It shouldn't have happened. I thought he pulled out before he—you know."

"Before he spent."

"He cleaned his—he cleaned me off with his handkerchief," she whispered. "But he didn't get it all and I could feel it drying on my skin all the way home. And then Mama was about and I couldn't wash. I knew it was the least of my problems but I was so unhappy."

Every word she said made Phoebe angrier. A little spunk wouldn't have bothered her, but anyone who knew Helen ought to have known that would be torture for her. "I promise it isn't always like that. There's a reason women want it. One day you'll find a man who makes you want to dance down the middle of the road."

"Down the middle of the road? Fee, that's dangerous!" Helen said with mock horror. She sniffed and giggled a little, and Phoebe felt as if her heart would break with affection. "Does Mr. Dymond make you want to dance down the middle of the road?"

Phoebe blinked, startled. Right now, Mr. Dymond mostly made her want to slink into a hole and hide. But if Helen had asked her this morning? "I don't know. I thought I just wanted to—to bed him. I thought I was lusting after his refined good looks and thrillingly patrician accent. Like daydreaming about Lord Byron."

"But you weren't?"

"I couldn't have been, could I? He touched me a great deal this afternoon, and I wasn't satisfied."

"You weren't?"

Phoebe blushed. "He was going to—well—I may have shouted at him for not being eager enough."

"What? Oh, Fee."

"He made me feel pushy!"

"You *are* pushy."

"I know, but—I wanted him to push back. I wanted him to want me as much as I wanted him."

"Men don't bed women out of charity, generally," Helen said with an air of superiority that was entirely unjustified.

"I know that, but you weren't there. You didn't hear him, he sounded so practiced and kind and as if—as if he were only trying to please me."

"And that's bad?"

"No…yes! I don't know. It wasn't really him. He hasn't always been like that with me. Sometimes he's talked to me, been honest with me. I wanted *that*. I know it was selfish, but I thought, just for a week—" Her voice was going to wobble. She pressed her lips shut.

Helen put a hand on her arm. "Don't get married next week. You don't have to. I'll go away on my own. I'll pretend to be a widow and work in a dress shop. Or—Tom Tuff would marry me, he's been after me for years."

Could they do it? Go to another town, start again, raise Helen's child together? Women did it all the time, certainly— but women were also ruined all the time when their stories were found to be false. Phoebe didn't want to live in fear for the rest of her life. She didn't want the threat of exposure hanging over Helen's child. She wanted this over and done with.

"You're not going to marry Tom Tuff," she said. "And you're not going anywhere. It's time I married again anyway. I'd like to be married again."

"I never thought I'd hear you say that."

"I never thought I'd say it."

"You want to marry him, don't you? Mr. Dymond."

"Of course not. I barely know him." On the other hand, she knew him better than she knew Mr. Moon or Mr. Fairclough. She tried to imagine being married to him—cooking him dinner, darning his socks and washing his shirts, sharing private jokes and annoying all their friends with how they couldn't keep their hands off each other. Going to sleep with a strong arm wrapped around her.

Of course, men like him had servants to cook them dinner and darn their socks. Probably his wife would have her own room and her own bed. And what friends could they have in common? "He can't marry me. You know that. He's from a different world."

"He could marry you if he wanted," Helen said stubbornly. "If he doesn't want to, he shouldn't be—doing whatever it is you did."

Phoebe put up her chin. "We are adults, we are being discreet, and I know ways to keep myself from getting with child. He wasn't taking advantage of me."

Helen snickered. "No, it sounds as if the shoe was on the other foot. Poor man."

Phoebe shoved her.

"Fee?"

"Yes?"

"What if I can't give up the baby?" Helen said quietly. "What if I see it, and I can't give it away?"

Suddenly Phoebe wanted nothing but to go back to bed and never get out. "Do you think that will happen?"

"I don't know."

This nightmare was never going to end. Phoebe tried to think. Could they raise the child together, saying it was a cousin's? Could they convince anyone it was Phoebe's own, and if they did, would Helen feel that Phoebe had stolen her child? Would Mr. Moon or Mr. Fairclough be willing to have a bastard in his home?

"If it does, I'll think of something. I promise." She ought to promise not to see Mr. Dymond again, too. But she didn't.

Chapter 20

Mr. Dymond didn't come to the printing office the next day. So that was probably that.

She didn't want to believe it. For the entire eleven hours that she worked on the paper, she listened for his uneven step and the rap of his cane on the sidewalk, no matter how hard she tried not to. Once she thought she heard it, but it was old Mrs. Briggs wanting to advertise for a lost watch.

The only good news she heard all day was that Mr. Jessop had hired Jeffrey back again. Maybe he was taking Mr. Dymond's advice.

"I like these," she told Mr. Moon late that evening, sucking on a coffee-cream bonbon. "May I have another?"

He grinned and held out the bowl. "Have as many as you like."

Across the kitchen, Peter was chattering quietly to Betsy as he washed the day's dishes. "Oh, stop your clapper about Shakespeare already," Betsy said. "You'd think you were the first person ever to read him." Phoebe was aware that her own smile was more for Peter than it was for Mr. Moon. She took another bonbon and set it on the counter by her.

"Only one?"

"Enough is as good as a feast." She grimaced. "I can't believe I just said that."

Moon looked inquiring.

"It's what my mother always used to say to me at dinner. Only for her, 'enough' was when I was still hungry."

Mr. Moon's eyes widened in horror. "She didn't feed you enough?"

She flushed. "She wanted me to be thinner."

Mr. Moon's eyes traveled over her body reverently. "A figure like that is the best advertisement for a sweet shop there is." Phoebe tried to feel warm with something other than embarrassment.

"What book did you bring today?" Peter called.

"*Histories or tales of past times, told by Mother Goose, with morals,*" Phoebe said. "Only the morals aren't always what you'd expect. It's rather an old book. Well, the *book* isn't that old, because it's a reprint. But the tales are, and they're based on even older ones, like the folk tales we have here in Sussex."

Mr. Moon frowned as he kneaded the last ball of dough. "Mother Goose is for children, isn't it? I know I'm not much for reading, but—"

"I like stories for children," Phoebe said, trying to sound cheerful and not defensive. "It's what I write, after all. I don't think it's always necessary to put away childish things. Simplicity is not the same as shallowness." That had definitely sounded defensive. Putting away childish things was another of Mrs. Knight's favorite aphorisms.

He nodded, laying a towel over his lumps of dough.

"What are you making?"

He gave her a small smile, his brown eyes sparkling. "You'll see in a couple of days."

"I can't wait." But it wasn't true. She realized as she said it that she didn't care a straw if she never knew. Mr. Moon was a very nice young man, but if she never saw him or his confectionery again, the thing she'd miss most would be Peter. She couldn't do this. She couldn't. She ought to tell him so, right now.

Better be sure of Mr. Fairclough first.

Phoebe wished she were a better person. Even more, she wished she were rich and could make all her problems go away. And more than all of that, she wished she could talk to Mr. Dymond.

She opened her book and began, "There was a miller who left no more estate to the three sons he had than his mill, his ass, and his cat…"

Phoebe waited for Mr. Fairclough to come and take her for a drive before church. Today she would tell him she would marry him, and that she wanted to meet his daughter.

Her stomach growled with mingled nerves and hunger. She hadn't eaten breakfast, ostensibly because there was work to be done at the printing office before meeting Mr. Fairclough. The real reason was that when she was anxious, all her bad girlhood habits came back. She took a deep breath to calm her nerves. It didn't work, so she took a deeper one. Her breasts looked like a fat Rowlandson caricature in the mirror as they heaved up and down. She tried to remind herself that that was a good thing when trying to charm a man.

She should have worn the green. Of course, he'd seen the green three or four times already, and he hadn't seen the lavender. But with her gray pelisse, she felt like a blob of the hideous shade you got when you mixed too many watercolors together. Perhaps she should wear her new Turkish shawl. Or would it clash?

Footsteps sounded on the stairs. That was odd; she hadn't heard horses stop. She opened the door, putting a coquettish smile on her face—and saw Mr. Gilchrist.

It was the first time she'd ever seen him at a loss. "Mrs. Sparks," he said, and stopped. His bow was too low.

Her heart hammered in her chest. "What is it?"

"I hate to be the bearer of bad news." He paused. "I abhor it, honestly. May we sit?"

She nodded, instinctively taking Will's armchair for reassurance. "Where is Mr. Fairclough?"

Mr. Gilchrist wrung his hands. Subtly, but it was a definite wring. "Mr. Fairclough isn't coming."

"Yes, but why not?"

He pressed his lips together unhappily. "He's withdrawing his suit."

Phoebe's heart plummeted into her boots. She couldn't even bring herself to ask why. All too many answers suggested themselves, none of them flattering.

"Mrs. Sparks, I hope you won't take offense at what I'm about to say. And you may rely absolutely on my discretion."

She doubted that. Mr. Gilchrist struck her as a born gossip. "Please," she said dully.

He looked about and lowered his voice. "Someone has told Mr. Fairclough that you're engaging in a clandestine *affaire*"— he said the word with a little French flair, probably to make it more discreet—"with Nicholas Dymond."

It wasn't what she'd expected. "I—but I haven't—" Guilt swamped her. Helen had been right. She'd selfishly risked too much and this was her punishment. "Is this—is this a common rumor? Is everyone saying—" She swallowed hard.

"No, actually. Your reputation is sterling; the worst anyone's said is that you should stop making calf's eyes at him before you give him false expectations. Believe me, I'd know if there were more. It sounded to me as if someone from the Whig camp spoke to Mr. Fairclough on purpose to put him off the match, and so I told him. He replied—" Mr. Gilchrist blushed. For all his show of worldliness, real cynicism seemed to elude him.

Evidently Mr. Fairclough had been insulting. Phoebe didn't blame him. He had his daughter to think of. But who would have done such a thing?

But what if you say no, and he's angry? Helen had asked. *He could tell everyone you kissed him.*

Nick wanted his brother to win the election. He wanted her vote. Could he have—?

Mr. Gilchrist cleared his throat delicately. "Is there any chance Mr. Dymond himself might have—"

"No," Phoebe snapped. "He is a gentleman."

Mr. Gilchrist raised his eyebrows. "I know more gentlemen than you do, Mrs. Sparks. Take my word for it, most of them are cads."

She drew herself up. "For all I know, you made this whole story up to put me off the Whigs yourself, sir."

"But I didn't," he said reasonably. "Now, I know this is a serious setback, but give me half a day or so and I'm sure I can find someone you'll like just as well—"

She leaned back against Will's chair. "I have to go," she said tiredly. "Thank you for coming to see me. And thank you for your discretion."

"As the grave," Mr. Gilchrist said. "Silent, I mean. Are graves discreet? I don't imagine much of note happens in their purview. But really, Mrs. Sparks—"

She rose from the armchair. "I have a paper to put out. If you need to talk to me again, I'll be at the printing office."

"If you wish me to escort you and your sister to church, I would be honored," he offered. It was generous, offering them the public backing of the Tory establishment. Unable to bring herself to snub him, she agreed, resigning herself to a morning of fashion talk. She had planned to avoid church—and Mr. Dymond—altogether.

As it turned out, Mr. Dymond wasn't in church. She wished she were more relieved and less disappointed.

After his exertions with Mrs. Sparks, followed by two days of hiding in his room and sitting still, Nick's leg hurt with a constant, distracting pain, like someone standing there screaming in his ear while he tried to go about his business.

Toogood set a folding table covered in breakfast on the floor beside Nick's bed. "Will you be going out today, sir?"

Nick's face heated with shame. Toogood hadn't said a word about his master's sudden relapse into hibernation, but then, he hadn't said a word about it in London, either. The valet had to know it wasn't normal.

But if he went out, he might run into Mrs. Sparks.

He wanted to see her, though. It had taken a strong effort of will not to go to church the day before.

The smell of fresh-baked rolls and fresh-churned butter wafting from his breakfast tray was a mere reminder of a duty: *I must eat if I don't wish to feel weak and sick later.* The image of Mrs. Sparks smiling at him as he walked through the door of the printing office, on the other hand, was irresistible.

She might not smile this time, of course. She might frown. He wanted to see that too, desperately.

He wanted to listen to himself, for once.

He looked at the rolls and thought, *If I leave without eating, I could see her a quarter of an hour sooner.*

"Would you like a robe? It's a chilly morning."

Until Toogood said it, he hadn't realized he was cold. Other people noticed when they were cold, he felt sure. He couldn't even blame it on the privations in Spain; he remembered being scolded by his tutors as a boy for omitting meals, going out without his coat, and reading with so little light he was sure to strain his eyes.

"I'd like to get dressed, actually," he said. "I'll stop in at the Honey Moon for breakfast. Have the rolls if you like, or return them to the kitchen."

"Thank you, sir." Toogood coughed. "Sir, if you will be returning to the printing office, I took the liberty of borrowing some older clothes from Mr. Anthony. Your wardrobe is not yet extensive enough to survive repeated ink stains."

It didn't sound like a reproach, but Nick felt the urge to apologize anyway. "Good idea. Thank you, Toogood."

Tony's clothes fit pretty well, which shouldn't have startled him, but did. In his mind, he still topped his brother by half a head.

The blonde shopgirl appeared when the doorbell tinkled. "I'll let Mr. Moon know you're here, sir." She bobbed a curtsey and ducked back into the kitchen.

Nick took his time walking to the counter, going easy on his leg. There was no one to see him. The Honey Moon smelled wonderful. Surely something here would make him feel enthusiastic about breakfast.

"Mr. Dymond, what a pleasant surprise! What can I do for you?" The pastry cook popped through the door like a jack-in-the-box, looking as nervous and eager as ever.

Nick's appetite faded. "I just dropped in to break my fast."

Moon couldn't seem to decide whether or not to be pleased about this. "Of course, sir. What do you fancy?"

"I don't know," Nick said, feeling as if he were confessing a deep, dark secret.

"I've a pound cake just out of the oven. Then there's one left of my currant kickels, a fresh lemon-glazed lavender cake like the one you had before, candied-orange-and-cinnamon turnovers—"

It wasn't panic, but it was a feeling like panic, a sort of blankness behind his eyes. His thoughts slipped away, and he found himself trying to reason out the correct choice. *If the pound cake is fresh from the oven, it must be the best* and *Perhaps he'd like to get rid of that last kickel, whatever that is,* and none of it to do with what he *wanted.*

Moon's forehead creased. "Is something amiss, sir?"

"I—do you know what the most delicious thing I ever ate was?"

Moon shook his head, eyes widening as if he thought maybe he ought to know.

"I was in camp with my regiment. A friend of mine had

brought us all some provisions from Lisbon. In my share, besides the usual sugar, anchovies, ham, and bad coffee, he had included—miracle of miracles—a sausage. But it had taken him two weeks to get back, and the sausage spoiled."

"Dreadful," Mr. Moon said on cue, but mostly he just looked confused.

Nick knew he should stop telling the story. "We had had almost no food for a week, but the sausage stank, and furry green mold was growing on its skin. I couldn't possibly eat it, so I threw it in the fire. I was sitting there, trying to write a letter, when a fellow officer walked by and asked what on earth that delicious smell was. When I told him, he drew his saber and plucked the sausage from the fire. Once he had, it smelled so fine none of us could wait, and we all burned our tongues."

Mr. Moon's mouth worked with ill-concealed disgust. "That was the bettermost thing that ever you ate?"

Nick nodded. He could still taste it, that hot burst of salt and grease and flavor after weeks of hard biscuits and empty stomachs. Soaked to the skin and less than a mile from the French lines, they had laughed, feeling warm and safe and happy.

"My parents' chef was a genius. I grew up on delicacies. But sometimes I still find myself longing for that sausage. And I have no idea what I want for breakfast."

Moon blinked, and Nick felt even less sane, and more guilty. This was the last man on earth he should be burdening with his troubles. Three days ago, he'd very nearly tupped the woman Moon hoped to marry. "I'm sorry. I'll have the pound cake."

Moon nodded, looking relieved, and went through the swinging door into the kitchen. He returned with a generous slice of cake and a dollop of blackberry jam on a plate and a steaming cup of chocolate. "That'll be a shilling and sixpence."

Nick paid him and took up the plate in his free hand. "I'll be back for the chocolate in a moment." He wished he could stop feeling embarrassed about his disability. He wished his leg would stop hurting so badly.

Instead of agreeing, Moon took up the cup and followed him to a table. He pulled out Nick's chair for him. "May I sit, sir?"

"Of course."

Moon tripped over his own chair getting into it. "Food feeds the soul," he said.

"What?"

"Folk think hunger's a thing of the body. But food is also nourishment for the spirit. 'Man does not live by bread alone.'"

"I don't think Our Lord meant he ought to have cake too," Nick said bemusedly. He hadn't expected metaphysical speculation from Moon.

Moon shook his head. "He didn't just ask us to remember Him with our hearts. He gave us bread and wine. When we take Communion and taste that food, we feel His love for us."

Nick had never felt much at Communion besides the dryness of the wafer and the poor quality of the wine.

"My pa was a baker," Moon said. "My ma worked in the bakery sunup to sundown, but she always found time to bake a cake for our dinner. Sugar's extra, don't you see. A mother makes a cake to give a child joy, not to keep him alive. When I eat sweet things, I feel as safe and comforted as when I was a boy." Moon laughed shyly. "Sorry, sir, I didn't mean to knabble on."

Nick took a bite of his pound cake. It was delicious. The

taste was perfect, the texture rich and dense without being heavy. Yet it didn't make him feel safe or comforted.

But in the end, he wasn't upset about breakfast. He was upset about Mrs. Sparks. "You're right. My problem isn't just about food. It's about everything."

"Sounds as if you were happy over the water," Mr. Moon said. "I'd not like to be a soldier myself, but I'm that sorry you had to give it up."

Moon was being kind to him. Nick felt awful. On top of everything else, he had grossly underestimated the man, assuming because he was poor and awkward that he was simple and stupid. He'd been a snob. Moon was the absolute last person he deserved kindness from.

Moon leaned forward, obviously trying to look casual. "So has Mrs. Sparks said anything to you about her intentions?"

Nick felt even worse. Moon had no choice but to be kind to him. Moon needed his help. He shook his head. "Pardon me for asking, but how much are your debts?"

Moon dropped his eyes to the table. "Fifty-seven pounds."

It was nothing to Nick's family, but to Mr. Moon, it could mean ruin. "Don't despair. I think she likes you." He said it because it was the right thing to say, the thing that would smooth the situation over. He didn't say it without thinking, precisely—but his thoughts seemed to run on a parallel track to his heart, his body. He knew Mrs. Sparks didn't like Mr. Moon. It was disgusting to pander for the two of them. It was awful to talk as if that was all she meant to him when, in his heart of hearts, he still hoped to bed her himself.

Moon didn't look much happier than he felt. "Do you?"

"Even if she doesn't, I'm sure we can help you with at least a part of that amount. You won't lose the shop." Nick privately resolved that if he still had a reliable income when this was all over, he'd pay Moon's debts himself.

"Aren't you going to eat the rest of your cake?"

"Can you wrap it up?" Nick asked. "I'm not hungry at the moment, but I couldn't bear to leave it here. It's wonderful."

The relief that washed over Mrs. Sparks's face when he walked in the door eased the knot in his stomach a little. "Good morning, Mr. Dymond," she said with an attempt at casual cheer. "Thank you for coming back to help us." She glanced nervously at Owen. It was very clear she'd never carried on an illicit affair before.

"Good morning, Mrs. Sparks, Owen." Nick bowed. "May I offer my assistance again? I've a couple of handbills my brother wants printed—two hundred copies each. Will you have time to run them?"

"By all means, sir," Owen said happily. He looked over Tony's drafts, asked a few questions, and went at once to work.

"I brought food today." There was a hesitant, hopeful note in Mrs. Sparks's voice. "There's ham and rolls and boiled eggs, and jam and mustard. Not that you'd want jam with mustard. Oh, and Miss Starling brought me some blackberries and fresh clotted cream so she'd have an excuse to ask about Jack and Miss Jessop, and I brought it with me." She blew a falling curl out of her dark eyes and watched his face to see if any of that tempted him.

It should have made him feel anxious. It did, a little. But in spite of all of that, she shifted in her chair, her legs moving below the table in some way he couldn't see, and Nick was suddenly roaringly hungry. He wanted jam and clotted cream. He wanted to lick jam and clotted cream off her breasts and stomach. He wanted to lick her. He rapidly recited a few stanzas of Pope—not "Eloisa to Abelard" but some of the dry, intellectual stuff—to stem the flow of blood to his cock. "That sounds wonderful."

Chapter 21

Nick gave Owen his pound cake and brought a feast back from the kitchen with him—a roll slathered in mustard and a slice of ham, and berries and cream and another roll with jam. When he sat down across from Mrs. Sparks, he could see by the purple stains on her mouth that she'd eaten some berries already.

He put a spoonful of berries and cream in his mouth and watched her reading the *Times*. The taste was obscenely sensual, the berries' skin breaking open against his tongue and spilling tart sweet juice, the cool cream sliding down his throat.

She was a fidgeter; he'd noticed it before. She leaned her chin on her fist as she read, which led to leaning her mouth on her fist, which led to biting her knuckles, which led to tugging on her lower lip, which led to—her heart-shaped face flushed crimson when she caught him watching her. Nick's senses sharpened even further. He had to have her. It didn't matter what he had to do, how he had to lay himself open, he had to have her.

"I was thinking," she said. "Would you be willing to write something for the *Intelligencer* about Badajoz? Or if you have some letters from friends, or something of that sort—people love to get war news that isn't dry official dispatches, or a reprinting of the London papers' reprinting of the Portuguese papers."

He didn't want to. "Badajoz isn't news anymore."

"This is Lively St. Lemeston, not London." She smiled at him. One of her front teeth was stained a light purple. Her left canine turned slightly to the side, making it look pointier than the others. Why was that suddenly erotic? "We define 'news' broadly. Besides, everyone is interested in you."

It was a small enough thing, he supposed. And if it helped sell papers, and renewed interest in the Dymonds, maybe it would strengthen Tony's position in the town. "I'll try," he said. "But it might be rubbish."

She smiled again, that pointy tooth catching at her lip. "If it's rubbish, we won't print it, that's all." She pushed a pen and some discarded correspondence across the table at him, and moved her inkwell to the center of the table. "You can write on the back of that."

He was so far gone that dipping his pen in her inkwell seemed scandalous. He made himself stop glancing up at how she leaned on the table and focus on the paper before him.

Twenty minutes later he was still staring at it. Anything that he wrote about Badajoz would only result in more people telling him he was a hero and then asking about his leg.

When civilians thought of war, they thought of battles. But war was more than that. It was long marches and laughter and empty stomachs and pretty Spanish girls and cards around the campfire. It was knowing that the man beside you was ready to give his life for England, and for you. As an officer, it was fighting to keep your men's spirits up, telling them you were grateful for their efforts when they felt forgotten by God—and by an England that wouldn't even send them decent shoes.

He remembered his speech to Mr. Jessop about the pro-war government, and how good it had felt to speak his mind.

He wasn't a politician. He wasn't a soldier anymore, obliged to publicly support the conduct of the war. He was, at this moment, a journalist, and his only responsibility was to the truth. His truth. He could say whatever he liked.

At that thought—*anything you like*—the pressure and panic rushed back, the fear that choosing for himself meant choosing wrong. Everyone in town would read these words. His family would read them.

And there was Tony to think of. What if this article damaged his little brother's campaign? Perhaps he should write a stirring account of Badajoz after all. He could do that in his sleep, and it would sell papers just as well.

But it was all one: the food and the article, the way he couldn't make Mrs. Sparks believe he wanted her and the way he couldn't manage to speak when Tony tried to talk to him.

He hadn't written Tony a word from Spain. When Tony had asked him point-blank about the war, had *tried* to be a brother to him, Nick hadn't had a thing to say. Tony deserved honesty.

You faced down the French guns, he told himself. *You can face down this.* And painstakingly, slowly, he began pulling words out of the quicksand in his mind and setting them safely down on paper.

Mr. Dymond hadn't spoken for hours. He simply wrote, slowly and carefully, his eyebrows a dark thoughtful line. He looked so straightforward, that open face and aristocratic, athletic body, and he was such a mystery. Of course another person's heart was always a mystery, but his very openness shut her out somehow, said, *You can have all this, don't ask for more.* She was wild to know what he was writing. Only the knowledge that he'd show it to her, and her own hatred of being interrupted when she was writing, kept her silent and focused on her work.

"I've got your handbills run off, sir," Owen said.

Mr. Dymond started.

"But let me know early tomorrow if you'll need more copies, as we'll want to reuse the type for the *Intelligencer.*"

"I'll do that, thank you." He turned to Phoebe. "What are those?"

She glanced up from the pile of letters she was sorting as if she hadn't been sitting there waiting for him to speak to her, painfully attuned to the sound of his voice. "Local contributions to the paper." She broke into a nervous babble. "Why *will* people send in this rubbish? Listen to this. 'On Saturday the 31st of October, Tommy McLaren, eleven years of age, of Slaugham, and deaf since the fever last spring, saw an adder transform into *him* and then back.' That poor child, as if he doesn't have enough new problems without people trying to make it out he has an affinity with adders! How does anyone even know that adders are deaf? Have they asked one?"

"*Him?*" He smiled at her elision.

She flushed, knowing it was common and uneducated to call the devil by that emphatic pronoun. She dropped another letter on the discard pile. "If we published every time someone's grandmother had the ague, the paper would be fifty pages."

Owen finished his cleaning and saw himself out with no more than a curious glance at the two of them. Her run of words dried up. Mr. Dymond took a deep breath. "Mrs. Sparks—"

"Thank you for coming back today," she blurted out. "I'm sorry about the other day. It was ridiculous and unkind to snap at you. You must do this sort of thing all the time, but I—I was nervous, I suppose. Of course a man like you needn't have bothered with a woman like me if you didn't want to."

"Don't. Don't disparage yourself for my benefit."

"But—"

"You were right. What you said was right."

There was complete silence in the room. Outside, a crow cawed, sharp and startling. "You mean," she said. "You mean you were only pretending."

"No!" His blue eyes glinted with a kind of desperation, as if he were chasing after words and couldn't catch them. It touched and confused her. For all her lacks, Phoebe had always been able to find words. "I wasn't. I wasn't at all. But I have before, more or less. And I don't think it would look much different from the outside. I wanted you. I wanted things to go well between us. I wanted things to go *smoothly*, so I wouldn't have to—" He broke off in frustration.

"So you wouldn't have to ask for anything?" she suggested.

He looked as if even nodding was a struggle. "And that… fear…it…I wanted it to go smoothly because I wanted you. But it has a life of its own."

This wasn't the conversation she'd imagined. It surprised her the way only the mystery of another person's heart could do. He looked more closed off than she'd ever seen him, and she was wildly grateful for it. She felt her way carefully. "Like being at a party?" she asked. "You spend so much time trying to look as if you're enjoying yourself that you forget to actually do it."

He nodded with relief. "Precisely. Half the time I don't

even know what I want. This morning I couldn't decide on what to eat for breakfast."

She frowned. "Isn't that normal? Sometimes I can't either, especially when I know I've to go out to the grocer's if I want anything other than stale buns."

He ran a hand through his hair, a quick sure motion. "It's the having to *choose*. If all I have are stale buns, I'll eat them. But if I'm at dinner at home, and the table is full of platters and bowls and everything smells splendid and all I have to do is help myself—sometimes I barely eat at all."

He leaned back in his chair, his strong frame and confident bearing a stark contrast to the black uncertainty he said he felt. She could hardly credit it. He took a deep breath and said, "There's something wrong with me." He watched her face closely, evidently waiting for her to be shocked.

She thought about what he'd said. "Did your mother ever tell you what to eat when you were small?"

"Oh, my mother told us all how to do everything. When she was there."

"Did she ever make you feel guilty about taking the wrong thing?"

He blinked, looking amazed at her insight into such a small, simple thing. She shouldn't want to laugh; it was heartbreaking. But affection flooded her, a giddy feeling. "When I was small, we couldn't eat anything with sugar," he said. "Only honey, because sugar was slave-grown. Then we couldn't have game at dinner because game in London was all poached and the Gaming Laws were destroying the countryside. We even gave up meat for a year when I was eight. It was noble, I know that. I'm glad I didn't eat blood sugar. It was the *way* she did it. The way anything"—he slowed, as if only now seeing her point—"anything I asked for was an indelible stain on my character."

"I can't eat at home either," she told him. "My mother always thought I was eating too much. I can't eat when she's watching me. I used to get up from the table starving and sneak back into the kitchen at night. I still feel guilty when I empty my plate, even if no one can see me."

He stared at her.

"I think when wanting something doesn't help you get it, there's maybe not much point to wanting."

She was right, of course. Unlike Mr. Moon, food did not mean love to Nick. It meant the family dinner table: anxiety and squabbling and a close scrutiny of his every move. Food had become separated from hunger. It had been, like everything else, something you did for effect.

He saw that the rest of it functioned on a similar principle. There had never been a point to asking for what he wanted; after a while, there had been no point to wanting at all. It should have felt freeing to finally see that. In a way it was, but he hated it too. He didn't want to do the hard work of sorting it all out, any more than he wanted to live with this damn pain in his leg. He wanted to be done with it.

She traced a design on the tabletop. "So you're afraid that if you ask me for what you want, I won't like what I hear. And I'm afraid that if I ask for what I want, I'm selfish and unwomanly."

He had to laugh. "The spirits of the wise sit in the clouds and mock us."

"They do indeed." She laughed a little too, stray locks of

dark hair shaking as they fell across her face. All at once he felt light-headed. Honesty was difficult, but this was his reward. His heart was in his throat, but he had faced down French guns. He could do this.

He leaned in. It was hard not to put on a seductive mask, not to let his voice go husky and his eyelids droop. Everybody knew how this moment was supposed to go, how he ought to sound, how a man ought to look at a woman he meant to bed. He could let momentum take over, say the words as if he were reading lines from a play that was already written. But she wanted more, and he wanted to give it to her. So he met her eyes straight on and said seriously, "I think we both want the same thing."

She swallowed. "Do we?"

He took a deep breath. "I want you. I want you very much."

There it was. No saying later he hadn't cared one way or the other. No pretending she hadn't understood him. No possible salve for his pride if this went wrong.

It was strange, but saying the words straight out like that, letting her feel the truth of them—*he* felt the truth of them. Wanting rose along his skin like the tide coming in. He held his breath, trying to keep the desire down, keep it in.

Her smile widened and widened, that one pointy tooth indenting her lower lip. Her face glowed like a bonfire on a rainy day, warming every tingling inch of his skin. He smiled back, helplessly.

"I have an idea," she said.

"You do?"

"It's—it's like a game." Her smile dimmed a little, turning uncertain again, but she forged ahead. "We'll take turns. Saying things we want. Just—little things. We can ask for anything, but we have to say it, not just do it. And either of us can always say no, and then we'll just ask for something different."

It wasn't going to be like any sex he'd ever had, but it sounded—fun. Not just arousing or wicked or bound to drive him mad—though it was all those things—but fun.

It was also going to be more difficult than any sex he'd ever had. But hell, he was ready for a challenge. He nodded.

"You have to go first this time," she warned him.

He considered for long, doubtful moments. In the end he decided on, "I want to go upstairs." He could leave it at that, but he added, "My leg hurts, and the bed will make things easier."

She beamed and stood. Strange how with her, speaking it aloud made the shame and self-consciousness less, not more. She went around to all the candles, blowing them out one by one and taking the last to light their way.

"Bring the berries and cream," he said.

Her eyes widened, but she cradled the bowls in her free arm. "Can you get the door for me?"

His leg had hurt that morning. Now it was also stiff from sitting still all day. He hobbled like an old man as he followed her to the door.

"We can wait until tomorrow if it hurts too much," she said. The obvious reluctance in her voice made him smile.

"I don't think I can wait until tomorrow."

She let out a sigh of relief. "Me neither. You just looked so miserable—"

"I'm not miserable. It does hurt today, but that isn't really the worst of it." He realized what the worst of it was, suddenly. "I used to be able to pass unnoticed. My leg makes everyone look at me. And it means—well, it means I'm not in control of what they see."

She laughed. "Try being fat and having breasts the size of footballs."

"You're not fat!"

She shrugged. "At least being fat doesn't hurt. Although these things make my shoulders and back ache some days." She waved the candle back and forth in front of her breasts. "I didn't mean to laugh at you. You're right, it's an awful feeling sometimes."

He felt the way he had talking to Miss Jessop or to Mrs. Sparks's friends—the sudden realization that he wasn't the only one. He wasn't Childe Harold with his unfathomable, solitary pain. He was just a man, with ordinary human problems that plenty of other people shared. It was lowering, maybe, but it was a relief.

He held the door open for her. "You don't mind that I like your breasts, do you?"

She threw him an incredulous, amused look as she passed him. "Did it seem like I minded on Friday?"

She'd rubbed herself against the front of his coat, face suffused with desperate, lovely desire, right here in this kitchen. His cock rose in an instant. No, it hadn't seemed like she minded.

"My leg also…" He swallowed. "It makes certain things more difficult." Like steps. He started grimly up the spiral stairs after her, watching his feet and wishing he could watch her arse instead.

She sighed. "I know. But I'm confident you can think of terribly wicked things to do, even if you can't—take me standing up." Her little hesitations and shames filled him with a curious tenderness. Neither of them were on solid ground.

Sparks had two small, orderly rooms above the shop. The

furniture was old and worn, but it matched, and there wasn't a speck of dust anywhere. "All the curtains are already drawn," he noted.

"I shut them all Saturday morning," she admitted. "In case you came back." There was a fire laid in the grate; she knelt to light it with the candle.

He wondered what else she'd planned, just in case. "It's your turn," he reminded her as she set the bowls down on the edge of the washstand.

She eyed him indecisively, her gaze dropping from his face to his chest, his hips, and down. His cock hardened further; he wondered if she could tell. What would she ask for? Her gaze ran back up his body. She chewed on her lower lip. He couldn't even imagine possibilities—his mind froze, waiting, completely empty of thought. Finally she said, "I want you to take off your coat." They were starting slow, it appeared. That was all right. Nick set his cane on the bed, pushed his coat off his shoulders and hung it from a bedpost. He shook out his crumpled sleeves, looking up at the sound of her boots on the floorboards.

"Mmm, I knew your arms would be splendid," she said in satisfaction, reaching out a hand to touch his shoulder.

He held the bedpost for balance with one hand and caught her wrist with the other, grinning. "It's my turn now." She made a moue of disappointment and waited, leaving her wrist in his grasp.

What did he want? He could have anything. This room was so homey and innocent, he found himself loath to simply be wicked. Then he remembered something he had wanted from her, the first time he'd been in this house. He let her go. "I want you to take that thing out of your neckline."

She unpinned her fichu and tugged obediently at it, baring the perfect tops of her breasts and the glorious hollow between them. Baring them for *him*. He reached out, fully expecting her to remind him that it was her turn. She didn't.

He ran his index finger down the curve of her right breast and up the curve of her left. Going back the way he had come, he dipped his finger into her neckline and tugged gently. She drew in a breath, her lips parting and her breasts rising on either side of his finger. "I want to touch your arms," she said.

He let his hand fall. She put her hands on his upper arms, squeezing and kneading through the worn linen of Tony's old shirt. She ran her fingers lightly down, humming. Nick felt each fingertip like a brand. Today, he meant to feel everything. No thinking. No ignoring his own sensations.

She took both hands and tried to circle his right arm. "I can't quite reach." She sounded almost smug, a little curl at the corner of her rosebud mouth, as if his strength had been created just for her. He didn't point out that she had small hands. Before the evening was over, she was going to touch him like this everywhere, that pleased, proprietary touch.

He was unbelievably warm. Could she feel it through his shirt? His cock pressed against the front of his breeches. It was uncomfortable, but pleasantly so, a reminder that this was real. He shifted, the buttons of his drawers scraping across sensitive skin.

"It's your turn," she said.

He hesitated. What if she laughed at him? What if she thought he was pitiful? He could always frame it as a simple favor, unrelated to their game, and she would never have to know how much he wanted it.

Damn it, he wanted to be naked with her—not just in

body, but in mind and spirit. He wanted her to see him. "I want you to take my boots off."

Her dark brows drew together in puzzlement; he felt an unexpected tenderness at the small furrow in her brow. Then she shrugged and gestured for him to sit, kneeling down on the floor in front of him. He held out one foot—the good one. It meant bracing himself with the other, and he gritted his teeth.

"Am I going to hurt you?"

"Not much. Please don't worry about it."

She took hold of his boot and pulled it off. He didn't wear them very tight, but she still hunched forward for leverage, giving him an unimpeded view down her neckline. She caught him looking and rolled her eyes, obviously thinking she'd figured out his motivations. His second boot snagged on his ankle, and she had to yank. He sucked in a breath, and her dark eyes flew to his face with concern.

Generally it was Toogood who did this for him, impassive and efficient, not flinching even if Nick made an involuntary sound of pain. Nick preferred it that way. But Mrs. Sparks set his boots to one side and ran gentle hands down his leg, and for a moment he imagined that she was his wife and she loved him, that they were so close her pity didn't sting.

She stood. "I want you to take my clothes off."

He blinked, his domestic fantasy dissipating like mist when the sun comes out. "All of them?"

Her face lit with amusement, her mouth folding in on itself with trying not to smile. Then she grinned anyway. "All of them."

He swallowed. "I can do that."

Chapter 22

S till sitting, Nick gathered her to him by her skirts and turned her around to get at her buttons. She reached down to gather up the hem, which pushed her generous arse towards him. He squeezed it.

She jumped, throwing him a minatory glance, but as she pulled her dress and then her petticoats over her head, the shape of her arse became even clearer. He tugged her towards him by her hips. "Sit here." He arranged her between his legs, that splendid backside snug against him. The curve of her neck was so near and inviting that he kissed it without conscious thought. When he leaned back to get at her laces, his erection pressed against her.

She squirmed her hips teasingly against him. For a moment, he forgot how to untie a knot—but only for a moment. He loosened her laces and she stood to pull the corset over her head. Now she was in nothing but her shift, stockings—and boots.

She laughed at the muddy incongruity and bent to untie them, facing him. Her unbound breasts dangled, swaying. He tugged loose the bow at the neck of her shift. Startled, she grabbed at his shoulder for balance. He caught her with a hand on each breast.

He thought she would scold, or at least glare, but instead

she laughed again and stayed there, pushing her breasts into his hands with the weight of her body as she toed off her boots. She was so close that the utter rightness of every line of her face, every delicate shade of color in her eyes and hair and skin, was almost too much. His heart beat wildly. He wished she were close enough to kiss, so he could shut his eyes.

He'd wanted this, though. He'd wanted it to be too much. "You're not naked yet," he reminded her.

They both instinctively held their breath as he lifted her shift slowly past her ankles and up over her calves. He snickered, and she craned her neck to see what he was looking at: the darn in her striped stocking, and the two small holes she hadn't bothered to darn yet.

She winced. "I—drat, I've no excuse."

"A careless shoestring, in whose tie / I see a wild civility," he said, quoting the Herrick poem again, "do more bewitch me than when art / is too precise in every part."

He loved the way she laughed. He loved *this*—it was strange and awkward, but at the same time it was more comfortable than he'd ever been with a woman. He'd never talked so much in bed. "That was always my favorite part of the poem," she said, "because if you say it with a Sussex accent 'civility' and 'tie' almost rhy—" She broke off as he bared her cunny to the cool air. The dark curls quivered as her muscles tightened.

Oh, she was splendid. The wide, luscious curve of her hips and the expanse of her thighs were a land of milk and honey. He raised her shift over her belly and the curves of her waist. "I am so, so glad that God created woman."

She took the fabric from his grasp, pulling it over her head and dropping it on the floor with her other things. Untying her garters without fanfare, she quickly peeled off her stockings—and then she was as naked as Eve, every last bit of her skin available for his delectation.

Even with the fire, she shivered under his gaze, her body moving in all the right places. "Your turn."

He wanted to touch her. He wanted to touch her everywhere. He wanted her pressed up against every part of him, and he wanted to feel it, close and vibrant, no barriers anywhere. "I want to be naked too," he said, quieting the little voice that said, *She'll be cold,* and *Would she rather I was clothed?* and *What if someone comes? One of you should look presentable to answer the door.*

She smiled as she undid the buttons of his waistcoat and pushed it off his shoulders. His shirt was stuck to his skin with the day's sweat. She leaned in as if to suck his nipples, clearly outlined through the linen—and snapped his braces over them. He jumped, and she snickered and did it again before pushing the braces off his shoulders.

Putting a hand flat on his chest, she shoved. He fell backwards obediently onto the quilt. Her nails dragged up his belly and chest as she pulled his shirt out of his breeches, her hands chilly against his hot skin. His stomach muscles contracted, sinking him further into the bedding, where he felt the quilted seams against the bared skin of his back.

She straddled him as he put his arms over his head, a steady pressure on his cock. He couldn't see as she pulled his shirt off, but he felt her weight shift as she braced herself on her knees. She lifted off him briefly; he pressed upwards, blindly chasing sensation. Then the shirt was off, and he looked down to see her bare cunny settling onto the flap of his breeches. Christ, that was nice. As much as he wanted to be skin-to-skin, he couldn't resist taking hold of her hips and encouraging her to rub herself against him through his clothes.

It was torture, the sensations filtering through nankeen and linen unpredictable and a little too rough, one moment a stab of unbearable pleasure and one moment just an awkward scraping. He liked it.

So did she, her breath coming in gasps and her dark eyes going darker than ever as she watched her hips move, her sensitive places dragging across the rough fabric and leaving it damp. He would let her spend first and take his time afterwards. He liked sated women, the lazy, satisfied way they moved.

Her clouded eyes met his and slid away. Then she looked back, her face almost solemn as she moved. She stayed there with him, acknowledged what they were doing. "Yes," she said. "Please—oh—" He couldn't wait to see her spend.

But she pulled away, sharply. "I was—you said—wait—" She fumbled to unbutton the flap of his breeches, because he'd said he wanted to be naked. "Let go." She climbed off the bed to pull his breeches and stockings off.

It bared his scar, a great ugly thing running half the length of his thigh. She sucked in a breath. "It's larger than I expected," she said, sounding a little awed.

"They had to make an incision to take out some of the bone."

She gave a high breathy giggle, flushing. "Oh. I meant—that is. The scar is large too."

He let his head fall back against the quilt and laughed at the low, whitewashed ceiling. "Thank you." Her hand closed around his cock. He yelped in surprise, and she let go immediately.

"Sorry," she said. "I forgot I was supposed to ask. I want to touch your—"

He discovered that her blush didn't extend past her neck and upper chest, but her upper arms flushed faintly on the outside. He was glad that he knew now. He was very, very glad.

"Yes?" he inquired innocently. "My what?"

She rolled her eyes. "Your cock, Mr. Dymond. May I touch your cock?"

He had thought he couldn't get harder. He had been wrong. "If you like," he said, attempting to sound careless but mostly sounding smug.

She didn't even try to look stern, only flicked his thigh hard with her thumb and index finger. He jumped, and she took his cock in her hand. The firm, even pressure after all the teasing had him on the edge at once. "I can stop, if you like," she said.

"I don't want you to stop." He shut his eyes and just felt, felt every slide and slip and fingertip. God. She was watching him. He didn't let himself think about what she saw. Unlike her, he wasn't brave enough to meet her eyes while she did this. "Is it still my turn, or did that count?"

"You can have two turns," she conceded.

It was probably ungentlemanly to accept. He opened his eyes. "I want you to spend while I'm inside you." It was the best feeling in the world, the way a woman's muscles rippled around a man.

Her mouth fell open. "I—um—"

"I'm close," he warned her. "If I tell you to pull off, you must listen."

She shook her head. "I know where to get herbs to bring on my courses. You don't have to worry about getting me with child."

Oh, thank God. After the last week, just being inside her might make him spend.

It was a close-run thing as she guided herself onto him. The slick heat and pressure as she sank down had him gasping and clutching at her thighs. "Touch them," she urged, arching her back to bring her breasts closer to him.

It shoved her further onto his cock. He groaned and took her breasts in his hands. Struggling to get closer, he levered himself up on one elbow, sucking her nipple into his mouth and teasing it with swift flicks of his tongue, matching the rhythm of his hips as best he could. They were naked and sweating and desperate, and touching her felt like touching himself, it made her shiver around him. She put her own hand between her legs and rubbed, her fingertips hitting his belly.

He switched breasts, rubbing his thumb over the nipple still wet from his mouth. Her hand moved faster, her movements more urgent. The wet clench of her around his cock was unbelievable. He realized he was gripping her breast tightly, and relaxed his fingers.

She gasped. "Do that again." He obeyed. She was bouncing against him now, panting, every movement sending jolts of sensation through him. He tensed, holding on to his control with all his might.

"Please," he said, his voice strung taut, and shoved his hips up.

She spent. Her body shook against his, her muscles contracting around him. The crest of his pleasure rose, the moment of unspeakable ecstasy before orgasm drawing itself impossibly out. "Oh," she said, "oh," and kissed him, her tongue pushing drunkenly inside his mouth just as her cunt gave one last, lazy ripple.

He shut his eyes as the wave of pleasure broke, plummeting him down into the sea. His blood crashed like thunder in the blind moment after lightning strikes. He buried his face in the curve of her neck and rode out the storm.

Phoebe felt drunk—that particular species of drunk she remembered from being a young girl trying to conceal that she and her friends had drunk an entire bottle of Martha's mother's blackberry cordial. Her body felt boneless, weightless; it seemed to move of its own accord, slower than usual but still faster than she expected. Her face kept trying to break out in a smile. It was raining, but her skin was suffused with warmth down to her fingers and toes.

Lord, that had been marvelous. Better than marvelous. And they could do it again tomorrow evening. Maybe even tomorrow morning, while Helen was at the library.

She opened the door to her staircase. For a moment her foot refused to lift high enough to get on the first step. She wasn't tired or sore. She just felt—lazy. As if nothing could possibly be important enough to justify that much effort.

She smiled to herself, tempted to sit down on the steps and relive the afternoon for a few minutes.

Her mother's voice came from upstairs.

There was a painful twang in Phoebe's neck as she tensed all over. She couldn't hear what Mrs. Knight was saying—evidently her mother was still in the die-away, long-suffering, painfully reasonable portion of the conversation—but she could hear that Helen's reply was tight with tears. She hurried up the steps and burst through the door.

"—encouraging you," Mrs. Knight finished, turning her reproachful gaze on Phoebe.

"Who's encouraging her to do what?" Phoebe demanded.

"She can't give up her child," Mrs. Knight said.

Phoebe tried to hold on to the serenity she'd felt a few minutes before. Failing that, she tried to hold on to her temper. "What do you want her to do, then?"

"I want her to marry the father."

"He's a bastard who doesn't deserve to live, let alone marry Helen," Phoebe said flatly. "If you wanted her to be happy instead of just wanting her to follow your self-righteous little code of behavior—"

"Don't you talk to me like that," Mrs. Knight said sharply, drawing herself up. "I am your *mother*."

"I'm glad to hear I'm still a member of the family," Phoebe snapped.

Mrs. Knight blinked, looking wounded and angry. "What is that supposed to mean?"

Phoebe glanced at Helen. She hadn't told her sister what their mother had said, about Helen choosing not to be part of the family anymore. It infuriated her that her mother was either pretending not to have said it, or, possibly, had actually forgotten. Mrs. Knight rarely remembered the unforgivable things *she'd* said in a quarrel. "It means I've asked you to let me know when you're planning to come over and visit," she said as calmly as she could.

Red spots appeared in Mrs. Knight's cheeks. "I don't understand why you feel the need to hide things from me."

"I'm not hiding anything," Phoebe said for the hundredth time. "I just don't like you to turn up unannounced, that's all."

"She came to see *me*," Helen said quietly.

"Yes, and she waited until she thought I wouldn't be here so she could bully you properly, didn't she?"

"I can talk to Mama without your help," Helen said. "Mama, I—" Phoebe felt a shock of mingled hurt and mortification. Was she just interfering? Oh God, she was.

Mrs. Knight didn't even wait to hear what Helen was going to say. "Come home, sweetheart," she said in a soft, affectionate voice she never used with Phoebe—maybe because Phoebe always snapped at her when she tried. "You've made a mistake, but you can fix it now. You know I want you to be happy more than anything in the world. And you never will be if you give up your child. If Phoebe were a mother herself, she'd understand that."

It was a low blow—and the worst of it was that Phoebe would never be sure her mother had meant it to be. She felt turned to stone, immobilized by anger, hurt, grief, jealousy. She had been hiding that even from herself, that she was jealous of her poor sister's pregnancy. She hated herself.

"Mama, I can't marry the father." Helen's face crumpled. "He's married already."

Phoebe was shocked out of her stupor. Helen had—she had knowingly helped a man make a fool out of his wife? If someone else had told her, she wouldn't have believed it.

Mrs. Knight looked shocked too. Her bloodshot eyes blinked rapidly, and she shook her head in denial. Helen watched like a little girl hoping desperately for her mother to tell her everything would be all right.

"If someone had told me that about you, I wouldn't have believed her," Mrs. Knight said finally.

Helen's mouth trembled. She turned and fled into the bedroom, slamming the door. The distinct, unpleasant sounds of heaving sobs came from the other side. Helen was still a girl, and some older married man had taken shameless advantage of her.

"Crocodile tears won't set this right, girl!"

"She isn't pretending," Phoebe said.

"Listen to her." Mrs. Knight shook with indignation. "Those noises are ridiculously exaggerated. She always does this. She wants to make me feel guilty."

Phoebe gritted her teeth. "That's how Helen cries." Her rage grew inside her, struggling to get free. She could feel herself turning splotchy.

Mrs. Knight started for the bedroom door. Phoebe blocked her way. If her mother decided to be stubborn, there wasn't much she could do, but she lifted her chin and crossed her arms and glared. "No," she said. It was hard not to back down. She felt hot and cold, her breath shaky.

To her complete shock, Mrs. Knight stepped back a pace. "I am her mother."

"That's not what you said a few days ago," Phoebe hissed.

"It's not right to hate your mother like this," Mrs. Knight said fiercely.

Phoebe knew that. She did. She tried to say *I don't hate you,* but she couldn't. Even that was giving too much ground. She felt sick.

Finally Mrs. Knight said, "I won't stay where I'm not wanted." She banged the door shut on her way out.

Phoebe sagged, wishing she could go to bed. "Ships? She's gone. Can I come in?"

"Please don't," Helen said, sniffling.

Phoebe knew she shouldn't be hurt. But she was trying so hard to help. She was giving up everything for Helen. And all she got was *Please don't come in* and *I can talk to Mama without your help.* If that were true, why was Helen living here, shutting herself up crying in Phoebe's room when Phoebe wanted nothing more than to curl up under the blankets, go to sleep, and forget the whole damn mess?

The father of Helen's child was married. That meant Helen had known from the beginning that if she found herself with child, there'd be no remedy. Phoebe tried not to resent that as well.

She sat on the settle—it was too narrow to lie down on—and pulled a blanket over her. She was hungry, but even going to the cupboard seemed a gargantuan effort. *Missing a meal will do you good anyway,* she found herself thinking. *The settle isn't too narrow; you're too wide.*

All it took was one conversation with her mother to bring her confidence crashing down.

If she couldn't sleep, she might as well write. She got up and lit the lamp. Her writing things were mostly in the other room, but she took up a pencil and wrote on the back of an old letter.

"Oh, sister," Ann wept. "I am more glad to see you than ever I was in my life…I have repented most sorely of the harsh words I spoke to you last."

"No matter," said her sister. Many tender words were then spoken, and many more went unspoken yet were understood, as is so often the case between sisters…

Chapter 23

The door of the Honey Moon seemed to weigh several extra tons as Phoebe pushed it open the following morning. What would Mr. Moon think, if he knew she had bedded another man the day before? That she hoped to do so again today? He deserved better. Everyone in her life deserved better, and she had nothing better to give them.

No one emerged from the kitchen. Going in herself and spending an hour with people who belonged together, trying to pretend she belonged there too—she couldn't do it. She turned around and walked out again, hurrying until she was out of sight of the windows.

She met Mr. Dymond in the street on the way to Jack's. "Oh, Mr. Dymond," she said, wishing she could sound arch. But her uncertainty and sadness *would* creep into her voice. "I forgot something at home. Would you mind going out of our way a little?"

"Not at all," he said promptly. "A morning constitutional can do wonders for one's health."

She smiled, feeling lighter already in spite of herself. "I think I can promise you a good bit of exercise." But she couldn't capture the flirtatious tone she wanted. He made polite conversation on the way; she could barely manage monosyllables.

"Is everything all right?" he asked when they were safely

in her rooms, free from prying eyes and ears.

"Helen's at the library and Sukey won't be by until the afternoon. Mrs. Pengilly's hard of hearing. If we're quiet, no one will disturb us." She sat to pull off her boots.

He frowned.

Everything was ruined. Everything. To her intense horror, she started to cry, one boot still dangling from her hand. Dropping it, she moved to cover her face before realizing her hands were muddy. She held them helplessly before her face and sobbed. She was a mess. Why on earth would anyone want to have an affair with her?

He handed her a clean handkerchief and sat beside her, putting an arm around her shoulders. "Tell me," he said. "Please."

"I can't. I can't tell you. It's just everything, and my mother was here last night, and you should send to London for that special license for Mr. Moon and me, and I'm disgusting and covered in snot and I just wanted—" She had just wanted to be happy. Maybe she was being punished for her selfishness.

He leaned in and kissed her wet cheeks. "You're not disgusting." He handed her a fresh handkerchief, dropping the first one on the floor. He was so rich he could toss handkerchiefs aside. Phoebe was still wondering whether she should go back for the one she'd left at the Drunk St. Leonard. She didn't throw *anything* away. She saved her fireplace ash for Jack to make lye. She blew her nose loudly, feeling poor and repulsive.

He kissed her neck. "Do you want to talk about it?"

She shook her head.

"Then we won't."

Afterwards, they walked to the printing office. Nick felt content, the brisk October air stinging pleasantly against his skin. Phoebe looked happier too, he thought. Well, he'd keep her mind off her troubles. He'd show her the fun in an illicit affair, in subtle flirting in plain sight.

It turned out to be an extremely double-edged sword. Every time he brushed their legs together under the table, every time he stretched or licked the tip of his pen or smiled at her and she shifted in her chair, eyes bright, or blushed just a little—it drove him wild. He was half-hard all day.

Maybe if he was very careful about exercising his leg for the next few days, he could risk taking her on her hands and knees by the end of the week. Or they could lie on their sides, and he could lift one of her legs over his hips, spreading her open for him—

She'd said he should send to London for the special license, he remembered suddenly. He'd been so distracted by everything that came after, he'd completely forgotten. There *was* no 'by the end of the week'. She'd be married to Moon then.

"We need to start printing soon. When do you think it will be ready for typesetting?" She pointed at his article. The article he'd barely managed to look at today, he'd been so busy thinking about bedding her.

"It's done," he said, and handed it to her. He regretted it the next moment. There was nothing politic about what he'd written. And what did he know about politics, anyway? Maybe he should run it by Tony first. Then he could put off her reading it. Christ, she was crossing things out already.

She glanced up and saw him watching her. "Just spelling

mistakes. Well, and some confusion between who and whom. Didn't you go to university?"

"I didn't study very hard." It was an understatement. He'd studied just enough to get by—in other words, hardly at all. The son of a peer had to make a really Herculean effort to not get by at Harrow and Oxford.

She smiled. "Jack is terrible for ending sentences with prepositions. 'Shakespeare did it', he used to tell me when I corrected him. But every time we printed one, the school-master in Nuthurst sent us an angry letter quoting Robert Lowth, and Will would be mortified and shout."

Will sounded like a lout, Nick decided. The failure of their marriage couldn't have been Phoebe's fault. She would do fine married to someone less, well, loutish.

A solution to their problems presented itself.

She sniffled, blinking rapidly at the last page of his article. "This is wonderful," she said, her voice a little thick. "*Everybody* will want to read it. Owen! Put this in the blank column and a half on page two. Label it 'An Account of the Conditions of Our Troops in Spain, by an Honorable Gentleman, until recently an Officer'. Perhaps 'Honorable' should be in capitals? Mr. Dymond, do you want us to put your name on it? Of course everyone will know it was you, but you can choose an alias if you'd prefer. And Owen, I don't think there's anything in there that could be considered sedition, but give me your opinion."

Everyone would know it was him. What had he got himself into? But everything in that article was true. What's more, everything in that article was his real opinion, said to please nobody but himself. "Put my name on it. Mrs. Sparks, may I speak to you in the kitchen for a moment?"

She frowned at him, but he couldn't wait. When he didn't

lower his eyes, she stood, sighing, and led him into the kitchen. "Nick, you really must be more discreet," she hissed at him— but she stood close enough to kiss. Somehow they'd slipped into using Christian names, this morning in bed.

"Phoebe," he said, "will you do me the very great honor of becoming my wife?"

Chapter 24

That silenced her. Her hands fell to her sides, limp. She sagged a little. It was definitely not the response Nick had been hoping for. "What?" she asked at last.

"If you're a Dymond, my mother will have to cover up Helen's scandal. And I know things haven't been working out so well with Moon."

"Yes," she said slowly. "But what do *you* get?"

"I get you."

Her brows drew together. Why couldn't anything ever be easy with her? "You told me you didn't know if you would ever marry. You told me that a week ago."

This was what happened when you were honest with someone. They knew things about you.

But why *should* she be grateful for a proposal from him? Why should she be pleased? Because she liked him a little better than Moon? That wasn't saying much.

I'm just trying to help, he thought. But it was a lie. If he said it, he would lose her. "Maybe I shouldn't marry." He kept his eyes firmly on the head of his walking stick. "I don't know how I'm going to support you. But I'll find a new profession. I'd have needed one anyway. I think I'd like to be married. To you."

"You've known me two weeks."

"You've known Moon two weeks."

"Yes, but he—" She went silent. He could think of any number of ways that could end. *He has his own business. He's a local man. He's of my own class. He's easier to make sense of.* "I know exactly what he's offering."

So it was *He's easier to make sense of,* then. That hurt even though he knew she was right. "Then I suppose you just have to ask yourself, do you want what he's offering?"

She glared at him.

Nick had put all his cards on the table. Either she wanted in or she didn't. He waited, refusing to try to charm her into this.

"You're right," she said finally, gruffly. "I accept your very generous offer. Thank you."

That wasn't—*what you wanted to hear?* he sneered at himself. She had to marry, and he was her best option. To say more would be a lie. "You honor me." He gave her a small, coaxing smile. "Come here." He put a hand on her waist and tried to draw her towards him.

She pulled back with a nervous smile. "Owen will have the proofs for pages two and three ready in a few minutes. We'll have to start printing soon if the paper's to be ready on time. We can—later. If you don't mind?"

"Just one kiss."

She let him pull her in, even responded willingly enough, but it felt different. He'd made it different. Before, she'd kissed him because she wanted to, a free gift. Now she was his future wife and owed him kisses as a matter of course when he asked for them. Her urgency was gone, and her eagerness. So much for showing her the fun of an illicit affair. He let her go. "I'll send to London for the special license directly. And I'll write to my mother."

Her eyes widened. "She's going to be angry, isn't she?"

"She was so certain I couldn't have you married to a Whig by election time she bet my father a hundred pounds," he said lightly, to cover his own trepidation. "She ought to be over-joyed. Not to lose the bet, of course, but the vote—"

Phoebe's jaw dropped. "She did *what*? A hundred pounds? Really? That's—that's so much money." She swallowed. "I suppose it isn't, to a countess."

"Listen. I—we're to be married. I ought to be honest with you. I made a bet with her too."

Phoebe's face twisted in distaste. "For how much?"

"Not for money." He looked away. "I told you she flinches when she looks at me now. I bet her that if I won, she couldn't do that anymore."

"Oh, Nick. And if you lost?"

"We didn't set the terms very clearly." He rubbed at his fore-head. "I should warn you my allowance is my only income at present, and she did threaten recently to cut it off. I don't think she'll do it if we marry. You're a prominent Orange-and-Purple and your brother-in-law is the town's newspaperman—it would be awfully risky to snub you. But it's not impossible."

She took a deep breath. "What about Helen? Is it possible she'd throw Helen to the wolves?"

"No," he said with conviction. "She'd do anything to avoid that kind of scandal."

Her eyes searched his face. "She's your mother. She's got to have some kind of motivation beyond political advancement."

Lady Tassell would be Phoebe's mother-in-law. He ought to encourage harmonious relations. But she'd meet Lady Tassell soon enough. She could judge for herself. Nick smiled in spite of himself; his mother might just have met her match.

"She has other feelings, without question. Other motivations for her actions? I haven't seen much evidence of it."

She nodded, hesitated, then gave him a hug so abrupt he almost lost his balance. "Thank you."

He waited for her to say more. To say anything. To say, *I'll stand by you, Nick, even if she won't.* Or just, *I love you.*

He wanted that desperately, he realized, wanted it so sharply he couldn't blot it out or ignore it. He tried to remember a poem, any poem, and all he could think was *A sweet disorder in the dress / kindles in clothes a wantonness.* One of Phoebe's cuffs was bent back so that it stuck out at an angle, and he wanted her to love him more than he'd ever wanted anything. More than he'd wanted his mother to be proud of him, more than he'd wanted to be warm and dry in Spain, more than he wanted his leg to be whole again. He'd always known he wouldn't get any of those things.

Somehow, he seemed to believe he could have this.

But she didn't love him. She wasn't here to make him happy. And she didn't say anything. Unlike him, her stock of words never seemed to run dry, but he'd silenced her.

"You're sure," he said.

She nodded. She didn't look sure.

"Let's put a notice in the paper," he suggested.

She hesitated. "We'd have to put your article in smaller type to fit it. Next week will be time enough."

Was that the truth or an evasion? He didn't dare press her. "I'll be back in an hour. The vicar has to send for the license today to be sure it will arrive in time for the polls."

"I think I must have misheard you," Tony said.

Nick shook his head. "I'm marrying Mrs. Sparks."

Tony rubbed the bridge of his nose, laughing incredulously. "That's insane. I don't need the vote that badly."

"Give me *some* credit, little brother. I'm not marrying her for the vote. Although of course I'll plump for you."

"Then why?" Tony's eyes searched his face, but Nick didn't get the impression he was really seeing anything. "Nick," he said in a low voice, "just because she's seduced you, you're not obliged to marry her. You're a man, and you've been lonely. A moment of weakness doesn't condemn you—"

Nick blinked, a little appalled. "She didn't entrap me into this. Don't talk about her that way."

"Then what?" Tony bit his lip and gave Nick an anxious sidelong look. "What did she tell you?"

Nick was touched by his concern. "I want to marry her."

Tony threw up his hands. "You *want* to marry her." Doubt dripped from every syllable. "A fat little widow without the least bit of breeding—"

"Stop it!" It came out in his officer's voice; Tony drew back, shocked. Nick softened his tone. "Tony, please, just apologize and let's—"

Tony's jaw dropped. "Apologize for what, my natural brotherly concern at seeing you tie yourself for life to a—?"

"Tony." Nick didn't try to keep the steel from his voice this time. "I'm going to marry her. If you're my brother, then you're her brother. Don't say what neither of us can forget. Say you're sorry and let's be done with it."

Tony shook his head, disbelieving. "You've known her for a fortnight, and you'll set her above me, above our mother, above— You really don't give a damn about this family, do you?" He turned and kicked at the log in the fire, setting off a shower of sparks.

Nick's temper rose. For once, he let it. "*Don't* tell me how I feel."

"Fine! I'm sorry. I'm sorry for trying to save you from yourself. God-damned officer and a gentleman." Tony laughed, angrily. "You've never been married. In six months you'll be wishing like hell you'd listened to me. At least I tried to talk you out of it."

Nick's temper fled, leaving a hollow gnawing in his chest. He *had* thought Tony shouldn't marry Ada when he'd got his mother's letter announcing their betrothal. He'd thought about saying something to Tony, even drafted a few letters, but in the end he'd thrown Lady Tassell's letter and the drafts on the fire together and thought, *No one cares what I think anyway.*

Maybe Tony would have cared. "Tony, about Ada—I'm sorry. I should have written to you. I should have—"

Tony laughed again. "Too bad you were busy not giving a damn at the time."

"I'm here now. I'm sorry, and I'm here now, and I'm not going anywhere. If you want to talk—"

"I think I'd rather have a drink." Tony headed for the door, then stopped. "Don't write to Mama until after the election, all right? She's sure to come down here and try to stop you, and I don't—" He actually looked a little green about the gills thinking about it.

Nick felt lower than ever. "I have to. I can't antagonize her right from the start."

"Nick, *please*. She'll find out—"

"Find out what?"

Tony hesitated and quite clearly decided there was no

point in talking to his brother further. "That I'm a failure," he snapped. "I wish you joy." He slammed the door behind him.

Nick started after him and ran right into Ada in the hallway. "Mrs. Dymond. Pardon me." He bowed and tried to move around her.

"It's no use speaking to him when he's like this." Ada went past him into the room. "Try again tomorrow, when he's calmer." Was that true? It felt all wrong, but the awful truth was that she knew his brother better than he did.

"What's got him in a temper now?" She sat down in front of the dressing table and regarded her reflection with a discontented sigh.

"I'm marrying Mrs. Sparks," Nick said.

"Who?"

It was amazing. All his mother's machinations, and she'd paired Tony with someone who cared about politics even less than Nick. "Mrs. Sparks. The widow with the votes."

She turned to look at him. "Oh, God. The one with that awful mother? Don't do it. Just for one vote? Tony wouldn't do it for you."

Nick sighed. "I'm not doing it for the vote. I want to marry her."

Ada turned back to the mirror, angling her head one way and then the other. She didn't seem happy with what she saw. She shot Nick a surprisingly wry glance. "Are you going to tell her ladyship before or after the ceremony?"

It was so tempting to wait. He didn't want her here any more than Tony did, and more than that he didn't want Tony to be angry with him. But Miss Knight needed Lady Tassell's help. "I'm writing to her directly."

Ada made a face as if to say, *Suit yourself, but I wouldn't be in your shoes for anything.*

"Ada, do you have a key to the campaign strong box?"

She nodded, looking more interested than she had through their whole conversation. "Why, do you want to steal some of the money?"

He shook his head and gave her an innocent smile. "Mother gave me fifty pounds for the license when I came down, but I need fifty more for election expenses. Do we have that much?"

Ada wandered down to the campaign office with him and handed him fifty pounds out of the cashbox. Nick hoped Tony didn't inquire too closely about it.

Dearest Mother,

I hope you are well.

I have asked Mrs. Sparks to marry me, and she has agreed.

Before you ask, I'm not just doing it for the vote. But I spoke with the vicar, and as I was baptized and confirmed here, I can be counted a resident. Of course I will cast my vote for Tony.

Please give my regards to Stephen. I know he'll win the county.

All my love,

Nicholas Dymond

Nick read the letter over with a deep-rooted sense of dissatisfaction. It wasn't the letter one ought to write one's mother on the eve of one's wedding. But he didn't know what else to say, so he sealed and addressed it and took it down the road to the postmaster in time for the mail coach to Chichester.

The vicar had already sent to London for the special license; his certification that both parties were legally eligible to marry should expedite the process. Maybe they could be married before his mother arrived. Nick crossed his fingers and prayed as he headed back to the printing office.

Phoebe woke early, her stomach a mass of nerves. For a moment she couldn't remember why, and then the previous day's events came rushing back.

She liked Nick. She liked him far better than either Mr. Moon or Mr. Fairclough. She thought she might even want to marry him.

No, she knew she wanted to marry him. But she wanted to do it because she wanted to, not because she had to. She wanted a choice.

Sighing, she heaved herself out of bed. It was chilly in her nightdress. She eyed Helen, still sleeping. She couldn't wake her sister just to tie her corset laces, and Sukey wouldn't be by for another hour at least. She ought to work on poor Ann's story.

She pulled on a fresh pair of stockings, checking them for darns, and imagined Nick taking them off again. Wrapping her night-rail around herself, she took some paper and a pen and went into the other room to light the fire.

Would she have a maid when she was married to Nick? Probably. That would be nice. She'd never had to light her own fires growing up.

The blank page stared up at her. It wasn't that she didn't know what happened next. She simply didn't want to write it. It felt like drudgery. But this was a job, not some fine lady's hobby. She dipped her pen in the inkwell and began.

In time, the virtue of Ann's sister gained her a worthy and prosperous husband, who aided Ann in setting herself up in a quiet sort of business...

An hour later she had finished the story. It was drivel, but with a little work she could turn it into something passable and get a few shillings from the *Girl's Companion*. It couldn't be any worse than the story she'd written in June about a chimney sweep's boy and the magical bird he found nesting in a flue, when Miss Starling's sister had a feverish baby and no money for the doctor.

Helen still hadn't stirred when Sukey came up the stairs with a kettle full of water for tea. "No tea, thanks," Phoebe said softly, feeling stifled suddenly by the low ceiling. "Help me into my dress." Helen had already been abed when Phoebe had finished at the *Intelligencer* last night; she was bound to be up soon, and then Phoebe would have to tell her about her engagement to Nick.

Sukey's eyebrows went up. Phoebe flushed. The maid knew she was a tea-guzzling slug-abed in the mornings unless something was wrong. "Getting cold feet, are you?" Sukey said. "Come along, we'll pack you a cloak-bag and you can be on the stagecoach before your sister opens her pretty eyes. No one would blame you."

"Thank you," Phoebe said sarcastically, "but no thank you. I'm going for a walk."

Chapter 25

Nick woke early and couldn't fall back asleep. That was unusual for him. But after tossing, turning, and reciting the entire first scene of Addison's *Cato* to himself with no effect, he heaved himself out of bed. Moving stiffly, he dressed without his sleeping valet and went out, hoping a brisk walk would ease the soreness in his leg. Yesterday's exertions hadn't helped.

He smiled, trying to decide how early he could justifiably call on Phoebe. Not for hours yet, probably. He stopped to look in the window of the bookshop—and there she was, her back to him, poring over a tiny volume.

At the sound of his cane on the stairs, she started and turned, trying to push the book back on the shelf. She didn't look happy to see him, although she did look eager to pretend she was. He affected not to notice. "Good morning."

"Good morning. You're up early."

"I couldn't sleep." He realized too late that that might seem an insult.

"Neither could I," she admitted. Yes, it definitely felt like an insult.

"What were you looking at?" The question didn't sound quite as casual as he'd meant it to. Why was he even striving to sound casual? There was nothing out-of-the-way in being curious.

She took the book back off the shelf reluctantly, her hands careful, almost reverent. "Will bought me this," she said. "When he took ill—I felt so guilty I sold my favorite books first, and this was the first of all of them. I can never believe no one's bought it in all this time. I know Mr. Blake has a strikingly original mind, but surely even in Sleepy St. Lemeston there ought to be someone to appreciate him." Her indignation seemed to conquer her self-consciousness. "Look how lovely it is." She hesitated for a moment in handing it to him. He set down his walking stick and took it with a show of gentleness.

The book was bound with plain covers—Will Sparks, unlike Nick, hadn't had the money to give his library matching calf-skin bindings. Nick opened it, expecting printed words, and blinked at the delicate wash of color.

"Mr. Blake is an engraver," Phoebe said eagerly. "Will sold—that is, Jack sells some of his prints in the shop. The decorous ones. Mr. Blake gave us this copy for only a guinea because Will told him it would be a sample for customers, and we kept it in the shop but it was mine." She sighed. "Luckily very few people ever really looked at it. My mother thought it quite shocking."

Nick listened with half an ear. The book was beautiful—a collection of watercolored engravings, the colors brilliant and impossibly delicate by turns, the shapes and figures soft and twining. Stopped by a bright wash of red on a fantastical flower, he read a poem entitled "Infant Joy".

I have no name
I am but two days old—
What shall I call thee?
I happy am

Joy is my name—
Sweet joy befall thee!

The style of the poetry, too, was like nothing Nick had ever seen. The whole book seemed composed of pure feeling. He looked up to see Phoebe's eyes brimming with tears. "I loved that one."

"We'll have children," he said in her ear, low enough the shopkeeper couldn't hear him. "I promise."

When he pulled back, she was looking at him, eyes wide and dark. "Do you think so?"

"I'm sure of it."

She smiled tremulously. "Would you like to be a father?"

He imagined Phoebe cradling his child. She'd watch its tiny face with all the wonder and intensity she possessed, tearing her eyes away only to give him a look that said, *Can you believe we did this?* "Yes. I think I would."

She looked happy for the first time that morning.

"Would you like me to buy you the book?" he asked.

There was a pause. Her mouth twisted with frustrated longing. "I—I'd like it very much," she said finally. "But a guinea meant something to Will. He scraped to buy that for me, and to you it's pocket change. I'd feel like a traitor, taking the same gift from you and being just as grateful."

No matter what he did, it was never the right thing. "Then be less grateful."

She laughed. "I couldn't possibly. I've been thinking about this book recently. I wanted to show it to Helen, but she won't come in here. She can't stand the layer of dust on top of everything. Look at this one." She flipped unerringly to the engraving she wanted and pointed at the opening verse.

Children of the future Age,
Reading this indignant page;
Know that in a former time,
Love! sweet Love! was thought a crime.

"Do you think it will really come?" she asked. "A time when no one will be ashamed?"

Quite shocking, indeed. Shocking to imagine a world where it would be the most natural thing in the world to take the person you loved to bed. A world where Phoebe wouldn't have to blush when she asked him to touch her. A world where Miss Knight could have her baby openly, and keep it without lies. It was unimaginable, even disturbing. "I don't know. Do you?"

Her expression hovered in uncertainty for another moment. Then she set her jaw. "Yes."

It was his mother's same stubborn insistence that what she wanted to believe was the truth, when it was only a wish. It should have annoyed him. It didn't. "Then let's not be ashamed," he murmured. "I'm buying the book."

A guinea was not, actually, pocket change to him. But he did have a guinea in his pocket. He set it down on the counter with a click.

The bookseller raised his eyebrows. "Auspicious day! I began to believe I would take that book to my grave despite all Mrs. Sparks's efforts to talk some wide-eyed gull into buying it."

"It's lovely," Nick said.

The bookseller shrugged. "Even with my spectacles the text is impossible to read."

Nick opened the book. The bloom of color and feeling

was expected now, but still startling. He didn't want to close it again. *Love seeketh not Itself to please,* he read.

"The clod believes that love is selfless," Phoebe said at his elbow. "But the pebble says love is selfish, and grasping." By the end of the sentence, her voice was tense. Evidently it was a question that troubled her.

"Which do you believe?"

"I don't know."

"Young people." The bookseller snorted, handing Nick a half-crown. "Both are true. Your change, sir."

Nick took the half-crown and the book. "Thank you." He waited until they were outside and out of sight to hand her the book. He felt a pang when it left his hands. He had wanted to keep it, he realized with surprise. He coveted it now. But Phoebe held the volume lightly, unconsciously sweeping her thumbs back and forth across the paper cover. Her lips curved as she walked, her eyes on the pavement. She wasn't smiling at him to thank him. She was smiling because she was happy.

His own face felt suddenly alien to him. If she glanced at him, he would know how to look. But without anyone watching, he didn't. Was he happy? Was he sad? He didn't know.

She glanced at him. He softened his expression. "I have to go back and tell Helen we're getting married," she said. "But—" She blushed and turned her eyes to the street ahead of them.

He ached with desire, realizing with a start that he was already hard. His tongue felt clumsy in his mouth. "Is there somewhere we can go?"

Her mouth curved again, that private smile, but wider. She looked down as if trying to hide it. He made her happy. He wanted to kiss her right there, in the middle of the street. He wanted to pull her into one of the Spanish dances he'd learned on campaign. "Owen isn't coming into the printing office until ten," she said.

Today Sparks's stairs weren't an unbearable gauntlet of pain and humiliation. They were just a frustrating chore that had to be got over with. And then they had been got over, and the two of them were in the room upstairs. Phoebe set the book down carefully on the nightstand. "Oh! We forgot the berries and cream."

"Are they quite spoiled?"

"I doubt it. It's been cold." She examined the bowl of berries. "This one's still good," she said, dropping it in his palm. "And this one—oh, and here—"

He popped them in his mouth and licked away the juice from his palm. Her eyes darkened as she watched him, eating a few berries of her own. They were a touch overripe. His tongue crushed them easily against the roof of his mouth, and the juice was too sweet. He swallowed. "If I sucked your nipple right now, it would turn purple."

When her lips parted, her tongue was stained dark. Her eyes sparked. "This time is for you. I promised."

All her talk of not wanting to forget—yesterday morning she had after all. She hadn't wanted to talk. So he'd made her forget, he'd given her what she needed and she'd promised desperately that next time would be for him. He could feel his senses dimming, the taste fading from his tongue. That had been easy, but *this* meant he had to tell her what he wanted, and he had to convince her it was true, and if she laughed at him— *You can do this,* he told himself. *It doesn't have to be perfect. There are plenty of things you'd like to do to her. Just pick a few.*

She lit the fire. Then she put her boot up on the chest at

the foot of the bed and began unlacing it, petticoats pooling around her knee. "I'll just take off a few things while you're thinking about it," she said teasingly.

He wanted to wrap his hands around her calf. He wanted to roll her stockings down. That was what he wanted right now. But what would he do after that, and after that? Would she enjoy it? "I want to stop thinking," he said. "I want to stop worrying about what I ought to do or say."

Her forehead creased.

His mouth was dry; he couldn't breathe. He sounded so weak, so unmanly.

"I don't know what that means," she said finally, toeing off her boots and shaking out her skirts. "I don't know how to do that."

If he laughed and told her never mind, she'd never accept it. "I want you to be in command." His heart was in his throat. "I want you to take responsibility. Just this once. So I can simply be here, and feel."

"You want me to be in command."

He nodded.

"So…whatever I want to do to you, I can do it," she said slowly, as if searching for the catch.

He nodded.

She grinned. "Really?"

She liked the idea. Nick's dead, crawling anxiety faded, leaving a deliciously buoyant flutter of nerves. He grinned back. "Why, did you have something in mind?"

Her eyes sparkled, those wisps of curls at her neck and temples bouncing as she nodded. "They sell naughty lithographs downstairs, you know."

"Really?"

She nodded. "There's something I've wanted to try forever. Will wouldn't."

There it was again, that flare of jealousy. She and Will had pored over naughty lithographs together, had they? He resolved inwardly that no matter how depraved her request, he'd do it just to show up Will.

"She—" That blush again. She bit her lip, that one pointed tooth sliding wickedly over rosy skin as she smiled. Nick wanted her a truly monumental amount.

He pulled her in for a kiss with a hand on her lower back, sucking her lower lip into his mouth and drawing back with a slow slide of teeth. She melted against him. She was his. They were getting married. She'd be his forever.

Her dark brows arched, half-rueful and half-naughty. "She tied him to the bedposts." She squeaked when his hand tightened on her lower back. "Is that—can I?"

He'd never done anything like that before. But he found he liked the idea. He wouldn't have to wonder what to do next, or what she wanted. He wouldn't have to worry that she might leave without warning. She could hardly leave him tied to the bedposts, after all.

"Would you let me tie *you* to the bed?" He slid his hand down her arm and circled her wrist, tugging.

She smiled. "Oh, I've done *that* dozens of times. It's fun."

His mind obligingly supplied an image of her naked and tied to the bed. Unable to do anything but beg as he teased her breasts. Unable to close her thighs against his caress if the pleasure became too much. Unable to hide.

Her face fell. "You don't want to. No matter. I'll think of something else."

Even though it was her idea, it was still hard to admit he

wanted it. It was embarrassing. "I want to."

Her eyes glinted black with surprised pleasure. She gave him a small shove, grinning shyly. "Take your clothes off, then."

A shock of arousal. He shrugged his jacket off, thankful his fingers still knew what to do with his waistcoat buttons even though his mind was no longer capable of directing them.

"Good boy." Her mouth curved sensually. He didn't quite understand it, but her hesitation had faded when he officially handed her command. Was it simply a role she knew how to play, as it was for him? Or had her shame come only from being unsure how far she could go? Either way, confidence and control fit her like a second skin. She was a queen, a goddess.

In a flurry and scramble, they both stripped. She wrestled with the last of her petticoats, making annoyed noises as she strained to pull it over her head. Her shoulders and head were enveloped in flannel, while the rest of her was exposed to view in only shift and stays. It was sweet and arousing at the same time.

"Ha!" She emerged triumphantly from the garment. "Undo my laces." When her stays were off, he reached for the hem of her shift. She shook her head and stepped back. "I didn't say you could do that. Stand up." She pulled the quilt off the bed and pushed it onto the floor. "Lie in the center."

He obeyed. Unsure what to do with his arms, he stretched them over his head in readiness. She could see every inch of him now. He was presented to her to take or leave, no words or seductive smiles to protect him.

The chilly morning air caressed his skin, his nerves strung doubly tight with fear and anticipation. Poems danced in his head but he quieted them, focusing on the tension growing in his belly and the ache in his cock. The very agony of waiting made it the most erotic thing he'd ever done. For the first time he understood the lure of gaming for high stakes.

She ran her tongue over her bottom lip, an unconscious gesture of hunger that aroused him unbearably, and took his cravat and handkerchief from the discarded pile of clothes. He could feel her proprietary gaze on his skin, warming him like a flame. "Give me your hand." She wound the cravat firmly and tied it. "Is that too tight?"

He shook his head. She dragged his arm up by the cravat and tied his wrist to the bedpost.

Just like that, he was trapped here. His breath caught, and when she rounded the bed and reached for his other hand, he pulled it back.

"Is everything all right?"

He nodded, knowing that in a moment this feeling of fear would pass. But a few seconds later, he said, "They held me down to operate on my leg." Of all the things one shouldn't talk about in bed, that filthy operating room topped the list. But letting her see his body and his thoughts was all of a piece. The words flowed with the same swirling tension as his arousal. "But it was understood that an officer shouldn't struggle. He shouldn't make a sound."

She sat on the edge of the bed. She listened with her whole body, mouth frowning, head tilting, shoulders leaning towards him, dark eyes focused on his face. He knew he must look ridiculous, but if she noticed, she didn't show it.

"I've never felt pain like that before or since," he told her. "But every time I moved or winced or strained against their grasp, I knew I'd failed in my manly duty. And I remember the shame more vividly than the pain."

She leaned down and kissed him; he gathered her up

against his side with his free arm.

"It's hard to be a woman." She sighed. "Sometimes I forget how hard it is to be a man." She traced a finger over his scar. He tensed, holding himself carefully still. The skin there was sensitive; her touch tickled and teased. "Is it perverse that I want to lick it? To you it means pain and shame. But all I see is you."

To him, the scar looked like an ugly growth, a cancer, something that would leave him clean if it could only be removed.

But he could feel her fingers on it. He felt it when she leaned down and ran the tip of her tongue up it. She couldn't really see, that close, and he felt it when she missed the jagged bit at the end. To her, it was just a part of him, like his fingernails or the dark blond hair on his chest.

Then he saw what he had tried to do: take his pain and his shame and put them in the scar, pretend they weren't really part of him. But they were, and they couldn't be amputated or lanced. He had to feel them.

He didn't want to.

"Do you want me to untie you?" she asked.

He shook his head, flushing. "Thank you for listening. It's not a very arousing story."

She laughed. "Oh, please! You've been seducing me with your war stories since the moment I met you." Her smile turned shy. "If you have a friend that loves me, you should but teach him how to tell your story…"

And that would woo her. Desdemona's line, when Othello told her stories of his life. Othello was a great general, not a mediocre lieutenant, but Desdemona hadn't loved him for his victories. She loved him for the dangers he had passed.

The tender, aching feeling in his chest when Phoebe spoke of her troubles—evidently it went both ways. He had never thought that his weakness could be loved as well as his strength. "No friend," he said. "Only me." It wasn't quite a declaration. He didn't have the courage for *that* yet. But he offered her his unbound hand.

Chapter 26

S he tied it to the bedpost, and then Nick couldn't reach for her anymore. She straddled him, up on her knees so they only touched where the inside of her thighs brushed the outside of his hips. The hem of her shift was just long enough to cover what he most wanted to see. She smiled. "You make me want to write erotic novels."

"What?"

"Something this spectacular is only supposed to happen in fiction." She ran her hands possessively down his shoulders and chest, her palms brushing across his nipples. He drew in a sharp breath. "But here you are. With me."

He felt warm from head to toe. "Yours to do with as you wish." Saying it, even playfully, made the warmth flare into abrupt heat.

She drew in a deep breath and arched her back. "Mmm. Mine." She smiled. He was on fire. "At the sight of him spread before me thus, like a rich banquet to a queen, so confused and excited were my appetites that I knew not which dish to sample first."

It was an apt imitation; she must read erotic novels. He imagined her curled up in a chair with a book, looking quiet and studious and all the while growing wet between her legs. She'd raise her head and ask him if he wanted to try out something obscene as if she were asking whether he fancied trout for dinner.

She would be his wife.

Suddenly he couldn't be still. He stirred restlessly, canting his hips towards her. *Touch me,* he thought.

"But as every meal begins with wine," she continued, "I thought I could hardly do wrong in first decanting the liquor offered me by the tall vessel between his legs." She crawled backwards, and without any more preamble than that, took his cock into her mouth.

He yanked at the bindings on his wrists. She couldn't fit all of him in her mouth, so she set her hand at the base of his cock and worked him swiftly as she sucked. With an effort, he raised his head to look at her. God, she was beautiful. The strap of her shift was sliding down one perfect round shoulder. A hairpin had slipped out of her bun and was on the verge of falling. Her mouth stretched around his cock was hot and wet and perfect; it was too much, he had already been close. He couldn't stop her, couldn't move away. "I'm going to spend," he warned her, head falling back. "I'm—"

Her other hand squeezed his balls, and he lost the power of speech. He lost the power to think in words. He could only feel the press of her tongue and her fingers. The pleasure radiated out along his nerves to his entire body. He yanked at his bindings again just to feel the linen against his skin. Her hands were everywhere.

He tried one last time to warn her, but as he opened his mouth she rolled one of his bollocks between her thumb and forefinger. "Aiaaaaaaah!"

Phoebe laughed, her mouth curving around his cock and the back of her throat vibrating. He spent.

She nursed him through it, hands slowing and mouth continuing its torturous slide. Only when he was still, his hands sagging limply in their bonds, did she sit up, swallowing his seed.

"But…" How would he pleasure her now? He couldn't even finish a sentence. He stared at the beams in the ceiling, feeling the rise and fall of his own chest with startling clarity.

"Think of it as priming the pump," she said cheerfully. "I wouldn't want you worrying about spending too quickly when you're actually inside me."

His cock was too tired to twitch, but the rest of him did. She smoothed a hand over his stomach. "In the meantime, I thought I'd go downstairs and make myself breakfast."

He jerked his head up indignantly.

She laughed, visibly pleased with herself. He'd never seen her this smug. Command suited her. "I couldn't resist." She lowered herself until she was on forearms and knees, the top half of her body resting on him. His spent cock pressed into her belly. As she wiggled, settling herself, pleasure echoed through him.

She slid her fingers into the dark blond hair on his chest, tickling pleasantly, and scratched lightly at his breastbone. Ohhhh. Why had no one ever done that before? In a moment he'd be purring like a cat. No, wait, that sound *was* him purring like a cat.

He felt drugged, floating. She leaned down to suck on a nipple, soft ripples of pleasure like a pebble tossed into still water. He hummed again, his hips tilting up of their own accord. She moved up, exploring his arms with fingers and mouth, biting lightly at his biceps. "You like my arms," he said.

"I *like* arms generally," she corrected him. "Your arms, I

adore passionately." She nipped her way up the soft skin on the underside of his forearm. "So large and perfectly proportioned. Like your…" She paused mischievously, shifting her attention to his other arm. It put her breasts inches from his face. He wrapped the cravat on his right wrist around his hand and struggled upwards. She stilled. "You really do like these."

"Ladies," he told them, "by yonder blessed moon I swear, that tips with silver all these fruit-tree tops—"

She pulled her shift over her head. "Don't worry. The love between you and my breasts isn't star-crossed in the slightest."

He smiled. "We'll grow old together."

She leaned in, presenting one rosy nipple. He sucked it eagerly until she pulled away with a wet pop and gave him the other. Her eyes glazed over; the game was arousing her too. She twined her fingers in his hair and held him there, her thumb tracing his ear. Her breathing grew ragged, and his cock stirred to lazy life.

He flicked her nipple with his tongue. He knew she liked that—such a small thing to know, and so many still to discover. She made needy, shameless noises. At this rate, he'd be hard again in no time.

Pulling back, she moved down to straddle his hips once more, her wet nipples leaving cool trails on his chest. Taking his half-hard cock in her hand, she rubbed the sensitive head over her slit, then up to tease her clitoris. Her head arched back, baring her throat.

He knew he couldn't reach to bite her there, but he tried anyway.

With a breathy laugh, she ignored him, seeking her own pleasure. His cock twitched faintly in her hand. She didn't seem impatient. It would be ready when it was ready.

So Nick lay back and waited, enjoying the view, enjoying the slow build of his pleasure. She moved her hips in slow circles, sucking her lower lip into her mouth, her lashes dark against her skin as she shut her eyes.

Then she slithered further down and—oh. She rubbed the head of his cock against her wet nipple. That was filthy. He watched her, enthralled. Her open, panting mouth still curved with shy mischief as she met his eyes, arching her back to give him a better view. Her areolas were darker than they had been a minute ago. The skin of his cock darkened too, a shocking contrast to her pale breasts. He thrust, throwing off her movements.

Her fingers tightened infinitesimally around him in reprimand. Just like that, he was hard again.

She glanced down in surprise, then tightened her fingers again, gently. He drew in a sharp breath. Her smile widened. He waited, breathless, to see what she had in store for him.

She captured his cock between her breasts, her nipples tickling the tender skin of his lower belly as she slid up and down. He'd wanted to ask her for this that first time in the kitchen and hadn't been able to.

"This isn't the best angle, but another time..." She trailed off, voice thick. "You look unbelievable."

He laughed. "Me?"

"Your hair's all mussed, and your mouth is wet and red, and your eyes are so, so—and when you do that the muscles in your arms stand out—" And all the while she was moving, the flushed head of his cock peeking from between her breasts and disappearing.

He tugged at his bonds. "When I do this?"

"Mm-hmm." She let his cock fall and climbed astride him.

"Do it again." So he wrestled up to meet her as she sank onto him. She was so wet for him that there was barely any resistance at all. Then she clenched around him, tight, and smiled triumphantly when he fell back against the bed, hips surging into her.

"You fit so perfectly." She settled down against him, her hips moving with slow purpose. "It feels so perfect. I could do this forever."

"Don't let me stop you." His voice cracked somewhere in the middle. He could see his cock sliding in and out of her. Even better, he could feel it.

There was no urgency to her movements; she was simply enjoying the sensation of being joined. For a few long minutes she kept that up. It was torture, and the most deeply satisfying thing he'd ever felt. His skin was on fire—the last thing he should be was comfortable. But he was.

"Touch me," he said, the first thing he'd asked for aloud since getting on the bed. She shifted to balance on her knees and ran her hands up and down his sides in long, slow strokes, gentling him like a nervy horse. He became abruptly aware that the mattress was lumpy when every muscle in his back relaxed into the bed.

She stroked up swiftly, her thumbs swiping his nipples. His nerve endings lit, his hips jerking. She gasped. Just like that, the mood changed. She put a hand down to touch herself, riding him faster. He moved to meet her, trying to get as deep as he could.

"Kiss me," she said, leaning down to press her mouth to his. Their lips met sweetly, gently exploring while below they coupled relentlessly. "Oh." Her mouth fell open. "Oh." She hovered over him for a moment, and then her intimate muscles began to spasm. She buried her face in his shoulder and rubbed herself furiously, drawing her climax out, her breath shuddering hot against his skin. The rhythm was exactly right one moment and all wrong the next, and somehow that only made it better, hotter, more intensely erotic. He strained upwards, unable to pull her closer, unable to do anything but take what she gave him.

She fell against him. He was still hard inside her, hard and entirely unready for this to be over. "Phoebe. Please."

She reached up and fumbled at the knots. "Drat. They've tightened." He thrust shamelessly into her as she shifted unpredictably, wrestling with the knot she'd tied. Stretching to reach his wrists, she kept her cunny and her thighs tight around him and let him use her as best he could.

"Ha!" she said, and one of his wrists fell free. He moved it to her hip, anchoring her in place. "I can't concentrate when you do that."

His other wrist came free. He rolled them both so she was beneath him. His leg twinged a protest but he didn't care. She was curvy and soft, and when he drove hard into her she spread her legs wider and made a sleepy sound of approval. He raised himself up on his elbows and watched her, her body bouncing with his thrusts, her heart-shaped face flushed and relaxed, her hair curling across the sheets. She breathed deeply and evenly, eyes closed, her exhalations holding the edge of a moan.

He let the pleasure consume him, taking her hard and fast until his climax flared white-hot and he spilled into her.

They would be married soon enough that she wouldn't even have to take her herbs, he thought with hazy contentment.

Phoebe took the stairs to her lodgings slowly. The door to her rooms was ajar. Through it, she heard her sister laughing, and a male voice that sounded familiar. Some friend of Helen's, no doubt. It was nice to hear her laugh again. She pushed open the door, smiling, and— "Mr. Gilchrist?"

The Tory agent stood politely, his oily smile diluted by the traces of genuine amusement still lingering at the corners of his mouth. "Mrs. Sparks. I'm so glad to see you. We've found a new suitor for you—"

"I'm sorry, Mr. Gilchrist," she said, "but please convey my apologies to him and tell him I've decided to marry a Whig." She felt terribly self-conscious. How would she explain to him that she was going to marry Nick when she'd assured him there was nothing between them?

Mr. Gilchrist's eyes popped. "You don't mean that, Mrs. Sparks. Marry that Moon-calf instead of the man of sense and substance I—"

Helen hid a smile with her hand, and Phoebe felt a pang of guilt. What was poor Mr. Moon going to do now? "That is unkind," she said sharply. "Mr. Moon has plenty of sub-stance"—even if most of it seemed to be sugar—"which is more than I can say for you, sir."

"Yes, but what about sense?"

"I'm sorry to have wasted your time. But I've made my decision, and I'd prefer you to leave."

Mr. Gilchrist glanced at Helen. "Use your influence with her. This is folly."

Helen flushed. "Once my sister's mind is made up, talking won't change it."

Phoebe wasn't sure how to take that. "Goodbye, Mr. Gilchrist. Thank you for everything, but I won't be changing my mind. I'm sorry."

Gilchrist took up his hat and went, but Phoebe saw him give Helen an *I'll-be-back* look.

"Are you really going to marry Mr. Moon?" Helen asked.

Phoebe shook her head. "Mr. Dymond's asked me to marry him. I told him yes." There, now it ought to feel real, less like a fairy gift that would be taken back if it wasn't kept secret.

It still didn't.

For a long, long moment, Helen didn't say anything. Her mouth worked, a little, as if she was trying to speak. Her face slowly drained of color.

"What is it, Ships? I know you read nasty things about the Dymond boys in the scandal sheets, but—"

"I can't come to your wedding," Helen said abruptly. "Fee, I'm so sorry. I'll help you with your hair and your dress, but I can't go. And—I think I'll go live with Mama again when you're married."

"What do you mean?" Phoebe asked, a sinking sensation in her chest. "We'd agreed you were to live with me. Do you know something about Mr. Dymond? If there's something I ought to know—"

"No, no, there's nothing," Helen said hastily. "You love him, and you should marry him. I wish you all the joy in the world, truly."

Phoebe tried to puzzle it out. Helen wasn't against the marriage. Then what would happen at the wedding, or in their home, that— *The Dymond boys have a reputation as heartbreakers,* Helen had said. She hadn't wanted to come to the Whig party, and every time Phoebe said *Mr. Dymond,* she twitched like a fox that heard the hounds.

Helen had shown Tony Dymond around town when he had arrived two months ago. And her seducer was married.

"Ships, is that baby Tony Dymond's?"

All the color rushed back into Helen's face. "No."

"You're lying," Phoebe said with conviction. "What did he say to you to make you lie for him?" But she knew. Helen had told her, that first day. *He said there's no money, and if I tell anyone, he'll ruin me. He'll tell everyone what I did.* "But he's rich, Ships. He ought to help you."

"He hasn't got any money of his own. He said his mother wouldn't help me. He said if I told her, I'd be ruining him for nothing, and he'd make sure everyone knew what sort of girl I was."

"What sort—what sort—why, that—" There were no words big enough for her anger. No words to express how much she hated Tony Dymond. She tried anyway. "That despicable, contemptible, swinish, foul, disgusting—"

Helen laughed. "Oh, Fee, don't. You and Mr. Nicholas will be happy, I know you will."

And that was when Phoebe knew she loved Nick. Because if she didn't, her heart wouldn't break with this awful, irrevocable crash when she realized she couldn't have him.

She couldn't abandon Helen. Not again. She couldn't let her sister go back home and live with Mrs. Knight's disappointment and judgment every moment of every day. She couldn't have Helen afraid to come to her house—afraid to come to her *wedding*, for heaven's sake—for fear of meeting the man who'd mistreated and abandoned and threatened her.

She could tell Nick. She could tell him everything and ask him to intercede with his family, and—

Then what?

Could she really ask him to bar his own beloved little brother from his home? Even if he agreed, Tony would be furious. He'd tell the whole town. He'd ruin her sister for spite.

Then she'd tell Nick and ask him to keep it secret—but she couldn't do that either. She couldn't know if Nick *would* keep it secret. He might think he had a duty to talk to Tony, or tell his mother.

Even if he didn't, she could never pretend to be Tony Dymond's loving sister-in-law, never. By marrying Nick, all she would do was keep herself and Helen firmly in Tony's field of vision, and sooner or later, he would realize Helen had told the secret.

Then the worst possibility of all presented itself. What if Nick took his brother's side?

He was fond of Tony. Plenty of men didn't think it a terrible crime to seduce a willing woman. She couldn't bear it if he stood there with his hands in his pockets and shrugged Helen's hurt away apologetically.

She could hear little bits of her heart rolling under the furniture.

But if there was one thing she'd learned as the clumsy daughter of a mother with a temper, it was that once you'd smashed something, it was no use trying to glue it back together. You could admit what you'd done and take the shouting and the slaps, or you could sweep up the pieces and bury them in someone else's rubbish heap and deny you'd ever seen the thing. Sometimes you even got away with it. But broken things never mended.

She gave Helen a smile. "Oh, don't be foolish. It's not as if I were in love with him. I only thought him the best of a bad lot."

"That's not what you said before."

She had known it was a mistake to confide in her sister. She had known it was a mistake to let her guard down. "You're my sister," she said, taking Helen's hand. "I just met him. I like him, but that doesn't matter. You matter."

Helen squeezed her hand. Love surged up where Phoebe's heart used to be, but there was nothing to contain it anymore. It spilled everywhere, dripping and spurting, and she couldn't tell what was for Helen and what was for Nick. "Everything's going to be all right," she lied, kissing the top of her sister's hair. "I promise."

Chapter 27

Nick was actually a little surprised when his mother's coach pulled into the courtyard of the Lost Bell just as they were finishing dinner. He hadn't been sure she'd leave the county election.

She alighted, nodded regally and smiled graciously at everyone she saw, gave Tony and Ada and Nick a motherly embrace, and inquired after the innkeeper's children and sundry other relatives. Then she said, "Nick, dear, may I speak to you privately?"

He took her to his room. "You didn't have to come." Her eyes searched his face. She was the picture of motherly concern.

Nick knew she *was* concerned. It wasn't an act. This would be easier if it was. "I think I did," she said. "Nick, is this some kind of joke? Are you punishing me for sending you out here?"

"*No*. Mother, I—"

She sighed. "I never dreamed you'd take this so seriously. Nick, there *was* no bet with your father. I only said so to get you out here. I was worried about you. I'd like the vote, of course, but it's Tony's first campaign and this is a difficult borough. I won't be surprised if he loses."

All his suspicions confirmed. "So there was no bet?"

She shook her head, looking tired. "Honestly, Nick, how

could you think there was? I'm not a monster. But of course you'd believe anything of me."

"I believed it because you *said* it. I should have known better." He had almost wanted the bet to be real, just so she wouldn't have lied to him. But she simply didn't see the point of honesty, or of the two of them understanding each other.

"I did it because I love you." Lady Tassell laid her bonnet down on top of his papers and quills and sleeve-links as if they weren't there. Such a tiny thing to make him so angry. "You needed to get out of those wretched rooms and get some country air and stimulation. You look a hundred times better. There's color in your cheeks." She came closer as if to touch his face.

He shied away. "You could have been honest with me. If you'd told me you were desperately worried and this would ease your mind, I probably would have come."

"Nick, we don't need to discuss this anymore. We need to discuss your marriage. You can't be serious."

"I am."

"I know you're doing this to spite me. What can I do to change your mind?"

"It's got nothing to do with you. I want to marry her. She's a wonderful woman."

"I'm not saying a word against her," Lady Tassell said with the engaging candor she was famous for. "I've always liked her very much. But she isn't an appropriate wife for you, Nick. Only think how awkward it will be, introducing someone of her station to your friends."

God, how Nick wanted to walk out right now, or to retreat into sullen silence. He wanted to think of something else—the curls at the ends of Phoebe's hair or—but he didn't want to use her to dull his senses. In the end it was only a subtler version of his mother's *We don't need to discuss this anymore* tactic, anyway. They did need to discuss it. "I've made up my mind," he said. "I'm marrying her. I think she'll make me happy."

Lady Tassell shook her head. "I don't understand how I raised such gullible children. Maybe that's all there is to it on your side. But do you think *she* doesn't want something?"

Nick felt his attention drifting and pinched himself hard. "She does need something, it's true. But you would have helped her if she'd married any Whig in Lively St. Lemeston. She chose me."

"And what is this little favor?" Lady Tassell said, with an air of *I knew I was right all along.*

"Her sixteen-year-old sister is with child, and the father can't marry her. She needs to take the girl away to have the baby, and to find a kind home to take it in."

Lady Tassell smiled. "Well, I can't blame her for preferring you to Robert Moon. You must have seemed like a breath of fresh air in this town." She reached out to brush her fingers through his hair. He made himself stay still and let her.

He shouldn't hate it so much, his mother touching him and smiling at him. But all he could think was *Flattery oils the hinges.* She might mean it, but she'd do it even if she didn't. "So you'll help them?"

"I'll help them." That, Nick did trust. She always made good her election promises. He relaxed. "Is the special license here yet?"

"I expect it on the five o'clock mail coach."

She nodding, glancing at the clock. "Well, I'd better get to know my future daughter-in-law a little better."

"Allow me to escort you." Nick offered her his arm.

Lady Tassell smiled again and didn't take it. "Oh, no, this is women's business. You'll only be in the way."

He smiled back, equally insincerely. "I'll just walk there with you, shall I?" He was almost looking forward to seeing Phoebe take on his mother.

Phoebe was going to have to go to Mr. Gilchrist and beg his forgiveness. She felt terrible for poor Mr. Moon, but there was no way— "No way in *hell,*" she said loudly, and winced despite all her attempts not to—she was going to give that bastard Tony Dymond one of her precious votes. Not today, not in the next election, not ever. If that meant marrying a Tory, then so be it.

Footsteps on the stairs. After a moment, she distinguished the telltale rap of a cane. Her stomach flip-flopped and the remnants of her heart ached. He had someone with him. Who? How would she get Nick alone to tell him what she needed to tell him? She should have gone to see him this morning, only she hadn't been able to bring herself to do it.

She went to the door and opened it. Coming around the corner were Nick and—her eyes widened. He had Lady Tassell with him.

Nick's mother was here, the mother he wanted to make proud. And Phoebe was going to humiliate him in front of her. Oh, God. It was beyond cruel, and he hadn't done a thing to deserve it.

She pasted on a smile. "Mr. Dymond, what an unexpected pleasure. I was hoping to see you." She gave Lady Tassell a deep curtsey. "My lady. Please be welcome to my home."

"Thank you, Mrs. Sparks." Lady Tassell sailed into the room with a warm smile and no notice of its dingy state. Of course not; this was what she did, wasn't it? But her crisp white linen and new shoes showed up Phoebe and her attic anyway.

Phoebe met Nick's eyes meaningfully. He gave her an encouraging smile, evidently thinking her nervous about meeting his mother. "She wanted to talk to you before our marriage. Don't let her intimidate you. She's already promised to help your sister, and I trust that."

He was so dear, and he looked—God, he looked happy. At his smile, the ruins of her heart made valiant efforts to knit themselves back together.

But her mind went coldly on. His words confirmed that his mother, as expected, opposed the match. Maybe there was something to be salvaged here after all—not her heart, of course, but her freedom. If Lady Tassell wasn't planning to bribe her to jilt Nick, then Phoebe was Empress of All the Russias.

The countess took off her neat bonnet to reveal charmingly arranged graying blonde ringlets. "Oh, run along, Nick," she said with an indulgent smile. "As if I would intimidate Mrs. Sparks. I just want to get to know my future daughter-in-law."

Nick leaned in and whispered, "The license will be here on the mail coach, no matter what. If you don't want me to leave you with her, I won't."

Don't leave me, she wanted to say. *Don't let me leave you.* Instead she took a deep breath and gave him a smile she thought might actually be convincing. "Don't worry about me. I'll see you soon."

"My money's on you." He squeezed her hand and headed out the door with a jaunty wave of his walking stick.

The door shut behind him. She and Lady Tassell regarded one another. *Sizing each other up,* Phoebe thought, resisting the urge to circle the other woman like an angry cat or a prizefighter.

"May we sit?" Lady Tassell asked with a smile.

First point to the countess for making Phoebe feel like an inept hostess. "Of course." She sat on the settle, and Lady Tassell took Will's chair with a regal sweep of her skirts. At least the hems of her petticoats were stained with mud, like an ordinary woman's.

"So you want to marry my son."

"Yes, my lady," Phoebe said. The countess waited, but she didn't volunteer anything more.

Lady Tassell leaned forward, the picture of motherly concern. "He told me about your sister. Is this really what you want, or are you only trying to help her?"

"I like your son very much."

Lady Tassell smiled proudly. "Of course you do. He's such a handsome, charming boy, isn't he? And more than that, he's kind and clever and he has a good heart."

Phoebe nodded, trying to swallow the knot of misery in her throat.

Lady Tassell sighed. "All of that, you could see on a moment's acquaintance. But I've known Nick all his life, and perhaps I see a little clearer than you can do." Her expression indicated reluctance and regret for what she was about to say. "Some men simply aren't meant to be husbands. Oh, he'd do for an heiress. Maybe for better, for richer, in health, he'd stand by you." She really looked pained. Did she believe what she was saying? Either way, Phoebe hated her. "But when worse, or poorer, or sickness sets in—he won't know what to do."

Phoebe knew she had to play this carefully. But oh, how she longed to give Lady Tassell a piece of her mind! Or a piece of her boot, one or the other. "He was an officer for years. You can't call that easy. My lady."

"Of course not." Lady Tassell sounded so damn earnest it set Phoebe's teeth on edge. "But that requires a different sort of strength of character than a profession in civilian life. All one has to do is follow orders, and give them to men bound on pain of death to obey. Naturally it's physically demanding work, but he was always such a strong, healthy boy." Her mouth twisted unhappily.

"He's still strong and healthy," Phoebe said. "It's only a limp."

Lady Tassell folded her hands on her knees. "My dear, I know how tempting it must be to go from this to being the Honorable Mrs. Dymond. But you haven't thought about what it will mean. Let me stand as a mother to you for a moment."

To her surprise, Phoebe thought, *I'd take my mother over you any day.*

"Our world, the world he comes from, is cruel. Perhaps his friends and their wives will be polite to you while he's watching. They won't be so polite behind his back. When the first flush of infatuation has worn off, he can't help but notice that you don't fit."

Her gaze swept over Phoebe's old gown and disheveled hair as if she could see to the mended stockings and messy heart beneath, that quintessentially motherly gaze of disapproval and disappointment that couldn't be resented because there was no malice in it. "One can't learn to be a gentlewoman, Mrs. Sparks. You'll never quite manage to speak as they do. You'll never dress or walk or sit on a horse the way they do. My dear, you'll shut doors for him, and you'll keep him from marrying a woman with money of her own. The annuity we give him might seem a great deal of money to you, but to a man of Nick's rank, it's very little."

Phoebe hated her. She hated her for the ways she was wrong, and the ways she was right. She hated that even if she hadn't already been planning to break it off with Nick, she would have had to offer him this chance to cry off.

Most of all, she hated Lady Tassell for the way she talked about Nick. All he wanted was for his mother to see him, really see him. And all the countess saw were his faults, and her own notions of what he was like.

Phoebe held her tongue, because if she let herself become involved in this conversation, she would lose her temper. She *could not* lose her temper.

"You're a strong woman," Lady Tassell said. "You've worked hard. You're talented and pretty. Among your own set, people can appreciate that. In my son's, all they'll see is that you aren't one of them. My dear, money is no substitute for happiness and self-respect."

Phoebe hoped *that* wasn't true, because she was about to trade both her happiness *and* her self-respect for money. She waited silently for the offer.

Chapter 28

L ady Tassell spread her hands. "I can't offer you the kind of financial security you'd have as Nick's wife. But I can offer you something. If you marry Mr. Moon, I'll help your sister *and* give you two hundred and fifty pounds as a wedding present."

Two hundred and fifty pounds. Heavens. This was going to be a better deal than she'd hoped for. She tried to be glad of that. "I don't want to marry Mr. Moon, my lady. But you—I think you might be right, about me and Mr. Dymond. If you pay for my sister to go far away to have this baby, and you find a good home for it—a *good* home, do you understand, with nice people, and Helen can meet them first and if she doesn't like them you'll find another—if you do all that, and give me the two hundred and fifty pounds, I'll call it off with your son."

Lady Tassell laughed gently, as if she were proud of Phoebe for bargaining. "Then what's to keep you from marrying him later, once I've lived up to my part of the deal?"

"What's to keep you from abandoning my sister, once I'm married to Mr. Moon? Besides, I thought you said Mr. Dymond had no staying power. Do you really think he'll still want to marry me in seven months? Once I've taken a bribe to jilt him?" He'd never look at her again.

"A new family with a failing shop would need that money,"

the countess said. "And of course, you would be Lively St. Lemeston Whigs, and I always take an interest in my family's supporters. A woman alone, with no votes to give…"

"Two hundred pounds."

Lady Tassell laughed again. "It's really too bad. You're a girl after my own heart. A hundred and fifty is all I can offer." She looked grave. "You're doing the right thing, Mrs. Sparks. I hope there are no hard feelings. It would be lovely to see you and your sister at the hustings with orange-and-purple rosettes. Plenty of non-voters come to show their support."

Phoebe hated Lady Tassell. She and her cruel, spoiled brat of a youngest son were ruining Phoebe's life, and they were doing it with smug smiles. For the first time in her life, she would rather have eaten worms than go to the hustings in orange and purple. Would Helen even do it?

Well, she'd have to. A hundred and fifty pounds would see the two of them truly independent. "If you give it to me now, I'll shake hands."

Lady Tassell pulled a roll of banknotes out of her reticule and counted out a hundred and fifty pounds. She had come prepared. Then she held out her hand, and Phoebe shook it. "What are you going to tell Nick?" the countess asked.

Phoebe drew herself up. "I'm going to tell him that I confided in you that I didn't really want to marry, and you made that possible. I'm going to tell him it's for the best."

Lady Tassell put a motherly hand on her shoulder and squeezed. "It's no more than the truth, my dear. You're a good, brave girl. Did many people know of your understanding?"

Phoebe swallowed a lump. "No one knew of it."

"We'd better keep it that way, don't you think? For both your sakes."

Phoebe picked up a copy of the *Intelligencer* and handed it to Lady Tassell, pointing to Nick's article. "Read this; your son wrote it. He's going to be a great man someday. Maybe soon."

Lady Tassell's eyebrows went up. "I'll be sure to read it carefully. Thank you, my dear. It's very much to his credit that he chose someone like you for his imprudent attachment."

Phoebe went to the door and held it open, silently.

Nick didn't like the pleased cadence of his mother's walk when she came down the stairs. And he definitely didn't like the sympathetic, crooked smile she gave him as she gestured for him to climb the stairs.

"What did she say?" he asked, heart sinking.

"I'll let her tell you herself. I'm sorry, Nick."

Nick swallowed the knot of fear in his throat. He could feel her watching him on the stairs, but just now he couldn't care what she thought about his limp. He went as fast as he could. When he opened the door, Phoebe was waiting, looking small and unhappy. Small and unhappy and beautiful. "Phoebe?"

For the first time, she didn't ask him to sit. Instead she stood, wrapping her arms around herself. "I'm sorry, Nick. But she's right, you know. It would never have done, you and me. You were only being kind, anyway. You wouldn't have offered if I didn't need to marry. You don't really want to *marry* someone like me, and introduce me to your friends—"

"Don't tell me what I want." He barely recognized his own voice.

She turned those big dark eyes on him, pleading. "She's going to help Helen without me marrying at all." It took the wind out of his sails. What could he say to that? He knew she'd never wanted to marry.

He should be happy that Phoebe was going to be free, not as blindly, selfishly angry as a child balked of a toy.

He tried to see her, really see her and not his own disappointment and misery. She looked wretched and guilty. Sorry for hurting him.

It was humiliating that she knew how much this hurt him, how much he'd wanted her. He couldn't shrug and pretend he'd never cared. She'd know it was a lie.

He had to be a man and take his lumps, and let her go without recrimination. It wasn't hard to do, only hard to want to do. But here was his chance to secure someone else's happiness first. He recited *Childe Harold* silently and slowly to himself. The furious, sick feeling in his chest didn't go away, but it retreated enough that he could give her a smile, and look like he meant it. "It couldn't have worked out better if we planned it, eh?"

To his surprise, that didn't help. If anything, she looked more miserable than before. "Nick, I—if I *were* going to marry again, I'd want to marry you."

He forced his smile wider. "And if I were ever going to marry, I'd want it to be to you." He leaned down and gave her a casual kiss on the cheek. "I'm happy for you, truly."

She didn't let him pull away. Instead she wrapped one arm around his neck and, just like that first time, went up on tiptoe and kissed him with everything she had. He kissed her back without thinking. His hunger for her opened like a pit beneath his feet, fiery and deep. He couldn't feel this. He couldn't, because he couldn't have her and it hurt too much, it hurt so he couldn't breathe or think or remember words.

He wanted to shove her away, but then she'd realize how he felt. So he tipped his head back, just a little, and gently reached up to disentangle her arm. "You don't want to send me back down to my mother looking thoroughly kissed, do you?"

For a moment her arm actually tightened—but then she let him go.

He'd thought he felt sick before, but real, physical nausea swamped him now, the kind you got when you'd been hungry for so long you didn't even want food anymore. He took in a breath and nearly gagged, nearly doubled over. This was the last time he'd ever kiss her, the last time he'd ever touch her. The last time she'd press up against him with everything she had. She had so much, and he had nothing.

"Nick?" She sounded concerned.

"It's nothing." He forced the nausea and the hunger down and away, straightening his shoulders. "Congratulations. Give my best to Miss Knight."

"I will. Thank you for all your help."

"It was nothing."

"It wasn't nothing, it was—"

He turned away. "My mother is waiting."

Mr. Moon was alone in the front of the shop when she walked in, refilling some half-empty jars of candy in the window. For the first time, she really understood what Nick had done for her. He'd saved her from this confectionery. It was a very fine confectionery, but it would never have been home.

She hadn't done anything for Nick except hurt him. *Even if he thinks he wants you now,* she told herself, *that doesn't mean he'll still want you in a year, or five.* Agreeing with Lady Tassell, even mentally, made her feel disgusting.

"Mrs. Sparks," Mr. Moon said with a nervous smile.

"Don't worry, Mr. Moon." Despite the heavy feeling in her chest, she felt a smile coming on. "I'm not marrying you, and you aren't going to lose the shop either."

He stopped pouring candy, looking wary. "Pardon?"

"How much do you owe?"

"Fifty-seven pounds, but—"

She set her book down on the counter, pulled Lady Tassell's money out of her sleeve, counted out a few bills, and handed them to him with a flourish. "You'll have to find another way to get the freedom of the city, but this ought to cover what you owe."

Mr. Moon's brown eyes turned the size of platters. "What—where did you get this?"

"I can't tell you that. And you can't tell anyone I gave it to you either. But it was legal, and safe, and neither of us have to marry at all."

He tried to push the bills back into her hands. "I can't take this. Mr. Dymond already gave me fifty pounds towards my debts."

For a moment she faltered. Nick had done that? "Please," she said. "Keep it. Buy the freedom after all. I don't want it."

"You're sure?" He squinted at her. "Is everything all right, Mrs. Sparks?"

No. It wasn't. She tried to say it was, and couldn't. "It will be. I didn't—" *I didn't sell my virtue,* she had been going to say, as a joke. But she had. She'd sold her goodness and her purity of heart. She'd sold Nick. "Don't worry about it. Please, take the money. I owe it to you."

He smoothed the bills through his fingers, his face alight. "I made you one last sweet. Would you like to try it?"

She shrugged. "Why not?"

He tucked the money into his pocket and led her into the kitchen. "Mrs. Sparks and I are not marrying," he announced to Betsy and Peter. "But when she does, we're making her wedding cake!" He went on into the cold room.

Betsy mostly looked relieved. But Peter said, dolefully, "I suppose you'll want your book back."

She almost gave it to him—but she liked it, and it had cost her a shilling ninepence. "Give it back when you've read it. You too, Betsy."

He grinned. "Obliged, ma'am. What should I read next?"

Oh, why not? "I'll let you use my subscription to the library," she promised recklessly. "I think you'll like *Tom Jones.*"

Mr. Moon came back in, holding a great bowl with a lid full of ice. He lifted the lid off carefully and took a spoonful of the contents. "Try it." He handed her the spoon.

She eyed it warily. It looked like brown-bread ice cream. She didn't mind that, so she tried it.

The gates of heaven opened in her mouth. She could hear the Hosannas as the cold cream melted on her tongue. It was rich and thick and satisfying and sweet and…salty. It should have tasted strange, but it was perfect. It was better than perfect. It was everything everyone had told her sweets should be, all her life. She wanted to eat a gallon of it. "Oh," she said helplessly. "Can I—"

Mr. Moon's face glowed even brighter as he dished her up a great helping. "I knew I could find it. There's one for everyone."

"What *is* it?"

"It's brown-bread cream ice with bacon," he said.

"*Bacon?*" She realized she was talking with her mouth full, and hastily shut it.

He nodded. "I baked some bacon and butter into the bread. And I cooked the cream and milk and egg yolks with bacon in it, then strained it through cheesecloth to make the ice."

She swallowed. "It's wonderful. It's the most delicious thing I've ever eaten. I don't know how I'm to eat anything else, now." Mr. Moon's grin looked as if it would split his face right in half. "I brought you one last book. A poem by Mr. William Wordsworth. Would you like to hear it?" He looked dubious, but he nodded. "When I've finished this ice," she clarified.

At long last, she picked up the book and opened to the marked page.

There was a time when meadow, grove, and stream,
The earth, and every common sight,
To me did seem
Appareled in celestial light,
The glory and the freshness of a dream.
It is not now as it has been of yore...

She looked up. He was listening, really listening, so she kept reading. It was a long poem. By the time she'd reached the bottom of the first page, Betsy and Peter had both gone back to their tasks. But when she got to *Shades of the prison-house begin to close upon the growing boy*, Mr. Moon set down his knife.

"Sir, I think the stucklings are burning," Peter said.

"Then take them out, there's a good boy," Mr. Moon snapped. "What was that about splendor in the grass, Mrs. Sparks?"

He was silent for long moments after she read the last line. "I never knew a man could do that with words. It's a whole—a whole feeling, and I never knew there was a way to say it. I thought it was just me that felt it."

She beamed. "A man can do anything with words."

Mr. Moon winked at her. "Not *anything*."

She laughed—and then she flushed, hearing Nick's voice in her ear, saying, *If you put your hands flat on the table, I could pull up your skirts and take you.* "You'd be surprised."

It was so splendid to find this one moment of connection with another human being, this one moment when she and Mr. Moon understood each other. With Nick she felt this way all the time. For the first time, today, she'd felt sorry for Wordsworth. She'd thought, *The glory hasn't passed away from the earth at all, you poor unhappy man.*

Nick had made her feel that way, as if the dull sadness of these last few years wasn't a natural part of being a grown woman at all. It was just a film that had formed over life's brightness, like dirt on a window, and all she had to do was wash it off.

He made her want to dance down the middle of the street. But that wasn't safe, and it wasn't respectable, and it didn't matter that her feet itched to do it.

Helen needs you, she told herself firmly. It didn't matter what she wanted, at all.

When Nick got back to the Lost Bell, the proprietor bustled up to him. "Mail from London, sir. Heavy, fine paper with a great big seal. It looks to be important." He handed Nick the folded letter with an air of pride at being the one to deliver such a vital missive.

Nick smiled so as not to disappoint him, but his heart sank. He knew what was written on that heavy, fine paper. "Thank you for giving it to me so promptly."

Upstairs, he broke the seal and spread the special license out on the table, reading every dull legal phrase with care. He lingered longest on two words, however, his eye tracing and retracing every stroke of the clerk's pen:

Phoebe Sparks.

The impulse to throw the paper into the fire built in his chest. He wouldn't even have to watch it burn; he could pack his things, hire a coach to take him to London tonight, and never look back, knowing every trace of this chapter in his life was gone forever. Every bone in his body ached to do it.

He forced his muscles to relax, breathing in and out until the urge ebbed a little. He couldn't go, anyway. Tony needed him. He folded the paper back up and tucked it into his coat pocket.

This pain, he chose to feel.

Chapter 29

"**I** can't go." Helen balked in the doorway to the stairs. "I can't face him."

"I'm so sorry, Ships," Phoebe said for the hundredth time. "I don't want to do it either. But it's just one evening, and then you never have to see him again, and we'll have Lady Tassell's help and money in our pockets."

"He'll be back next election. Maybe I should just leave town."

Phoebe put an arm around her shoulder and squeezed. "This is your home, not his. You shouldn't have to run away. I couldn't have changed the deal without telling Lady Tassell the truth. She wants you there because you're the prettiest girl in town, you know that."

"I hate being pretty," Helen said flatly.

Phoebe didn't know what else to say. She desperately didn't want to go either. Nick would be there. "All right," she said, trying to sound warm and not quite managing it. "I'll tell her you ate something that disagreed with you. See you tonight."

Helen's shoulders drooped. "No, I'll go."

Phoebe felt like the greatest beast in the world. "You don't have to."

"It's just one evening." Helen's fingers traced the orange and purple ribbons she'd braided into her hair, her mouth thinning miserably. Phoebe realized she was doing the same thing with her own rosette and hastily dropped her hand.

The streets were crowded with townsfolk on their way to the hustings, but Phoebe elbowed her way through without difficulty, Helen following in her wake. Ahead of them, a carriage was having less success; the crowd filled the road. As they passed the mired vehicle, a familiar voice called to the driver, "We'll get out here, that's all." The door flew open, and there stood—

"Jack!" Phoebe cried. "You're back."

Jack grinned broadly at her. "That I am, and so is the new Mrs. Sparks." He jumped down from the carriage. "I told you we'd make it in time for the polling." He climbed up on the roof to retrieve an old sedan chair lashed there. "Oi, clear the way!" he bellowed, shoving his way to the sidewalk with the chair.

Caroline Jessop—Caroline Sparks now—leaned out of the open carriage door, red hair and happy face ablaze against her dusty, travel-stained cloak. "We're sisters!" she shouted.

Phoebe smiled at her, trying not to feel gnawed apart by envy for their new-wed bliss. "Welcome to the family."

"Nobody touch this chair," Jack shouted to the passersby behind them, and then he was back lifting Caroline out of the carriage. She slung an arm comfortably about his neck, and he leaned in to kiss her.

Several long moments later, she pulled back, eyes shining. "Your sisters are right here."

Jack winked at Phoebe. "Oh, you should have seen her and Will when they were first married."

Phoebe felt a truly Wordsworthian pang of nostalgia for something that could never have lasted. She and Will *had* been happy at first, deliriously happy. *Where is it now, the glory and the dream?* Maybe it was better this way, better to be an old maid than to take that risk again.

Jack settled his wife in her new chair. She made a face. "Ugh, I hate this chair."

"We bought it off a man in London," Jack explained. "He was peddling people about in it. It was cheap. Well, you can see why."

It certainly didn't move as smoothly as the expensive one Caroline had left behind as Jack started pushing it towards the square. But Caroline said, "And then he said, 'Don't drop her, ducks, there'll be plenty of time for tumbling later!'" She and Jack dissolved into laughter.

"I suppose you had to be there," Caroline got out between giggles. Phoebe glanced at Helen to share an eye-roll, and caught her watching them with the same naked envy she felt. Poor girl. Helen deserved that innocent, uncomplicated joy.

"So how are the numbers looking?" Jack asked. "Will our man win?"

Our man. Phoebe remembered that of course Jack was still planning to vote for Tony Dymond.

"That bad?" Jack said. "Then it's a good thing we shelled out for the post-chaise. We nearly didn't make it, you know." He looked Phoebe up and down. "You don't look married."

"I'm not." She tried to sound happy about it. "Lady Tassell agreed to help us anyway. I'll tell you about it later."

Jack clapped her on the shoulder. "That's splendid news."

She forced a smile. Jack didn't notice; he was looking at his wife.

Their progress was slower after that, but neither Phoebe nor Helen minded. She tried to avoid her friends, pretending not to see when Martha Honeysett waved at her from across the street. She caught sight of Mr. Moon passing out sweets and Sukey holding a banner with a group of her friends. The hustings were tall and festive, covered in bunting in the colors of both parties. It was, objectively, a hideous clash, but until now Phoebe had always liked it. It had seemed cheerful and rowdy, like the elections.

The Dymond family stood in a cluster to the left. Nick slouched discontentedly against the back wall, his eyes fixed on the old church without seeming to really see it. Occasionally he shook his head or nodded in response to a question from his brother or mother, but he didn't turn to look at them. Her heart smote her. He wanted to be here about as much as she did.

Mr. Gilchrist was up there too, talking to Lord Wheatcroft's daughter. He saw them immediately and tapped Mr. Jessop on the shoulder, pointing out Caroline and Jack. Mr. Jessop pushed his way down the stairs and disappeared into the crowd. Phoebe stiffened, expecting a scene.

Nick's head turned to follow the direction of Mr. Gilchrist's pointing finger without any real urgency. His eyes fixed on her at once. Their gazes held—and then he gave her that charming, boyish, practiced grin of his and went back to looking at the church.

Phoebe felt lower than worms. She linked her arm through her sister's, ostensibly to give Helen support but really because she needed it herself. The poor girl was rigid as a board. "It's only a few hours," Phoebe said. Helen nodded silently, looking anywhere but at the hustings.

Mr. Jessop appeared in the crowd a few feet away, crying impatiently, "Make way, kindly make way." Phoebe had forgotten all about him.

"Father." Caroline looked small and pale again, suddenly.

Mr. Jessop gave her a narrow-eyed look children the world over would have recognized as *We'll discuss this later.* Then he smiled and embraced her. "Caroline Maria, you naughty puss!" he said in a carrying voice. "What a fright you gave me." He clapped Jack on the shoulder. "And you, young man. I've half a mind to knock you down." He shook his head indulgently. "Welcome to the family, boy."

Jack looked pole-axed. Phoebe waited a moment, then elbowed him. "Thank you, sir," he said hastily.

"I've got your chair at home," Mr. Jessop said more quietly to his daughter. "I'll have it sent round to your new lodgings at once."

Caroline's smile trembled, and her eyes were bright. "Thank you, Papa."

He gave her a crooked smile back. "I love you, puss."

"I love you too."

"Well, I—" Mr. Jessop sniffed, jerked his head in the direction of the hustings, and dove back into the crowd. His progress this time was slowed by handshakes and congratulations, which he took with remarkably good grace.

"I suppose he *is* a politician," Phoebe said. Caroline nodded in proud agreement.

She sneaked another glimpse at Nick, who was quite plainly snapping at his mother. But he was here. He'd come to support his brother. Of course, he didn't know that his brother was a low seducer and terrorizer of defenseless girls. She'd lied to him about everything, and he'd been trying so hard to find the truth. How would he feel if he knew?

"Ah, Mrs. Sparks," said a familiar smooth voice at her elbow. "I thought you were marrying a Whig."

"I was," she told Mr. Gilchrist. "But I've come into some money, instead."

His eyebrows rose, and he leaned in confidentially. "Not from the young pig-Whig, I hope."

"For heaven's sake," Helen said crossly. "How long have you been waiting to use that bigwig pun?"

He smiled. "Oh, I use it frequently." He stepped neatly around Phoebe and looked Helen up and down. "The cuffs are genius."

She smiled up at him, dimpling.

Phoebe looked at her sister's spencer. She'd added gold braid and tassels to the front in accordance with the latest craze for frogging, but instead of covering the width of the breast, she'd done a shortened version and piped embroidered ribbon on either side. The effect was very modern and gay, and Phoebe had complimented her on it, but she hadn't even noticed the cuffs. Now she saw that Helen had added narrow, short frogging to the buttons as well and meticulously given the closure a zigzag edge.

She looked between the cuffs, her sister's beaming face, and Mr. Gilchrist's oily smile, and had a very bad feeling about where this was going.

Sure enough, Gilchrist said, "I'm leaving town after the election, you know." He paused. Helen's face went carefully blank. "Maybe even tomorrow morning, if we can send you Orange-and-Purples packing without a poll." He waited for the expected enthusiastic denial.

Neither sister obliged him. Instead Helen said, in a rather colorless voice, "I hope you have a very safe journey."

Mr. Gilchrist glanced at Phoebe. "Have I your permission to ask your sister to marry me?"

"What?" Jack demanded. "No! No you don't, you Tory rodent, and I—"

Phoebe put a hand on his arm. She would have liked to back him, but Helen was regarding Mr. Gilchrist with the white, strained face of someone who had been offered her heart's desire and knew she couldn't have it.

"You can ask," Phoebe said. "But if she says no, I hope you'll be less of a nuisance about it than you have been about my votes."

"I promise nothing," Mr. Gilchrist said. "Miss Knight, please allow me to tell you how deeply I worship you. Will you make me the happiest man on earth?"

Helen opened her mouth, but if she made a sound, it was lost in the noise of the crowd. Then she said, so quietly they could barely make it out, "There's something you don't know."

Mr. Gilchrist blinked. "I am all-knowing," he said, striving for a joke, but he looked very young and anxious as he said it.

Helen glanced around, then stood on her tiptoes to whisper in his ear.

His jaw dropped, his eyes going to Helen's still-trim waist. "Ohhh."

"Yes," Helen said. "Oh."

He looked, mostly, terribly disappointed. "But—who?"

Helen glanced up at the hustings, so swiftly Phoebe thought Mr. Gilchrist might not have noticed. Then she burst into tears and fled.

She didn't move very fast through the crowd. Her vision was blurred by tears, and she'd never been very handy with her elbows. Phoebe caught up with her easily and dragged her into the church, an empty, echoing oasis in the midst of chaos. The opaque walls of the deserted box pews made her nervous, as though they concealed crouching, sanctimonious eavesdroppers.

"I love him," Helen sobbed. "I love him and he'll never marry me now. I'm ruined."

"You aren't ruined," Phoebe said, startled at this ardor for fox-faced Mr. Gilchrist. "You aren't. If he doesn't marry you, he's a fool, that's all. No one else knows. We can still get through this unscathed. Put up your chin, and we'll go back out there—"

"If I hadn't been so *stupid* I could have had him," Helen said furiously. "If I'd just waited two dratted months— I *hate* Tony Dymond. I hate him. I can't bear to go out there and cheer for him. I can't bear it that he's going to win and I've lost everything."

Phoebe had striven and sacrificed, had done everything but bleed, to get this bargain for Helen. She'd given up Nick. And she'd thought she'd finally come out on top.

In that moment it all fell apart: Helen felt as if she'd lost everything.

Helen had been against Phoebe's election-marriage plan from the start. Phoebe had pushed her into it, had ignored it when Helen said she wanted to leave town and keep her baby. She hadn't really listened. Maybe it had been for Helen's own good, maybe it was even the safest choice—but it ought to have been Helen's choice to make, not hers.

She thought of poor Ann in her quiet line of work, and her virtuous sister. Phoebe had made herself the heroine of Helen's story.

Nick had *told* her. He had told her that when you looked at someone you loved, you should only see them.

Love, she realized suddenly, didn't mean putting another person's happiness above everything else. It didn't mean giving up everything. Loving someone meant letting him choose, letting her put herself first. "What do you want to do?" she asked. "We can stay, and keep the money. Or we can walk out right now."

Helen swallowed, looking frightened. "What do you think I should do?"

Stay, she thought. "It's up to you."

"It's another vote for Reform in the Commons," Helen said slowly. "And he could tell everyone. The scandal would be so hard on you and mother—"

That stung. She'd wanted so much to protect Helen from scandal, and all Helen had seen was that she was afraid of scandal herself. She'd organized Helen's life according to the same stupid rules that governed Improving Tales.

Once, Phoebe had believed in progress and possibilities and risks. She meant to believe in them again. "What about you, Ships?"

Helen put a hand on her stomach. "I could always go somewhere else, if I had to." She was so young. She couldn't go off somewhere by herself and raise a child.

Phoebe would deal with that when she came to it. It was terrifying, but maybe it was time to let Helen reach for a real happy ending. "It's up to you," she repeated. "I'll stand by you no matter what you choose."

Helen straightened her shoulders. "Let's get out of here."

Phoebe nodded, unpinning her rosette and dropping it on the floor. Helen set her heel on it and ground it into the stone floor, looking more cheerful and sure of herself than she had in weeks.

"What about Mama?" Phoebe asked. "Do you want to tell her?"

Helen faltered. "Do you think I should?"

"People in this town care what she thinks," Phoebe said. "If she leaves, it might sway a vote or two. It might not, and I don't think we can be sure she'll keep it to herself. And then there's Jack. The same goes for him. What do you want to do?" *Don't tell them,* she thought. *Don't tell them. It isn't safe.*

"I don't want Jack to vote for him," Helen said, in almost a pleading tone.

"I don't either." She had to make sure Helen understood the risks. "But he could make a scene. Or he could tell his wife. She's a Tory. This is valuable information that could change the course of the election. It's up to you, sweetheart. If you want to tell them, I'll be right there with you. Just remember, it isn't cowardice to protect yourself."

Helen laughed. "You don't want me to tell them, do you?"

No. "I want you to think about what *you* want."

Helen's lips twisted. "If I'd done that earlier, maybe I wouldn't be in this mess. But I was thinking about what *he* wanted, and whether he'd be angry. I'm so frightened, Phoebe. I've been so frightened."

"I know, Ships. And if you want to just slip away, now—"

"You don't understand," Helen said. "I can't go on like this. I have to feel strong again."

"Nick, that piece you wrote for the *Intelligencer* was wonderful," Lady Tassell said.

"Thank you." He ought to be pleased that his mother was proud. But he couldn't feel anything but annoyed and self-conscious that she'd read his article. He didn't mind it being in the paper for half the county to see, but the idea of his mother reading it still made him squirm.

She turned to Tony. "Maybe he should have written your speech." Tony stiffened, shooting Nick a resentful look.

"Mother, Tony is quite capable of writing his own speech."

Lady Tassell gave a dissatisfied frown. "It lacks conviction."

"So does Tony," Ada muttered.

"He can't possibly lack conviction as much as I do," Nick said lightly.

His mother regarded him thoughtfully. "So I would have said. But that article— Where did they go?"

Nick, grateful her attention had been distracted, went back to counting how many shop signs he could read at this distance.

She swept forward and leaned out over the low wooden wall that separated their part of the platform from the voters', gaze searching the crowd. "I made a deal with her, and she and her pretty sister disappear just as Tony is about to give his speech? I don't think so."

Nick froze.

Tony took her elbow. "Mama, just let them go. It doesn't matter."

"Tony, they have influence with the voters in this town," Lady Tassell said severely. "And look, there go her mother and Mr. Sparks, who have more. With his Tory wife—oh Lord, and Dromgoole's election agent. This is a disaster. Where are they going?"

Nick could have told her that Phoebe and Miss Knight had gone into the church five minutes ago, but he didn't. "Let them alone."

"Let them *alone*?" Lady Tassell was incensed. "Wait here,

Tony. I'll take care of this." She started down the wooden steps.

"Mama, no!" Tony hastened after her, with a last vicious glance over his shoulder at Nick. "This is all *your* fault."

What did Tony mean by that? *It doesn't matter. Phoebe's not your concern anymore.* But even after ten full verses of *Childe Harold*, he hadn't pulled back or distanced himself in the slightest. He went after them.

In a crowd, no one noticed his limp or made allowances. He made his way as best he could, not doing so badly until a matron in an enormous orange-and-purple bonnet turned unexpectedly, jostling him so hard he fell. Pain shot through his leg.

Gritting his teeth, he stood and dragged himself the final ten feet. Bracing himself to pull the heavy door open hurt.

"Phoebe, what happened to your rosette?" Mrs. Knight was asking when he got inside. "Honestly, you wouldn't lose things so often if you'd only pay attention."

"I took it off," Phoebe said. "Lady Tassell, I'm giving you your money back. All except fifty pounds. I already gave it to Mr. Moon, for the freedom of the city. You would have bought him that anyway."

She'd given away fifty pounds. And she was giving back the rest. *Why?* His heart pounded. Had she changed her mind? Did she want to marry him after all?

Lady Tassell gave her a strained smile. "This isn't about the money. Or the *other* things I promised you. Your party needs your support. Please, come back outside."

"I don't need the other things, either, now." Phoebe took a deep breath. "And we won't be coming back outside." Miss Knight was deathly pale, clinging to her sister's arm as he'd never seen her do, but her face was resolute. What the devil was going on?

"I don't know what the Tories have promised you, Mrs. Sparks, but you cannot rely—"

"Mama," Tony hissed. "Come away." He threw a desperate look at Phoebe and her sister. "Please. We needn't lower ourselves by haggling with these people—"

"Tony! Where are your manners?" Lady Tassell snapped. Tony actually took her by the arm and tried to drag her away, but she yanked free.

The fox-faced Tory agent looked entertained but confused. Miss Knight was trembling, her wide eyes fixed on Tony. And Phoebe—Phoebe alternated between watching her sister and shooting Tony glances of such vitriolic hatred they rocked Nick back on his heels.

Oh, God.

"Tony," he said harshly. "Tony, tell me you didn't."

"Didn't what?" Lady Tassell asked. "Will one of you boys kindly tell me what is going on here?"

"Shut up, Nick." Tony's voice was low and intent.

Nick felt sick. His brother—his little brother—he couldn't wrap his mind around the enormity of it. Lady Tassell, evidently, could. Her jaw dropped.

"Edward Anthony Fitzhugh Dymond," she began, drawing a deep breath.

Nick looked at Mr. Sparks and his new wife, unabashedly confused and curious. Mrs. Knight and the Tory obviously didn't know, either.

"A little discretion, if you please, Mother," he rapped out in his officer voice. Phoebe shot him a grateful look. He felt the beginnings of an emotion coiling in his chest. He wasn't sure yet which one.

Lady Tassell actually subsided, nodding. "Tony, we'll

discuss this later," she said through her teeth. Tony blanched. "Your brother, at least, is a gentleman."

Enlightenment dawned on Gilchrist's face. The Tory agent glanced between Tony and Miss Knight, eyes widening as he realized what this could mean for his party. Phoebe, seeing it, looked devastated. Damn it all to hell.

"Miss Knight," Lady Tassell said, "I would love for us to become better acquainted. May I call upon you tomorrow? And Mr. Gilchrist, if I might speak with you—"

To Nick's surprise, the young man stepped forward and put his arm around Miss Knight's shoulders. "This young lady is my future wife," he said. "Please don't call; I don't much care for her consorting with the Whig leadership." Miss Knight stiffened, and Lady Tassell raised her eyebrows as if to say, *Too late for that.* Sometimes Nick couldn't believe how rude his mother was. Gilchrist screwed his face up and squeezed Miss Knight's shoulders in apology for his poor choice of words.

"Then you have no plans to make this public?" Lady Tassell said.

"None," Gilchrist said firmly. Miss Knight leaned against him, just a little.

"Splendid," Lady Tassell said. "I will, of course, be happy to contribute to the infant's—"

Gilchrist smiled blandly. "No. You won't."

Lady Tassell shrugged. "Congratulations, my dear," she said to Miss Knight. "I'm glad things have worked out well. I'll still call on you before I leave town, if your overbearing young man will allow it." She turned and swept from the room. Before following her, Tony shot a warning glance at Miss Knight, who shrank back fearfully.

Nick saw red. He barely waited until they were outside to

grab Tony, turn him round, and slam him against the wall hard enough that his head cracked against the stone. He recognized the feeling in his chest now. It was rage. At every single damn person in his life, including himself.

Chapter 30

"Helen, has this Tory coxcomb been letting you dangle all this time?" Jack demanded. "I don't think much of a man who—"

"He isn't the father," Helen said softly.

Mr. Gilchrist shrugged. "If we're married when it's born, I will be."

Mrs. Knight had taken all this time to absorb what was happening. Now she crossed her arms, giving Mr. Gilchrist a watery glower. "Preening Tory peacock. How do you even know this man, Helen?"

Helen gave her a pleading look. "Mama, I can keep the baby."

Phoebe couldn't believe it. Mrs. Knight had treated her like a criminal, and here she was, crawling back for approval.

Mrs. Knight was silent for long moments. "He isn't—well, men set store by such things, you know."

"My aunt raised me, myself," Mr. Gilchrist said. "I've always thought she loves me as much as her own children. Babies, don't you know—God must have designed them express. If they weren't so infernally sweet-looking, they'd have a hard time getting food. And then, if it were mine, we'd have to worry about it having a terrible pointy chin." He watched Helen, trying to look confident.

Helen glowed. "Thank you," she said. "Thank you. I—I never thought I'd be this happy again."

Mr. Gilchrist lightly ran his fingers over the orange and purple ribbons in her braided hair. "I'd like to get these out." But he didn't muss her hair, Phoebe noticed.

"Does he have a name?" Mrs. Knight asked.

"Reginald Gilchrist at your service, madam."

Mrs. Knight held out her hand, and Mr. Gilchrist bowed low over it, kissing the air an inch above her glove like an old-fashioned courtier. Mrs. Knight eyed him suspiciously—but Phoebe could see her softening. "Helen, he's a Tory."

"I noticed, Mama," Helen said with a small smile, running her finger along the inch of Mr. Gilchrist's bright pink-and-white waistcoat that showed below his coat. "Don't worry, you can give our children as many pamphlets as you like."

Mrs. Knight's eyes brightened with tears. "Oh, my baby girl, getting married!" She pounced on Helen in exactly the way Helen hated, squashing the carefully arranged linen fall of her fichu. Helen let her.

"So who *is* the father?" Jack demanded.

"How *could* you?" Nick's fists tightened in Tony's coat. "You knew all this time? You *abandoned* her?"

Tony's eyes flew to their mother, over Nick's shoulder. Nick slammed him against the wall again. "Look at me."

"Nick, that is quite enough," Lady Tassell said furiously. "The pair of you are about to lose us this election. Tony, I had credited you with some judgment. Evidently I was too generous."

"Judgment?" Nick said incredulously. "*Judgment?* The *pair* of us? He—he—" People were watching. He couldn't say aloud what Tony had done. Tony had known their mother would help Helen, and he'd obviously threatened her to keep her quiet. "He sacrificed decency for your good opinion. That's not *ill judgment.* That family has been going through hell, you selfish, despicable—"

"She seduced me," Tony said desperately, still looking past Nick to Lady Tassell. "Who knows if the child is even mine?"

Nick was suddenly afraid of what he would do. He forced his fingers to unclench from Tony's coat and leaned against the church wall, trying to breathe through the fury filling his lungs. *He's your little brother,* he reminded himself, but he couldn't quite remember why that mattered.

"Mama, you have to believe me. I doubt I was her first—"

Jack Sparks erupted from the church just in time to hear those words. He called Tony a truly impressive name and hit him square in the jaw with one of his enormous fists. Another massive swing sent him crashing to the ground, where Sparks straddled him and dealt a few more heavy blows. "I'll kill you," he growled, the ring of sincerity in his voice. Tony struggled, landing a punch or two, but he was obviously outmatched. Nick tried not to feel deeply satisfied by that.

Helen Knight burst through the door, sobbing and holding her fist to her mouth. "Jack, please!" Behind her tumbled Gilchrist, Mrs. Knight, and last of all Phoebe, trying to maneuver the heavy door and the new Mrs. Sparks's wheelchair. Nick inched his way along the wall and held the door for her, setting his jaw against the pain in his leg. She shot him another grateful look. He turned away.

"Stop it, Jack," she called. "You'll be jailed for assault.

Think of the fines!"

"Jack, please," his wife added sharply.

It had absolutely no effect. Sparks roared and hit Tony in the face again. Everyone in a ten-foot radius was watching now. Miss Knight looked petrified, her eyes darting wildly around the crowd.

Nick put his fingers in his mouth and gave a piercing whistle. "*Gentlemen,*" he roared in his best officer voice. "Desist at once. You are making a spectacle of the ladies."

Sparks froze, turning his head to glare at Nick. It was a somewhat frightening glare, but at least he was distracted from Tony. Nick met his eyes coolly. The key was looking absolutely certain you'd be obeyed. "Hand me my stick, will you? Then get in the church. Now." He jerked his head imperiously.

Sparks reluctantly climbed off of Nick's little brother. Tony gave a feeble moan, and Lady Tassell rushed forward to feel his jaw and nose. "Oh, sweetheart. I don't think anything's broken. You'll just give your speech, and then we'll go home and put a steak on your face and—"

Ada broke through the first row of spectators. "What—? *Tony?*"

"Church." Nick snatched his stick from Sparks's hand, put an arm around Ada's waist, and hustled her into the church himself. Inside, she looked around—at Tony's battered face, Jack's scraped hands, and sobbing Miss Knight. Ada was no fool.

"You son-of-a-bitch." She slapped Tony across his bruised face. "Oh, I'm terribly sorry, Lady Tassell, I didn't mean you," she added with angry insincerity.

"Me?" Tony reached into his mouth to feel a tooth. "He attacked me. I ought to call the constable."

"I *knew* you had a mistress in this town," Ada said, her voice choked. "I just didn't think it would be a respectable virgin. I didn't think you'd make a scene at the hustings. You're determined to humiliate me. It's not my fault you asked me to marry you, Tony."

"It's not my fault you said yes!"

Nick's eyes instinctively went to Phoebe. Her face was suffused with incandescent anger; she was clearly about to boil over.

"What did you tell her to get her in bed, I wonder?" Tears slid down Ada's flushed cheeks. "I doubt you said *she* was too plain to keep a man's interest any other way."

Gilchrist took Miss Knight's hand. "You are all laboring under an insulting misapprehension. I must ask you to immediately cease speaking in such terms of my fiancée."

But Miss Knight stepped forward, her eyes on Ada. "He told me not to be a spoilsport. He said I ought to know what a temptation my looks presented. I think—I think you're very pretty."

Bile rose in Nick's throat.

The fox-faced little Tory drew himself up. He wasn't very tall, but it was with a great deal of dignity that he said, "Name your friends, Mr. Anthony."

Lady Tassell dropped her son like a hot potato. Tony stumbled and almost fell, but Lady Tassell was already sweeping over to Helen. "You poor girl. Why didn't you come to me? Apologize at once, Tony."

"Because he said if she did, he'd ruin her reputation," Phoebe burst out. Even though Nick had known it was coming, it still turned his stomach. She rounded on Tony. "You selfish, vicious, weak... You don't deserve to live, let alone sit in Parliament!" She trembled, her face gone all blotchy.

"Name your friends," Mr. Gilchrist repeated.

"Mr. Gilchrist," Miss Knight said. "Don't, please."

"There's no need," Lady Tassell said. "Tony will apologize." She turned and looked at Tony.

Tony wobbled where he stood. His eyes were bright and desperate, and his skin, where it was not already beginning to bruise, was very pale. He looked to Nick for support. Nick couldn't move. "I'm sorry," Tony said, sounding terribly remorseful. "Miss Knight, I didn't mean to—"

"Is that supposed to be good enough?" Phoebe demanded.

"Phoebe, keep your voice down," Mrs. Knight interjected.

"Don't tell me to keep my voice down! None of us will ever vote Orange-and-Purple as long as you're running," she told Tony.

Gilchrist led Miss Knight away into one of the pews and sat beside her, her hands in his, talking quietly.

Somebody had to take command of this situation.

"Tony isn't running," Nick said. "Tony is stepping down."

His mother and brother gaped at him. "What?"

"You really mean to inflict your continued presence in this town on this poor girl? You're stepping down. Make up a reason—your health, your wife's health. You'll explain the fight by saying you confided your intentions to Sparks and he was angry with you for ruining the Whigs' chances at the last moment."

"But we can't find a replacement candidate in time," Lady Tassell said.

Nick shrugged. "The Tories will win again. It's a shame, but it can't be helped."

"You'll have to take his place," Lady Tassell said briskly.

Tony gasped. "People in town seem to like you. We might lose a few votes, but—"

Nick ignored her. "Tony, will you step down?"

Tony's eyes met his defiantly—and then they dropped. He nodded.

"I want a separation," Ada said, and ran out of the church.

"Nick," Phoebe said wildly.

He looked at her. She was still quivering with energy while he felt bone-tired. He wanted her, and it made him angry. Somehow, perversely, that only made him want her more.

"I'm giving her money back." Her voice shook. "I want— if you're still interested, I want—I'd marry you, if you asked again."

Jack Sparks looked floored, and his wife clapped her hands together with delight. Gilchrist spared them an interested glance from his pew.

"We had an agreement," Lady Tassell protested.

Phoebe turned on her. "What kind of woman says her own son simply isn't meant to be a husband?" She stopped, her hand going to her mouth and her eyes going to Nick.

Lady Tassell gasped. "Nick, I didn't mean it—I only said it because—"

"You only said it to make her break off the engagement. I know." Nick knew, too, that she wouldn't understand why that didn't make it hurt less.

"Nick, I'm sorry," Phoebe said. "I shouldn't have repeated it, I wasn't thinking—"

"So you'd marry me now?" Nick interrupted curtly.

Phoebe nodded. The truth of it was all over her heart-shaped face; she did want him, desperately.

"This is why you cried off, isn't it?"

She nodded again, curls bouncing against her neck. "I couldn't tell you, you have to understand—"

"I don't *have* to understand, actually," he said. "Of course you couldn't tell me about Tony. But you could have told me there was a reason. Instead you made me think you'd never wanted to marry me to begin with."

She flushed. "I couldn't risk it. And I thought for your sake I ought to make a clean break—"

"For my sake," Nick repeated. "*I* thought the truth meant something between us. I thought we—but in the end, you told me what you thought I ought to hear. Just like everybody else."

She drew back, crossing her arms protectively over her chest. She looked small and defenseless and he wanted nothing more than to hold her. "Nick, please—"

"No." He smiled at her. "Unusual word for me, isn't it?" He hefted his cane.

"Nick, I—"

He walked away.

His family, unfortunately, followed him. "I'm sorry, Nick," Tony said quietly. "I should have told you I knew why Mrs. Sparks cried off. I wanted to tell you the whole story when you arrived. But I was afraid you'd—"

"I wouldn't have told Mother. I'd have said it was mine."

"You would have done that for me?" Tony said disbelievingly.

Nick nodded, because three weeks ago, he would have. He would have missed the chance to fall in love with Phoebe for the illusion of being a good brother, of being relied on. He would have been that stupid. "I'm not a good brother, Tony. I never have been. I'm sorry for that. But I can't—I can't forgive what you did to that girl. I can't forgive the things you said tonight."

"I know," Tony said miserably. "I was just under so much pressure with the campaign, and I needed—I needed a little fun. You've seen her. She's beautiful and she *admired* me—I never intended—"

Nick wanted to cover his ears.

"I should never have let you run for this seat," Lady Tassell said. "I knew you weren't ready."

Tony slumped.

"*Don't*," Nick said to his mother. He couldn't seem to stop telling people what he thought, now he'd started. "Don't. Why do you think Tony was afraid to tell you? Hell, why do you think this happened in the first place? You've been whoring him out to voters' wives and daughters since he was in leading strings. Teaching him that that caddish smile is all he has to offer. That if he can't win over voters, he's worthless."

"Oi!" Tony said. "What's wrong with my smile?"

"I can't be part of this family right now." As Nick said it, he realized how true it was. "I can't—"

"Family isn't something you choose," Lady Tassell said.

"It can be. Go make your concession speech, Tony. I'm going back to the Lost Bell to pack my things."

"Nick…" Tony began pleadingly. But he obviously didn't expect Nick to stay. That hurt worst of all—he wanted to stay, wanted to fix this, but he couldn't. Love wasn't selfless, and it wasn't selfish either. Love was equality. It was saying that another person's self was just as important as yours, and expecting them to feel the same way. That was something his family couldn't give him—that he wasn't sure they could give anybody. It was something he didn't yet have the strength to expect from them.

Lady Tassell talked right over Tony. "Nick, you can't just—"

It would be so easy to ignore her, to just go back to the inn and slip away. He made himself look her in the eye. "Yes. I can. I don't want to speak to either of you. I don't want to see you. I can choose not to do those things. Don't write. Don't try to see me. I'll come to you, when I'm ready." If he was ever ready. "I'm sorry, Tony."

Tony turned his back and began making his way back to the hustings alone. He was nearly as tall as Nick, but he looked small and slight, somehow.

Lady Tassell recoiled, her lips parting, her eyes bright with tears. "Nick, what are you saying? Please, just listen to me…" She kept right on talking.

To his surprise, it didn't even matter that she didn't listen. He had said it. That was what mattered. "Goodbye," he told her.

To his shock, his mother began to sob. "Nick, how could you punish me for what Tony's done? How can you blame me? It's horrible. You know I love all three of you terribly, I love Tony, and I can't bear that he's done this—"

"Bear it." He took her hands. "Just this once you have to live here, with us, in the world. You have to see that we aren't perfect. Not even close, and we never will be no matter how many instructions you give us! Tony did this, and you have to bear it. Listen to him. Try to understand how he ended up here. If you ever want things to be all right with me, you have to make them right with Tony first."

She squeezed his hands tight. "Then stay. Stay and help me—"

"I can't."

He headed out of the square. Behind him, he heard his mother still crying—but she didn't follow him. She blew her nose and went after Tony.

Phoebe sat on her wooden chest, holding up a hand to the window so she could see a patch of cloudy sky instead of her own reflection. Her ears rang faintly—from the shouting crowd, she knew, but it felt as if the day's events had deafened her.

Helen and Mrs. Knight were in Phoebe's bedroom, excitedly planning Helen's wedding. Mr. Gilchrist, evidently, was still obliged to leave town to finish the county polling, but he would be back in a month to be married, and take Helen on a wedding journey to Brighton to stay in a fashionable hotel and visit the shops. He had high hopes of being hired by Lord Wheatcroft to stay on in Lively St. Lemeston, although of course he would occasionally be needed to lend a hand elsewhere.

Phoebe, meanwhile, would be right back where she started. Alone in her attic rooms, writing stories for other people's children.

She would come to enjoy it again, she knew. She loved these rooms. She loved her Improving Tales. But right now, it all seemed very stale.

Maybe when Helen was gone she'd write a nice spot of pornography to liven things up. She could sell it anonymously. *A Merry Widow and Her Three Suitors,* she could call it: one woman courted for marriage by the baker and the mill owner, and courted for pleasure by the duke's son. She could bed all of them in a variety of daring locations and positions.

She couldn't write something like that with her sister and mother in the house, but to soothe herself, she began silently narrating it.

I was born of simple, honest English parents during the first months of the Revolution in France. No one present at my birth, seeing my golden curls and cherubic countenance, would have suspected the depths of sin to which I would one day sink. But the French Saturnalia must have got in my blood; by the time I was five, my hair had darkened to black, and I had learned that an angelic smile procures forgiveness for most any trespass in a pretty girl...

"Fee." Helen stood in the doorway to Phoebe's bedroom. "I'm sorry about Mr. Dymond. But you know he won't stick to it."

Words fled, leaving only an aching sadness in Phoebe's chest. Part of her almost hoped he did stick to it, for his sake. He had a right to be angry.

"Come join us," Helen said.

"Indulging your melancholy will only make you feel worse," Mrs. Knight chimed in, behind her. Helen made an apologetic face at Phoebe, which their mother couldn't see.

A dozen hot retorts on the subject of Mrs. Knight and indulging one's own melancholy sprang to Phoebe's lips. Instead, she smiled and stood. She was in the bosom of her family. Surely she shouldn't feel so desperately lonely.

A pebble hit the window with a sharp crack. Phoebe jumped, startled, and hit her head on the ceiling. Ignoring her mother's and sister's exclamations of concern, she whirled round and knelt on the chest to peer into the darkness. She couldn't see a thing. She cracked the window—but only a little, in case more pebbles were on their way. "Is someone there?"

"It's me," Nick's voice called up, terse and rueful. "I couldn't face the stairs without being sure you'd let me in."

Her heart pounded. "I'll be right down!"

Helen beamed at her. "I told you he'd be back."

"We don't know what he's here to say."

"Maybe *you* don't."

Phoebe hesitated. "You really wouldn't mind, me marrying a Dymond?"

Helen sobered. "I won't see his brother. I'm sorry, I know it will make holidays difficult, but I won't. I've no objection to Mr. Nicholas, however."

Phoebe gave her sister a fierce hug and ran down the stairs.

Nick was waiting by the door, looking uncharacteristically stiff and awkward and holding a valise.

Phoebe's heart stopped. "You're leaving?"

"Not exactly," Nick said. "Well, perhaps. I've left my family, anyway."

"Oh, Nick, because of—"

He nodded. "It means I'm penniless," he said. "I'm sorry I walked away from you, before. I think I should have stayed and had it out with you. I don't trust myself not to be ridden roughshod over."

"And I'm sorry I wasn't honest with you, as far as I could be." The words tumbled over each other in their eagerness to be said. "I should have trusted you. I should have honored the things we shared. I shouldn't have listened to your mother when she said I was unsuitable. I shouldn't have made myself into a martyr to give myself consequence."

"Love isn't selfless," he said. "It's not selfish either. It's two people each being just as important as the other."

"I know." She smiled tremulously. "Love?"

His mouth twitched, but he nodded, solemn and apprehensive. It reminded her of the way he'd said, *I want you very much,* that first time she'd asked him for the unvarnished truth and he'd given it to her. He'd come so far. They'd come so far, together. So they still had a ways to go; that was all right.

"I love you too. Very much. Absurdly. And I'll try to do better next time. I *will* do better. You deserve better."

The tension drained from his body. He set the valise down. "Our first row."

"It wasn't so bad," Phoebe said in surprise. She'd never felt like this after a row with Will, never believed either of them would do anything different, or even that Will understood what she wanted.

She trusted Nick to try. She trusted herself to try, with him.

"Will you marry me?" he asked. "I don't have much to offer you. No money. No profession. No valet—I'm sure I'll be much less handsome in future. I don't know yet what I want to do with my life. But I know I want to do it with you."

"It doesn't matter about the money. In the meantime you can get some Spanish translation work, and I'll write erotic novels. It pays much better than Improving Tales."

"Erotic novels?"

"Why not? I am, after all, a modern woman, free from conventional prejudices." She drew him nearer by his lapels. Something crackled in his coat.

He drew out a carefully folded paper. He opened it and showed it to her, smiling. Their special license. "No prejudices against short engagements then?"

Exhilaration lodged in her throat, so that she had to take a shaky breath before she could speak. "None at all."

"Any against being kissed in your front garden?"

"Quite the opposite. Really, if you think about it, it's our duty to strike a blow for—" In general she disliked being interrupted, but in this case, she would make an exception. She stood on her tiptoes and kissed him back.

Epilogue

NEW YEAR'S DAY, 1813

Nick put a tray of bread and cold tongue on Phoebe's writing table. She set down her pen and looked up with a quick smile. "Thanks. I just need to finish copying this out before we leave." Nick watched her spread mustard on a slice of bread with a liberal hand, smiling to herself. Even after almost three months in their new ground-floor lodgings—modest, to be sure, but not quite so modest as her old rooms—things like having enough money for mustard had not lost their novelty for her.

"I'll need you to lock our trunk while I sit on it," he said, making himself a sandwich. "A cart will come from the Lost Bell in the morning to carry it to the coach." Nick's article on life in the army had turned into a series, and the *Times* had offered to send him to the Peninsula for a few months as their correspondent. Their *paid* correspondent. Doing for himself and going without luxuries he'd learned in the army, but until now Nick had never realized how satisfying even a little money could be, when you'd earned it.

"The coach." Phoebe sighed happily. "I can't believe I'm really going to see Spain. I've never even seen the *sea*." She'd borrowed Bewick's *Water Birds* from the library and had been poring over it all week.

For a moment he felt sad. Tony had decided to go on an

expedition to South America. (Ada was living with her parents again.) He'd sent Nick a letter from Portsmouth before he left, with a sketch of a seagull in flight. Even reading the salutation had called up too much churning anger to continue, so Nick had put it in the fire and watched the seagull blacken and crumble into ash.

He looked down at his wife scribbling a correction in the margin of her erotic tale, bound for anonymous publication in London. The sadness faded. Not even the best drawing could show the way seagulls flew, or their insolent honking calls, or the way they could catch a thrown piece of bread in midair. Nick couldn't wait to see Phoebe's face.

"You're sure the trip won't be too hard on your leg?" she asked, not for the first time.

"It won't be easy," he said again. "It will hurt sometimes. But I want to go."

"And you're sure we'll be back before Helen has her baby?"

He nodded.

"And you're sure—"

"Are *you* sure?" he asked gently. "We don't have to go."

She shook her head. "I want to go. I'm just nervous." She gave him a sidelong smile. "I want to see the sunken glen, whose sunless shrubs must weep."

He poked her. "That's one of the most beautiful passages in the poem, and all you can do is laugh at the sunless shrubs? What about the tender azure of the unruffled deep and the orange tints that gild the greenest bough?" She'd read *Childe Harold's Pilgrimage* twice now, but he thought she enjoyed Byron's notes about his travels better than the poem itself.

Her smile widened. "Are the colors really brighter in Spain?"

He looked out the window at the gray English January, at pale light filtered through clouds. Then he looked at his wife, and he couldn't imagine any colors brighter than her hair and skin and eyes. "You'll have to decide for yourself. The sunlight might be richer there, but I like the colors here fine."

"I want to go." This time she sounded sure. "I want to go with you," she added, flushing a little.

He leaned down and kissed her. "I can't wait to introduce you to my friends." He'd actually written to them to say he was coming. To his surprise, despite the unreliable mail he'd already got replies from three of them—men he'd ignored for almost a year now—full of congratulations and cheerful entreaties for him to bring them equipment, books, and food.

She smiled shyly. "Really? You mean it?"

Nick's anger at his mother for the cruel things she had said to Phoebe rose—but it was less sharp than it had been. He'd spoken to her once more after the election, after Stephen and his father had both come to town to remonstrate with him. She'd begged him to let her write to him, and he'd agreed she could send one short letter a week. She was mostly sticking to it. Maybe, someday soon, he'd try writing back. He'd stopped really talking to her so long ago. Maybe he was ready to give her another chance to listen. "They'll all be unbearably envious," he said with perfect sincerity.

She raised her eyebrows and smiled, as if she thought he was talking nonsense but didn't really mind.

He knelt beside her chair and kissed her neck. "Who *wouldn't* be envious of us?"

She beamed and turned in her chair. "Good point. We're probably the happiest people in the world."

"I would assume."

Her hand wandered to his coat buttons. "I have to finish copying this." She sounded as if she were trying to convince herself more than him.

He undid the buttons for her. "You can spare a quarter of an hour."

"Yes, only it never *is* a quarter of an hour, is it? I don't know what I did to deserve such a demanding muse." But she let him pull her out of her chair and towards the bed.

"I don't know either, but it must have been very naughty."

"Mmm." She smiled. "Maybe by the time we come back home, I'll be pregnant."

"I'll do my best," he promised.

Author's Note

Thank you for reading *Sweet Disorder*! I hope you enjoyed Nick and Phoebe's story.

Would you like to know when my next book is available? Sign up for updates at RoseLerner.com or follow me on twitter at @RoseLerner. You can also support me on Patreon, and receive weekly sneak peeks at what I'm working on!

Reviews help other readers find books. I appreciate all reviews, positive and negative.

You've just finished Book 1 in my series about the little market town of Lively St. Lemeston. Book 2, *True Pretenses*, is about Lord Wheatcroft's daughter, Lydia, pretending to fall in love with a traveling con artist in order to get her hands on her dowry. (And we all know what happens when you *pretend* to fall in love…)

Book 3, *Listen to the Moon*, is about Phoebe's wisecracking maid, Sukey, and Nick's long-suffering valet, Toogood, who marry to get a plum job. And by popular demand, Book 4, "A Taste of Honey," is a sexy novella about Mr. Moon, his shopgirl Betsy, and lots and lots of dessert! (The dessert is *mostly* not involved in the sexy parts. Mostly.)

Visit my website for *Sweet Disorder* extras, including free short stories (there's one set in an alternate universe where Nick is a vampire and Phoebe is a dragon), deleted scenes, recipes, and historical research. There's information about Byron, Sussex slang, the British electoral system—there really were women with voting privileges of various kinds!—and lots more.

Turn the page to learn more about my other Regency romances.

MORE BOOKS BY
Rose Lerner

LIVELY ST. LEMESTON
True Pretenses
Listen to the Moon
A Taste of Honey (novella)

To find out when new Lively St. Lemeston books release,
sign up at RoseLerner.com!

RYE BAY
(f/f Gothics set in the world of Lively St. Lemeston)
The Wife in the Attic (an Audible Original, coming February 2021)
The Wife in the Attic (print and e-book, coming late 2021)

To find out when new Rye Bay books release,
sign up at RoseLerner.com!

NOT IN ANY SERIES
In for a Penny
A Lily Among Thorns
All or Nothing
(novella, first published in the *Gambled Away* anthology)
Promised Land
(novella, first published in the *Hamilton's Battalion* anthology)

TURN THE PAGE for an excerpt from *True Pretenses*,
in which a small-town heiress marries a traveling con artist
to get her hands on her dowry.

True Pretenses

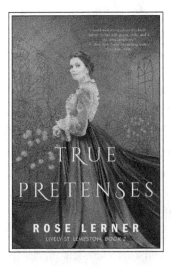

Something borrowed...

Through wit and sheer force of will, Ash Cohen raised himself and his younger brother Rafe out of the London slums and made them (in his unbiased opinion) the best confidence men in England. Ash is heartbroken when Rafe decides he wants an honest life, but he vows to give his beloved brother what he wants.

When Ash hears of a small-town heiress scrambling to get her hands on the dowry held in trust for when she marries, he plans one last desperate scheme: con her and his brother into falling in love. After all, Rafe deserves the best, and Ash can see at once that captivating, lonely Lydia Reeve is the best.

Lydia doesn't know why she instinctively trusts the humble stranger who talks his way through her front door and into her life. She just knows she's disappointed when he tries to set her up with his brother.

When a terrible family secret comes to light and Rafe disappears, Lydia takes a big risk: she asks Ash to marry her instead. Did Ash choose the perfect wife for his brother...or for himself?

Chapter 1

B elow them in the darkness, a clock chimed half past two. "Just once, I'd like to leave somewhere in daylight," Rafe grumbled under his breath as they crept down the stairs. "Wearing my boots. I'd like to take my trunk with me too."

"Shh." Their trunk and its contents were worth twenty pounds. If Ash Cohen could have brought them away safely, he would have, but they meant exactly that to him—twenty pounds. The only thing he had that he couldn't leave behind was two feet in front of him, sulking.

His brother knew perfectly well that they left places in daylight with their trunks all the time. Only certain jobs—like this one—required sneaking off in the dead of night. But Rafe was always at his worst just after a successful swindle.

Ash supposed it was natural to feel empty and frustrated when an enterprise you'd spent weeks or months on was abruptly over. Ash himself would feel giddy, if his brother didn't insist on ruining his mood. Now instead of fizzing like a celebratory mug of ale, his chest cavity filled with—butterflies was too pretty a name for them. Moths, maybe, dirty-looking gray-and-white ones, swarming about and clinging to his innards.

At least Rafe didn't let pique spoil his concentration. He stepped unerringly around the squeaking, creaking places they'd scouted in the staircase, eased open the door on hinges they'd oiled, and shoved his feet silently into his boots. Ash did the same and followed his brother out into the night.

Rafe had never been able to hold a grudge for longer than ten miles, if Ash resisted the urge to cozen him. Today, it was nine and a half (calculated with their average speed of walking and Ash's watch) before he gave Ash a sidelong, apologetic smile and said, "I could eat a whole side of beef right now."

Ash relaxed. He wished he could be less sensitive to Rafe's moods, but it had been this way for twenty-five years now and showed no signs of changing. When baby Rafe had smiled and waved chubby little arms in his direction, nine-year-old Ash had felt special, important, as if he could vanquish lions. Before Rafe, he'd been nothing, one of an army of little street thieves. Ash smiled back and gave his brother a shove. "I've no doubt you could. Giant."

Rafe laid a large hand atop Ash's head. "Midget." Actually, Ash was of average height, and greater than average breadth. But Rafe towered over him, and that was Ash's greatest pride and accomplishment: one look, and you knew he'd always had enough to eat.

And people did look. Heads turned when Rafe walked into a room, huge and golden. Dark, sturdy Ash looked like an ox or a draft horse, his brute strength meant to carry others' burdens. Rafe was a thoroughbred. Maybe if Ash hadn't shared so many dinners with his little brother, he'd be a giant himself, but he had no regrets.

Another five miles and they were in complete charity with one another, and probably safe enough from pursuit to buy something to eat at a crowded inn. Rafe, more memorable, waited outside with his hat low over his face while Ash bought pasties and ale to be consumed a little way down the road.

Once the food was gone, however, Rafe's good spirits went with it. When he began worrying a worn handkerchief between his hands, Ash knew something was very wrong.

The scrap of fabric was all Ash had managed to keep when his mother died. Since he couldn't split his memories with his brother, Ash had given him the handkerchief as soon as Rafe was old enough to safeguard it from boys wanting to steal and sell it. He carried it always but almost never took it out.

"I'm sick of swindling," he said at last, with a heavy finality that Ash didn't like.

"You say that after every job. You'll be right as rain when we've found another flat. We always get on best when we're working."

"I'm sick of flats. I'm sick of a profession that hurts people. I want to be able to point to something I've done at the end of the day, something *good*."

Ash patted his pocket. "Two hundred pounds is a damn good thing, if you ask me."

Rafe frowned. "Other men give something back for money. They leave something behind them. We only take. I liked Mrs. Noakes."

"I liked her too," Ash said, stung. He liked everybody. That was why he was so good at his job. You couldn't swindle a person you couldn't get on with. "And she can afford to lose two hundred pounds."

Rafe turned his head away. "It isn't the money. Think of how she'll feel."

"Think of how we'd feel if we starved," Ash snapped. "We have to take care of ourselves—"

"—because no one will do it for us, I know." Rafe rarely raised his voice when he was angry. Most of the time, when he was trying to express an emotion other than happiness, he slowed down. It only meant he was struggling to find words, but in his deep voice, it gave every word a weight and echo, like a church bell tolling. Ash hated it. "I just want to make someone happy for a change."

You make me *happy.* The words stuck in Ash's throat. They really meant, *Don't I count?* They were weak and childish, and he knew the answer was no, anyway. He had brought Rafe up to take him for granted, to believe him strong and capable and impervious to the world's blows. He had wanted his brother to feel safe, as he himself never had. Fear, anxiety, illness, sadness—he'd protected Rafe with fierce care from them all. It seemed bitterly unfair that this was his reward.

"I don't enjoy the work anymore," Rafe said. "I'm sorry. I've tried and tried, but I find myself wishing the lies were true. That we were really shipwrecked Americans, or speculators who'd found copper on Mrs. Noakes's land, or anything other than thieves."

"You can't get—"

"—too fond of your own lies, I *know*. But haven't you ever, Ash?"

The dirty little moths settled back into his stomach and chest and clung. He had exactly one secret he'd never told Rafe. Sometimes he forgot about it for days on end, and when he remembered, it was worse than stepping out of a warm shop into a snowstorm.

"Once." The word scraped his throat like a dull razor.

Rafe waited, but didn't press him. Ash wished he would. He wished Rafe would make him tell, because by now it was obvious he'd never find the courage otherwise. "Then you know what it's like," Rafe said finally. "I want to leave."

Everything stopped. The birds singing in the bare branches, the sun rising in the sky, Ash's heart beating in his chest—they all went silent and still. "Leave?"

Rafe held his gaze, earnest and sorrowful. It was the look he gave flats when he told them their money was gone, there'd been a ship lost at sea, a horse gone lame in the first lap, a bank failure. That was what made Rafe such a brilliant swindler: he had an honest face. Ash wanted to put his fist in it. "You can keep most of the money," Rafe offered. "I've thought about it. I could join the army—"

The money? Rafe thought he cared about the *money*? "You'll join the army? Even you can't be that stupid. Starve and fight and die for what? For England? What did England ever do for you? Men slice into their own legs with an ax to get *out* of the army!"

"Or I'll go to Canada. I've got to leave, Ash." He said it so slow and heavy it was like a judge pronouncing sentence. "I've done everything with you. Always. I don't know how to stop, without *stopping*. I won't be able to stick to it if you're there to talk me round. We both know it."

Resentment seared Ash's throat, sticky and hot as pitch. That was gammon. Rafe was the easygoingest man in the world right up until he dug in his heels, and then there was no moving him.

Rafe was going to leave, and Ash would be alone.

Instinctively, he bought himself time. "Well, if that's how you feel, I won't try to change your mind."

"Thank you for understanding. I didn't think you'd—you're the best of brothers." Rafe put an arm around his shoulder, his face glowing with...*relief*, Ash thought. Relief that Ash hadn't made an unpleasant scene. In spite of himself, Ash's stupid heart eased a little, that he'd made Rafe happy. "Thank you for everything. I'll—I'll miss you. I'll write you horribly misspelled letters, if you can think of a safe place to send them."

Mrs. Noakes had been a nice woman. Ash had liked her. But she'd grown up with a family, a home and plenty of food and clothes. She'd always have those things, two hundred pounds or no.

The world had given him and Rafe nothing, and they'd proved they didn't need it. Ash looked around at the muddy little clump of trees they stood in. The morning was cold and their breath misted in the air, but they were alive and well, with food in their bellies, good coats on their backs and good boots on their feet. The two of them against the world, and Ash would put his money on them every time. This little slice of England was all he'd ever wanted.

All Rafe wanted was to be somewhere else. Anywhere else. Now that Rafe had said it aloud, had given it shape, it made sense in a way Ash's idyllic picture of Two Wandering Jews never had. Rafe's depression between jobs was real, and his cheerfulness during a swindle was a brief intoxication. Ash had seen it too many times—dull-eyed, hopeless men who only found a spark of life when they could forget everything but the roll of the dice, the turn of the card, the pounding of the horses' hooves. He should have recognized it in his brother.

When Rafe had been hungry, Ash had found him food. When Rafe had been cold, Ash had got him clothes. When Rafe had been sick, Ash had brought him a doctor. He'd begged, borrowed, bargained, whored and stolen to do it—stolen every way he knew, and then made up a few new ones. He'd made it look easy, so Rafe would never feel how close they were to starving, freezing, dying of fever in a gutter some-where and being dumped in paupers' graves.

Who would he even be, without Rafe? What right did Ash have to expect more than he'd already got?

What good did it do to be so angry, when he couldn't make Rafe want to stay anyway? It was twenty-five years too late for any sleight of hand. Rafe knew exactly what life with Ash was like, and he'd decided he didn't want it.

If Rafe wanted a new life, a respectable life, Ash would find a way to steal that for him too—one with no cannonballs or long sea journeys in it, either. And then, to keep himself from changing his mind, he'd do something he'd never done before. He'd give back something he'd stolen.

He'd tell Rafe everything.

Read the rest of Chapter One and buy the book at smarturl.it/pretensesdotcom

CPSIA information can be obtained
at www.ICGtesting.com
Printed in the USA
FSHW011422060321
79247FS